MEMOIRS
of the MOP

Dear Tara:

The public schools rock!

J. R. WARNET

J. R. War[signature]

Copyright © 2022 J.R. Warnet
All rights reserved
First Edition

PAGE PUBLISHING, INC.
Conneaut Lake, PA

First originally published by Page Publishing 2022

ISBN 978-1-6624-7029-5 (pbk)
ISBN 978-1-6624-7030-1 (digital)

Printed in the United States of America

DISCLAIMER

All events, places, people, scenarios, and timelines in this book are fiction. Nothing in this book is even remotely true. All things herein were fabricated in the sick, twisted mind of the author. Opinions written in this book were written purely for entertainment purposes. If you don't know what fiction is, I suggest you google the term, then proceed to call your old high school English teacher and yell at them for not properly educating you on the difference between fantasy and reality. Thank you for your understanding.

J. R. Warnet

To my mother and my wife. To my mother, please stop trying to sell this book to every single person you meet. To my wife, please try to read this one this time.

J. R. Warnet

CHAPTER 1

Well, I'm Still Here

Yes, you heard that correctly. I'm still stuck in this outpost of humanity called my job. All those promises and dreams I embarked on in the last book, well, it's complicated. Not the part about quitting or moving to another state. That would be easy if I only had the balls to do it and about $100,000. You see, it's easy to say you're going to do things until you actually have to do them. Remember when you said you would backpack around Europe after college? That shit costs money. A lot of it, to be blunt. Tell me, did you ever make it to Switzerland or the Roman Colosseum?

I would love to leave this place, but it's hard out there to find a job with my credentials. College degrees are like high school degrees nowadays. Even with the right one, you could fuck yourself in the foot by having too much of an education. Employers don't want to pay for a master's degree, because it's more money, to start, Unless you have a doctorate and are willing to take pennies on the dollar, you might as well pick up a mop like me and start chugging away. We're always looking for a few good dummies to master the art of mopping.

I'm keeping my options open at this point. The classifieds aren't offering too many dream jobs for an overweight, bearded janitor who likes to write stories about other fucked-up janitors. I guess I'll stick around for a little longer to see what shit comes down the pike. I need more fuel for the creative writing fire.

Let me fill you in on what's been happening since our last conversation. Most of my coworkers are gone. They either quit, got fired, or died with a broom in their hands. Poor Tyrell Jones. I haven't heard a thing about him. After he got shitcanned, he's been off radar. I heard he got locked up on a drug bust outside of Paterson. I also heard from a buddy up north that Tyrell was shot in a crossfire near Trenton. Two months ago, somebody with the same name was gunned down outside a club in Miami, fighting over a woman. Any of those stories can be true for Tyrell. He sure did love him some drugs and women. I miss him so much. This place just isn't the same without him. No more awesome stories about cocaine snorting in the back of a limo with Dr. Dre and Patti LaBelle.

My head boss, Mr. Poloski, finally had enough and went off like a tank. He was tired of interviewing druggies who stole laptops shortly after being hired. Do you know how many heroine packs you can get for a laptop? Even a shitty laptop can bring a hundred hits or so in junk. Polotski had a nervous breakdown during a board meeting, where the big bosses tried to pin all the problems on him.

Normally, Polotski was a whiny bitch who complained a lot but never took action. Well, he took action this time. He grabbed the superintendent by his throat and chokeslammed him near the bleachers. It was amazing! He looked like the Undertaker when he lifted Yokozuna off the mat. Old-school WWF, baby. That superintendent bounced off the ground like a racket ball.

It must've felt wonderful to powerslam his boss. I bet you would like to chokeslam a member of your management team, right? Half of you just thought of that one son of a bitch you would crack with a hockey stick right across their stupid little face. Too bad Polotski's in prison. I kind of liked him toward the end. When he gets out in three to five years, he'll probably apply for a job as a janitor here.

Remember Roswell Murphy, that head case who moved to Montana? Well, I got a postcard from him last week. I know, right? A postcard. Fucking guy still doesn't trust the government. He couldn't just pick up a phone or send me an email. He had to get a postcard, buy stamps, handwrite the letter, and mail it old-school. I'm surprised he didn't send a carrier pigeon or hire someone on horseback to deliver it. Anyway, he's doing fine out in his nuclear bunker in Bozeman. He's never been better. I'm sure Roswell's pension and social security are affording him all sorts of extravagances. Maybe he'll buy a new car or take a cruise to Iceland. If I know him, he'll probably spend most of his government check on peyote and incense.

If my math is correct, we have about ten people still here from when I was hired. When I first took up the plunger, we had 150 moppers. Due to budget cuts and the aforementioned issues, we're now down to sixty or so people. Each cleaning solider is working twice, sometimes even three times, as hard as they should. I'm all for doing my fair share, but how many times can one be screwed by management before they break? The remainder of the Old Guard and I are like an endangered species. Pretty soon, if no one intervenes, we will go extinct in a matter of months.

A few holdouts from the last book are haplessly calling this place home. Mr. Sanders is still scurrying around here like the vermin he is. Frigging slimeball just won't die! Each year, he gets more and more grotesque. It's like he makes a sacrifice to Beelzebub and his black heart is revitalized. Christ, now he looks like someone who's been burned alive in the Salem witch trials. One minute, you think he's dead; then the next, he comes in with a different tie, fresh as a daisy. Same shitty old gray suit, though. That suit's older than the Acropolis. What a cheap fuck. I'm sure he'll pop up in a few stories in this ever-raging battle of good versus evil.

Don't worry, I have a fresh new lineup of dimwits, imbeciles, and blockheads to tell you about. We've got some real winners here after the last hiring wave. One guy slipped on a wet floor he had just finished mopping. He mopped the floor soaking wet, turned around to get his coffee cup, and walked back down the saturated hallway. He went straight up in the air and landed back first. He broke three vertebrae and burned himself with the coffee he was carrying! He looked like Wile E. Coyote after a bad slingshot accident. This is what management hires, and they wonder why our workers' comp claims are through the roof.

This was his first day on the job, I shit you not. He didn't even make a full shift before filing his first accident report. Now he's got a workman's compensation case with a lawsuit. He'll win it; I bet my life this dude will walk away with tons of money. That's why management won't give us raises, because of shit like this. They keep giving morons thousands of dollars for settlements. Maybe if they hire responsible workers instead of dipshits, I could get a decent wage.

I've encountered a small pushback from several people over my last book. Some of the smarter ones I work with see shades of themselves in those pages. They've confronted me about the book, stating their displeasure over what some people might consider an unflattering portrayal. I thought most of them couldn't read, let alone comprehend what was being written. After many hours of careful consideration, I decided not to care about it. That book—and this one, for arguments' sake—is fiction. I tried to explain the difference, but no one seemed to understand. If they're not smart enough to know what's real and what's not real, then that's their fucking problem. There's a reason they push a broom for a living.

But darkness looms in the distance of Janitorland. An evil has descended across the countryside, causing the townsfolk to run screaming into their panic rooms. I'm saying a few fuckers have come out of the woodwork and are trying to take my job away. That's what I'm getting at. I had to drama it up a bit to set the mood. It's me versus them, a priomordial battle of good against evil, winner takes all.

The title of my new saga is *Memoirs of the Mop* because it's most definitely a love story. I have a love-hate relationship with my job—and with this profession, for that matter. I love the fact that I can write these stories and create a humorous scene for my readers. I hate the amount of bullshit I deal with to come up with those stories. Had I not seen these things firsthand, I wouldn't believe half the shit I write. But it's my burden to undergo. Every true artist struggles to create art. There must be some kind of agony to create beauty, so I gladly accept my torture to give you a hoot. Get ready for more mopping analogies and poop references from the guy behind the dustpan!

CHAPTER 2

Why the Public School System Blows

We should start a discussion on why the public school system needs to be abolished. I figured that will get your attention. If there is ever an institution in need of a serious overhaul, the public school system would be at the top of the list. I would love to tackle a more daunting topic like the government or economic crisis or even global warming, but I've got a word count to stay under.

Before I started this book, I truly believed in the American education system. What's not to love about achieving your dreams or making learning a lifelong pursuit? I put two feet forward in school, ultimately plotting a course toward graduating, then I discovered what every else already knew: College is a brutal pyramid scheme designed to suck the life and your money right out your asshole. True, some degrees are worth the trouble, like being a lawyer, for instance. These fuckers are the real organized crime, circumventing the law to bleed a bank account down to negative numbers. School administration is another degree where you get to pilfer money hand over fist. But your average Joe or Jane comes out of college overeducated yet underpaid.

In my seventh or eighth year of college—yes, it took me that long to finish school—I became very bitter about the whole thing. Why in God's name would anyone attend college if they knew what awaited them after graduation? Do you know how many jobs are available once you get your degree? Fucking zilch. Nada. Very few people work in the field they go to school for unless you count the

10 percent who actually land a career they study in. One out of every ten—those useless guidance counselors never gave me that statistic.

Imagine if they tell you the truth about college. "Okay, Chloe, here's the scoop. You'll never get a job as a fashion designer, but we'll let you try anyway. You'll spend four years of your life racking your brain on the verge of a nervous breakdown just so you can be in the debt until you croak. But before you die, you'll work for free as an intern until the company says you're not good enough to get paid for the work you've already done.

"By that time, your student loan debt will exceed any salary you'd ever make as a part-time hairdresser, which, coincidently, is the only job available with your qualifications. You'll have no credit, no money, and no assets to help pay the interest on your astronomical student loan debt. Anyway, here's a pamphlet for a school that meets all your needs!" Poor Chloe should just enroll in plumbing school, because everyone in the world takes a shit, and someone has to run the pipes to flush it all out to sea. Okay, so I'm a little cynical, but I've got a right to be. Most of you have gone through the same crap as Chloe would have, whose one dream is to see her dresses in an haute Parisian boutique.

How did we get to this point in the educational system? When did we all stop getting good jobs with a pension and health benefits? Well, the system that educated us is completely fucked. It's busted, both figuratively and metaphorically. From the moment you step into kindergarten, everything costs money, lots of money. It's known as the PPCS, or per pupil current spending, a stupid term probably thought up by some asshole who actually has a good job in the US Department of Education. Basically, it's the number of dollars it costs to educate a student. In some states, the number is low, like, around $7,000. I'm looking at you, Alabama. Other states can spend over $20,000 on average per student annually. Think about how many students are in each classroom in each school in every district in the United States.

You would think that with all the money this country spends on education, we are leading the world in educational initiatives. Wrong again, kind reader. America is currently ranked seventeenth in educational performance in the world. That means, if my math teacher did her job correctly years ago, that sixteen other countries are more prepared then the United States. How is this not pissing everyone off?

This country spends the most money on education, and we're not even in the top ten. America is ranked twenty-fourth in literacy. Are you kidding me? There's a library in every city in this country, sometimes more than one library. If you're fortunate to have some spare change, you can visit one of the remaining bookstores to buy a book. Goddamn Liechtenstein is ahead of us in literacy. The county's the size of a Walmart Supercenter. How the fuck are they beating us in reading?

I may be a janitor, but I'm a janitor in a public school. I see how and why the students of this great country aren't getting the best education possible. It all comes down to money. Schools cost money to run. Think about the size of your kid's school. Do you know how much it costs to keep the lights on in that big-ass building? The heating and cooling system, electric bills, and daily and weekly repairs alone run into the millions in larger districts. Then add in personnel salaries to the mix. That's the thing that really fucks a school budget. School principals make $125,000 a year, school administrators can tap out at $200,000, and superintendents stretch the budget at close to $225,000. Don't forget all the teachers who can max out over $100,000 a year while only working ten months.

So there's a lot of money involved. Think about what typically happens when a large governing body gets ahold of a massive amount of cash. That's right, everyone skims a little off the top! By the time the money filters down, you're lucky if you get to smell it, much less use it toward the greater good. Do you actually believe your child benefits to the fullest extent when they attend a public school? If they do, then the world won't need charter schools, private schools, Catholic schools, private tutors, etc. Take a look at the statistics to see how really bad our public schools are when they rank with private educational systems.

I know it's a lot to think about. Hell, I nod out at the very mention of numbers in a math equation. But bear with me just a little longer. Here's why we're not in the top ten in education in the world. Your average American school year consists of 180 school days per year out of a possible 365 days. That's 186 days out of each calendar year that your kid is not in school. All those holidays, weekends, snow days, etc. add up. Then count in the days little Joanne misses because she's sick or goes to Orlando to have breakfast with Tinkerbelle. Let's round it out and say your kid misses two days a month due to illness or family vacation, so 165 is the number now. Compare that to Japan's educational system with a school year consisting of 240 days. Two more months of learning per year matters. Japan's number two on the list, and we're number seventeen. Think about that for a minute.

Do you think your kid gets an exceptional education with all the staff budget cuts over the past four decades? Schools are top-heavy, meaning a lot of the staff is maxed out on the pay scale. Once you've spent twenty-five years or so doing the same task, people tend to veg out. Retirement years are what those top-step teachers are thinking about, not your kid's future. Most teachers nowadays are the lowest bid. The bosses don't hire the expensive, multidegree professors. They hire the fresh out of college newbies who are willing to take a pay cut to get the job. The more money a business administrator can save, the better. They hire more bosses to watch the remaining staff—at top salary, no less. Why does a school need so many bosses to evaluate the staff anyway? Those dollars can be spent hiring more qualified teachers, ones who actually want to prepare their class for their next stage in life.

Enough with the math lesson. Let's talk real for a minute. American classrooms share a great deal in common with a slaughterhouse. Every day, cattle—or students, if you like—are brought into the facility on a large transportation system, aka buses. They go through the conveyor belt to the processing plant—from hallways to classrooms. The cattle are usually fed beforehand so they're nice and plump for the slaughter, which is not so different from school cafeterias. After the cattle have been run through a long corridor to warm up the meat—gym class?—the cattle are then brought to the killing table, or final exams. If the cow is of good enough quality, it gets culled and sent to the packing plant, the next grade. If the cattle are defective or not good enough for human consumption, they get rejected, or fail the grade and go to summer school.

This is exactly how the American educational system works, whether you want to admit it or not. It's one long line of processing until it reaches its final destination: the grocery store. Oddly enough, once most high school students graduate, they get a job in a grocery store, stocking the meat freezer with hamburgers and steaks. If the education they've acquired isn't good enough, which it normally isn't, then they stay at the said grocery store, making minimum wage for the next thirty years. It's mildly alerting to know we share the same destination as a pork loin or rump roast once we graduate.

Why does this happen? Why does a majority of students leave school not fully able to take on the world? The short answer comes back to money. If schools spend the money they get from taxes properly, each kid will have a shot at being the next president. As I said in my first book, *The Day I Clean My Last Toilet*—consult your local bookstore, if it's still in business—most of the taxed school budget goes to operational expenses. Salaries bleed a lot of those dollars out, as does crumbling infrastructure repairs. Things break or need to be updated frequently. What's left of those millions doesn't buy a lot of hope for the future.

Think about how many photocopied papers your kid lugs home in their backpack. Each year, a school burns through pallets of copy paper, only to be discarded the next day after it's handed out. I know this because I'm the dumbass who has to truck twenty pallets of paper into the school each summer and then throw out the garbage at the end of the day. A more efficient system would be for the teacher to actually teach the content on a whiteboard instead of simply giving the students a sheet of paper. This way, the student learns firsthand while saving a few acres of trees.

Why do so many schools spend millions on sports programs but hardly anything on trades, like home repair or car maintenance? I can't tell you the last time I made a jump shot in a championship game, but I sure as hell know when my fucking radiator blew up. Knowing how to change oil is a helluva lot more useful than knowing how to throw a spiral.

The same goes for math, that class where they mix numbers and letters to confuse the shit out of everyone. Algebra is a waste of time. I've never seen an algebraic equation on my pay stub. What I really needed to learn in school was how to budget my paycheck to accommodate student loans. They never teach students those calculations, do they? The last time I started compounding numbers for my student loans, the fucking calculator caught on fire.

Speaking of calculators, they're exactly what every student needs in today's schools, because no one knows how to do the new math they're teaching. Have you seen this yet? It doesn't make any sense whatsoever. You need a good calculator to figure this stuff out. There's more money you have to spend, some fifty bucks, on a Texas Instruments calculator! The funny thing is, one of the guys who made a boatload of money with Texas Instruments has an amazing home in Bermuda. It's beyond luxury, complete with a five-story atrium. He's worth millions because every kid in America needs one of his calculators for school.

The same goes for laptops at hundreds or so apiece. Shouldn't the school be supplying these things to every student? Some school districts are so screwed that they're requiring parents to spend hundreds in school supplies. I've heard of some districts asking parents to bring in boxes of tissues and toilet paper at the beginning of the school year. I'm out of a job if they start telling parents to add plungers to their back-to-school shopping list!

If I need to supply my kid with pens, notepads, calculators, a book bag, a laptop, tissues, toilet paper, running water, and gas money for the bus, then what the fuck does the school system actually do for the children? Not teaching, apparently, as we've seen the results of statewide testing in some districts. You'll complain in a restaurant if your steak comes out not cooked the right way, won't you? Imagine millions of steaks being served half frozen each year. Now you have a good idea of how not prepared your kid is to face the real world.

You can spot these anomalies in your daily life. Just look at your cellphone bill when the carrier adds in little expenses. Each person has to pay x amount of money to fund services, like the dreaded administrative charge. Administrative fees are money you pay so the company can hire more bosses in case the ones they have now aren't doing their job right.

Take a gander at your school's board meeting minutes sometime. Look for things like summer training seminars or board of education getaways. They're usually hidden toward the end of the board minutes, because John Q. Public gives up looking after the first few pages. These so-called training seminars are designed to teach school board members how to pilfer more money from the budget. The people who control the checkbooks in a school district are spending your tax dollars to learn how to fuck you even harder. That's why your kid has to bring toilet paper to school, because there's not enough money in the budget to account for it.

All I'm saying is, open your eyes to see what's really going on in your kid's district. See how and where the money goes. It's weird how all the top-tier school officials get a guaranteed raise each school year while your taxes never decrease. Funny how that works, huh? That's because they control the money, your kids' money, which can be been spent more wisely. Maybe that's why America ranks seventeenth after all.

CHAPTER 3

The J Word

Didn't your mama teach you the golden rules in your childhood? Remember them? Treat others the way you want to be treated. If you don't have anything nice to say, then don't say anything at all. Always turn the lights off when you leave the room. And the most infamous golden rule of all, never use the J word.

The last one is my own addition. It's not as well-known as, say, the Code of Hammurabi. You know, an eye for an eye? But it's just as important as the others, especially in my world. Using the J word is considered vulgar. It behooves us to think of ourselves as custodians, although we sometimes use the J word in informal speech. Come to think of it, I never used the J word until I started writing my books. I always told people I was a custodian if they asked what I did for a living. Even I didn't want to say the J word aloud.

Here's the part of the book I call the academic section. Get ready for some knowledge you didn't know you needed to know. It all began many moons ago with the Romans. Yep, those wine-soaked, orgy-having Etruscans everyone can relate to. The word *janua* in Latin means "door." By adding *-tor* to the end, you get a word that means "a keeper of the door." A person who guards the door or is a doorkeeper is often called a janitor. Now you know why we have so many goddamn keys. It's because of all those frigging doors we have to watch.

The Romans loved the term so much that they named one of their gods Janus, the god of beginnings, endings, gates, time, transitions, and doorways. He was the bad mofo who oversaw entrances and exits. He was usually depicted as having a two-faced head—one that was staring into the future, straight ahead, and one that was staring into the past, behind him. Janus was forever looking into the future and the past at the same time. I know quite a few janitors with two faces, but that's neither here nor there. We also get the word *January* from Janus. The Julian and the Gregorian calendars have January as the first month because it is the entrance to the new year.

Not for nothing, but of course, it had to be the Romans who gave janitors their name. They were the same pricks who invented the aqueducts. Imagine the little giggle the architects had with that one. The same system that brought water in and out of the public bathhouses was named around the same time as the janitor. Good God, can you imagine having to clean up those Roman bathhouses after all those drunken orgies?

Anyway, we got our first taste of the word *janitor* in the English language toward the end of the 1500s. It was used to describe an usher in a school. Later, in literature, we saw janitor being referred to as a doorkeeper in the early 1600s. Some biblical texts showed that Saint Peter was called the janitor of heaven. Imagine old Saint Pete himself sweeping up after the helpless souls waiting to get into the promised land. "Excuse me, miss. Can you pick up that candy wrapper you've dropped? Yeah, yeah, the one by your foot, stuck to the cloud. Look, I saw you drop it. If you don't pick up your trash, it may affect your getting past those pearly gates over there."

So when did the janitor go from the Roman god of doors to today's negative image? In a word, toilets. Unlocking a few doors here and there is an image one can live with, but scrubbing up piss and shit? That evokes a disturbing scene, one most people relate to as lower-class. The thought of human waste is disgusting to many. It's a bad mental image that suggests filth or uncleanliness. Janitors, in turn, are considered unclean by association.

As the years went on, janitors started to take more of a cleaning role instead of the keeper of the door. The janitor went from opening the door to cleaning the fingerprints off the door itself. I bet the building supervisors thought that one up. "Hey, you know that guy walking around, opening and closing doors all day? Let's make him clean the place too." Typical supervisors, saving money and pissing people off since the beginning of time.

The janitor underwent a weird metamorphosis throughout history. First, they kept watch on the door so no undesirables came into the building. The ancient Mayan city of Tulum on the Yucatán Peninsula had plenty of janitors on duty during its years of activity. Tulum, which meant "wall" in the Yucatec language, had a massive stone wall around the perimeter. Three sides of the city had a sixteen-foot stone wall surrounding it while the side facing the ocean was built thirty-nine feet above the cliffs. It was Central America's "first gated community," as one tour guide told me on a recent vacation.

All jokes aside, it must have needed the wall for some reason. Tulum was known to be the primary location for all trade in the Mayan civilization at one point. The ability to keep all maritime trade under lock and key, so to speak, was imperative to the Maya. Armed sentries were posted at the door entrances leading into Tulum. They brandished weapons on anyone they deemed hazardous to the city. I wish someone would give me a spear or a club sometimes. I won't have people who disrespect me so often if I have a poison blow dart at the ready.

A janitor's role evolved as history marched along. I would like to think that janitors of the medieval era had the same respect they did as during the Roman Empire, but I highly doubt it. You know the janitors were the ones who had to pick up all the dead bodies during the Bubonic Plague. No one else wanted that job. History can call them body collectors or cartmen if it wants, but they were janitors, trust me! "Hey, door guy, on your way to picking up all the shit buckets, can you throw a couple of corpses on the cart? You know, just a couple million bodies on your way to swab out the latrines. Pay no attention to the black, pus-ridden tumors all over their bodies. They're harmless!" Come to think of it, I bet that was where the term "janitor cart" came from. It's not that far a stretch from the dead carts the people of the Black Death pushed along.

Along with watching the door and picking up dead bodies, the janitor also had to empty the piss pots before indoor plumbing was a thing. The term "chamber pot" was derived from the pot you placed under your bed where you relieved yourself at night. Most chamber pots were emptied out of windows into the streets due to the lack of sophisticated plumbing. Guess who got the lovely job of hosing down the streets too? Freaking janitors!

The lowly chambermaids cleaned up after the rich until they had enough of their shit. I'm willing to bet the French Revolution wasn't all about the "let them eat cake" remark. Once you've emptied a few thousand steaming chamber pots for low pay, you might be a little disgruntled. I would like to believe a few janitors bashed those rich fuckers over the head with a chamber pot on their way out of the Bastille, scoring one for the working class.

Moving right along, we find janitors in all societies throughout history. The first flushing toilet was invented in 1596 by Sir John Harington. He designed it for his godmother, Queen Elizabeth I, but she refused to use it because she said it was too loud. I guess the sound of her taking a huge dump into a bedpan wasn't as loud as water flowing to and from the house. Then again, she was rich enough to have some poor sap clean up after her. Alexander Cumming is credited as patenting the first flushing toilet in 1775 in England. It seems odd how America declared its independence from England less than a year later. I guess we were tired of England's shit too.

Modern flushing toilets weren't easily available to the public until around the mid-1800s. Even though innovations to indoor plumbing have improved, the need to clean the bathroom remains the same. Today, we find that your average janitor has a laundry list of things they do daily. Gone are the times of being considered an honorable profession; people only know we exist if there's a problem. Usually, the bathroom runs out of toilet paper or the toilet itself is clogged beyond flushing. So why do so many people look down on the janitor? Perhaps the guilt of looking at someone who cleans up after them is too much to bear.

I read an article in *National Geographic Magazine* about latrine cleaners in Haiti. These workmen were called *bayakou*, and their job was to remove waste from the latrines. Most *bayakou* would not admit to their profession, fearing rebuke. People threw stones at them in the streets. They encountered horrid conditions, working at night to hide their shame. Without these workers, the city of Port-au-Prince would be backed up with raw sewage due to their ineffective sewer system. Had it not been for these latrine cleaners, the city would be riddled with cholera and other transmittable diseases. No one thanked the *bayakou*, though, just like most janitors around the world weren't even acknowledged.

I've never had stones chucked at me; but pencils, crayons, and wads of paper, yes. Some children think it's okay to throw things and call me names. This isn't a trait children are instilled with from birth. It's a learned ability, just as one learns how to count to ten or ride a bike. I'm sure they've learned it from another kid, who has most likely learned it from a parent. These traits are not born into us; they are taught. The same can be said for violence and other harmful tendencies. No one wakes up one day thinking of how to demean another person.

Perhaps the reason people are afraid to speak to us is that they fear what they do not know. How many times have you told your kids not to talk to strangers? Now think about this: Why is it acceptable for children to talk with teachers in a school but won't speak to the janitor? I've seen it in kids of all ages, even through to high school. They won't look at the janitor, but they see a teacher and say hi all the time. Why is that? I believe it's because society tells them not to have the same respect for the janitor as they do for the teacher.

It's a cultural aspect, if you think about it. Teachers are held in higher regard than a school janitor. Even the terms are different today. A teacher is someone who instructs or educates another. I bet you didn't know where the term *janitor* came from before I told you about it earlier in this chapter. The emotions one feel when they hear the two terms are astonishingly different from each other. Bring it up in conversation sometime. Start talking about a teacher to someone. Now bring up the school janitor and watch as their demeanor changes. See how the word *janitor* resonates with them. I bet their face cringes or their body language changes dramatically.

The word *janitor* brings about a cultural dissonance, much like the word *plumber* or *garbageman*. These so-called undesirable professions almost always do. The semantic change from doorkeeper to toilet cleaner has ruined it for all of us. That's why I never use the J word in public, and neither should you. Try something a little more acceptable, like custodian or sweeper of the night. Anything is better than *janitor*, believe me.

CHAPTER 4

Types of Workers in the Public School System

One would think that with all the emphasis on education, an institute such as the public school system would hire the brightest people they can find. Things can't be further from the truth. All those so-called intelligent people with multiple college degrees and eons of experience hire the most mentally inept individuals. Each department has at least one worker who exemplifies the characteristics of a bad, shit-for-brains troll who makes it impossible for everyone around them.

I don't think public schools started out hiring these goblins when the education system first came to be. Decades of budget cuts, outsourcing, and so-called restructuring have decimated what was once a great system. The world of public school service workers has been muddied by what the bosses now call their kind of employee.

Through my more than two decades of insight, I've created a guide to help you understand the types of workers employed by the public school system. Below is a rough outline of what these people do and how they drive away good workers. For argument's sake, I'll limit my research to the likeliest you'll encounter.

Each type of worker has an obvious namesake. I've also added a military rank. Not only will it give you an idea of where they fall on the totem pole, but it will also make the list that much funnier. These rankings apply to all departments in the public school system, not just janitors. I'm certain you can find these people everywhere within the system in one capacity or another.

Note: Before you start criticizing my ranking system or point out which ranks are higher than others in the actual military, just remember one thing: it's all for fun. I recommend you try it with your job. It makes the days more bearable.

At the top of our list, we have General Desk Rider. This person is exemplary at sitting behind a desk all day long. When I say all day, I mean it. General Desk Rider doesn't move. The only time you see them move is to take a piss or get more food to stuff in their pudgy face. I've seen generals demand someone bring them a snack so they don't have to move. Without moving, generals appear to be dead. The only way to tell if they're alive is to rattle a small bag of chips or open a box of Girl Scout Cookies. The sound of the wrapper will free them from their self-induced coma.

Unless you hear a deep, bronchial wheeze or see froth gathering in the corner of their mouth, it's best to let them sit. It's impossible to combat a general due to the overwhelming number of support soldiers flanking them. Generals are untouchable for the most part. As the name implies, this worker plants their ass at their desk, doing little, if any, work. They give orders either through email, phone call, or scribbling a note on a Milky Way wrapper and throwing it at you. This is not to say that all General Desk Riders are fat and out of shape, just a couple, like Mr. Caravaggio, head of all the generals. (Don't worry, you'll meet him soon enough.)

Orders are given and are always expected to be followed. General Desk Riders are normally heads of departments or top supervisors. These workers make an insane amount of money for the work they output. It's something like a thousand dollars per command. No wonder they stick around for so long! If someone offers me a six-figure salary to sit behind a desk, barking orders and filling my gullet with snacks, you bet your ass I'll take it. I guess that's why it's so hard to get rid of a general.

Our next ranking officer is called Captain Clipboard. You guessed it! They sling their weapon around, constantly checking off orders from their generals. I've never seen a captain without his or her clipboard in hand. Much like a soldier carries their rifle, so does Captain Clipboard carry a clipboard. Have you ever seen the movie *Full Metal Jacket?* Do yo remember that part when they sing about their rifles? Yeah, that's exactly what Captain Clipboard looks like, strutting around all day, grabbing their prick or twat. Some captains go so far as to have a coffee cup in the other hand to complete the look. Tell me, how does one write shit down on a clipboard if your other hand has a cup of coffee in it? Logic implores me to believe a captain must put down the coffee first before jotting down any important information.

    Captains normally have a long list of work on their handy-dandy clipboards. The top sheet may have important intel, like which employees to watch like a hawk or which ones they haven't interrogated recently. Captains decipher orders from the generals, in turn passing it down the chain. A lot of captains pass along misinformation, further confusing all those who receive it. Other than holding the clipboard and occasionally checking things off, Captain Clipboard doesn't accomplish much.

    Directly below the captains is one of the most useless ranks in the public school military: Brigadier Bullshit Artist. These individuals are most excellent at talking out of their ass. We've all met a brigadier before, haven't we? Work to them is all about the schmooze. Brigadiers talk more than work. No one knows where brigadiers get their info from; not much is known about their profession or how they got the job in the first place.

    If they are assigned a weapon during basic training, it would be the machine gun since they constantly fire off round after round of bullshit. Most of what they say is incomprehensible. They proclaim having done this job for many, many years. In my experience, Brigadier Bullshit Artist doesn't know what the hell they're doing. They have no cognitive skills and no work habits worth mentioning and usually laugh or joke a lot to cover up their faults. The only thing they are good at is spreading manure. I guess their commanding officers are complete imbeciles, not knowing their brigadiers are blowing smoke up their asses.

Since they have the term *artist* in their name, it bears mentioning their most successful trait. They can paint you a serious picture of chaos and disarray once provoked. If called out for not working, the brigadier is amazing at concocting a brilliant story to stave off punishment. They can manufacture a story for any occasion, usually making it up as they go. Under normal conditions, the brigadier is an unskilled worker without much in the smarts department. It is not known why or how they're still employed.

Going forward, we come to learn about Sergeant Stupid. This worker is, by far, the dumbest worker ever hired. Their intelligence is so low that they display signs of mental deficiencies. Sergeant Stupid shares the same capabilities of early Cro-Magnon species. Sergeants, believe it or not, have a tremendous number of workers directly under them. You would think it's counterproductive to have so many people following orders from an actual caveman, but the public school system is a strange and often idiotic establishment.

I've witnessed sergeants causing tremendous amounts of damage without a notion that they're doing anything wrong. Millions of dollars have been lost due to their stupidity. The only thing these workers do with efficiency is blame those under them for their mistakes. Perhaps some primordial instinct kicks in, enabling the sergeants to throw a lesser-ranking worker under the proverbial bus. In any case, Sergeant Stupid isn't going away anytime soon.

Next up, we can find a most unusual worker no job is complete without. Lieutenant Hands in His Pockets is a staple on the job. Although not as prevalent as Sergeant Stupid, these workers are found in all levels of the work environment. Whenever real work is afoot, Lieutenant Hands in His Pockets snaps into action, sticking both hands directly into their pants. You can observe these soldiers under any condition, but they primarily come out during times of particularly strenuous activities.

This specific job title doesn't have to involve heavy lifting or manual labor. I've seen many upper-level managers stick their hands in their pockets as soon as anyone mentions a hard task. They can also be found having one hand in their pocket with the other hand on a smartphone or other electronic device, avoiding the topic of work altogether.

I cannot stress enough how lieutenants are one of the worst people to work with. Nothing is more annoying than working next to someone with their hands in their pockets every fucking time you see them. Are they jerking off in those pockets? Do they not wash their hands and, therefore, need to hide their fingers out of shame? We are not meant to know these answers. With any luck, Lieutenant Hands in His Pockets will go extinct or get promoted to another rank in another department.

The worst coworker to have on your team is Admiral Ass Licker. This type of worker do nothing but kiss ass any chance they get, but not physically, although I have heard rumors as to that kind of behavior behind closed office doors. Their work performance, much like all the rankings highlighted in this chapter, is subpar at best. An admiral also has the highest number of complaints of any other ranking. This person is a little bitch.

Admirals turn their fellow coworkers in by naming names. This practice makes Admiral Ass Licker the scourge of the workplace environment. Once accused of being an admiral, it's over for this worker. All communication should be ceased immediately with admirals until they have been eradicated. Do not confuse Admiral Ass Lickers with its close counterpart Rear Admiral Rat Bastard, who does nothing but rat out their coworkers. Both individuals in the admiral class squeal on their coworkers, but it's important to know the difference between both rankings. One is strictly an ass-kisser while the other is a rat fink. Under extreme conditions, you may encounter these two rankings combined to form a Mecha-Admiral, a coworker who rats on friends while kissing the boss's ass. This person is never to be trusted and should be destroyed immediately.

As we descend further into the ranking system, I encourage you to keep your eyes peeled for these next few. They are more common than you expect. Use caution while on patrol; they have an uncanny ability to adapt to any circumstance. Always defend yourself vehemently while working. The remaining rankings are lethal and can inflict bodily harm within seconds.

Corporal Kill Themself is a dangerous worker. Corporals are easily-led dummies who follow any command without hesitation. They've been known to follow the most blatantly harmful instructions, even to the point of fatality. They disregard safety protocols. They push machinery to the limits of its practical use. Above all, they lack a sense of reality, making them a danger not only to themselves but also to anyone within a fifty-foot radius.

I've witnessed a corporal use hazardous chemicals without proper safety equipment. Without fail, the person had their skin burned off and now has disgusting marks all over their body. What's worse is, they've been known to do this on multiple occasions. This indicates that they cannot learn from their mistakes and will continue doing harmful things until they expire. Please give these cretins a wide berth.

Corporals believe anything they are told. Think Chicken Little meets a lemming. They're dumb and extremely incompetent. Do not engage a corporal under any circumstances unless, of course, you have a death wish and want a loved one to cash in on a lucrative life insurance policy. Upon receiving this, you'll then be classified as a Corporal Kill Themself. Good job.

Major Runaround is like Corporal Kill Themself in a lot of categories. Majors will sprint in all directions at once, causing panic to those around them. This is usually accomplished at maximum speed. A major is known to possess tremendous energy, normally induced by excessive amounts of caffeine or an illegal controlled substance. It's okay to be vivacious and energetic, but majors tend to get absolutely no work done. They simply run around, trying to work but ultimately ending up tripping over a mop bucket.

Use restraint if forced to work in close proximity to a major. They can and will get you hurt! Most times, you'll have to redo any work they've attempted to complete. I know it's ridiculous, but at least they try unlike most rankings above them.

Be on the lookout for this next person even though you will probably never see them in action. Comandante Hide-and-Seek is a very tricky worker indeed. These people have been known to stay hidden for hours. After years of incognito training, a comandante is highly skilled in the art of disappearing. You could be right on top of them, and you wouldn't know it. Their level of camouflage is so advanced that it has been adopted by the US Marine Corps during the development of the ghillie suit.

They are masters at becoming one with their surroundings. A theory suggests that all comandantes can turn invisible once they've reached a certain number of years on the job. This is unproven but should be taken into consideration just in case. Comandantes are typically bad at work, thus their need to be hidden. Should they put the same amount of effort into working as they do into hiding, they could be an unstoppable force.

You can find our next ranking in every workplace across the globe. They are so prevalent that I almost considered adding this rank to all other rankings listed thus far. Field Marshal Fuckup, as their name implies, is a catastrophic worker. Field marshals infect a workplace by spreading germs to other workers. They've been known to mess up anything they lay their hands on, even while not working. I've seen field marshals be promoted, and within seconds, that entire area is now contaminated. Once a field marshal is detected, whatever project or task they've been assigned is now doomed to fail.

You can identify a field marshal by listening to how they speak. Once you hear a coworker talk about how they can do the job better or how you should do it this way, start running. Consider field marshals as contagious as the plague. Avoid them as if your life depends on it! You've been warned.

These next two rankings aren't so much dangerous as they are a pain in the ass. Special Agent Sick Days and Wing Commander Workman's Comp are a nuisance, plain and simple. They tend to be absent a great deal. Special agents are out of work due to some invisible illness or ailment only they can see. Witnesses say that a majority of special agents are lying about their illness, pretending to be sick so they don't have to come to work. When at work, a special agent will complain incessantly about their affliction, saying things like, "My doctor says I have irritable bowel syndrome because of the stress I'm under while working here." This, of course, is a lie and should be disregarded. The same can be said of all things special agents say, because they're habitual liars. They may also possess characteristics of someone suffering from a multiple personality disorder.

Wing commanders make similar statements. These workers claim to be injured while on the job even though no witnesses can substantiate their claim. The fact is, wing commanders are most likely injured at home or have an existing injury. Their plan is to cash in on some of that workman's compensation money thinking no one will catch them. Many are repeat offenders. A system has not been devised to counter their claims, thus making their termination an exercise in futility.

Both rankings bring down productivity. Since you must complete both your job and their job, it's clear why most workers despise these creatures. Be especially wary of wing commanders; they've been known to ask you to sign a piece of paper declaring that you saw the whole accident happen and that you believe the job was to blame for this worker's injuries.

The last ranking is so rare. Not many have been documented in the workplace. Private Good Worker is an ancient ranking from a time long ago. It has been said that a private does their job correctly and does not interfere with others' job performance. As this claim is so exaggerated and obviously fake, it is not to be contemplated. No worker in the public school system does their job properly. Such a claim is unheard of.

Sightings of privates have been so low that I fear they have been driven away from the public school system. Last spotted during the so-called good old days, privates were once an abundant class. They used to roam workplaces of yesteryear, contributing to the betterment of others. Sadly, they are thought to be extinct. They exist now only in folklore, much like griffins and dragons. But they live on in the hearts of people who claim to have seen a Private Good Worker in action.

Last year, a scientist doing field research allegedly stumbled upon a private in the wild. His thirty-page document stated that he witnessed a private "doing its job without hesitation or complaints." The scientist also went on record to proclaim that this individual "had a smile on its face" and even appeared to be "whistling a pleasant tune." Without proper documentation, like a clear video or a sound recording, this claim has been classified as a rumor until proven true.

I hope, for the sake of us all, that this sighting is not of the self-proclaimed Ensign Great Worker from years past. This fucker lacks any proof of its great work ethic, opting to rely on speculation instead of physical evidence. Ensign Great Worker has been identified as a con artist on more than one occasion by several witnesses. Despite its wildly horrendous claims of working circles around their coworkers, ensigns are horrible people. It is said that all privates evolved into ensigns many years ago, thus eliminating any potential return of a good worker.

There you have it. That's just a smidgen of the ranking system I've devised to help navigate the complex world of the public school worker. I'm sure you have several rankings of your own or know of a few ranks I've failed to include. Be sure to send a message or comment to my email or social media account. If, by chance, you think you've encountered a previously undocumented worker rank, then consider yourself blessed. New ranks are being discovered daily, and you may get the chance to name one if you're lucky!

Take care for now, and be sure to use caution while in the workplace. You never know when you could encounter one of these mysterious yet useless workers.

CHAPTER 5

Mr. Polotski, the Boss Who Went Off the Deep End

Do you ever get the feeling that you're going to snap at work? Like, one day, you'll get fed up with everyone's shit and may do something drastic? All it takes is one prick to make a comment, right? You see red, and a whole lot of it. Most of us never get past the seeing red part. Mr. Polotski, on the other hand, saw red and reacted like a deranged bull, and you can't stop a charging bull once it has seen red.

A worker will quit within a week if they know they can't hack it. The ones who work for years, letting all that hatred stack on top of itself, are the dangerous ones—"Longtime employee takes out years of frustration on unsuspecting crowd. Details at 8:00 p.m." or "Woman who spent decades being quiet flattens boss with steamroller. Shocking video to come." There ain't jack shit you can do when they blow; just pray to the heavens they crack on your day off.

Richard Polotski, forty-eight, from Wilshire Falls, Delaware, had been my boss for twelve years. He started working at the board of education after the last numbnut was caught selling supplies at the flea market. Yes, you read that correctly. The big cheeses noticed the inventory for cleaning supplies was low, so they investigated. Sure enough, the dum-dum was caught selling plungers, toilet paper, mop handles, etc. When asked why he did it, he stated he didn't think his salary was high enough. These were the types of people the board of education hired, the ones who thought it was perfectly acceptable to steal supplies to sell at a dumpy flea market.

Mr. Polotski started working a few years after I took the janitor oath. He was a decent enough guy, a little rough around the edges maybe. He wasn't the type of person to compliment you on a job well done. In fact, he wasn't the type of person to engage you in conversation unless you cornered him and practically begged him to speak to you. Come to think of it, I don't think Mr. Polotski ever said a nice word about anybody, especially me. You know what, on second thought, maybe he was an asshole after all. Fuck that guy. But he's an integral part of the overall story, so I guess I must tell you about him.

Mr. Polotski was the head of my department, the head supervisor of all the broom pushers, grass cutters, and wrench turners. Think of him as the top guy in my department even though there were, like, twenty other departments in the board of education and our department was laughed at by all the other departments.

He came to the board of education out of sheer necessity. He figured, with his college degree, he could walk into an easy job for a few years until his dream job had more available positions. Mr. Polotski had obtained a Bachelor of Science in Park and Recreation Management degree. His dream job was to watch bison all day in Yellowstone while wearing a dark-green uniform and frumpy hat. What he got was a cramped office with fake wood paneling, a crappy budget, and around one hundred or so numbskulls to babysit. "How hard can it be to manage a few janitors and order supplies?" he must have thought. As long as he didn't pilfer those supplies to sell in a muddy market, he was already better than the last putz.

I guess he figured he would bang out a few years of state worker pension until he had the chance to move out west to follow his passion. Then the recession hit, causing him and about 125 million other Americans to put their dreams on the back burner for awhile. Giving Mr. Polotski the job of managing our department was one of the dumbest things ever to happen at work. Anyone who worked with him saw a volcano on the verge of eruption.

That man should have never been in charge of other humans. He had absolutely no people skills whatsoever. He was like a grizzly bear woken up from hibernation every time he spoke with you. He even had the hairy exterior sticking out from his long-sleeved, button-down shirts. Talk about big and powerful! This guy had the body frame of a bouncer with a doughy face and stacked arms. Let's just say Mr. Polotski could have thrown a vending machine halfway across the highway if provoked.

Mr. Polotski was more interested in nature than the human race. Animals and trees were his jam, not people. He was trained to handle matters in the National Park System—you know, how to save an endangered species on the brink of extinction or find a creative way to make mushrooms more fascinating. Mr. Polotski tried to run the department like it was a national park, and he failed almost immediately.

The public school system is very different from the great outdoors. To start, you cannot use a tranquilizer gun on school grounds. True, it's a fun way to handle aggressive coworkers, but it's not acceptable in most circumstances. You must also maintain strong communication skills to succeed in a school environment. Mr. Polotski communicated by screaming and slamming the stapler on his desk—not an effective way to manage subordinates.

There are rules to follow when working in an office setting, and Mr. Polotski ignored them, opting to do as he pleased on many occasions. Instead of attending mandatory meetings, Mr. Polotski raged out of his office, got into his way-too-small pickup, and sped down the highway. Needless to say, Mr. Polotski was the typical embodiment of a fight-or-flight scenario.

I didn't see Mr. Polotski on a regular basis. I bet you see your boss from time to time. Mine was MIA. He was hidden in his office, behind a huge CRT computer screen, constantly checking company emails. He had eight immediate bosses, not counting multiple school principals, vice principals, heads of departments, and so forth. They all sent him emails regularly, to which he took days, if not weeks, to reply. He typed as if he had boxing gloves on, mashing the keys instead of isolating one letter and tapping it softly.

I'm sure he tried the one finger at a time trick, got frustrated, and went full berserk. It probably took him an hour to answer a simple question via email. One of his old secretaries joked that he busted a keyboard, on average, once a month. The board of education stopped replacing them after the first year, so he had to buy his own. Imagine being so frustrated with work that you smash your keyboard to pieces.

When a boss sends you an email, they expect an answer within seconds. Even if you're on vacation, riding a donkey on the beaches of Aruba, they don't care. Mr. Polotski fell behind from day one. By the time he answered one email, he had several more waiting for a response. What happens if your boss doesn't hear back from you in a timely manner? They send another email. If that doesn't get answered, they have their secretary start calling your office. Before he knew it, Mr. Poloski's office looked like one of those telethons you see on public access TV.

The first time I met him was about a year after he was hired. I was called to his office to have a face-to-face meeting about an altercation. It was so long ago. I'm sure whoever I had told to go fuck themselves is already dead. Back in the good old days, you could tell someone to go fuck themselves and fear no repercussions, but times were changing rapidly during those years.

When I arrived at his office, he had the door closed, which was never a good sign. This meant the person behind the door was not approachable. His secretary told me to "just knock on the door. He'll answer." She looked terrified when she said this. So I did. I heard a muffled, "Yes?" I stated my name. Mr. Polotski, who let out an audible sigh, finally agreeed to let me in. "Yeah, it's open!" But he shouted it. It was like anytime the man spoke, his volume was cranked up to 11.

I walked into his office, only to be smacked by the whiff of a dirty hamster's cage. You know the scent I speak of. He didn't look to be a soiled, unwashed individual, but I guess keeping the door to your office closed for twelve hours a day would produce a certain aroma. I sat down in front of him, not knowing what to expect. As soon as I sat down, I looked at Mr. Polotski and remembered something from my childhood.

Have you ever watched that show *Dinosaurs* back in the nineties? Do you remember the main character? Not the mama. He had a boss, the one who was always screaming in a tiny office. He had horns on his head. Sherman Hemsley voiced the character. Well, that was what Mr. Polotski reminded me of—not the horns, just the size factor.

He was a large man, gruff and unpolished. His hair was brown but thinning and graying at the same time. His outfit consisted of a long-sleeved, button-down shirt with brown stripes crisscrossing a yellow background. Only one of his sleeves was rolled up. The arm he used to control his computer mouse was rolled up to his elbow. I would say he was about twenty years older than I was, but something had aged him rapidly. He looked damn near thirty or forty years years older than I was. This is what they mean when they say stress will kill you faster than cancer.

Mr. Polotski had one hand on his cheek and the other on his computer mouse. Every ten seconds, he would pick the mouse up and slam it on the desk. That poor mouse. I was sure he had to pay for his own computer mice too. It became apparent that Mr. Polotski was agitated. If forced to guess, I would say he didn't have a clue on how to use his computer. Gradually, he closed his eyes after groaning for a minute, then looked at me.

"Damn software update," he said.

"Oh," I said. "I hate when that happens."

"Yeah!" said Polotski loudly. "I hate computers altogether. Useless pieces of plastic, wires, and mercury." He stopped fiddling with the mouse, turned his eyes to a piece of paper on his desk, and sighed. "I'm Mr. Polotski, the new supervisor of the department." He stopped briefly. "Nice to meet you."

"Nice to meet you as well." We shook hands over his desk. I thought he would crush my fingers like a handful of pretzel rods. Goddamn, what a grip! His desk was small and boxy, much like an old desk from newsrooms in the 1950s. Most of the desk was taken up by a black computer screen. This was the early 2000s, kids, so you have to think big monitor and big tower. The remainder of the items on his desk were piles of papers, a nameplate with a wooden background, and a huge red coffee mug with the logo of the National Parks System on it.

Mr. Polotski looked down at his pile of papers. The top sheet I could see had my name on it. It was a discipline write-up. I had seen this quite a few times over my tenure, and I had become accustomed to the routine. The discipline write-up was a bullshit form. The people who submitted these things realized nothing would ever happen. This was a state job for one, and the leeway was pretty lax. Then the union put their two cents in, and before long, it was all forgotten.

It was almost like detention. If you had one or two detentions a semester, you were okay. It was a slap on the wrist, really. The trick was to know the acceptable limit of write-ups. The magic number was five. If I got five complaints over the course of a year, I might get moved to another post. That year, I believe I only had one previous write-up, so I was good.

"It says here on this discipline sheet that you told Mr. Johnson to go fuck himself," said Mr. Polotski. He had a loud, booming voice. At first, I didn't know if he was yelling at me or if that was his regular talking voice. I broached the situation cautiously.

"No, I didn't say that," I said. "I told him to back up and leave me alone."

"So you didn't tell him to go fuck himself?" asked Mr. Polotski.

"No, no, I didn't. I'd never say that to a coworker." I almost lost it on that one. Since this guy didn't know me, I tried to set a precedent for the future. Who knew how long this joker would last? The previous couple stunods were tossed after a few months. If Polotski were to last a few years, surely he would see me again for more discipline write-ups about my unsavory usage of the English language.

"Well, I'm not sure what you said, because I wasn't there, but I did go over your previous write-ups from former supervisors," said Polotski. Ah, shit! The new guy wasn't a complete fool like the last dummies. He might have looked like a dopey bear, but Polotski wasn't stupid. Mr. Polotski brought out three other pieces of paper, all with similar write-ups. "Here's one from three years ago saying you told the same Mr. Johnson to go fuck himself with a broom handle," he said. He shuffled the papers around. "And this one here from two years ago says you spoke to a Mrs. Humi, advising her to, quote, 'Back the fuck up, you ugly fuck.' Do you want to explain to me why I see several write-ups containing the word *fuck* with your name on them? This is a serious offense, mister. What are we going to do about this?"

He was extremely loud now. This speaking tone was intense, full of power. I believed this was the first time a boss actually yelled at me. Sure, I had been in verbal fisticuffs before, but with numbnut coworkers. The previous supervisors were all morons and were easily led. Perhaps I could derail the Polotski train the same way. While sitting in his tight office, my mind started to wander. *Think, my good man, think!* I thought. *Find his weakness and use it against him! Everyone has an Achilles' heel. Find his!* With Polotski barreling his gaze down at me, I went for my move.

"Is that a National Parks coffee mug you're drinking out of?" I asked.

"Um, yes, yes, it is," said Mr. Polotski. He sounded dumbstruck. "I bought it at the visitors center in Red Rock Canyon. It's not a national park, but it should be." His angry boss face slowly faded. "It's twenty-five miles outside of Las Vegas. Really, really nice trails and so close to Vegas."

"Oh, nice," I said.

"Have you ever been there?" he asked. His massive jowls were arched up, smiling. He looked like a bulldog panting.

"No, not yet," I said. Before I could speak again, he went into his story:

"Boy, it sure is an amazing place. The colors from the rocks and cliffs reflect so beautifully off the natural landscape. They have this interesting artist in residence program on-site. You can apply in January to paint in the desert during off-peak hours. Simply marvelous!"

"Oh, wow," I said. "That's something."

"I highly recommend a trip out west. You should see it in the morning, just as the sun's starting to come up. Pure magic, plain and simple!"

He went on and on about the glories of Red Rock Canyon for another twenty minutes. From the "super cool trails" to the "really neat interactive center," this place was the bee's knees according to Polotski. Christ on a cracker, this guy wouldn't shut the hell up about national parks and his coffee cup collection. I mean, yeah, they were cool and all, but still. At this point, being suspended would have been a welcome experience.

Once Polotski ran out of trip photos to show me from a huge photo album he kept in his desk, he went back to the paper in front of him. "Just, ah, just lay off the cursing to coworkers, okay?" he said.

"Got it," I said.

I left his office an hour and a half later with a new appreciation for the term administrative punishment. My fucking ears were bleeding after listening to Polotski drone on about the National Park System. True, my use of the term *fuck* was out of control. I admit I had a problem. But Polotski had a problem too. Whenever he spoke about parks, he was a great guy. It was the other 98 percent of the time that he was a complete dickhead.

As I look back now, years removed from our first meeting, I like to think of Mr. Polotski as *Dr. Jekyll and Mr. Hyde*. His entire attitude changed frequently and without cause. Whenever I saw Mr. Polotski, he was either completely confused or extremely pissed off. Mind you, I only saw him a handful of times over the years, but those times were jam-packed with emotions.

About six months after the Red Rock Redrum, I witnessed Mr. Polotski's full fury. The board of education had one of their dipshit meetings at my school. It was all a big show, where they discussed topics pertaining to the running of a school district. They talked about nonsense for three hours, congratulated themselves on yet another job well done, and then headed off to a redneck dive bar. This meeting, however, had a bit of drama.

Mr. Polotski was tasked to drive to the administrative complex, pick up a box of binders, and bring it to my post for the meeting. The issue was with the box; Mr. Polotski, whose job it was to set up their meeting, brought the wrong one. I heard a loud commotion in the cafeteria around six o'clock. They normally had these meetings in the cafeteria, which had a stage with a curtain area in front of it. Of course, I ventured down to see what the noise was. I snuck behind the curtain on the stage to peek at the action. There, I saw a confused Mr. Polotski being yelled at by Mr. Sanders.

"How could you bring the wrong box, Polotski? This is unacceptable."

"I'm sorry, Mr. Sanders. I thought you said to bring the financial box," said Mr. Polotski in a Golly Gee Willikers manner.

"No, I did not tell you to bring the financial box. I specifically instructed you to bring the administrative box. I clearly wrote that in the email!"

"I'm sorry. They look similar to each other," said Polotski.

"Similar?" said Sanders with venom in his speech. "Similar, Polotski? Does the sun look similar to the moon?"

"No, it doesn't." He was starting to pick up the box when Sanders dug into his ass even more.

"Don't answer that question! It's rhetorical. Do you know what that means?" asked Sanders. Mr. Polotski stood there, not sure whether to answer. "Well, it seems funny how you know the answer to a complex question but not the difference between two clearly marked, very different boxes!" Mr. Polotski was starting to repack the box while Mr. Sanders and his cronies were sitting in their comfortable, high-back chairs, annoyed. Sanders slashed into Polotski yet again. "It's quite a simple task: bring the administrative box to the building. How could you have fouled it up, Polotski? Perhaps I should hire someone who understands simple tasks instead of screwing them up."

Mr. Polotski did not answer the question in fear of another lambasting. He picked up the box, placed it onto a handcart, and wheeled it back to the loading dock, all with his head hung low and his tail between his legs. As he wheeled the cart down to the loading dock, I followed in tow—out of sight, mind you. I was hiding in a classroom connected to the back of the stage with the lights off. I had a front-row seat to the madness.

Mr. Polotski was walking so fast that he tilted the box onto the ground, causing the binders to spill out. He growled upon seeing the mess. I had never seen anyone growl at something before. It was quite disturbing. With ten or so large binders splayed out on the floor, Mr. Polotski went into robot mode. Each time he bent down to pick up a binder, he was a metallic fiend. Each motion was mechanical in nature. Instead of placing the binders in the box, he slammed them with force.

I stood there in that dark room watching Mr. Polotski pick up a paper binder, raise it high above his head, and then slam it down as if he was trying to drive it ten feet into the earth. The violence in which he slammed those binders was astonishing. He looked like Zeus throwing lightning bolts from the top of Mount Olympus, eagerly trying to smite the villagers below.

After he smashed the last binder, he tilted the handcart back and proceeded down to the loading dock. I didn't move from my hidden location until I knew he was gone. Boy, did he have some power on him! Good God, if he ever unleashed some of that power on someone…

If you talk to some of the old-timers and ask them about Mr. Polotski, they'll start laughing uncontrollably not because Polotski was a funny man but because he was the butt of everyone's jokes for a long time. You know how people get when they see a new employee, especially a boss. Think back to high school, when the jocks made fun of the nerds. They would haze them and pull their pants down in class and maybe give them a wedgie or two. This was what, theoretically, happened to Mr. Polotski. Once the broken keyboard thing got out, the rumor mill revved up production. Then came jokes about his love of national parks. Mr. Polotski was the big, dumb beast everyone made fun of from then on out.

It started with a little teasing over handheld radios. Mr. Polotski would call a worker on the radio about something—"Polotski to Post 718. Come in, Post 718." The responding janitor would call back, "Yeah, go ahead, Smokey the Bear. I'm all ears!" Then some morons would laugh over the airwaves. They would key up the radio and laugh like hyenas. Sure enough, someone would call out, "Only you can prevent forest fires!" over the radio. Hearing laughter pissed him off royally, but the more he yelled into the radio for them to stop, the more he sounded like a real animal. Mr. Polotski would try to stop the banter, only to be met with growling and barking in return. After five minutes of random animal sounds, an administrator would call Mr. Polotski over the radio, yelling at him to call their office. Imagine having to deal with immature workers all day and then be yelled at by your boss because you can't control them.

Mr. Polotski brought out his grumpy side soon after the radio incidents. Nobody fessed up, but everyone knew who they were. Polotski, after getting his ass reamed out numerous times, went on the offensive. The suspected culprits were given more of a workload in retaliation. An all-out revolution followed. A clique of workers bucked against Mr. Polotski and his punishing ways. These few individuals started a riot among the department, paving a path to insubordination and rebellion.

Before long, more workers had joined in. They called him Ranger Rick, Boy Scout of the Year, Smokey the Bear, and all sorts of mean shit. Jokes about him wearing a 5XL Boy Scout outfit ran all throughout the department. One of the more artistically inclined workers started drawing caricatures of Mr. Polotski and faxed them all over the district. They were crude cartoons of him holding one of his National Parks coffee cups. Some depicted him taking his oath with hairy arms raised high or sewing a patch onto his sash. Much like the radio calls, no one was ever caught, and Mr. Polotski was yet again laughed at for simply being a passionate person.

More heavy workloads were doled out. The union got involved. Bickering back and forth led nowhere; it was a mess. Then the hazing took a horrible turn. Mr. Polotski had a wooden shelf in his office with a bunch of animal figurines aligned on it. He showed me his collection during that long conversation when we first met. He said he bought them from his travels around the parks. There were things like a moose, some wolves, and a few bear statues; it was kind of like your grandmas Bradford Exchange collector's plates. By my count, he had around sixty animals. Well, one of the wrench turners got ahold of a key to his office and rearranged his personal possessions.

Mr. Polotski came in on a Monday morning to find that his animals had thrown themselves a little party. Someone had arranged his figurines in naughty, provocative positions. They had put a lot of thought into their placement, like, a ridiculous amount of thought. The bears were all in lewd positions—some in a sixty-nine position and some straight-up screwing. The wolves were engaged in a pack humping session, like, ten of them in a row. I didn't know how the person got them to stay like that, but they had a conga line of wolf sex going strong. The poor bird figurines were all in a drunken stupor. The vandal had put empty airplane liquor bottles under their wings.

The crowning achievement of the attack was the desecration of Mr. Polotski's famed National Parks cup. Some heathen filled it to the brim with dried dog shit. On Polotski's desk was a piece of white paper with magazine cutout letters glued to it. It read, "EAT SHIT RANGER RICK." Regardless of how I ever felt about a previous boss, nothing had ever driven me to fill their coffee mug with feces. There were certain lines one did not cross.

Mr. Polotski went fucking ballistic, and rightly so. A few of the wrench turners who were stationed near Mr. Polotski's office witnessed the whole tirade. Mitch told me about it a day after it happened.

"Dude, you should've seen the look on his doofy face!" he said. "This dumb son of a bitch started whooping and hollering about how he's 'gonna get someone good for this.' He looked like he was foamin' from the fucking mouth like a rabid coon!"

"Jesus Christ," I said.

"Yeah, buddy, Polotski sure did cause a scene. He threw a bunch of tools around the office, pounding his fist on his desk like a gorilla who'd been shot with a BB gun!"

"Who did it?" I asked. "Who broke into his office?"

Mitch, who had been grinning the whole time while talking to me, smiled with a look of self-congratulation. "I don't know," he said smuggly. "Must've been someone Polotski pissed off real bad."

"That's low, man. Whoever did it went too far with the dog shit," I said.

"Come on, man," said Mitch begrudgingly. "Whoever did this heinous act must've had reasons for doing it. I mean, Ranger Rick had it coming, ya know."

"Aren't you the guy who has all those hunting dogs?" I asked.

"What?" said Mitch. He had a befuddled look on his face.

"Don't you breed hunting dogs to sell? I heard you have a pen behind your house. You raise Labs and pointers, don't you?"

"Maybe I do," said Mitch. "And maybe I don't."

"A man who raises a lot of dogs would always surely have an abundance of dog shit on hand," I said. Mitch suddenly remembered he had a work order to fix a busted pipe at another post. He left abruptly, looking perplexed.

Mr. Polotski filed a police report after the attack. Unfortunately, there wasn't much they could do. They took notes and a few photos and questioned people, but in the end, it went down officially as a misdemeanor vandalism. "What about the ransom note on my desk?" asked Mr. Polotski. "Isn't that classified as some sort of intimidation? Can't you dust for fingerprints?" The police told him they didn't have much to go on. Without cameras or credible witnesses, they couldn't do much.

Mr. Polotski appealed to his bosses for help, but he got nowhere. "I'm sorry your little toys were violated, Polotski," said Mr. Sanders. "But the police have informed me it was a random act of vandalism."

"Mr. Sanders, you know it was an inside job. The door wasn't broken in. They used a freaking key for God's sake! This was a deliberate attack, and…and I'm requesting cameras to be installed in my office to prevent this from happening again."

"Not a chance, Polotski," said Mr. Caravaggio, the head of the district. "There's no money in the budget for that."

"But, sir, this was done by a couple of maintenance workers. I know Mitch and Greg were hanging around outside my office late Friday night. I think one of them did it!"

"Do you have any proof?" asked Mr. Caravaggio.

"Well, no, but I know—"

"Polotski," said Mr. Sanders, "you can't go around making bold accusations about employees unless you have proof of their guilt. That's how we get sued!"

"But, sir—"

"Enough with your useless talk." Sanders's demon snarl came out. "Listen here, Polotski. If you had better control over your workers, maybe they'd respect you. Between the radio calls and the cartoons…" Sanders looked pitifully at Mr. Polotski. "Get some control, Polotski, or find yourself a new job!"

I felt sorry for Mr. Polotski. I really did. Poor dude was double screwed. Not long after the Cup O'Poop incident did we see a very different side of him. He answered questions with one- or two-word answers, learning not to blow his top. When provoked by rowdy employees, Mr. Polotski simply ignored them. There were no more outbursts on the radio, yelling at people when they badgered him.

Mr. Polotski stood tall in the face of juvenile behavior. Take, for example, when Mitch started a rumor about how his wife was an actual bison from Yellowstone National Park. Normally, Mr. Polotski would have jumped into his tiny pickup truck and torn out of the parking lot in anger, but not anymore. He ignored the hazings.

For years, no one heard a word from Mr. Polotski. He took his daily torture from employees with poise. People like Mitch and Greg tried their hardest to break him, but it didn't faze him. Soon, the cartoons, radio calls, and hazing altogether had no impact on the man.

I've known several people who don't give a crap anymore about stuff at work. Tons of workers hit a wall, say, "Fuck it," and give up trying to fight. They take their hits and keep it moving. I think once Mr. Polotski knew he had no help from his bosses, he learned to operate on autopilot. I mean, everyone can expect a level of disrespect when working in a public school. Unfortunately, it's par for the course. You don't get to clean up garbage for so many years and not expect to be treated unfairly. I think that was Mr. Polotski's biggest downfall. He thought that because he had a college degree and he was only going to be there temporarily, he could have left anytime he wanted to.

Mr. Polotski let this place destroy him piece by piece. Once you become complacent, it's ever so easy to ignore quitting a shitty job. A person can fool themselves into believing it will get better. Soon, you get run over by the dump truck of reality. I didn't think he saw it coming until he was under the tires. Instead of leaving after the first few incidents, Mr. Polotski stayed on thinking it would get better. He kept telling himself, "Only one more year. Just a few more months until I apply for a good job in the Parks System." Before he knew it, the job had him stuck in quicksand up to his thick neck.

The last time I spoke with Mr. Polotski, he was at my post, setting up for another meeting. His job was to make sure the meeting was all set for examination from Sanders and Caravaggio. There were six-foot tables to align and water pitchers to set out in front of wired microphones. He called me over the radio to meet him in the cafeteria to help move a large projector screen. As I walked down to the café to help, I heard familiar animal sounds over the airwaves. I remember shaking my head as I walked toward him. *What a bunch of children,* I thought.

A minute later, I was walking across the empty cafeteria to help him. There he was, flannel shirt and all, calmly placing nameplates in front of high-back office chairs. As I walked up to Mr. Polotski, the noises continued to get louder and more animalistic. This night, the district was especially infantile. It sounded like a recording of the jungle in the middle of mating season. All I could hear were gorilla grunts and howling monkeys. Mr. Polotski looked at me to say hi. I saw a defeated man.

"Hello, Mr. Polotski. How are you?" I asked.

"Good evening," he said. Mr. Polotski stated his words without emotion. His face was sunken in and tired looking. "I'm fine. How are you?" He didn't say it in a condescending tone. He sounded more like a person who had been through the mill and needed a vacation.

"I'm okay," I said. "Where is this screen going?"

He stopped placing placards on the tables. "We'll move it over to the right side," he said. "That's where Mr. Sanders wants it this time. Last meeting, it was on the left side, near the exit ramp. I guess he decided it would be better over here, near the water fountains.

Each meeting, the floor plan changes. He changes it each time and wonders why it looks different when he shows up."

He was referring to Mr. Sanders and his vile pack of hangers-on who hosted these events. I shrugged my shoulders, trying not to engage Mr. Polotski either way. "I guess we can move it now before he storms in here, trying to change it all over again," he said. We started to move the screen when the radio waves woke up again. "Hey, Ranger Rick, eat shit!" Both our handheld radios echoed throughout the empty cafeteria. Of course, laughing sounds came across the airwaves.

I had heard this line no more than a thousand times over the years. I didn't laugh anymore; it became an annoying sound to me. It was sort of like a police siren in the city. As we moved the screen, I let out a short huff, shaking my head. "You'd think those guys would have something better to do instead of that stuff, you know?" I said this as we moved the heavy screen. "I mean, Jesus, what the hell?"

"Yep," he said. As we placed the screen down, more antics came.

"Look at me. I'm getting a dog shit badge for my stupid sash!" This was followed by more laughter and screeching. Hearing these sounds while I was right in front of Mr. Polotski was painful. I felt remorse while standing in front of him. I felt pity for a man who didn't deserve this kind of treatment. He always seemed fair to me. Even with his loud voice and humdrum demeanor, Mr. Polotksi was a decent man. It had been almost a decade after the whole dog shit incident too. What kind of losers still talked about stuff like that for years?

I stood there for a few seconds, keeping eye contact with him as the noises howled from the radios. We both reached down to our radio volume knobs to turn them lower just so we couldn't hear the nonsense anymore. Mr. Polotski started to walk away to rearrange something for the meeting. He had taken a few steps away when I stopped him. I wasn't sure what to expect when I spoke up. I felt the need to make the moment more human.

"How do you do it?" I asked.

He stopped walking. He had his back to me at first, then turned around to put his head up. Mr. Polotski walked back toward me, stopping a few feet away. "I don't know anymore," he said. "I really don't know." He put his hands in his black jeans' pockets. He took in a long breath, then blew it out through his nose.

"This is bullshit, man," I said out loud. "How come you can't fire someone? This ain't high school. This is supposed to be a professional job." A little anger came out with my words. Mr. Polotski shrugged his shoulders with a look of bashfulness. I was more upset than he was.

"Nobody cares," he said. "Everyone laughs it off like they have for years."

"I mean, it's Mitch who's doing this crap. Everyone knows it. That jerk-off and his buddies are nobodies. They…they can't keep doing this. It's embarrassing to hear that shit!"

"Not anymore," he said. "I've heard it so many times it doesn't affect me anymore."

"Can't Mr. Sanders or Mr. Caravaggio stop this from happening? Isn't it illegal to block airwaves with nonemergency talk or something like that? Mr. Sanders is the boss of us. He needs to stop this!"

Mr. Poloski laughed and took his hands out of his pockets. He folded his arms in front of his chest. "He doesn't give a shit if they mess with me. He's the one who gave them the key to my office in the first place," he said.

"What?"

"He sure did," said Polotski. "When I first took over, I changed the locks with my own set of locks. I had only two keys made from my own locksmith: one key I always kept on my key ring and the other key I gave to Mr. Sanders in case I lost my key or was locked out. No one ever got to my keys because I had always kept them on my personal key ring in my pocket. My guess is, Sanders gave Mitch or whoever the key and told him to go wild."

"But why?" I asked. "I mean, I know Sanders is the biggest asswipe walking, but why would he do that?"

"Because he can't fire me without a good reason. My contract states that administration cannot terminate me without due cause. If they do, then I can sue the hell out of them. But they can't get rid of me because I perform up to the standards of my contract. Each year, I exceed the requirements of my duty, and it kills them not to fire me. Sanders has had it in for me from day one. He couldn't fire me legally, so he got some maintenance men to start harassing me."

This was the only time Mr. Polotski ever spoke without screaming or waving his arms up and down. It was as if he was sedated, like a tired person who had given up.

"You know, Mitch and Greg work for Mr. Sanders on side jobs. They fix all those broken-down tenements he rents out under Section 8 housing."

"I...I didn't know that," I said.

"Yep. Sanders has his little foot soldiers taunt me week in and week out. Do you know I asked for another supervisor to help me? Yes, I have. According to the bylaws of the department, I'm supposed to have two other supervisors work directly under me to help ease the burden of the job. Each time I ask, Sanders tells me there's no money in the budget."

"Really? I had no idea," I said.

Mr. Polotski looked over to his left. He was staring off into space, thinking about something. "I've been harassed at home too. I get people egging my house, shooting paintballs at my truck. I had to buy a home security system because someone broke into my house three times."

I stood in front of Mr. Polotski, listening to his speech, not knowing what to say. He sounded like one of those head cases who thought the world was out to get him, but I believed everything Mr. Polotski said. I saw it in his face. He wasn't lying.

"I had no idea that happened," I said. "I'm sorry they did that to you." Mr. Polotski had a mixture of emotions behind his eyes. If it were me, I would have broken down a long time ago. He was steadfast in his speech. He turned back to look me in the face.

"I come to work each day and do my job as best I can because I can't let them win," he said, "not after all I've put up with. I won't give them the satisfaction of firing me."

With that said, Mr. Polotski unfolded his arms, turned around, and began setting up the remainder of the nameplates. As I walked away, I saw him reach for something on the middle table. It was his red coffee cup. I know what you're thinking: "Why didn't he throw that dog-shit-filled cup out?" That was what I would have done! I hoped it wasn't the same cup. Maybe he bought the same one to replace the other crap-filled one. Then again, he really loved that cup from what I heard. I mean, you can bleach it out and really clean it thoroughly. I was guessing that along with anger and rage, coffee was one of the only things that kept him going. I watched as he took a long sip and proceeded to work on getting the meeting set up perfectly.

About two hours later, I got a call to come help disassemble the tables after the meeting was done. Usually, when the meeting was adjourned, Mr. Polotski called for help with the heavier items. So I gathered the crew to help with moving the big tables and projector screen. Breaking down after the meeting was a chaotic scene. Chairs were moved and the microphone wires were wound back onto their reels. It was a lot of people walking around in circles until the head bosses left. The head schmucks lingered around, bullshittting the night away, as we slaved under their watchful gaze.

Polotski was already grabbing nameplates from the tables as we came into the cafeteria. As I walked in, I saw the evil Mr. Sanders rubbing elbows with the head guy Mr. Caravaggio and some other board members. They were smiling it up, no doubt enjoying the sight of Poloski and the rest of us lowly workers clean up their mess. I walked toward one side of the tables with a coworker named Tommy. We started to break down as usual. With all the commotion going on, tables being dragged and all, I heard a sharp sound. I stopped to look. There on the white tile floor was a shattered red coffee cup. It was in several pieces, resting in light-caramel-colored liquid. Mr. Polotski must have brought it with him when he started disassembling the meeting and left it on one of the tables.

The room went quiet until the sound of bitter laughter erupted from behind a table. "Whoops!" said Mr. Caravaggio. "Look out!" The fat man, who resembled a bull elephant seal, was staring at the broken coffee cup, laughing out loud. Mr. Polotski was standing about five feet away when he stopped to see his beloved cup in ruins. I looked at the poor ceramic cup, then at Mr. Caravaggio, then over to Mr. Polotski. *Should I get a mop or maybe a sweeping pan to clean up the mess?* I thought. "Must've tipped the table there, huh?" said Mr. Caravaggio, who was tapping Mr. Sanders on the shoulders to gloat. "Sorry, Polotski. Too bad about your cup." Anyone within earshot heard the lack of caring in his voice.

"That fat bastard knocked his cup over on purpose!" said Tommy. "Did you see that?"

"Looks like it," I said.

"Should we clean it up?" asked Tommy. He was whispering, but his voice carried a little.

"Um," I said, "yeah, maybe go grab the—"

"Are you fucking kidding me?" Mr. Polotski shouted. This was said so loudly that anyone within a two-mile radius could have heard it clearly. Polotski slammed the nameplates he was holding and stared at the heavyweight boss. The room was silent; even the mice in the walls were quiet. All eyes went to Mr. Polotski, who, at this time, was unhinged from his regular complacency.

"Woah, woah, woah," said Mr. Caravaggio in his best Tony Soprano voice. "Watch your language, Polotski."

"You tipped that table on purpose! I watched you do it. I saw you out of the corner of my eye!" Mr. Polotski didn't care who was listening. He had taken enough shit from his overlords for three lifetimes. "You broke my cup on purpose!"

"Who do you think you're talking to there, Polotski?" said the fat man. "You're crazy. It was an accident." He said this with a smile, like a "Screw you" smile. Mr. Polotski saw this look and went off. He started to walk closer to the group of supervisors.

"Oh, shit, here we go!" Tommy said out loud.

Mr. Polotski pointed to the table. "I watched you waddle your fat ass over to this table right here, look around to see if anyone was looking, and then you bumped it enough to knock my coffee cup onto the ground!"

Mr. Polotski had the attention of everyone in the room. Nobody moved, and nobody spoke. It all happened so quickly. Mr. Polotski grabbed the table in front of Mr. Caravaggio, flipped it over, and proceeded to step two feet closer to Mr. Caravaggio's face. At this point, members of the board moved in close to try to settle things down. People remaining in the crowd tensed up, waiting to see the outcome of the standoff. Here was the scene: Mr. Polotski was standing inches from the fat, flat face of Mr. Caravaggio.

"Don't do anything stupid, Polotski!" shouted Mr. Sanders, who, not surprisingly, was about fifteen feet away, slowly slinking into the shadows.

I watched Mr. Polotski stare into the eyes of his boss. He pointed toward the puddle on the ground. "Pick it up," he said. "Pick up the pieces of my cup and apologize right now."

"You better watch your tone," said Mr. Caravaggio. "You know who you're talking to?"

"Don't care," said Polotski, shaking his head from side to side, never unlocking his gaze. "I'm tired of being harassed and bullied by you and your minion Sanders over there." He pointed his left arm to Sanders, letting him know he saw him slithering away. "Pick up each shattered piece of my coffee cup now, or else."

"This sounds a lot like insubordination, don't it?" yelled Mr. Caravaggio. He was pretty ballsy for a short, round man. He spoke as if he was untouchable like a mafia boss with ties to Sicily. "I think this warrants grounds for termination, don't you, Mr. Sanders?" Sanders didn't say a word. He was busy making an exit strategy. He knew what was coming. Mr. Sanders was inching his way closer to the exit door. "Right?" said Mr. Caravaggio. He looked over to his right to look for Mr. Sanders. He was no where to be found. Mr. Caravaggio, who was still smiling, turned back to face Mr. Polotski.

"Oh, we're past termination now, you fat fuck!"

With that remark, Mr. Polotski lunged for Mr. Caravaggio's chubby neck, clamping onto his gullet. Mr. Polotski straightened his arm, drew upon all his strength, and picked up his obese boss. I know it sounds cliché, but no one had time to react, least of all Mr. Caravaggio. He didn't realize what was happening until he was a good foot off the ground. Screams arose from the congregation. Audible gasps pierced the crowd. With Mr. Caravaggio wiggling, Mr. Polotski let out a vicious war cry. The tubby boss looked like a plump fly trying to free itself from a sticky spider's web. I saw his tiny eyes pop out of his fat face while in the death lock of Polotski the Terrible. I now know what pure fear looks like after seeing the face of Mr. Caravaggio as he struggled for oxygen.

After three seconds of holding his boss, Mr. Polotski screamed once more, then chokeslammed him into the nearest folding table. It was like something out of WrestleMania, I swear to Jesus. Pens, paperwork, a few notepads, and a water pitcher scattered outward, away from the epicenter of impact. I remember seeing that chunky son of a bitch bounce off the tile floor. Mr. Polotski slammed him so hard he actually bounced!

Although his hang time wasn't that great, Mr. Polotski got some good distance in his throw. The table was about two feet away from where he originally grabbed his prey. When the papers and pens finally settled, the usual ass-kissers rallied around Mr. Caravaggio—"Someone call an ambulance!" "Oh my God, Mr. Caravaggio, are you okay?" and "Get the police here now!"

With his boss writhing in pain in front of him, gurgling in agony, Mr. Polotski casually walked to where his broken coffee cup lay and began picking up the pieces. Ignoring the yells from those surrounding him, he casually gathered what remained of his cup and turned to exit the building. He never spoke a word after planting his boss into the table. He simply took the wet pieces of ceramic in his hands and left.

As he walked toward the exit, Mr. Sanders, seeing that Mr. Polotski was halfway across the cafeteria, called out to him. "Consider yourself terminated, Polotski! And don't bother coming back. You won't get in any school building ever again! I've already alerted the police department, and you'll rot in prison for this, you animal!" It was pretty big talk for a man who ran damn near fifty feet out of harm's way when the shit hit the fan—a typical coward for you.

I stood there stunned with the feeling of pure adulation. Oh, the feeling of slamming a scumbag boss through a table, then walking off like a champ. Sure, he would be fired, arrested, and charged with second-degree assault; but for those few, precious seconds, I bet Mr. Polotski felt like a god. Too bad he couldn't have grabbed Sanders with the other arm. I would have donated both eyeballs to science after seeing that feat knowing that surely I would never witness anything so amazing ever again.

I'm sure you can guess how Mr. Polotski's story ends. He's out on bail now, awaiting a short and swift trial. After all, the board of education has the best and most diabolical lawyers taxpayer money can buy. I'm positive he'll spend a year or so in county lockup for his actions. I guess spending a year in prison will be a breeze after being tortured for years under the hooves of Sanders and his ruffians.

The show must go on, as they say. My department is interviewing for Mr. Polotski's job next week. Maybe I'll put in for it. Nah, you can't pay me enough to put up with the shit Mr. Polotski dealt with. I'm shocked he lasted so long. If it were me, I would have cracked a lot sooner than he did.

CHAPTER 6

Guess Who's Back

It was only a matter of time until he came back. You couldn't hold a good brother down, as he once put it. So here was the scene: I was walking down a corridor late one evening with headphones on, oblivious to the world. My head was down, as it normally was when I was sweeping the floor. While slowly chugging along, I looked up to see a set of metallic-gold sneakers dead stopped in my path.

There, decked out in what one could only call thug clothing, was Tyrell Jones. My boots squeaked a little as I came to a stop. Standing in front of me was the greatest man ever to swing a mop; his arms were outstretched, waiting to deliver one of his patented bear hugs. I yanked my earbuds out so fast they wrapped around the broom handle in my hands.

"Surprise, mothafucka!" Tyrell screamed. He fluttered his fingertips, beckoning me to come in for the hug. My heart was still hiccupping a few beats, startled.

"Wha-what are you…," I tried to say.

"That's right, baby!" said Tyrell. "It's the man himself!" He lunged forward into my chest, hugging me aggressively, laughing as he swayed. He snatched me up so quickly I almost fell forward on top of him. I believe the broom handle was stuck in between us when he came rushing in for his love. Tyrell was singing aloud, his voice echoing in my chest cavity. "Guess who's back…back again. Tyrell's back. Tell your mothafuckin' friends!"

My brain had just shit itself. I hadn't seen this man for years, too many years. Nobody had heard a word from him in such a long time, yet there he was, grabbing me like a drowning man holding on to a life jacket. Tyrell was giggling to himself, hooting and hollering the whole time. He let go, stepping back a little, still smiling.

"What are you doing here?" I asked. "How the hell did you get in?"

"Well, my chubby compadre…" Tyrell paused, closing his eyes in a dramatic fashion. He tilted his head back, just like the Rock used to do when he was about to say his tagline. "I'm back, baby! Tell it from the highest mountain peak! Tyrell Jones is back. Back in action, you dig?"

"What…what do you mean back? You were fired years ago," I said. I was still astonished that he was standing in front of me, in the flesh, with a curved Boston Celtics hat and golden basketball shoes.

"They can't hold me back, man! These mothafuckers are so damn dumb, I'm telling you!"

"Who?" I asked. "Who's dumb?" Tyrell was slowly dancing in a circle, doing his rendition of the dance move called the percolator. Once he finished jamming around, he stopped, looked me in the eye, and said, "Captain Cupcake is gone, my brotha."

Let me refresh your memory from the first book. Tyrell Jones was fired after numerous years of slacking off. He spent most of his janitor career calling in sick and refusing to do any real work for a good ten years. He got away with a lot of garbage because he was a super smooth liar. Tyrell could talk his way out of anything. Above all, he was a con artist. When lying failed, he turned to straight-up buffoonery. He used any angle he could to get out of trouble. This included falsifying doctors' notes, lying about dead family members, and reporting the board of education for what he called racist-ass bullshit.

But years of crying wolf caught up to him. That, and the number of complaints reached a tipping point. He was fired by Mr. Polotski, the head boss. That was almost seven years ago. A few weeks ago, in today's time, Mr. Polotski was terminated for less-than-professional behavior, i.e. the chokeslam into the tables situation. Tyrell always used to call Polotski Captain Cupcake because he looked as though cupcake was his primary food source.

"That's when I seized my moment, man," said Tyrell. "My boy C-Rod told me about the melee at the board meeting. He was there. His kid was at the meeting, receiving an award for band or some shit. He saw Captain pick up the tubby superintendent and slam his ass into the table." He was finger-pointing to me, trying to illustrate his story—not in a bad way but more like a "Keep listening" sort of way.

"With Captain Cupcake gone and the ad in the paper looking for help, I figured it was worth a shot."

"No way!" I said. "They hired you back? Who hired you?"

"New boss man, Ginger or Geiger. I don't know. Something white sounding." He was referring to the new head boss named Mr. Genger. At this time, I feel the need to explain, dear reader, that I am indeed Caucasian, and Tyrell is most definitely not Caucasian. Just to clarify any confusion.

"And they hired you right there, on the spot?" I asked.

"He interviewed me today," said Tyrell.

"No. I don't believe you. How...how can they hire you back? You were shitcanned."

"I don't know," said Tyrell. "I walked in, handed over my application, new boss man gave me a ten-minute interview, and poof, I start tomorrow at this building! Aha! You believe that shit?"

I stood there befuddled and elated. He was back, alive, standing three feet from my face. It felt totally unreal. My skin had goose bumps up and down, turning from smooth to bumpy every thirty seconds. The fact that he was here at my post was enough to make me believe in miracles, but to be rehired at the same job he was terminated from? It didn't make any sense. Then again, this place hadn't ever made sense. Rationale was a misnomer in the public school system. Just ask any teacher who had to buy their own school supplies.

Since Polotski was the head guy for our department, he had control over everything. He did all the hiring, firing, and supply ordering. You name it, this guy did it. When he was fired, the board rushed to hire a new boss named Philip Genger. Without access to old records, he saw no reason not to hire Tyrell. Being constantly shorthanded, he interviewed and hired anyone who walked in the door. How could the new boss have known the man sitting across from him at his desk was forcefully removed years before?

"You're lying," I said. "They're stupid, but not that stupid. Nobody hired you back." I was in disbelief, utter and complete disbelief, of yet another one of Tyrell's short stories. This guy lied about his own mother dying to get a paid week off. Of course, he would lie about being hired back just to grind some old axes.

Tyrell kept turning around behind him as he talked to see if anyone was coming. He looked nervous, like he had broken into the place. A part of me believed he did until he brought out a set of keys from his back pocket, jingling them.

"Lookie here!" Tyrell said. "Lookie what I got!"

"Get the fuck out of here!" I said. "This is crazy. Did you mug someone in the parking lot?"

"Nope. I told you, man, they stupid. Boss man said my résumé was—what did he call it?—superlative. Some college word. And my letter of recommendation was on point!" Tyrell pulled a folded piece of paper from his other back pocket. It was a letter from someone in the Newark school system. "I had my pal Johnny Boy from PS 24 write me a glowing letter. He's the vice principal at one of them elementary schools." Tyrell laughed again. "I never worked there, man. They not gonna check."

"But they're going to check here!" I said. My raised voice echoed a bit down the empty corridor. "You know once someone recognizes you, you're toast."

Tyrell gave me one of his jerk-off motion hand gestures, smirking the whole time. Nothing ever fazed him the way it did most people. He didn't seem the least bit concerned with the notion of getting fired again the very next time he walked into the building.

"Look, man, I gotta split. I'm not supposed to be here until tomorrow afternoon. Just pretend like you don't know me when I show up. I'll fill you in on everything else. Peace out!" He flipped two peace fingers up, then clapped my hand and bounded down the hall. I would have expected Liberace or Mother Theresa to walk into the building before seeing Tyrell ever again.

J.R. WARNET

The next day, Tyrell used his new set of keys to enter the building, go directly to the custodians' office, and begin introducing himself to the rest of the crew. I was the only one who remembered Tyrell, because none of the other workers were around when he was fired. I'm not even exaggerating when I say we had no less than two hundred new employees after Tyrell left. The other three workers at my post had a combined two years total time between them. As Tyrell introduced himself, he never looked at me until he came up to shake my hand. "Hello. I'm Tyrell Jones. It's a pleasure to meet you, sir." That sly son of a bitch.

The night boss, who had even less time in the district, started to show Tyrell around the building. Tyrell laid it on thick too, pretending he had never been inside the very same building he was terminated from. "Oh, so this is the band room, huh? That explains the musical instruments. Wow, look at that, the cafeteria. Is this where the children eat they lunches?"

Any second now, I was expecting to hear someone blow his cover. I was sure Tyrell sexually harassed half the teachers in the building, but I couldn't remember who was around long enough to remember him. Had it really been that long since he was gone? It wasn't like he left thirty years ago. Surely someone was around when Tyrell wreaked havoc during his first tour.

The day went along with quiet refrain. *This isn't happening,* I thought. *How is he here?* About an hour into the shift, I started searching for him. I needed to know what in the actual fuck was going on. I found Tyrell by the soda machine, trying to count out a dollar in change. He looked over his right shoulder, smiling as I approached him. He put his index finger up to his lips in a shushing motion. I made sure no one was within earshot as I walked up next to him.

"Are you kidding me?" I said in a whispered tone. "You're gonna get caught. You won't last a day here, dude. They're going to fire you, maybe even lock you up for pulling this."

"Relax, my brotha," said Tyrell. He started to put coins into the slot. "I got it all figured out."

"Oh, really? How do you figure that?"

"Easy," said Tyrell. "If someone catches on, I'll tell them to prove I was fired in the first place." Tyrell pushed the button for Diet Pepsi, casually waiting for it to drop.

"Huh?" I said.

"Yeah, man. If they can't prove it, then I guess I wasn't fired." Tyrell bent down to pick up his soda, releasing a grunt of old age as he came up. "Perhaps I quit the first go-round, which means it's okay for me to reapply." He tapped the can lid, wiped it clean, and popped the tab on his drink. His logic reminded me of how a serial killer must operate. I wondered how long he had spent working this little scheme out in his warped mind.

"So that's it? You're going to hope they don't have that massive folder with all your write-ups and incident reports and union grievances highlighting the path of destruction you have left?" I was sounding very much like a parent at this point.

Tyrell took a long slug from his drink. Cooler than an iceberg he was. He let out a satisfying burp. "Damn, man, don't cha have any faith in me? You still paranoid as fuck! How many times have I told you? Don't sweat the small shit." He looked around to check the scenery, looking for any stool pigeons, as he called them. He leaned in close to me. "The stupid mothafuckas threw out all of Captain Cupcake's files. When he got fired, the head boss threw all his shit out, everything that was in Cupcake's office—his papers, his files, his damn briefcase! All that shit was chucked to the curb! I drove by when they was doin' it."

Tyrell started laughing loudly now. His shoulders were bouncing up and down with glee. "Captain Cupcake is still in the joint, waiting on a bail hearing. He's locked up! How's he gonna collect his shit from prison? All his stuff was taken to the dump, man! My file is probably covered up with fifty thousand pounds of trash on top of it by now! I bet all those bullshit certificates and degrees on his wall were smeared with doo-doo before they chucked it!" he said.

Once Polotski was fired, the head supervisor ordered all his stuff to be removed from the building. Every personal possession was collected and sent to the county garbage facility, such as every last National Park animal figurine; from the mighty bison down to the tiniest sparrow. Word was, his family photos and personal items, all of it, were destroyed.

In theory, Tyrell was right, believe it or not. No evidence of him being fired was kept digitally. The district started digitizing all records a few years after he was booted. It would have cost too much money to scan all the records from years ago. Only the old files were kept in paper form. Mr. Polotski kept all the personnel files of past employees in his office in case he ever needed to produce them legally. Tyrell knew this. With all traces of Tyrell's extermination gone, he was free to start anew.

Even if he ran into someone who knew him from years ago, there wasn't any formal record of him being fired. No one could legitimately prove Tyrell was terminated, only that his payroll record was set from this date to this date. All he had to do was deny he was fired.

If this sounds like the most fucked-up scenario in the history of scenarios, then you're right. Most jobs keep files from all its employees regardless of how long ago they worked. But then again, most bosses don't physically assault their supervisors. The superintendent was so pissed off and embarrassed after the incident that he got rid of all traces that Mr. Polotski existed. In doing so, he wiped the slate clean for all the employees who no longer worked there. Too bad they kept all the files of current employees in a separate location. If they didn't do that, then all my sins would have been forgiven as Tyrell's were. I would give my left nut to have a clean slate just so I could start causing more havoc.

Tyell's return reminded me of an old saying that former employees use when they leave this junk heap: "A lifetime gone in an instant." Years of dedication are undone instantaneously. All your hard work, your struggles, and your selflessness to the job are simply forgotten the minute you're off school grounds. I've known teachers, janitors, and bus drivers, all with decades of service, being forgotten before they're out the door. We had one guy who worked for nearly fifteen years who passed away suddenly. His job was posted within an hour of the news. The poor schmuck wasn't even stiff yet. I specifically remember one of the bosses complaining about how he had to pick up the slack for half a day because the guy died. That's the kind of monsters who run a board of education, the kind who doesn't give two shits about a man's life ending because it inconveiences them for a few hours.

Now if you're a top dog, then the story changes. If you're a boss, specifically a high-ranking member of the board, they name things after you—countless bronze plaques, statues, and street names. It seems the more evil you are, the more things they dedicate in your honor. It won't be long until the head scumbags of the school system get entire towns named after them. It's kind of like how Stalin and Alexader the Great changed the names after they conquered the lowly peasants who had the misfortune of being in the path of their war machine.

Poor Tyrell never had anything named after him. In most people's mind, he had never existed, a figment of an overworked imagination carelessly discarded like an empty Dasani bottle. Not many people liked Tyrell. He was a man whom you either loved or hated. I loved the crazy bastard and was beyond thrilled to have him back. After the shock settled, we caught up on seven years of lost time. I needed to know everything. Tyrell had been a busy little beaver during those years. He filled me in with his euphemisms and slang dialect, so I'll paraphrase as best I can:

The night Tyrell was fired, Mr. Polotski was the one who took his keys. Polotski, along with two of his fake-ass union lackeys, showed Tyrell a video from a surveillance camera in the parking lot. It showed Tyrell in his car, waiting in the driver's seat, when another car pulled up. The video showed Tyrell handing something to the other driver. This was, in fact, a small potatoes drug deal. "That's right, man. They got my slingin' on tape. I fucked up. They had my ass good."

Tyrell was so stoned when he came to work that day that he forgot about the security camera. Frigging dumbass parked right in direct view of it. Polotski watched Tyrell every day on the security monitors in his office, just waiting to nail him hard. He finally got his chance when he caught Tyrell dealing on school grounds.

Without a job and no money, Tyrell went back to doing what he did best: hoodlum activity. "I stole, I drug-dealed, and I robbed mofuckas in the streets," he said. "I even started runnin' with my old gang back in the projects." According to Tyrell, it lasted about a year before he got out of the game. "Look here. Do you know how hard it is to keep up with these young cats now? Shit! I can't be doin' that no more. These suckas are dealin' in H. I ain't slingin' H! That shit is dangerous. Weed is all I know. It's what I'm good at. Heroin will get all over your clothes, man. And that Fentanyl shit? No way! I ain't trying to catch a charge for China white! Cops will throw my ass away for good with that crap."

After leaving the street game for good, Tyrell tried to go straight. He worked in a Foot Locker for a few months. He traded selling drugs for selling LeBrons, as he put it. Minimum wage didn't sit too well with him, though, so he quit. "I stole about twenty pairs of shoes over the course of three months, but I can't be livin' off no ten dollars an hour. That's bullshit wages!" Then Tyrell's big break came. He left the state for a few years to enter into a new business venture, one perfectly suited for a man with his qualifications.

"I sold all the unnecessary stuff I had, packed a U-Haul trailer, hitched it to my Lincoln, and drove out to Colorado," said Tyrell.

"Why would you do a thing like that?" I asked.

"To enter in the weed game, baby!" said Tyrell. "They legalized weed out there. I got a job in a dispensary selling lab-quality cannabis and CBD oil. Do you know how much money I made out there? Legal money too! I didn't get shot at one time while I was out there in the mountains, slingin' gummies, oils, brownies, and vape cartridges. Call me the new American dream!"

I should have known it had to do with drugs when it came to Tyrell. He lived in Boulder, Colorado, for five years, working in all aspects of the cannabis distribution system. He said he cleared close to eighty grand a year on average in addition to all the weed he could smoke.

"I'll tell you what. I made a killin' in Colorado. Bought me a new car for the first time in my life with legally made money. It was drug money, but it was legal drug money. Scored some serious poontang out there too! Those five years, I was on top of the world, man, literally on top of the world. Do you know how high those mountains are? Just about as high as I was on the regular!"

"So why'd you leave?" I said.

"It's too fucking cold out there!" said Tyrell. "I was tired of shoveling snow all day."

"Yeah, but if you were making all that money and free weed, why did you come back?"

"I missed livin' here," said Tyrell. "All my peoples are here. I made my money, enough money to put a good chunk of it in the bank, not in a coffee can like I used to. But it was too damn cold. My fucking car kept getting stuck in the snow!"

"You know, they make a Lincoln SUV with four-wheel drive, Tyrell," I said.

"Fuck that," he said. "I had my share of mountains for a lifetime. Besides, I had to give up weed for a little while. They made me take a piss test before starting work again. I don't know how the fuck I passed that one!"

During those years, Tyrell had gotten married, gotten divorced within a month, and then gotten remarried to the same woman a month after that. They took a honeymoon to Tahiti, where he subsequently got divorced for a second time. "We hooked up now and then for, like, two years after our divorces," said Tyrell. "She wasn't my Ms. Right. She was more like Ms. Right Now. You feel me?"

Tyrell traveled extensively while working in the cannabis industry. What began as an entry-level gig turned into a career, complete with paid trips to California every other month. "My boss called it research and development, but I called it Tyrell's Road Trip to Toketown!" he said. "The boss asked me if I was interested in testing new strains of weed to sell. I said, 'You goddamn right I'm interested!' My luggage was packed in less time it took to fill up the gas tank. Everything was a business expense—the hotel, the food. I got to claim rolling papers on my taxes. I never heard of this before in my life! That shit was unreal."

We spoke on and on the entire first week he was back. It was beyond words to be working with him again, listening to all his adventures. I missed him more than anyone ever realized. All his stories were straight out of a fairy tale book. For most people, these would be fairy tales. Who else but Tyrell would make a ton of money in the marijuana industry? Once he heard the government legalized it for good, his old Lincoln was tearing up the pavement on I-76.

Life was always about the right place at the right time, Tyrell used to say. A person needed to get in at the precise moment in order to make it. It was sage advice from a man who drove a U-Haul trailer across the country attached to a hunk-of-shit town car.

The next big moment in Tyrell's life came during his second week on the job, when he was reintroduced to a staff member from his past. That following Tuesday, I heard one of the loudest crashes ever while working. The sound of breaking glass caught my attention as I pushed my janitor cart out of the closet. This was followed by the phrase, "Get out of my sight, you sick bastard!"

I was surprised Tyrell had remained incognito for this long. I jogged down toward where the yelling was coming from. I made out words like *perv* and *sexual deviant* emanating from the room in question. I entered the room to find Tyrell in a corner, dodging small objects, namely whiteboard markers. Glass was littered around where he was standing, along with flowers and a small puddle of water.

"How dare you talk to me like that?" said the teacher. "You get the hell out of my sight!"

Tyrell bopped from side to side, trying to get words in between the barrage of projectiles. "I was only playing, Mary. Ow, don't be like that, girl. Ow! Quit it!"

"Don't call me girl, you sicko!" she said. "You remember what you did to me on our last date? You…you…" She noticed me standing in the doorway, watching her rage unfold. She stopped throwing anything in arm's reach and addressed me. "Tell this man to get out of my classroom!" she said while pointing at Tyrell. "He's a sick human being!"

"Mary, Mary, come on now, baby." Tyrell was pleading with her in a devilish manner. "That was a long time ago, sweetness." He was moving toward me at the doorway, staring at the teacher as she whipped another marker at his head.

"Don't you Mary me, Ty," she said.

"What? You don't want me to marry you, Mary?"

"Get the hell out of here!"

Tyrell shuffled past me, briefly using me as shield. I didn't say a word. I turned back around and exited the room, following Tyrell, who, at this point, was grinning ear to ear, strutting down the hallway. "Friend of yours?" I said jokingly.

"I guess not!" said Tyrell. "We had a good thing going years back, but I guess she don't remember how good we had it."

"Oh, I think she remembers perfectly, Ty," I said. He grinned, silently laughing as he walked away from the room. "Are you actually trying to get caught?" I asked him. "I mean, really?"

"What?" asked Tyrell.

"You know she's going to call someone, probably some union dick. Once they start looking into it, you're done."

"Fuck them. Let 'em come for me. I'll be waitin' on they ass." He had a look in his eye like he had it all planned out. Seconds later, his lady friend came out into the hallway with a handful of roses.

"Take these ratty flowers out of my face, you jerk-off!" She threw the wet flowers in the hallway, then stormed back into her room.

"Did you bring her a vase with flowers?" I asked.

"Yeah, so?" Tyrell said. "What's wrong with that?"

"You think she'd forgive you, dash back into your arms, after doing whatever the hell you did to her years back?"

"Well, not necessarily," he said. "I thought she'd wanna get together like the good old days." Tyrell was out of breath. His lungs were shot from his time in the Rocky Mountains. "Ah, fuck it. Next time, I'll just get the flowers without the vase so she can't throw it at me!"

Sure as shit, she must have called someone on Tyrell, because he had bosses waiting for him the next day. The next afternoon, after school let out, they came for him, ready to intimidate. I saw two bosses' cars in the parking lot, along with Mr. Sanders's car. You would think that Sanders drove a hearse, being a messenger from Satan and all, but he rocked some ugly-ass, sensible compact car.

As I came into the custodians' office, I saw Tyrell at the table, his arms folded, staring at the bosses with his mouth open. The two bosses and that reptile Sanders all turned to look at me when I entered the room. For once, they weren't there for me. I was told to make my way to my section for now; the meeting wasn't for my eyes or ears. So I turned and walked out.

As I left, I remember two sights: One was Sanders's scaly face, burrowing his mystifying gaze at me. I swear I saw a forked black tongue jot out and back into his mouth. And two was, Tyrell smiled and waved. It was his "I'll see you later, buddy!" wave.

I went about my business, expecting police to roll into the parking lot any minute. Two hours later, all four men were still locked in the small office with varying degrees of shouting coming from inside. At the three-hour mark, I heard the door slam as it opened with Sanders rushing into the hall. He was followed by his two minions in tow, gathering their padfolios as they walked out abruptly. Tyrell emerged from the doorway, his left hand in a mock talking gesture in the direction of Sanders. Picture a duck quacking. Tyrell mouthed silently as he did it.

"We will see about your so-called case, Mr. Jones!" said Sanders. He was exiting the building, looking back to point at Tyrell.

"Yeah, right. Yeah, go ahead. Go on wit' your dead-looking self," said Tyrell. He had his phone in his other hand, checking for messages. "I done told you I quit before. You aint got no proof on paper that I was fired!" Both men had a little bass in their voice.

"You're a fraud, Mr. Jones. I will find your record soon enough, and you'll be out of here before long. You'll be hearing from the school's solicitor about this very soon!" said Sanders.

"Prove it, mothafucker. Prove it!" said Tyrell. He was still looking at his phone, not giving one shit about cursing at the district's head snipe man. Tyrell turned his attention to me, looking up from his phone. A smile came across his face. "Hey, man, ain't it time for break?" he asked. He put his phone away, then dug into his pocket, collecting loose change.

I walked up to him, staying out of the view of the bosses as they drove away quickly. Tyrell stood at the all-glass corridor, waving to the men outside as they peeled out. "Are you fucking mad?" I said. My voice was cracking. "They're gonna nail you to the wall! What are you doing cursing at Sanders? You can't be antagonizing him like that!"

"Dig this, man," said Tyrell. "If they had anything concrete on me, I'd already be gone." He was clanging coins in his pocket, no doubt heading to the soda machine for a refreshing drink. "That old skeleton Sanders ain't got one bit of proof, and he knows it. Come on. Let's go get a Pepsi. I'm buying."

I walked with Tyrell to the drink machine, constantly looking over my shoulder, waiting for the hit squad to come back. The few remaining teachers in the school poked their heads into the hall, searching for the cause of the commotion. Tyrell addressed them as he walked toward the soda machine, no doubt sizing up his next one night stand. "Afternoon, ladies!" he said. "How y'all doin' today?"

What I loved about Tyrell, other than his attitude and hilarious stories, was his ability to handle a serious situation with relative coolness. Yes, he was caught by management lying, and he cursed out the bosses without fear of repercussions. But Tyrell knew how to stay calm under pressure. If it were me, I would have cracked under intense questioning, especially if I knew I was 100 percent in the wrong. My man Tyrell was used to pressure. A round of questioning from three superiors was like a brisk autumn walk to him. He grew up in the projects of Newark, where the streets had made him harder than an iron-forged sword.

While inserting coins into the machine, I got nosy. "Dude, what the hell is going on?" I asked.

"Don't worry about it, man," said Tyrell. "I'm straight. Like I done told you, they can't prove I was fired, so they ain't got no case."

"Yeah, but what if someone comes forward from years back, claiming you threatened them or say something bad about you? Sanders will be all over you for that."

"They can't, man!" he said. "It's past the statute of limitations. The last time I worked here, it was over seven years ago." Tyrell paused to push the Diet Pepsi button on the machine. "The legal time limit for fraud or trespass or even legal malpractice is six years." The soda fell to the slot. As Tyrell picked it up, he looked at me and smiled. "They ain't got jack on me!"

He started rattling off statute codes and numbers. Tyrell said one of his longest friends was a lawyer in East Orange, who filled him in on the legal jargon. Before he went on the job interview, Tyrell told his friend the situation about Polotski leaving, the files being thrown out, and all the other scenarios he could think of. According to Tyrell's lawyer friend, the board of education had no recourse. His buddy gave him the all clear and told him to call him if he needed legal help. "I'll tell you what," said Tyrell. "If they really want to fuck with me, I'll sue 'em for false termination. I'll get they asses for seven years back pay!" Tyrell said.

Over the next few weeks, Tyrell had meeting after meeting with Sanders and the rest of his hooligans. Tyrell remained steadfast in the face of interrogation, and along with his lawyer, they fought off threats from the board of education. After the fourth meeting, Tyrell's lawyer filed a suit for harassment in the workplace. Once he did that, Sanders let up. That was all the board needed, another round of reporters asking questions and writing headlines. It was bad enough the school district was in the news a few months before for Polotski's cage match. The board of ed offered Tyrell a small settlement to make the lawsuit go away. It wasn't enough to retire, but it was enough to raise some eyebrows. Tyrell took the offer and could keep his job. Sanders never found any concrete files on Tyrell, so he couldn't fire him, especially now.

It was a fairy-tale ending after all for Tyrell. He made his triumphant return. He slayed the evil dragon known as Sanders for now, and he lived happily ever after, mopping floors next to his sidekick, me. Instead of the hero getting the girl, Tyrell had many girls, again due to his fat settlement against the board of ed. He spent a nice chunk of his legal winnings on date nights for multiple princesses in the kingdom.

It was a happily ever after for me as well. I got my Tyrell back. He's still here, with an ironclad, sealed document saying the bosses won't fuck with him anymore. If they do, I'm sure his lawyer will send off another lawsuit claiming discrimination. All I know is that it's good to have him back. I've missed him even if no one else at the job did. I could spend a lifetime listening to him tell the same old stories. It's a lifetime worth living.

CHAPTER 7

Butch Cassandra and the Schmuck-Faced Kid

Let me paint a picture for you. Say you're working at this place and you have a boss. You've got other coworkers at your job, some of whom are cozy with the boss. They believe they run the joint because of their coziness. One of your boss's little friends thinks they can boss you around. Do you (A) go along with the program because you're a good worker and want to be a positive team member or (B) tell the bitch and the even bigger bitch to fuck right the hell off?

This happens in every job that's ever been classified as a job. I bet you a hundred drachma that when the Greeks started building the Acropolis, one asshole stonemason thought he could push around another stonemason because he knew the head guy at the quarry. Jobs aren't supposed to have thirty bosses. Just one or two dingleberries should be sufficient. The reason for a limited number of bosses is to avoid the whole place from turning into a shit show. Random people calling their own shots and dictating mindless orders can turn your workplace into a havoc-filled free-for-all. Bosses are supposed to create an orderly, efficient workplace, not turn it into a looting riot.

Such is the case at my current post. If you've been following along since the first book, you know I'm in charge of the night janitors. Don't clap your hands. It's a meaningless title. Well, there's this bitch named Cassandra who works during the day with my immediate boss, Taylor. She's nothing to me, not even close to a boss, yet she tries to push her weight around. I'll give you a scenario. You work at a bank. You're a bank teller. All is good in the world of monetary exchanging. Then comes the dilemma. Your boss, who doesn't do shit, tells his pal to boss you around. This middle person has a tendency to be power drunk and starts yapping away. How do you resolve such a situation?

Most times, this scenario is resolved relatively easily at a reasonable establishment, but I can't do that at my job because this place has no rules. Basic workplace etiquette went out the window decades ago. People go rogue, making their own decisions. This is where we meet Cassandra Mastiffson and Taylor Gregors.

Taylor is my immediate boss, and I don't like him. I can't stand him and his stupid, scrunchy face. His whole frame looks like someone crumpled him up, like you do with junk mail. It angers me to get junk mail, and it angers me to be in Taylor's presence.

Cassandra is Taylor's coworker during the day, and I can't stand her either. She's his muscle in more than one way. This broad should've been named Mongo or Brutus, because she's a roadblock of a woman. She frightens me, and I'm pushing six-four and 350 pounds.

When I first started working here, back when BlackBerry was king, I heard of Taylor and Cassandra. I asked around and got a positive report from all my sources. "Yeah, Taylor's great! He's my son's Little League coach. He throws a nice end-of-summer barbecue each year." I got the same happy response about Cassandra. "You mean my neighbor for almost twenty years Cassandra? Oh, she's a hoot! You'll love working with her!"

Never trust what people say about someone until you've actually worked with them for an extended period of time. Cassandra and Taylor were nice people to their friends, but if they didn't like you, they made your life a living hell. It all started about three years ago, when I was transferred to my current post. I've been all over the place, at different schools, for various reasons. I won't get into it extensively, but let's say I'm not a well-liked person around these parts.

I was told by several high-ranking officials that this was the last place I could be moved mainly because I had made enemies everywhere else. I think management says those things to scare you into being a better worker. I knew a maintenance guy many moons ago who killed a coworker and kept turning wrenches for months. Accidents happen, as they say. He ended the guy's life, and he still collected a paycheck, so I was not too worried about this being my last chance.

When I arrived at my current post, I was welcomed with open arms by Taylor. Well, they were sort of open arms. This guy had the shortest arms I had ever seen. He was kind of like a T. rex. When we shook hands, I was afraid I would rip his arm off. Picture shaking the hand of a fragile department store mannequin child.

I towered over him by at least two feet. I'm not going to say he was a dwarf, but he had dwarflike attributes. Taylor's body frame looked as if it wasn't fully fused together yet—a work in progress, so to speak. And his eyes were too close to each other. When God created Taylor, he took his fingers and pinched his face inward like you would do to wet clay. These were all signs of a sickly person. Regardless of his physical appearance, I tried to make nice with the little fellow. But in the end, I believed the rumors gave Taylor a jilted view of my persona.

"Nice to finally meet you," said Taylor. "I've heard so much about you." But when he said that line, it wasn't in a flattering tone. Most times, when someone say they've heard so much about you, it's to build up your confidence. Taylor said it as if he really wanted to say, "Great. Now I'm stuck with you." I didn't take offense. I was used to this kind of treatment. But I'll admit, I'm somewhat hostile with a limited number of incidents in the past. I clenched his feeble hand a little more aggressively after hearing that remark.

"Nice to meet you too," I said, all while extending our handshake a few seconds more than necessary. Since Taylor didn't put out a stern handshake, I added some pressure to mine. My gorilla grip damn near crushed his tiny chicken bone fingers. He let out a little sound when I turned up the volume on the handshake.

"Let me show you around, give the lay of the land here at the high school," said Taylor. "Here's where we keep the extra mops in this storage closet, and that brown door over there is where we store the hazardous chemicals. See the skull and crossbones sign? It means there are harsh chemicals stored therein. Be careful not to open a bottle of ammonia with students in the hall. Their little, underdeveloped lungs can't handle the smell."

Taylor was the very last person to be talking about lung size. His mousy voice matched his miniature demeanor. You know what I'm talking about. Don't make me say it out loud. Okay, here it goes: He sounded like a midget. There, I said it. He wasn't a midget, though. He was more like a hobbit. He could pass for an adult in a roller coaster line, but reaching for something on the top shelf might have given him some difficulty. It made sense that his voice had a tinny, shrill sound to it, but it still freaked me out. It was like touching his toddler-sized hand during our initial meeting.

As we walked down the hallway, I noticed his feet moving ever so quickly. Since my stride was longer than his, it took Taylor more steps to keep up with me. His tiny shoes squeaked on the tile floor as if he was jogging instead of walking. Between that sound and his voice, he reminded me of a cartoon character. Once I thought about it, I couldn't help laughing to myself as we walked. He noticed my chuckling and wasn't too pleased.

"What's the matter, guy? You okay? You find something funny about this place?"

"No, no, nothing's funny," I said. "Just thinking about something earlier." Yeah, because that excuse always smoothed out a volatile conversation. Taylor knew I was full of shit. I was sure he had been made fun of a lot about his stature, so upon seeing me laugh while he spoke, he took it as an insult.

"Are you sure, pal? You seem to be laughing about something awfully hilarious while I'm giving you the rundown of the job."

"Nope, not laughing about anything here. I...I was thinking about a comic I saw earlier today in the paper, that's all." Even I wasn't buying that line.

"Gotcha," said Taylor. He continued his spiel as we walked further into the school. "If you ever need to report an accident, there's the nurse's office. She can help you if the need arises to administer first aid."

Really? You're telling me the person who can help me with things like cuts or burns would be the school nurse? I never would've figured that little gem out. All I kept thinking about during his blatantly obvious speech were his voice and those size six and a half shoes squeaking down the hall. Once the thought of him buying shoes from the kids' section popped into my head, I lost it.

"Hey, buddy!" said Taylor. He stopped walking and stared at me. He put his hands on his hips, and I almost pissed myself. That image of him standing there in a disgruntled pose got me giggling. I was immediately brought back to my childhood in the eighties. He looked like a Cabbage Patch Kid; all he was missing was a blue denim set of OshKosh B'gosh overalls and a Pound Puppy under the crook of his arm. The urge to laugh overwhelmed me. I now had a massive smile on my face while my immediate supervisor stood there judging me.

"You must've had a dose of laughing gas before coming in. You sure as hell seem like you got something to say."

"No, man. I'm just overtired and thought of something funny earlier today."

"Sure about that, guy?" he said. "Tired, huh? Laughs a lot too." Taylor nodded as he spoke with his chicken wings perched on his hips. "Maybe you like to use marijuana. That's the only thing I can think of when someone laughs a lot and they admit they're sleepy."

The more he kept talking, the wider my smile became. Once you've got a laughing fit, nothing can stop it. Add in the fact that my new boss looked and sounded like a munchkin and I was off to the races. He just looked so impish standing there.

"Look, I'm just overtired and overwhelmed here a bit," I said. My face started to hurt like it did after you had been crying for minutes on end. The more I tried to fight it, the more I wanted to laugh. Ever since I can remember, the sight of a midget gives me a laughing fit. I know I'm going to hell, but it's an uncontrollable, knee-jerk reaction. It's in my subconscious, like when people cry when they hear bagpipes.

As we finished our tour around the school, I saw an object off in the distance slowly coming into view. I didn't know it at the time, but Taylor recognized his protégé from halfway across the school. "Well, Mr. Funnyman, I think it's time you meet my right-hand man at this post. Say hello to Cassandra."

There she was, all six-six of her, pushing the scales at close to four hundred pounds. As she came into view, I realized she was swaying her arms like one of those mall walkers. She met us in the center hallway, extending her hoof out to meet my hand. Her hand looked like a bunch of bananas, only with hair and a case of eczema.

"Hello there," she said. "It's nice to make your acquaintance."

I had never heard such a deep, manly voice coming from a woman. The sound hit my chest like a sonic boom. "Hi." That was all I could muster. The sight of her put me off-kilter for a few seconds. I believe she was the largest woman I had ever met in person. I'm a big guy myself, but Cassandra was a beast of a woman. There is nothing wrong with being a big girl at all, but she looked like someone you would hire to guard a pouch of exquisite diamonds you were transporting to a bank vault.

"This is the new night head at our post, Cassandra," said Taylor. "He's a bit of a laugher, if you ask me, so try not to say anything too funny in his presence."

"Oh, I think that won't be too much trouble," she said. She stood there eyeballing me, evaluating my presence like a beat cop sizing up a thug.

As the three of us stood there in that empty hallway, I couldn't help but feel out of place. Taylor and Cassandra had been coworkers for quite some time and started a conversation between themselves as I stood there. I was no bump on a log, so I tried to talk with them, you know, the polite thing to do, but the two buddies weren't having it.

"Those new desks came in a few minutes ago, Taylor," said Cassandra. "I'll move them later today."

"Good job, Cassandra. I know I can always count on you."

"Thanks, boss," said Cassandra. She cleared her throat as if she had a severe case of postnasal drip.

"What kind of desks do you mean?" I asked. "I can try to move them tonight after I get situated."

"I'll handle it!" said Cassandra. She sounded like a grizzly bear letting out a dominant growl to the other animals in the forest.

"Yeah, let's let Cassandra take point on this. Besides, you might get too excited by laughing and drop a desk on your foot," Taylor said. He and Cassandra had things to do, so he pointed me down a separate hallway to my section.

As I stood there, looking helpless and lost, the two buddies walked away. I got the feeling I wasn't allowed to hear their conversation. I watched them converse with each other, Taylor moving his twiglike arms erratically while Cassandra kept turning her massive neck to keep an eye on me. Had I made a move to join them in their walk, she most likely would have charged me, grunting and shooing me away. I started to laugh again as I watched them shuffle off, Taylor looking like a bouncy third grader with an ice pop and Cassandra closely resembling a linebacker for the Chicago Bears.

For those of you who don't know the hierarchy of the janitoring world, I'll explain. Every post has what's called a day head janitor. The day head is the first person in charge of the building. Second in command is the night head janitor. A night head is to report to the day head and give instructions to the evening crew. Cassandra was only a swing shift janitor. She was basically hired to assist Taylor because he was so goddamned helpless. She did things like put him in his stroller and burp him when he was done with his sippy cup. I'm sure she did other important janitoring things, but she was a nobody, not management or a boss of any kind.

Taylor was the day head, and I was the night head. That was number 1 and number 2, if you're still listening. Since our rocky introductions, Taylor hadn't given me any directives or assignments. He had given his standing orders to his ogre, Cassandra. In my first few days at my new post, Cassandra treated me as if I was her personal slave. She tried to assign her work to me, saying Taylor wanted me to do these things. I had been around long enough to know what my job duties were, so I immediately called her on her actions.

Cassandra, in turn, threatened me with bodily harm if I didn't abide by her orders. "Taylor told me to give this work to you, so you better do it, or else!" Then she would clip-clop down the hallway, swaying her arms like a bull elephant clearing brush with its trunk.

I approached Taylor on lunch break one day to surmise what was going on. He was consuming a Lunchables box and Go-Gurt. I shit you not. In between bites of ham and Swiss on Ritz Crackers, Taylor smiled and explained he was very busy and needed me to comply with whatever orders Cassandra gave.

"Listen, buddy. You're new here. This is how we do things at my school."

"Your school?" I said. "Did you pay for it? I think it belongs to the taxpayers." I might have hit a nerve with the comment, but I had worked there too long to beat around the bush anymore. "I'm the second in command now. Why is Cassandra giving me orders and threatening me on top of it?"

"Well, because I said so," explained the wicked little man with cracker crumbs on his chin. "I'm the boss here, and I feel it's necessary to have Cassandra be my emissary when it comes to working detail."

"But that's not how it works," I said. "You're supposed to give me orders and work instructions. You haven't said shit to me since I started here a week ago."

Taylor, who viciously tore open his Go-Gurt, smiled again. "Really? I haven't talked to you since then, huh? Hmm, I hadn't noticed. I must've been too busy laughing about something I saw earlier in the newspaper." Touché, micro man. Touché.

I had limited contact with the gruesome twosome for the next few weeks. Each time I came into work, they watched me but never came to see me. I got the strange feeling I was being evaluated. They didn't actively look for me when I came in, but they knew where to find me when they needed to conduct their surveillance. If I was filling up my mop bucket in the janitors' closet, I would turn quickly to see Taylor studying me. You would be surprised by how quiet an elf could be, their little elvin shoes muffling the sound of their footsteps. "How's the new post? Have you been getting accustomed to the new school yet, chief?" he would ask.

Don't you hate when people call you chief or boss or pal? You don't fucking know me. Don't be jovial in my face, then stick the bayonet in my back as soon as I turn. The tone in Taylor's voice suggested he was going to abuse his position until further notice. I called it the Napoleon Syndrome. These tiny chaps had been made fun of their entire lives by bigger people. Now that Taylor had a little power, he would use it to punish me. I was guessing that when someone stole his lunch money or dunked his head in the toilet, it scarred him deeply. Now I would have to pay the price for Taylor getting his ass kicked every day after school.

The same outlandish behavior came from Cassandra, who made just a tad more noise when she walked. She couldn't sneak up on a statue with all her bodily groans. I would pass her in the hallway while she gawked at me with her gluttonous mouth open, breathing heavily.

"Hot one today, ain't it?" she spouted. It was the middle of fall with the thermometer reading forty degrees.

"Yeah, it sure is," I said.

"Tell me about it!" said Cassandra with sweaty pits and a chafing sound coming from her thigh region.

She might have made squishy sounds as she passed, but I knew what her intentions were. She was sizing me up for an attack, but not verbally or mentally. I didn't think she had the capacity for a battle of wits. Physically, she might have given me a run for my money. I'm not saying she would have beaten me in an arm wrestling contest, but it would be close. Cassandra looked like she would have no trouble picking me and hurling me like a hacky sack.

During my first month at the job, I saw Taylor five times. Never once did he give me instructions. He simply smiled while evaluating me. Five minutes later, I would see Cassandra pass, slowly hunting me like a great white shark terrorizing a Cape fur seal.

"Taylor said for me to tell you to move the pallet of art room clay upstairs," said Cassandra.

"Why, because his little arms can't steer the heavy load?" I asked.

"What?" spouted Cassandra.

"Oh, nothing," I said. She grunted like a pig. "Hey, how come Taylor couldn't tell me that when he passed me a few minutes ago?"

"I don't know!" Cassandra said. She seemed confused and angry at the same time. "He told me to tell you, so I did what he said!"

"But you're not my boss. Technically, I'm your boss now. Why are you—"

"You better do what I said!" she interrupted. She seemed very perturbed now. Cassandra drew her hand down onto a nearby locker in the hallway. Her huge meat hook created both a dent and a massive thud, bellowing down the hall. She then walked away at a furious pace, no doubt to relay her anger to her leash holder, Taylor.

Nine times out of ten, both Taylor and Cassandra would be up each other's ass, avoiding me like a smallpox outbreak. Since Taylor and Cassandra worked during the day and I worked at night, we didn't see much of one another. We had a few hours of overlap in between shifts. Taylor was a lead custodian, meaning his job was to open up the school at 7:00 a.m., switch on a few lights, and find a good place to hibernate. Cassandra was his shadow when she came in around noon. Basically, she was his bodyguard, watching over her master while he slept.

In most jobs, your boss will give you directions or some form of action for your duties. I was ignored. Taylor spent his working hours being flanked by his enforcer, who would stare at me each time I walked up to them. Whenever I had a question, the two BFFs gave me an obnoxious answer. I asked Taylor about a setup at the school that evening, and he gave me a snippy response.

"Gee, buddy, I don't know where you'd find several long tables," said Taylor. He had a tiny cup of coffee in his hand with his freakishly small feet up on his desk. "Smart guy like you should be able to procure them in a relatively short period of time. Start at one side of the building, and look for them until you locate them." Sure enough, there was Cassandra, sitting next to him in her chair with the chair legs creaking under her. She crossed her tree trunk arms to watch me as I walked away, frustrated. She didn't say anything, more like sat there, breathing through her cowlike nostrils.

Two days later, I needed to fill out a work order. I came to tell Taylor about a broken window, only to get a shitty response again. "I'm busy working on an important project with Cassandra," he said. "Why don't you try to figure it out yourself?"

The evening crew, whom I was in charge of, came in at 4:00 p.m. and didn't speak to me very much either. They were nice but not welcoming. I figured they were just trying to get acquainted with me, saying hi here and there. I would give them orders about work, which they complied, but that was about it. I didn't get to talk with any of them too much unless I initiated the conversation. After a month and a half of being standoffish, I called for a meeting to ask them if they had any questions or issues with me. I got blank stares at first. Once prodded, they told me what was really happening: Taylor and Cassandra were spreading rumors.

I'm not one to believe in office gossip. I tend to take people as they are. You may seem like a dick at first, but I'll make my judgments after I've worked with you a few times. First impressions can be rough. My guess is, since I rubbed Taylor the wrong way, so he informed the rest of the crew I wasn't to be trusted.

The evening crew reluctantly told me what Taylor said. One coworker named Bethany asked me if I had a problem with women. "I don't want to be a nosy busybody, but Taylor said you were thrown out of the other building because you hate women. Is that true?" I assured Bethany I was not a male chauvinist. A couple of seconds later, Roderick asked me if I had ever been arrested for animal cruelty. "I don't know how to say this, but did you kill a dog a few years ago in a dogfighting ring? Cassandra said something to that effect last week, but I told her it doesn't sound right."

In the world of janitorial arts, rumors are a part of the job. We've got a ton of Chicken Littles around here. A majority believe anything they hear. I put the crew's minds at ease by having a nice, long chat. When they seemed at peace, I started a rumor of my own, because if you can't beat them, join them.

"Don't you guys think Cassandra and Taylor spend a lot of time together? I mean, they're always with each other. Maybe they're starting rumors about me to take attention away from their situation." That was all it took to lead the sheep. The night crew started discussing the possibility of Taylor and Cassandra being more than work associates.

"You know what," said Bethany, "I didn't want to say anything before, but they do spend a lot of time together."

"That's right!" said William. "They've been working here for years! Who knows what's been going on?"

"I know I'm new here," I said. "But I can see something more than a working relationship between those two." The remainder of the crew started talking all at once about past things they had seen or heard.

"I know neither of them is married, right?" said Andy.

"You know," said Mason, "I remember one of the maintenance guys saying something like this two years ago when I first started working here. I didn't believe it, but it kinda makes sense now."

Instead of being thought of as a woman-hating dogfighter, I was now the voice of reason to the crew. All it took was a simple push, and the hens were out of the coop. The crew squawked away for the rest of the night, talking about Taylor and Casandra's possible romantic involvement. The thought of Taylor and Cassandra having sex repulsed me to no end. Maybe I made a comment that turned the conversation to that point. Maybe I didn't. Either way, the idea of the warlock and the gimp getting it on came up. It was beyond childish, but this was what this job did to people. Before you know it, you're making rude conversations about how Taylor may need a grappling hook and a rappelling line to mount Cassandra during intercourse.

The crew found it hilarious, and everyone's inner sixth grader came bursting out. We all had an extremely satisfying laugh, which was just what I needed to get the crew on my side. I didn't, however, anticipate the rumor and proceeding jokes to get back to Taylor and Cassandra so quickly.

The next day, I was met by both of them as soon as I walked in. Taylor, with his baby hands perched on his hips, had a look of intense anger across his mongoloid face. Cassandra had her forearms crossed, resembling a smoked meat log you would see hanging in an old-world Italian deli.

"What do you think you're doing, guy?" asked Taylor. He was as intimidating as a SpongeBob piñata. Cassandra, with drool frothing from her jowls, was quite scary, though.

"Why? What's up?" I asked. I might have smirked when I said it.

"You know what the hell I'm speaking of! Who do you think you are to spread rumors about me and my associate? How dare you besmirch us this way?"

"Yeah!" grunted Cassandra.

"I don't know what you're talking about," I said. "What are you insinuating?"

"Well, gee, I don't know. Maybe it's because I heard from several of your evening crew that my coworker Cassandra and I have been carrying on a romantic relationship for years. You have no evidence to substantiate your claims, buddy! We don't take too kindly to your blatant accusations!"

"Yeah!" uttered Cassandra, this time a little louder with a few teeth showing.

"Look, I don't know what you're talking about, okay? Maybe you should ask the same person who spread rumors about me why they find it necessary to flap their fucking gums in the first place."

"Oh, okay. I get it," said Taylor. He threw his miniature hands in the air in a frustrated manner. "You come into our post, laughing hysterically in our presence, then start making obviously false rumors about two other employees' sexual interactions?"

"That's not nice, what you did!" said Cassandra. She pointed at me as she spit saliva all over the place. "Why'd you do that?"

The three of us argued for the next few minutes. Taylor used big words and long phrases inaccurately, all while his forest troll Cassandra stood ready to spear me. I, being the civil one in this conflict, told them both to lick my taint. Eventually, the argument touched upon the grappling hook comment from the previous night. Taylor's rage reached critical mass.

"I heard about your little mountain climbing analogy too! You're a sick pup, you know that? I've worked with my dear friend Cassandra for the past twelve years, and I've never entertained such a thought. You should be ashamed of yourself for saying such a thing! That comment will be brought to the attention of human resources ASAP. You've gone too far, mister. Do you hear me? You've gone too far!" He stormed away with Cassandra in tow after she let out a snort in my direction.

So the battle lines were drawn. It was the tag team of Taylor and Cassandra versus me. I've been on the outs with them ever since. I had no mal-intent when I came to my current post, but something so silly as a laugh started yet another war at work. It's been a real blast coming to work and hearing bullshit rumors from two people who belong in a freak show. I'll tell you more about it as we go deeper into the book. I'll just have to compose myself and go about my day without them getting the best of me. It's tough when your job forces you to be a dick just to get by.

CHAPTER 8

A Trip to the Human Resources Office

It was bound to happen sooner than later. There was only so much shit I could talk until someone reported me to HR for inappropriate language. Honestly, I didn't know how I didn't get flagged years ago. You should have heard the names I used to call people. Do you know how many different people, both male and female, I've called a twatwaffle? A lot. I've called an inordinate number of coworkers a twatwaffle, albeit all for good reasons. Many colorful words have been used with varying degrees of success, but *twatwaffle* seems to be the best all-around derogatory term.

I got a letter in my mailbox two days ago with the term *confidential* stamped on it. That was never a good thing to see on an envelope. It didn't mean you had won the Publishers Clearing House big cardboard check prize. It meant you had either taken out a pension loan recently, or you got a meeting coming up with management. I was broke, but I was not desperate enough to take out a pension loan. Those thieving bastards charged more interest than a loan shark. I would rather borrow money from a guy with no fingers than borrow from my pension. So I knew it was one of the hierarchy admistrators who beckoned for me.

Meetings with management were never a good thing. They didn't single you out for janitor of the month awards, complete with a pizza party and a gift card to Walmart. A meeting with management translated to, "You're fucked." You needed to bring a union representative, a lawyer, a priest, a vial of holy water, or some other religious artifact to ward off damnation.

This letter could be from any number of incidents from my jilted past. I was leaning toward the current bullshit with Taylor and Cassandra, although it could have been from when that teacher reported me for terrorism. Oh, you didn't hear about that one? This lady wouldn't let me in the building one time when I forgot my work keys. I left them in my wife's truck over the weekend and simply forgot to put them back in my center console. I was at the mercy of a teacher who was passing by the door. She asked me who I was several times even though I was wearing a uniform and an ID badge.

"I've never seen you before!" she said. "For all I know, you might be a terrorist!"

"Are you fucking serious?" I said. "I've worked in the building for over three years now. Look, I'm wearing a uniform and an ID badge around my neck with my photo on it."

"Doesn't matter," she said. "You look like a terrorist with that beard. I'm not letting you in the building."

I was 99 percent sure you couldn't say that to someone, especially in a school. My boss finally came by twenty minutes later to calm her nerves, saying I was indeed an employee who worked at that building. Ever since then, I made it a point to say hello as I passed her. Even though it had been a year since the incident, I was never given an apology or explanation as to why it was acceptable to call someone a terrorist. What did a terrorist look like anyway? Don't answer that. Never mind.

This letter might, in fact, be a hogwash letter telling me it's safe to return to work regardless of my beard's social status. Since the board of education took its sweet-ass time doing anything, I wouldn't have been surprised. The board of ed took longer to accomplish a task than any other entity in this country, including the government. They weren't really on time with anything. It took seventeen years to remove moldy floor tiles in the oldest school in the district. They still had asbestos pipes in a few schools, and that shit had been outlawed since the late eighties. *Punctuality* wasn't a term I would have used when describing the public school system.

I opened the letter to find a masthead from the human resources department. They were advising me of an "impersonal employee review" with the new HR supervisor.

> Please be advised that you have been selected for an impersonal employee review with the new human resources department head supervisor, Ms. Janet Rillings. She would like to speak with all employees to advise them of upcoming changes to the public school curriculum for the new school year. Please make sure you bring your work history records and any employee review letters you have been given over the past eighteen months. This is not a voluntary meeting. We look forward to talking with you and working on a positive note in the new school year!
>
> Sincerely,
> Ms. Janet Rillings, Esq.
> Head Supervisor / Human
> Resources Department

Let's dissect this letter in real-world terms, because it's purposely vague. First, these meetings were never impersonal. They were biased as all shit. HR departments simply didn't see how you were doing after you had been working at a job for twenty years. They were prompted to call a meeting because someone had filed a complaint. My money was on Taylor ratting me out. I didn't think Cassandra had the mental capacity to read or write anything other than a grocery list.

Secondly, I had nothing to do with educational curriculums in a public school because I didn't educate the children. I mopped the floors they walked on and dusted the window ledges they stared out of. That was the extent of my involvement with the children. Why did I need to be aware of the educational changes? I saw this as a farce. They needed a reason to call me to a meeting without tipping their hand. Had they written, "You called someone a twatwaffle, so now we need to punish you," I might not have been so skeptical.

Come to think of it, I had never had an employee review since I had my initial interview. I wish I were making this up; but none of the countless bosses, managers, or supervisors had ever given me a formal review since the last millennium. I could have honestly said that none of the twenty or so bosses I had had over the past umpteen years had ever given me a review, either written or formal. I'm sure you've had a quarterly or even a yearly review with a boss about how you're progressing as an employee, but nope, not me. This place didn't do that sort of thing, which led me to believe that either I was doing a fantastic job, or none of the bosses gave a crap.

What does that tell you about a job when no one monitors you on a professional level? If you aren't evaluated on anything, then what's the point of having a boss? Hell, I think the managers at Wendy's check on the fry guy once in a while. I come in year after year without reviews, assessments, or even conversations on my performance. In my mind, that's the most unprofessional thing I've ever heard. How would you feel if your boss just ignores you all the time, letting you do whatever the hell you want? Sure, it sounds cool, but what's the point of putting your best foot forward if no one watches you do it?

Even though human resources had a new supervisor, it was unlikely they wanted me to pop in for a friendly chat. The last guy who ran HR retired after twenty-five years because he was tired of doing his useless job. Who in their right mind wanted to sit in a stuffy nine-by-nine office, listening to one asshole bitch about another asshole? It was the pettiest job in a public school, other than crossing guard.

Regardless of the salary, which I hear is mind-boggling, I believe HR departments are a complete waste of time. People don't get along for a multitude of reasons. You're not going to pressure someone into not being a dick head. I don't care how positive your attitude is.

The most important part of the letter to my ears was, "This is not a voluntary meeting." That set the tone right there. I couldn't opt out of it. I guess the secretary had to write that line in case I didn't show up. I was under the impression that everything at this job was done on a voluntary basis. I wonder where I got that idea from. Maybe it was because I had never met with HR before and I had never had an employee review and I had never been informed of previous changes to educational cirriuculm. I had meetings before, plenty of them, but never had I been asked to come in for a checkup. Suddenly, it was mandatory. I asked a few coworkers I was still cool with if they received the same letter as I had. None of them had. My mind started to stroll down the streets of Dookie Lane and Asswipe Avenue.

The meeting with HR was scheduled for 9:00 a.m. on a Wednesday. This may sound like an ordinary time to have a meeting, but remember when janitors work their normal hours. I was on the second shift. I worked from 4:00 p.m. until 12:00 a.m. By the time I got home, showered all this shame off, and unwound for the night, it would be around 2:30 a.m. I was lucky if I got to bed before three o'clock. Dragging my ass into a 9:00 a.m. bullshit meeting was close to sacrilege.

Ms. New HR Department Supervisor didn't have meetings after 3:00 p.m., during my work hours. I found this out the hard way when I called a day before the meeting to change the time to something more accommodating to my schedule. So I was pissed off before I even stepped foot into the meeting. Let's make that abundantly clear.

The human resources department was located in the administration complex, the hub of all asinine activity in a school district. It was where all the administrators congregated to sip cognac while reviewing their latest stock portfolios. This wolves' den was all about money. If your salary was under $100,000, they scowled at you as you walked in.

The administration complex had an armed guard at the front desk. It seemed odd that a board of education building needed a man with a Glock 17 handgun to protect them. Perhaps there was a perfectly good reason this guy was packing heat. Several spiteful taxpayers and nosy reporters had been banned from the premises before. Remember, the regime didn't like people asking questions about where the money went. Rumors of fatalities and mutilations had been bandied about, and stories of people being dragged out the back door and into a blacked-out Cadillac DeVille were common.

As I walked into the HR department, I was smacked with snowflake propaganda. It was way too bright in HR. The walls were painted sunflower yellow with all kinds of horseshit in my face. I counted fourteen posters and textual art sayings before I made it to the front desk. *Motivational* was the word to describe the feeling one got when they arrived in HR. Had I not been so pissed off about having this meeting, I might have wanted to scale a nearby mountain or conquer my fear of loneliness after reading such inspirational wall decor. Upon reading these things, I was reminded of how jilted the worldview of an HR department truly was.

"May I help you, sir?" asked the spry and perky millennial behind the desk. She had a voice filled with jubilation, as if no one had ever ruined a single day in her young, naive life.

"Yes. I'm here to see Ms. Rillings for 9:00 a.m.," I said. The sound of sleepiness in my voice was deep, like a trucker after his third pack of Marlboro Reds for the day.

"Oh, sure. Let me check to see if she's in her office yet. I think she's running a little late this morning." She picked up the phone to call the director, but all I could think was, *Wait, why is she running late? I've got maybe five hours of sleep for this stupid meeting. This bitch better be here!* Sure enough, a brief call down the hallway informed me I would be waiting longer. "Ms. Rillings said she is busy at the moment and will have to push your meeting back."

The secretary's mousy voice enraged me. "You're kidding me, right?" I said.

"No. I'm sorry, sir. Ms. Rillings is very backed up with paperwork at the moment."

"I, ah, I don't understand," I said. "Didn't the office just open at 9:00 a.m.? I mean, I'm the first meeting, right?"

"Yes, sir, but Ms. Rillings is extremely busy this time of year with the new curriculum changes. She said to tell you if you'd like to take a seat, she will be with you as soon as humanly possible!"

"Listen. I'm very tired. I...I work nights, and I got up really early for this meeting, so is there any chance she can meet me now so I can go home and get some sleep before my shift this afternoon?" The secretary wasn't comprehending. People didn't understand there were shifts other than nine to five.

The good news was, I had my choice of seats in the waiting area, because no one else was there to have a meeting this early in the morning. Minutes passed as I stewed in an uncomfortable chair, eagerly awaiting to have my name called. Several things bounced around in my head. First and foremost, I was the only putz waiting for a meeting. Sure, other people walked in, like the mailman and an office delivery boy, but no other employees ever showed up. My meeting was most definitely not a random thing. There were no important curriculum changes this lady had to go over with me. I was there to have my shit pushed in, as the kids on the street say nowadays. This meeting, whatever its real purpose, was a setup.

I fumbled in my phone for a union rep's number just to have someone on my side in case it got serious. The only numbers I had were of people I had burned bridges with a long time ago. Not a single one of them would have showed up to defend me against the upcoming onslaught. Half of them were incompetent while the other half had been less than cordial since our last interactions. They usually didn't come to your aid after you called them a bitch-ass puppet.

It was my fault, I knew. I had a problem with people who got paid a boatload amount of money to represent the worker, then backed down because they had no balls. Bosses owned the unions nowadays anyway. Gone were the times when the mere mention of a union would have the boss shitting in his slacks. Now unions were simply a formality. No one was standing in picket lines anymore. You paid union dues because it was mandatory, and if you didn't pay the dues, then you didn't have the so-called protection of the union. Once you stopped making those union-due payments, the bosses could fabricate a story to fire you without cause.

Both the union and adminstraton were making money hand over fist while plowing the average worker down like a field of dry cornstalks. Union dues went to numbskulls who talked in circles and to inept mouth breathers who tripped on their shoelaces at random intervals. These clowns couldn't negoataite their way out of a wet paper bag, let alone save someone's job.

The boss told the union what to do, reminding the union reps not to rock the boat, or else they would lose their position as a union representative. Why would a person making an extra forty grand a year as a union rep jeopardize losing their money? Doing the right thing wasn't a reason to lose a second paycheck in their greedy eyes. It was all a big game, usually one the average worker lost in the end. I never had much faith in my union in the first place. So I put the phone away, folded my arms, and stared out the window for a few minutes.

At approximately 10:15 a.m., I was awoken by a fairylike voice telling me Ms. Rillings would see me now. Yeah, I fell asleep sitting there. I told you I was tired, so don't cast judgment. I stumbled down the hallway, trying to wipe the sleep from my semicrusted eyes. Halfway down the hall, I overheard the secretary pick up the phone. Her voice was muffled, as if she was relaying vital information to an informant. Seconds later, I arrived at the front door of a disgruntled-looking older woman with a telephone receiver on her ear. The fucking mousy secretary dimed me out for sleeping. Goddamn millennials!

Ms. Janet Rillings was not a young woman, as I assumed when first seeing her name on my letter. There was no *Ms.* here. She was in her late fifties and very Caucasian with deep trenches on her face that could have been mistaken for the Nazca Lines of Peru. She had years of bitterness written on her mug. I would say she previously worked for the DMV, where intimidation and lack of giving a fuck were a job requirement. Her jawline was flat; you could have put a level on her mouth, and it would have been perfectly balanced. She sported a short gray hairdo similar to a retired nanny's.

Her office decor displayed the empowered, strong woman starter pack, as I liked to call it. A Rosie the Riveter "We Can Do It!" poster hung on the back wall. To the left of that was a Hilary Clinton campaign donation plaque saddled by one of Ms. Rillings's numerous degrees. Don't you hate seeing that, an office wall covered in inane awards? Who gives a shit if you've taken one hundred hours of professional business management classes? I once got a certificate for my dog for graduating from obedience school. The gold seal on his certificate looked exactly like the one on Ms. Rillings's certificate.

On her extremely tidy desk were family photos of who I assumed were her children. None of the photos had a husband figure in them, and I know this sounds a little sexist, but there wasn't a wife figure in them either. It was just her and her adult kids. This told me that Ms. Rillings either adopted her children or went through a painful divorce. Also, the photos were facing away from her. You get this, right? Her family photos were facing the person who sat across from her at her desk. Won't you want pictures of loved ones to be looking at you instead of whoever you're interviewing? This didn't make sense to me.

"Good morning," said Ms. Rillings. "Sorry to keep you waiting."

"No, it's okay. Nice to meet you," I said.

She didn't offer a reason for making me wait, and I didn't expect one. It was not like I mattered or anything, not like my time was precious. She shook my hand with a lot of force. This handshake could have been performed by a lumberjack or someone who crushed things with their bare hands at keggers.

Ms. Rillings extended her hand out to the single chair in front of her desk and said, "Please have a seat."

It felt as if I was being interrogated by a vice detective in one of those rooms with a two-way mirror. As I settled into yet another uncomfortable chair, she rifled through a thick manila folder. She didn't speak. All she did was keep her gaze on the folder as she flipped through different-colored papers. This, ladies and gentlemen, was my work file. I had never actually seen my work file before. There it was, plump and packed with all sorts of documents—numerous work write-ups for abuse of sick days, several handwritten accounts of incidents among coworkers, and a strange number of pink carbon copy sheets. I was guessing those were all the union meetings where I outsmarted people like Mr. Polotski and Mr. Sanders.

Not to brag or anything, but I was impressed with the folder's girth. She was a hefty one! Those pages told a story of my struggles among moronic management and chaotic coworkers. God only knows what vile things were written on those pages. Ms. Rillings, on the contrary, didn't seem impressed with my work history. As she studied each page, sitting there in an olive-green pantsuit, she didn't speak. A few huffs and bellows came from her throat with varying degrees of volume. Those ticks told me all I needed to know about how she viewed me as an employee. She looked up from her pile as I shifted in my seat after five minutes of silence, watching her evaluation.

"Would you like some coffee?" she asked.

"Ah, yes, please. Thank you," I said.

She pointed to the coffeepot resting on the counter behind me. "Pot's right there behind the doorjamb. We don't have any milk or creamer left. No sugar either." She never took her eyes off my file.

That was a dick move, wouldn't you say, asking someone for coffee like you were going to get it, then pointing to the coffee maker? Why wouldn't you just say, "Help yourself to some coffee. It's right over there"? As I got up to pour myself a cup, Ms. Rillings let out an extra loud huff. I turned around momentarily to see her holding photos—not professional pictures but something you would print out from a cheap, all-in-one printer used at home.

While pouring my black-as-night coffee, I peeked to see what she was excited about. They appeared to be photos of a classroom. Only one schmuck could I remember taking photos of my work, that Irish beast Greg O'Sullivan. He was that hard-on supervisor who tried to shitcan me, acting as Sanders's enforcer. He was always walking around with some crappy flip phone, snapping pictures of my work—that and jingling a pair of toenail clippers in his pocket.

I blew on my coffee no less than eight hundred times while standing there. Since Ms. Rillings displayed no intention of addressing me in the first nine minutes of our meeting, I decided to break the ice. "How long have you been the new HR supervisor?" I asked. She didn't respond immediately the way most people did when you asked them a question politely.

"Six months," she said after a few seconds. "But I've been in human resources for over thirty years."

"Oh, very nice," I said. "I've been here a little over twenty years with custodial myself."

Ms. Rillings finally took her eyes off my file. "Yes, I can see that," she said.

Ms. Rillings went back to shuffling my papers as she started to take notes on a steno pad. This reminded me of movie scenes where the shrink jotted things down during a session. "Tell me, when was the last time you had a murderous thought appear in your head?" More silence followed for the next few minutes as she took detailed notes on one particular piece of paper. I directed my eyes toward the headline, though it was backward to me from my side of the desk. It read, "Formal Employee Termination Sheet."

This was the infamous three amigos situation from years ago, where three pieces of caca almost had me out the door. Had it not been for a miraculous video and one amazing Spanish-speaking friend, I might be collecting toll money from a cramped green booth on the Turnpike. Ms. Rillings burned through a good two pages on her steno book over this document. She let out a little "Hmm" while she wrote too.

At this point, being a respectable employee was not high on my list of things to do. After making me wait an extra hour and ignoring me for thirteen minutes in her office, this entire situation irked me royally. Was she for real? Who the fuck did she think she was? There I sat with a cup of coffee—if you could call it coffee—watching some pencil-pushing thug criticize me silently. I was beginning to lose my shit sitting there, all angry and such. Jesus, lady, get to the fucking point already!

At the fifteen-minute mark of silence, I made an executive decision. Since she was so fond of making noises, I made a few of my own. Each time she gave an internal groan, I took a sip of my coffee. I slurped that putrid concoction loudly. You know which sound I speak of. It's the same ear-piercing sound a dumbass makes when they want to create noise for no reason. Those coffee sips matched her judging *ahems* in stride. If she was going to make stupid sounds, by God, so would I.

My coffee slurps got her attention and riled her rage. Ms. Rillings closed my fat file and folded her hands onto her desk. "I've been evaluating your work file for the past fifteen minutes," she said.

"Yes, I can see that," I said. I could be a sarcastic fuck too.

"It appears you've had quite a colorful history here at the board of education." Ms. Rillings still had her hands folded together while she glared at me.

"Well," I said, "define colorful." *Let's start out with the dumb routine and see where that goes,* I thought.

"I mean, you seem to have had several unprofessional incidents with coworkers. Can you tell me why that is?"

She was bold and to the point. I liked it. She finally directed a shot across my bow. "I don't know what you mean," I said. "I guess I've had a lot of problematic workers accost me for no good reason."

"I see. According to your personnel file," she said as she tossed open the folder, "you have been moved quite a few times in your career. Do you happen to know why you were transferred back and forth to each school in the district several times?"

"Maybe because other employees quit and the post needed a better worker to take their spot."

"No, it doesn't seem that way," said Rillings. "It seems like you've had multiple discrepancies. It says here on one transfer paper that you moved due to a situation with a Mr. Johnson." She was referring to one Brother Wade Johnson, whom I might or might not have called a stupid cocksucker and a Jesus freak.

"Nah, I really don't remember him all too well," I said.

"Hmm. You don't remember him?" She gaffed. "Perhaps you don't want to explain why your actions caused a tremendous amount of strife with this individual."

"Oh, you mean that Mr. Johnson? Actually," I said, then I cleared my throat, "that case has been sealed due to a police report, so I'm not at liberty to discuss it."

"I see," she said. "Maybe you can explain why you've been here over twenty years and only have three sick days left. Most employees have over one hundred sick days banked at this point in their careers."

"I get sick a lot," I said. I put my hands over my mouth and coughed a dry cough just to spite her.

"Okay. I see," she said.

Ms. Rillings was trying to goad me into a confrontation. That was what these meetings wee all about. One minute, you were having an innocent conversation; and the next, you were standing in line at social security, dealing with another equally stern-faced pencil pusher. I was moderately annoyed with her line of questioning at that point. I was going let her blow and blow until she was out of breath. She couldn't fire me; I was union and tenured. She didn't have the power to take my job away regardless of how shitty I looked like on paper.

Ms. Rillings noticed that her standard interrogation process wouldn't affect me. I was a person who abhorred redundant questioning. Perhaps my sleepiness was getting to me. My bed was calling to me from inside my tired little soul, but the bitch still pushed onward, creating a tense environment. She persisted with her line of questioning.

"It seems you have a long record of attendance issues coupled with employee infractions," she said. "Do you consider it to be a positive working atmosphere you've created?"

"Well," I said, leaning back, thinking for a second to coordinate a snarky yet poignant response, "what does my file say? You seem to know exactly the type of person I am despite having only met me twenty minutes ago. I'm assuming you want me to say something incriminating, don't you? I have no idea what you're getting at, lady. Why don't you just come out and say it so I can go the hell home and get some sleep already?"

If this twatwaffle was going to get pushy, I would push right the hell back. With no union rep, I could have called off the meeting at any time. It was called invoking my Weingarten Rights. This meant that since I paid union dues, I had the right to representation if questioned by management. But no one in their right mind would have come to my rescue; they would laugh insensately if I called them. Plus, since Ms. Rillings was playing hardball, I wanted to take her on by myself. It probably wasn't the smartest thing I had attempted while working for the board of education.

Mr. Rillings settled back into her chair as well. She placed her pen down on the desk slowly, all while never breaking her concrete smirk. I had poked the bear. I had stirred the proverbial hornet's nest. I was sure that during her life, both personally and professionally, Ms. Rillings had rejoiced when offered the chance to berate a confrontational person, especially a man. As she settled in, I regretted my actions to piss her off immensely.

"What I'm implying with my questioning is that you are a terrible worker. Your track record for overusing sick days combined with your lack of respect for fellow coworkers tell me all I need to know about you. You have no drive to produce quality work. Your attitude is vulgar at best. You're crude, brazen, and unashamed of your decadent ways. You also appear to be a horrible person, although I only got halfway through the incident reports in this bulging file, so I can't determine that confidently."

"Hmm," I said, sort of stupefied. "Why don't you tell me how you really fucking feel?"

I didn't mean to say that out loud; it just kinda came out. Perhaps it was not my finest moment. My momentary lapse in judgment was a huge mistake. The bitch got what she wanted: I cursed her out. Had I not been overtired, I might have stymied my words. Nonetheless, Ms. Rillings had what she wanted.

"Excuse me?" she said. "Cursing at a superior member of management is a fireable offense!"

"Management?" I said. "Superior? Aren't you a guidance counselor or something like that?"

"How dare you question me like that," she said.

I slurped my coffee one last time before smiling in my seat. "Because you don't know me and you're casting judgment. You don't know a thing about me. You've been nothing but disrespectful to me since I got here, yet I'm supposed to let you treat me like crap because you've got some fancy papers on the wall?"

"Disrespectful? I see. Falling asleep in the waiting area is a sign of respect, I assume?"

"Look, lady," I said, adjusting my posture in the chair, "I got done working at midnight, and you call me into this meeting with less than five hours of sleep. Then you make me wait another hour, then ask me rhetorical questions on top of that. You're the one without respect here. I don't care how many degrees you have on the wall. You don't know shit about me."

"Well then," said Rillings, "you've left me with no choice."

"For what? You can't fire me. I'm union, and I'm not answering another question until I have a union rep present."

"Oh, it's far too late for that, mister." Ms. Rillings took my file, dropped it onto another pile off to her left, and then took out a form from her desk. "I've seen and heard all I need to make my decision. I'm recommending your work contract be terminated on the grounds of insubordination. Your actions have forced me to call for a full termination. I suggest you get your things in order and await the board's decision."

I stood up fast, pushing my chair back with just a tad too much force. It fell backward, hitting the ground with a thud. It wasn't thrown or slammed, as a certain bullish woman would have you believe. It sort of toppled ever so slightly onto the carpeted floor. Since she was trying to fire me, I might as well go the whole hog with my rant.

"Termination?" I laughed out loud, a defiant gesture. "You're joking, right? Who the hell do you think you are, huh? I'm union and tenured in. You ain't got shit on me! You get me out of bed with limited sleep, start throwing baseless accusations, and expect me not to get defensive? Lady, you don't know who you're fucking with!"

"Get out of my office!" she screamed. "I will submit my report to the superintendent, and you will await their decision as to your working relationship with the board of education." Ms. Rillings pointed to the doorway.

"My working relationship? I'm just a vulgar, scumbag janitor, so you're going to have to explain what working relationship means. Are you firing me or not?"

"You are now under review. I suggest you leave my office now before I call security and have you escorted from the building!"

"Your little report doesn't mean dick to me! Get fucked, lady!" I said.

Once my brain comprehended the word *security*, I realized it was time to leave. I was on fire inside, burning like street tacos in Mexico City, where they used the really hot sauce. The stuff that was brownish red and sort of paste-like? That kind of fire. It took all my might to not grab one of the Things Remembered engraved trophies on her desk and throw it like a hand grenade.

As I stormed out of her little hovel, I passed the secretary standing at her desk. She had her mouth covered by her delicate hands, her face plastered with a look of horror. As I walked past her, she gawked at me as if to say, "Oh my God! The vile beast is on a rampage!" I didn't deserve her judgment. It wasn't fair to be labeled a monster regardless of how many f-bombs I dropped within earshot. She didn't know me either, yet there she was, probably afraid for her life.

I left the administration complex a bitter and embarrassed man. The granite-faced Ms. Rillings called down to the front desk to ensure my departure was speedy and without altercation. That gun-toting security guard eyeballed me as I passed his desk. I gave him the stink eye back knowing all too well what he and the other front desk workers were thinking: "There goes that horrible person."

That's the thing about being a villain; you can never become a hero once you've been marked as a bad person. My work file didn't have any of my accomplishments. There was no mention of the numerous times I worked alone, doing the work of two or three people a night. I didn't see one piece of paper thanking me for helping someone when they needed advice.

Do you know how many times I've helped coworkers fill out paperwork for loans or other job applications because they didn't understand the wording on it? How about the time I left work to change a tire for a teacher who got stuck in the rain with a flat or even that one time I saved a coworker's life by calling 911 because he was having a heart attack? I bet those papers weren't in there, were they?

When I got home, I had a voicemail from the superintendent telling me I was on unpaid suspension until the review board had a chance to look at Ms. Rillings's report. Now I'm sitting home, not getting paid, waiting to see if I still have a job in a few days. I don't know about you, but I need a paycheck each week. It's not in my budget to lose a week's pay. I called the head of the union to see if he could do anything even though it was a long shot. He didn't seem hopeful, but he said he would try to use my years of service and tenure to get me a second chance. I didn't know if he was sincere when he said, "I'll do the best I can for you."

So that's where I'm at now, waiting for a tribunal of overlords to look at Ms. Rillings's recommendations to see if they have enough evidence for termination. And to top it off, I can't fall back asleep now that I'm home. I'm too pissed off to sleep, thinking about how this shit has gone down. If I had only kept my big mouth shut.

CHAPTER 9

Mandatory Sensitivity Training

I was angry, sports fans. It would be an understatement to say I was livid beyond belief. That was saying a lot given what I had been through in this latrine for the past 7,000 or so days. The good news was, I still had a job. I didn't know how good it was, but yes, for the time being, I could still pay my rent and eat fairly well. My union president called me late on Friday night to tell me I was still a card-carrying member of the board of education. Fucking whoopee. Despite Ms. Rillings's scathing report to the board, it was determined that they didn't have enough evidence to terminate my contract.

"You're lucky the board is allowing you back," said the dopey teachers union president. "They had a tremendous case against you with Ms. Rillings's report and all. I had to beg for your job and promise them you'd turn over a new leaf."

"Oh, wow," I said. "Thanks for begging on my behalf."

"Hey, no problem. That's what I'm here for. That's what union dues are for! I really had to pull some strings for you, so make sure you'll do the best job you can when you come back."

"Yep. You got it." *What do you want, dude, a fucking bouquet? That's your job. Defend your union dues-paying workers against accusations, and false ones at that.*

"Yes, indeed. They had a good case too. They said this was the last straw," he said.

"Uh-huh." If I bit my lip any harder, I would slice it in half like a ripe banana. *Focus,* I told myself. *Don't say anything other than thank you.*

"You know, I had to call in a favor from a union rep in another county to have them review the case," said my hero. I was holding the phone away from my ear, trying with all my might not to let my mouth say what I really wanted to say. I made one of those sounds a person made when they agreed with someone even though they wanted to smash their face in with a shovel.

"Mm-hmm."

"You start back Monday at your regular hours, at the same post," he said this with a slight pause at the tail end.

"Okay. That's good, right?" I asked.

"Yep. You got your job back, but we agreed you need to make a little concession before you return," he said.

"What kind of concession? What do you mean?"

"Well," said the union president, "you need to attend a seminar this weekend before you can come back."

"Seminar?" I said. "What are you talking about?" I began to feel a warm sensation blanket me. My internal teapot was boiling away.

"It's a special class offered by the state to ensure you have the right disposition for the workplace. It won't take long. I signed you up for tomorrow morning, so you need to complete it before coming back to work. Just bring your ID, maybe a notepad to take notes, and a checkbook. Hey, dude, you'll do fine! Hello? Are…are you there?"

I was—for the first time ever, I believe—speechless. My brain turned itself off. It was kind of like when you blacked out from drinking. It was a safety precaution so you didn't die from alcohol poisoning. I couldn't formulate words or thoughts for a few seconds. I was kind of glad I didn't say anything, because had I said what I was feeling after the conversation, I definitely wouldn't have a job anymore.

Management suggested I take a class in sensitivity training due to my confrontation with Taylor and Cassandra. That was what this whole clusterfuck was about. That small-handed freak Taylor called HR to tell them I was spreading rumors about him and Cassandra having sex. Once the harbinger of harassment, Ms. Rillings, got wind of it, she made it her duty to terminate me. I knew she tried vehemently, but since I had so many years of service and I was union, she couldn't shitcan me outright. Her only concession, since I blew up in her face, was to have me attend a training class on proper workplace etiquette.

I won't say I had it coming, but maybe I had it coming. Sure, I spent a majority of my career referring to coworkers as twatwaffles or the like, but who hadn't? Maybe if the board of education didn't hire these cretins, I wouldn't have called them such names. Seriously, this place practically begged me to call them out on their stupidity. Don't put dipshits in my way and not expect me to have altercations. That's like putting a cake in front of a fat person. You know they like cake! Don't tempt people like that.

The union president sent me an email with all the info on the class. After reading the first few lines of the description, I almost reached for my old PetSmart uniform in the closet. Scooping goldfish seemed a hell of a lot more appealing than spending five minutes in a class made for the criminally deranged. "Shh! Let's Not Say or Do That: Your Guide to Proper Workplace Speech and Attitudes" had all the appeal of a mass shooting. I didn't think they called it anger management anymore. They had to retool the name after numerous incidents involving flying chairs and overturned folding tables.

The online pamphlet resembled a recruitment paper you would see for a well-funded cult. It showed happy, multicultural people laughing while appearing to get along just swell. Motivational phrases like "Let's do it together" and "We can find a solution" were plastered all over this trifolded nightmare. Did these organizations actually thought jobs operated like this? I had never once come into work thinking about how I could brighten a coworker's day by complimenting their new haircut.

This class was designed to let people know "what [was] acceptable workplace talk and what [could] be left out in the gutter, where it [belonged]," according to their website. That sounded exactly like the same shit hanging in the office of one Ms. Janet Rillings. It pissed me off to think about going to this massacre, but since my old PetSmart shirt was about six sizes too small, I had to go.

The class was ninety minutes away from my house, in some crappy-ass town I had never heard of. I was glad I left early, because this place was in an old Main Street church with absolutely no parking. I didn't like to parallel park, but doing it with a cunt hair's room between the front and back bumper was what I was left with. Once I got through that, I wandered around the church, politely asking people for directions. There was nothing like getting silent stares from church folks when you asked where the heathen classes were being held.

As I made my way down the creaking stairs, I got the feeling that I had been there before—not that exact place but as if I had done this class before. It felt like I was going to an AA meeting, to be honest. I had a few of those in my day, as I'm sure you have. If not, then you've missed a great opportunity to feel shitty about yourself. It was all about what bad decisions you made in life and how your actions caused others great pain. I was pretty sure my drinking never killed anyone, but the last instructor made me feel as if it did. This new guy wasn't nearly as intimidating as my AA instructor, but he still pissed me off nonetheless.

Andrew Scribens from Mount Holly, New Jersey, was the embodiment of what sensitivity training classes were. Complete with girlish hips and a blond soul patch, he exuded a glowing persona one would find in any motivational speaker. His endless arm-waving while he spoke irritated me. I was positive this guy was a recovering drug addict or drunk or maybe even a sex addict too. Those were the type of people who taught these classes. He had the look of a former smack addict who saw the light after his sixth or seventh OD.

Just play nice, I told myself. *Get your stupid class completion token and be on your way.* As I walked into the class, I found Andrew beginning his spiel on how to think before you spoke. "Are you here for the positive speech class?" he asked.

"Um, yeah, I think so. Is this the sensitivity training thing?" I said.

"You bet it is!" he said. Andrew put his hands on his hips in a flamboyant manner. He was so positive when he said it. "Although we don't call it sensitivity training here. We like to think of it as more of an attitude reaffirmation class, but you'll learn that later. Please, come in and take a seat. We're just about to begin our session!" He handed me a packet of papers with worksheets and one separate piece of paper, which was the enrollment form.

"You can review the papers later as we go over them in class. Just fill out the order form with today's date, and make out the check to the company listed in bold," said Andrew.

As he went back to his speech, my eyes were drawn to the numbers at the bottom of the form. The attitude reaffirmation class, as Andrew called it, cost $400 with an additional fee of $75 made payable to the church for using the building. Motherfucking asshole union president never told me it would cost me almost five hundred bucks to get my job back! I almost fell out of the way-too-small folding chair once I saw that shit.

That was $475 to have some fruit loop tell me what I could and could not say at work. And how did the church get out with charging $75 for room rental per person? Didn't they give drug addicts a free place to stay until they got off meth? I never paid years ago when I went to AA meetings. What the fuck!

So the drunks and junkies got free stuff while I paid because I called someone a naughty name. Perhaps I should have downed a bottle of RumChata while spiking up. Then my class would have been free. To top it off, this useless powwow was four hours long on a Saturday. Who in their right mind wanted to talk about feelings for four hours? That was a cruel and unusual punishment if I ever heard of it.

As I signed my name on the check while spreading my butt cheeks, I thought about how fucked up this situation was. These things always boiled down to money. The same thing happened for any so-called infraction. Speeding tickets, DUIs, drug possession, and even worthless meetings on why we didn't call people names all revolved around cash. You could break the sound barrier in a stolen car while a hooker gave you road head just as long as you paid your fine. Anything short of genocide could be paid off with court fees and class tuition. Just as long as the government got their cut, you could do whatever you damn well pleased.

Andrew Scribens, with his velvet notepad and zany Trolls pen topper, was born to teach motivational speaking classes. He appeared to be in his late forties, but given his young demeanor, he could pull off being in his early twenties. I didn't normally judge a book by its cover, but this flake was extremely cheery. He wore rust-colored pants with a bright-green polo. These colors clashed with his blue glasses' frames and his white watch. Did he care? Not one bit.

I also noticed a few of those colorful silicon wristbands. Awareness bracelets people called them. I was sure he didn't have all the afflictions labeled on his arm. Perhaps he supported family members who did. I was sure someone with his level of positivity had plenty of friends who gave him these accoutrements. I don't mean to sound shrewd, but what is an acceptable number when wearing awareness bracelets? Three? Seven? I counted twelve between both arms. His hands looked like they had oversized Life Savers above them.

"All right, everyone," said Andrew. "Let's begin down the road to redemption! We're going to get through our problems with our potty mouths and learn a few things to calm us down when we are confronted with situations at work. Who's ready to be a positive worker again?" No one in the room, except Andrew, raised their hand. The only sound I heard was the low hum from the coffee urn resting next to the Dunkin' Donuts box in the corner. At least they had snacks on this shit safari.

"All righty! Well, we'll just have to work on that, shall we?" Andrew looked dismayed. He made each of us stand up to state our names, where we lived, and what led us to take this god-awful class. The first contestant looked like she had been shot out of a cannon and into a row of spears. She had track marks all over her deeply scarred arms, arms she covered with a well-worn jacket as she left the room without saying a word.

"Oh, Jackie," said Andrew, "please try to stay with the class this time. This class can help, Jackie!" She was halfway up the stairs before

Andrew finally gave up pleading to her. "I hope she comes back. That's her fourth time walking out." He left out a short, "Hmm," then addressed the next classmate, a postal worker. I knew this because he had his uniform on and displayed the same bitter disposition as my letter carrier. With some coaxing, Andrew was able to talk him into sharing his story.

"Well, ah, my name is Gary, and I...ah...well..." He stammered back and forth, trying to get his train of thought out of the station. "I...I don't like talking with people because they drive me fucking nuts."

"Oops!" said Andrew. He put his hand across his mouth. "Let's not use those types of words while we're here, okay, Gary? It's okay to be upset. Believe me, I feel your pain. But this class is all about getting to the root of the problem. Let's try it again, okay?"

Gary composed himself and tried once more. "My name is Gary, and, ah, I...I don't like talking...talking about my feelings, so just go to the next guy, okay? There. You happy?"

"That's a good start, Gary. Tell us why you've come here today. I'm not letting you off the hook that easy now! We have to face our problems so we can fix them the next time we have them."

"My boss told me I need to take the class because I, um, because I called a customer a stupid bitch," Gary clenched his fist around his jelly doughnut, causing it to squirt raspberry filling all over his hand.

"All right, Gary. How about you tell us where you're—"

"And I ran over her mailbox," Gary interjected, trying to lick jelly from his hand.

"Okay. Well, how about if—"

"And her Havanese. I ran them both over," said Gary, "with my mail truck."

"Oh," said Andrew. He tried not to show utter disgust, but it was all over his face. "Well, um..."

"I didn't do it on purpose, you see. I...well...it's just that she pissed me off so much, and it sorta happened."

"Well, Gary...," said Andrew. He took a second to piece together a response. "I hope this class can offer you some closure to what happened to that poor lady's dog."

"Yeah, sure thing," said Gary. I noticed that he was breathing in and out slowly through his nose. I was guessing it was a trick he learned from years of holding back rage. "I want to say, for the record, that I…ah…I did have to pay for a new mailbox for her inconvenience, but…ah…she didn't give me a price to replace the dog. I hope…I hope she gives me the bill soon, and maybe it will help with her loss or something," said Gary.

"Okay. Well, let's move along to our next classmate, shall we?" said Andrew. "How about you, miss? What's your name?" He pointed to a small, short woman who had her arms crossed and who had a pissed off look on her face. This woman did not want to talk about a damn thing, especially her feelings. She sat in the folding chair with wire-framed glasses and tight jeans and with her legs crossed. Her upper leg was bouncing up and down in a seesaw manner. She let out a long breath before she spoke.

"My name is Jen, Jen Tolbert," she said.

"Hi, Jen! How are you?" asked Andrew.

"Fine."

"How about you tell us what brings you to our seminar today?"

"I'd rather not!" she said quickly. "Just here to get my paperwork and go back to my stupid, pointless, meaningless job." Jen's leg bouncing became more pronounced as the questions went on. I saw the mercury rising as she tightened her lip and brushed her short hair back behind her ear.

"Okay, Jen. Where are you from?" Andrew asked.

"Cherry Hill."

"What do you do in Cherry Hill, Jen?"

"I work for the goddamn social security office," she said. That leg bob of hers was kicking like a Rockette in training. She looked like a caged puma who got caught in one of those wildlife traps, pacing back and forth, ready to pounce on the first person dumb enough to open the gate.

Andrew, the do-gooder, kept poking her with questions. "Well, Jen from Cherry Hill," he said in a coy, joking manner, "what do you do at the social security office?"

"I used to take shit from my boss," she declared. "But not anymore!" She shifted her legs to uncross them and put the bottom leg on top of the other leg.

"Oh, okay. What do you mean exactly? Try to use action words to describe what you're feeling, okay?" Andrew seemed oblivious to the volcano about to erupt. I knew she would go berserk, as did everyone else in the room. Perhaps Andrew enjoyed watching car crashes unfold in slow motion, 'cause that was what happened after Jen spoke next.

"Well, I told my shit-faced boss I'd strangle him one day, but he didn't believe me. He kept doing the things I told him not to do. I said, 'Ya can't keep working me shorthanded all the time,' but that's what happened. Yep, just me all the time working the window by myself with no relief helper. My dirtbag of a boss kept pushing all the new applicants onto my work pile even when I told him I was already knee-deep in old applicants. Unreal. Fucking unreal!"

"Oh," said Andrew.

"And that's not the worst of it!" Jen said. Her legs were uncrossed now as she leaned forward to dig into the conversation. "My piece of crap boss simply would not stop putting DN paperwork on my desk even when I specifically told him it wasn't my job to file those, but he did it anyway, because he's a stupid, moronic, ass-faced jerk-off who got exactly what was coming to him! I warned him if he did it one more time, I'd strangle the life right out of his fat round face."

Holy sheep shit, this chic was a murderer. She was, as my aunt used to say, an itty-bitty badass. Nobody messed with a short girl with an anger streak, nobody except Jen's boss, who might be or might not be six feet under. Andrew didn't know how to proceed after Jen's tirade. You would think that someone like Andrew knew how to handle psychopaths, but he looked mortified.

"Oh, well, um…," said Andrew. "Jen, I want you to know you're in a safe zone here. No one is asking you to do any work here today." He had his right hand up in a calming posture, trying to recap Mount Jen, who sat back in her chair, rolling her eyes and refolding her legs and arms. All she kept saying under her breath was, "Unbelievable." When the tension in the room had stymied a little, Andrew went back into his Q and A session with the remaining students. He was only two people in, and already, I knew I was in the wrong place. There I was, surrounded by dog squashers and boss stranglers, yet my harshest crime was only saying two people had sex with each other.

Andrew went on to talk with workers from all over. Most of them were employed either at a state or government job. One guy from a civil service field office chucked his boss's leather chair out of a six-story window. Thank the heavens his boss wasn't in the chair when he did. Another woman, who seemed zonked out of her mind, said that one of her coworkers kept making fun of her clothes while in the break room. Her response was to grab her coworker by her ponytail and continuously slam the copier lid onto her head.

I was surrounded by violent offenders. Seriously, these people belonged in prison. I wondered who had let them out of their shackles in the first place to attend this pointless class. When Andrew came to me, he seemed worn out from listening to maniacs. I was last to speak, so I guessed he thought I was the worst degenerate this side of the Mississippi River.

"And last but certainly not least, please tell us why you're here, Mr...?"

"I'd rather not say my name," I said. "Just call me Mr. Mop. I'm a janitor in the public school system."

"Okay, Mr. Mop," said Andrew. "What brings you here?"

"Well, I...I called someone a twatwaffle," I said.

"Okay. Go on," he said. "What else brings you to our discussion?"

"That's about it. I spread a rumor that two of my coworkers were having sex, and I yelled at an HR supervisor."

Andrew seemed almost shocked at my response. Maybe he viewed me as an ax-toting butcher who chopped up coworkers on the weekends. He seemed relieved about my situation. "That's it?" he asked.

"Yep. Nothing major here. Just called some people a few bad names. Shame on me, right?" The other group members let out disappointing huffs like I was wasting their time. They seemed like they wanted to call me a pussy or shoo me out of the room so they could get to the real meat of their own problems.

"Oh, well, that's not too bad, isn't it? We can work with you on that!" said Andrew.

"You didn't punch anyone?" asked Gary. He seemed disappointed in me.

"Nope. Just said some BS," I said. Even Andrew was looking at me like I was in the wrong place.

After the brutal introductions, Andrew put us in groups to work on what he called problem employee scenarios. We were given a sheet of paper to formulate a response to various situations regarding hostile coworkers. It was kind of like group work back in school where the teacher wanted you to solve an equation. My group consisted of myself; Jen, the strangler; Walter, an avid fisherman who pulled a knife on his immediate supervisor; and Stephanie, the airport TSA screener who beat a passenger with a baton over a seating change.

We were given a mock scenario to work out to see if we could alleviate the conflict without violence. This could have been resolved within minutes, but Andrew suggested we take the next hour working out a solution in which each person wins in the end. He said we should all work on our own outcomes first, then share our answers with our group to see who had the most peaceful answer.

Here was our group's dilemma: Your name was Ed, and you worked the drive-through window at a local burger chain. You had a confrontation with someone over their order. The customer stated that you gave them the wrong flavor of milkshake and wanted to speak to your manager. You gave them chocolate, which was the flavor they ordered, yet they insisted that you gave them a strawberry milkshake. After a few choice words were exchanged, the manager decided it was your fault even though you knew you did your job correctly. Your boss berated you in front of your coworkers and the customer. The boss then asked you to replace the milkshake for the disgruntled customer. What would you have done next?

My initial answer was to use sarcasm or quit the useless drive-through job. I wanted to say all sorts of things to both the asshole customer and my useless boss. Perhaps a few poignant remarks about their stupidity would have satisfied my anger. But alas, I needed to get my job back regardless of how trivial this exercise was. Andrew told us to work out the problem first on paper, then to discuss it within the group as a whole. My final answer was to swallow my pride, remake the milkshake while smiling an excessive amount, and then to apologize to both the customer and the manager.

My fellow groupmates, not to my surprise, had more elaborate opinions on how to address the problem. Jen suggested that Ed strangle the customer first, then once they were unconscious, wrap her hands around the boss's neck. "It's his fault I'm working shorthanded at the window anyway!" said Jen. We all decided this was not the best way to fix the problem. It was not worth it getting arrested over a milkshake.

Walter had a more creative approach. "I say you make the milkshake over, but this time, take a shit in the cup first. They'll never know 'cause it's a chocolate shake!" This, too, caused a problem. If the customer became ill over the tainted shake, it would undoubtedly be linked back to the feces found in the cup. When asked what Stephanie would do in that situation, she stated that she wouldn't be caught dead working in a fast food place ever. "I wouldn't be serving no fucking assholes in no burger place," she said. "That's fucking minimum wage! I got kids to support. I'd quit that job after the first time someone yelled at me over a milkshake. You'd find me selling weed again like I did back in the '90s before I'd wear a paper hat, dunking french fries!"

Stephanie's answer made the most sense, but still, it didn't solve the problem at hand. When it came time to discuss our answer with the rest of the class, Andrew found my conformist answer to be the most positive and helpful. He walked over and drew a smiley face on my paper, telling me my answer displayed courage and good worker appeal. "You'll be working your way up the corporate ladder in no time!" he said. This wasn't a comforting remark. Maybe I could squeeze back into my old PetSmart uniform one last time and see if they were hiring. Anything was better than this holocaust of dispshittery.

Our next in-class activity was a word association exercise. Andrew started writing words on the chalkboard and told us to say the first thing that came to mind. Class participation started off slower than expected. "It's okay, everyone!" said Andrew. "This is a judgment-free area. Just say whatever pops into your head!" I believed that Andrew wasn't ready for a majority of the responses. He wrote words like *customers* and *clients* on the board, only to hear things back like *morons* or *pricks*.

The next words on the board revolved around coworker interactions. Andrew wrote the word *supervisor*. The level of classroom participation skyrocketed. "Dickface!" shouted Jen. "Useless!" said another classmate. I even threw a couple of my all-time greatest insults out there when Andrew wrote "human resource officer" on the board. "Twatwaffle!" I said. "Assclown!" Gary said. "Cunt muffin!" said the quiet guy in the back of the room.

We hit every filthy word combo in the dictionary, much to the chagrin of Andrew. "Okay, guys, let's try to be a little more passive with our word choices, all right?" Andrew probably would have preferred we used nicer words, but we made breakthroughs nonetheless. The whole class was smiling and laughing like children in our own demented little way. Apparently, screaming *fuck-face* was a good way to relieve some work-related stress. I'll have to try it if ever given the opportunity to clean toilets professionally again.

Finally, Andrew wrote his last word on the board: *termination*. The room fell silent. You could almost feel the class pondering their worst thoughts at this point. If any one of us said what devious thoughts were rolling around in our heads, we would kiss a passing grade goodbye. No instructor wanted to hear how many pieces you could cut your boss into or how much weight was required to chain a body down to prevent it from floating back to the surface. Nobody said anything out loud.

Andrew seemed pleased with our silence. "Hey, wait a minute, guys. No one here can think of any words to describe what it feels like to be fired? Well, I'll tell you what, you're starting to think like positive workers again! Remember one of the golden rules: 'If you can't say anything nice, then don't say anything at all!'"

I preferred thinking that none of us wanted to spout out what hideous things we would do once we had been fired. It was better this way. I was sure Jen or Stephanie were going to chime in, but they didn't. We all sat there with complacent looks on our faces, hoping Andrew would change the subject before someone implicated themselves.

As we approached the fourth hour, I started to think this class was all just a test to see who was going to crack first. I mean, how many times can you say you're not going to snap at work ever again? If you've spent the past decade or so putting up with stupid people's shit, don't you have the right to voice your opinion? What's to say you won't go off the rails the next time someone pushes your buttons?

While looking around the room, I saw potential crimes waiting to happen—the office worker who crammed a stapler up his boss's butthole or the city bus driver who took the entire bus off the nearest bridge when someone asked for a change of a hundred-dollar bill. These people were lunatics. I saw that after the first few minutes. Did they view me as a lunatic as well? Was I really as bad as the rest of my inmates? My only crime was calling someone a bad name. I never strangled anyone at work, although if given the chance, I did have a mental list ready to pull names from.

Andrew erased his writing on the board, moved the chalkboard to the side of the room, and picked up the nearest folding chair. He walked over to the person closest to the door and placed it in front of them. "This is the last thing we're going to talk about in this class," he said. "I want you to look at me and tell me you're not going to say or do horrible things at work anymore." Andrew, sitting backward in the folding chair, sat in front of each of us and asked us all the same question: "Are you ready to go to work and not cause any problems?"

The first guy was a little dazed by the question but answered, "Yeah, sure. I guess so."

Andrew reached out his hand. "Congratulations. You're ready to be a positive member of the workplace again! Your certificate is on the table behind me. Have a great rest of the day!"

And that was it. There was no written test or oral exam—"Poof, you're healed! Don't forget your parting gift on the way out." These people were in no way ready to reenter the workplace. Half of them were still threatening violence as they gathered their stuff to leave. "Oh, I can't wait to show my stupid, fat-faced boss!" said Jen. "He's gonna regret ever giving me all that work now!" All we had to do was pay the fee and promise not to do it again. I would have bet solid money that half the people in that room were going to commit a major crime once they returned to work. I guaranteed one of them would be in jail within a week.

When the time came to sit in front of me, Andrew looked me square in the eye. He asked me the same question as all the others, and I said a resounding, "Yep."

"Congratulations, my friend! You've graduated from Positive Reaffirmation Class! Don't forget your paperwork on the table to bring back to work!" He shook my hand and moved on to the next guy.

I grabbed my authentic-looking document as I left, thinking just how stupid this truly was. Was this what it was all about, pay some money and you were good? But then again, that was how the system worked. Look at people who got DUIs. Their insurance went up, but not much else happened to them. Sure, they lost their license for half a year, but I bet most of them drove anyway, praying they didn't get caught in those six months. You would still have to get to work or pick up kids from school, right?

None of those people in that meeting were rehabilitated, myself included, but according to the state, we were. It said so on our paperwork. Just as long as the checks we wrote didn't bounce. I would bet that Andrew had to ask us individually if we were okay just to clear himself and the state of any liability in the future. If Gary decided to flatten the next dog, I bet the United States Postal Service would be in the clear because they had sent him to the new and improved anger management class.

Nobody cared if you had learned your lesson. The next time you choked someone out, it was another guaranteed $475. That was the hook here. It was a constant flow of money to the state, who knew damn well a repeat offender was a sure bet. That was why they offered the class in the first place!

I returned to work that Monday and was met with blank stares from ugly faces. No one said much to me that day. It took a few days for a nosy coworker to ask what had happened. I told them exactly what had been clawing at my soul for the past week or so: "Yes, I'm a changed individual. I've learned the error of my ways. By golly, I'll never call anyone a foul name again so long as I work here. You've heard the last bad name or random insult out of my mouth, so help me Jesus!"

CHAPTER 10

Father Bob Is a Fucking Asshole

The one good thing about my job—and any job, really—was overtime. School systems always had sports or academic programs going on during the weekends, so I tried to cash in. I could give two craps about who won the state wrestling championship, but if they hosted it at my school, I would hear cash register sounds go off in my head. Overtime was my way of getting even with the job. Sure, I gave up a few Saturdays here and there. But most days on overtime, I milked that shit like a ripe cow.

Since I was a union member, we had a fixed rate of one and a half times the hourly rate when we did overtime. I would sit there all day, making time and a half babysitting some basketball game or math olympics. It was easy work too. I was there to do a little cleanup and to watch the boiler. That was it. There was no mopping of dried blood or polishing walls, just hours of money coming my way. I came in, opened up the building, turned the lights on, and let them play their games. When they were done for the day, I raced around and dumped a few trash cans, and I was out the door. On a good day, I could net ten to twelve hours depending on the schedule.

Like most larger buildings, a school needed a boiler to keep hot water. It heated the pipes to bring hot water to all parts of the building. Remember those jokes you heard about the janitor hiding away in the boiler room? Yeah, that was me. Laugh all you want, but guess what, boiler operators made sweet money. You needed a brain to use one of these things. If you had a boiler's license, you made more money than your typical janitor. It was not enough to buy a mansion in Rumson, but it did help. Plus, when the bosses handed out overtime, they had to give it to the guy with a license.

The Holy Grail of overtime was the elusive Sunday OT. This, my friend, was when the real money started flowing. As per my union contract, any person who worked on a Sunday must be paid two times their regular hourly rate. Double time, *mi amigo*! I would drag my ass to work on a Sunday any day for twice the pay. I only did a Sunday one time, and it was glorious. We had a soccer club who needed my school as a training facility during the winter. I guess they couldn't use the soccer fields when there was a foot of snow on the ground.

I banked eighteen hours that day. That was almost like another whole paycheck. All I did was turn the lights on and throw out the Gatorade bottles when they left. Easy money, man! I would do nasty things to get double time. I'm talking crimes against humanity.

Sometimes, life gives you lemons. Other times, life gives you a diamond-encrusted platinum lemon. As luck would have it, a little bit of divine intervention fell into my lap. One day, my boss asked me if I had any plans next Sunday. It turned out that a church group wanted to use our school as a base for their congregation. The Sons of Gabriel Fellowship had an old church in need of massive renovations, and they needed my post as a fill-in for God's house.

"Sure. I can do it," I said. I didn't even let him finish talking. "What, just this Sunday?"

"No, it's going to be more than just one day," he said. "Probably at least the next six months."

"What?" I said. My mouth started watering like I was watching a steak being grilled to perfection over an open flame. "Like, every Sunday for six months?"

"Perhaps longer. More like six months, at least," he said.

Right then and there, I heard angels singing in the distance. The sound of trumpets calling out in the wind permeated my ears. I was told I could have each Sunday because no one else wanted it. The whole time my boss was talking, I saw a light slowly envelop his body. This was a sign, a very green, dollar-filled sign, telling me to take the money as fast as I could.

"Holy shit! Damn. Well, how long do they need me to be here? A couple of hours?"

"Well, they have several groups coming in. I think the pastor told me twelve hours each day."

"Are you fucking serious?" I said and slowly realized I was being loud. "Sorry. I didn't mean to say it like that."

He laughed and smiled. He knew exactly what I was thinking. "It's okay. Just try not to spend all that money in one place. I hear the father is a real nice guy too. You'll meet him at 7:00 a.m. Sunday."

I felt weak in the knees after our conversation. Math was never my strong point, but I was crunching numbers like a son of a bitch. Four or five Sundays a month for a minimum of six months with twelve hours each day at double time—let that sink in for a second. I didn't have a calculator that could add that high. My mind began to wander on a glorious stroll. All I could think about was all that money. Finally, after so many years of making shit wages, I was going to be pulling in some serious dough. I didn't know anything about church or Jesus, but for all that money, I would dress up like an altar boy and light the fucking candles myself.

The first Sunday came, and I was pumped, beyond pumped. I showed up half an hour early with a dozen doughnuts and a box of coffee. It was my little way of saying, "Thank you, sweet Lord, for this bounty you have provided for me." The lights were on, the hallways were sparkling, and the chairs for their church services were perfectly aligned. I was contemplating buying paper doilies for each chair, but I didn't want to overdo it. Everything the church asked for was in place when his holiness arrived.

A knock at the door came exactly at 7:00 a.m. There, in the doorway in all black, except for his collar, was the reverend father Robert J. Skininski. I introduced myself, and he said, "Please, call me Father Bob." He was alone with none of the churchgoers there yet.

"Sure, Father Bob. I think everything is set for your congregation. There's the seating over there. The bathrooms are down that hallway, and I even set up coffee and doughnuts on that table there."

"Oh, thank you so much, my son," said Father Bob. "My congregation will be so pleased to see such a nice reception!"

"Yes, you are welcome, sir." I never called anybody sir, but I figured this guy was a priest, so I should show some respect. "I think everything is ready," I said. "Is there anything else you will be needing today?" I was just trying to be a nice person instead of my shitty normal self, and right before I was going to walk away, Father Bob asked me for something else.

"Well, yes, there is, my son. You see, our church, St. Vincent's on Eighth and Park—you do know of it?" I lied and said it was a nice place even though I had never seen it. "Our house of the Lord is in much need of repair. That is why we are using this building instead of our own proper house for the Lord. I was wondering if you could see it in your heart to help our parishioners, who have already undergone so much strife as is."

"Okay. I...I don't know how I can help out with that," I said.

"You see," said the pastor, "our renovations are of a great cost to us. We need a lot of donations to help give God's house the rightful face-lift it needs. I would like to ask if you can help those who need it most."

I was confused and kind of embarrassed because I didn't know what he was asking. Did he want a couple of bucks for the silver plate they passed around? I already bought the doughnuts. "Well, I don't know what you're asking of me, sir." I could see that Father Bob was inching toward something, so I prodded him to get to the point. I had a cup of coffee already myself and needed to use the bathroom.

"To be honest, my son, to use this facility each week is costing us a great deal of money. It's quite a bit of money to pay for the usage of this school when we didn't have to pay at our church. Can you please see it in your heart to donate your daily wages to our cause so that we can be free of any financial burdens to our already encumbered church?"

And there it was, the old payola speech, the whole green paper in white envelopes trick. He was asking me to donate the money the church was paying for the use of the school. You'll have to excuse me if I sound like a creep, but this shit ain't gonna fly. "Oh no, I'm sorry.

I can't do that," I said with a little bit of a laugh. "I'm working here to pay off bills myself."

"Bless you, my son! I do understand life has a way of sneaking up on all of us," said Father Bob. "I wouldn't have asked for it unless we truly needed it for a greater cause. Our church members would so appreciate your patronage. I would be willing to make a special prayer in your name during my service for your troubles."

Yeah, that sounded fair. A couple of sentences to a group of people whom I didn't know was totally worth my giving up all my Sundays for half a year. Don't call me a greedy fuck. You would have said the same thing. I was broke as shit. My bank account laughed at me when I checked my balance. I needed this money. I was not religious to begin with, and it was because of shit like this. True, I was being greedy, scoffing up that overtime. But I was not the one begging people for 10 percent of their paycheck each time I saw them, aka tithings.

"I'm really sorry, Father, but I can't donate the money. I have bills too." I was referring to the new Ford F-150 I was going to purchase in a few months, but he didn't have to know that part.

Father Bob's jovial smile slid off his face. He cupped his hands, giving me a shit-eating grin. I knew what that look meant. Then the preacher tried to put the fear of God in me so I would give up the money. "Well, I do appreciate your honesty, my son. But you know, the Lord requires us to make sacrifices for the betterment of others. Perhaps if you were to think about the consequences of your actions, you would see it's for the best."

Now it was getting uncomfortable. I met the guy for five minutes and he was already threatening me with eternal damnation if I didn't pony up the funds. Who the hell did this guy think he was? I knew it was his job to scare his flock, but I wasn't one of his sheep. I stopped the nice guy routine and hit him with some realness. "I'm not giving you my paycheck. If you need anything else, just give a holler down the hall."

Father Bob was not pleased. I guess not many people told the reverend no. As I walked away, he let out a little huff while clearing his throat. "Thank you for your help this morning. I'll be sure to tell your boss tomorrow how well you did." But he said it in a bitter tone. You know, like, "I'll be calling your boss tomorrow, asshole!" kind of tone.

"Anytime, Padre," I said. Fuck that guy. I should have taken back the doughnuts and the coffee.

Sure enough, first thing on Monday morning, Mr. Father Bob, the bringer of doom, phoned my boss to report how cold and unfriendly I was. This guy tried to extort me, and I was the asshole? I told my boss exactly what happened. Do you know what my boss said to me? "No, he's a reverend. He wouldn't do that!" It was useless to argue over what happened, so I figured I would come in next Sunday to try and talk rationally with the pontiff.

At exactly 7:00 a.m. the following Sunday, a loud knock came at the gym door. This time, the knock had a little more pizzazz to it, an "Open the damn door!" knock. I opened it, and Father Bobby waltzed into the gym. He was on a mission now. He was making sure the chairs were aligned correctly and checking to see if the lighting was right. "Have you given any more thought to donating your salary to the church, my son?"

The balls on this guy were massive. They were like two scruffy coconuts hanging from a palm tree. "Yeah, that's not happening, preacher," I said.

"Well, then," said Father Righteous, "perhaps you can raise the temperature in here a few degrees. It seems a bit drafty. Maybe open a few window blinds in here as well. We need more light to fill this room. And we'll need a few more chairs today too. Some nice parishioners want to hear the truthful Word of God in this cold, breezy gymnasium."

"Sure. No problem," I said. That was all I needed, to piss off a priest. Believe me, I had enough enemies. I did not need one with a direct line to God. By the time I came back, a few of the church members had started to file in. "Anything else you need, Bobby?"

"No, that will be all," he said while shooing me away with his wrinkled old hands. As I turned to leave, he spoke again. "And that's Reverend Robert," he said with an air of distaste. His head was held so high you would think he was trying to hold back a nosebleed.

Now I got a money-grubbing man of the cloth who wanted to torture me just because I wouldn't pay his ransom. He wasn't the pope! I'm sure I'll go to hell for that remark, but it's the truth. I had heard plenty of stories about priests who acted more like a mafia don than a holy man.

With another Sunday in the books and another sweet-ass overtime check, I cleaned up the school and went home. It was nothing big, only a few scraps of paper on the ground and a couple of bathrooms to clean. I hoped Father Fuckface would let the situation alone, but on Monday afternoon, when I came to work, I had a love letter from my boss.

> I got another call from Reverend Robert this morning. He said you were very rude to him and his congregation yesterday. He called the superintendent and wanted to have someone else work instead of you. I don't know what happened, but the superintendent is mad. Bring a union rep with you if you want.
>
> Sincerely,
> Mr. Genger

Over the years, defending myself had become more of an art form than a necessity. If you ever worked in an environment where you were surrounded by people of lesser intelligence, you exploited their stupidity. When faced with adversity, a person must use their skills to rectify themselves. Back in 2001, when a part-timer said I called him a faggot, I proved he was lying. By secretly hiding a fellow employee around the corner of a hallway, I got the part-time jerk-off to confess to my innocence. The following year, when a teacher claimed I had stolen her Disney x Dooney and Bourke purse, I took pictures of her leaving the school the next day with the very same purse in hand. Both individuals were fired after I reported their asses to the union.

If pushed to answer, I would have to say that I had been in over thirty administrative meetings. What can I say? I worked with a bunch of dickheads. I always defended myself gracefully, bringing witnesses, evidence, and sometimes video clips. This time, I had no evidence or witnesses to back me up, but I did have one thing going for me. A coworker told me the priest and the superintendent were old golfing buddies. They had some minor business deals years ago. Now we're talking! That, my friends, was my ace in the hole. Don't fight fire with fire; fight fire with a flamethrower.

During the meeting, the superintendent and the union danced around a bit but ultimately ended the meeting when I brought up the father and the superintendent's relationship. "I heard you and the reverend had some property deals go south many years ago, like, lawsuits and litigation, before either of you had the prestigious jobs you have now. Maybe the newspapers would want to hear about you guys being friends," I said. "I don't know. Sounds kind of fishy if you ask me. Maybe the taxpayers want to know, because it sounds like a conflict of interest to me. I mean, there's a lot of money at stake here with the church paying the school system and all."

It was a ballsy move on my part. If the superintendent wanted, he could have burned my ass right there. He might have been a putz, but he got a few brain cells rolling around in that fat head of his. He excused himself to make a few phone calls. Minutes later, he came back to end the meeting. On some insane level, it worked. No one wanted to see their name in the newspaper. Catholic priests and school superintendents had a fear of being plastered all over the headlines. I guess years of child molestation and embezzlement charges had put them on the defensive. The meeting ended with a note in my file, and a note didn't mean shit to me. I could publish a book with all the paperwork in my file.

I had never met someone I couldn't easily defeat at work. I'm not saying I'm a genius, but most of my coworkers weren't smart enough to set the timer on a microwave, let alone debate against me. But now I came across an enemy who would be harder to defeat. This demon, Monsignor Motherfucker, abused his title to mess with my money. Not cool, man. I don't know about you, but when I go on a warpath, I usually make sure my foe is completely eradicated.

Let's talk a little history. Back in ancient times, the Roman Empire did something wicked to one of its enemies. Have you ever heard of the Punic Wars? Carthage versus Rome? Google it, brothers and sisters. It wasn't enough to simply kill the men and rape the women for weeks on end. No, no, Rome went all psycho on its North African nemesis. After winning the war, the Romans burned the city of Carthage to the ground for seventeen days straight. Then they tried to destroy the buildings of Carthage brick by brick just in case the raping, burning, and slaughtering didn't work. To top it off, the Romans shoveled tons of salt into the ground so nothing would grow in the soil for a thousand years. The civilization of Carthage was almost completely wiped clean from history books. The point is, if you're going to beat someone, make sure the fucker won't get back up to fight again.

Father Bob was an adversary worthy of my full attention. He had good connections, an army of followers behind him, and oh yeah, he was a reverend. Who was gonna believe a janitor over a reverend? That was a no-brainer if I ever saw one. But my mama raised no fool, you see. This task would require all my skills in unison. To defeat an evil force, one must dig deep into their soul to find the answer.

During the week leading up to our next confrontation, I forged a battle plan. It took me hours, but I devised a scheme to combat the dark lord known as Father Bob. I called it Operation Angel Slayer. Don't ask me why. It just sounded cool, okay? First, I would show a sign of weakness to the father. I dug out my old cross necklace. The chain was a little tight. I'm not gonna lie. But I made sure to wear it on Sunday so he could see it. Then I would use his faith to screw him royally. Reverends always loved a fixer-upper. They thought they could save the world. I would play the role of the helpless sinner who needed his guidance.

I needed hard evidence if I stood a chance against him. Since I was fresh out of incriminating photos, I used the next best thing. I placed a digital recorder in my pocket with a microphone line drawn up through my shirt. Who would have cared if it was legal or not? Extortion was illegal, and so was two grimy shysters using a school board as their personal bank account, but I guess their illgal activities classified as circumventing the laws instead of breaking them. They simply fudged the numbers, as their sleazy lawyers would say. I would get Father Bob to admit a few things when no one else was around. This way, when the time came to turn his ass in, I would have him dead to rights.

I wasn't sure if the superintendent told the reverend of my threats, so I had to gauge his expression when I opened the door the following Sunday. I switched the recorder on.

"Good morning, Reverend," I said. My voice was low and full of sorrow, as if I was a defeated man.

"Morning," he said as he sped past me. "Is the heat on? It still feels drafty in here."

"Yes, it's all set, Reverend Robert. I turned it on before and opened the blinds already."

"Good. Make sure you come back and close the blinds at 11:00 a.m. The sun spills into this room, and it nearly blinds my parishioners."

"Yes, yes, of course." I tried to make my voice sound like Snuffleupagus, all somber and dopey. "Is there anything else you need, sir?" I asked.

"No, no. I think we shall be okay."

Then he spotted my necklace. It shone like a lighthouse in a storm, a beacon calling out to the father, letting him know, "Hey, I'm on your team." I saw his eyes fixed on it for a brief second, then I spoke again. "I…I wanted to apologize, Reverend Robert, for my behavior these past two weeks. It's just that I…I didn't want to. I'm sorry. Nevermind."

"Well, it's okay." He was looking at me, half expecting me to continue talking. That was when I tugged the fishing line a little more.

"It's just been so hard lately, and I…I…"

"Go on," he said. "Is there something wrong?"

"Well," I said while trying not to lay it on too thick, "it was foolish of me to not offer the money you asked for. It's…it's just that I have a problem." Father Bob gave me the same look he gave all his charity cases, that faint look of disappointment mixed with a little shame and disgust. "Father, I can't give you the money because I have a gambling problem."

The atmosphere in the room changed. It went from anger to remorse; the feeling of hatred now subsided into a calmer situation. Even if Father Bob was a greedy con artist, he was still a reverend first. This meant he had to make some sort of effort if I came crawling to him for an answer, and he also knew that if he could get me to stop gambling, he might have a chance at that money he wanted. He took the bait with a nibble.

"Oh boy," he said. Father Bob crossed his hands in front of himself while tilting his head to one side. "Are you betting heavy on the horses or the lottery, my son?"

"Well, it's more of an Atlantic City sort of deal. I play on Saturday nights at the blackjack tables in Harrah's."

"Oh Lord, my son, that's the worst kind! Those games are fixed, you know? You're betting against yourself and the Lord each time you do that!"

He was getting a little preachy, which was exactly what I wanted. I loosened him up a bit and reeled in some fishing line. "Yes, yes, I know," I said while staring at my shoes. I felt like a little kid who just got caught stealing from a 7-Eleven. "But I can't stop. It takes ahold of me. One minute I'm up, winning hundreds, and the next, I'm down a couple thousand dollars, Father."

Once I said "a couple thousand dollars," his ears perked up. I lost all guilt for what I was doing when I saw his eyes light up like a slot machine. A real man of God wouldn't have done that. No, if he was a person who really wanted to help the needy, he wouldn't have tipped his hand when I spoke about money.

"Well, my son, I know the temptation is hard, but you must follow God's will when it comes to life. I can offer you guidance if need be." Father Bob's game face was on. Five minutes ago, he didn't want shit to do with me, but dangle a packed money clip across his nose and an instant savior was born.

"I don't know, Father. It's hard to resist the urges. I mean, I want to stop gambling. It's just—maybe if I didn't have money to spend, I could avoid going to Atlantic City all the time."

"Well, I know of a way you can avoid the urges while helping out someone in need," he said. "If you choose to help my congregation with our repair bills, I can offer you counseling from the disease which afflicts your soul."

What a fucking louse. The dumb shit took the bait hook, line, and sinker. I set the hook. "I guess that's okay," I said. "If I don't have the money to spend, then I can't gamble, right?"

"Exactly!" said the father. He was like a greasy car salesman rushing to hand me a pen: "Here. Just sign on the dotted line!"

"I would be willing to help you right now before any of my parishioners came in. We have a few minutes before the first service if you want to donate to our cause."

I had his ass teetering on the ropes. I just needed Father Bob to spell it out so I could get it on the digital recorder. Carefully, like a vice cop working an undercover case, I had Father Bob say on record that he would take the money I was working for on Sundays to use at his church. Think about it. The church was paying a school for services and then taking that same money back to use in their remodeling expenses. I was no lawyer, but I believed Father Bob was breaking plenty of laws—and sinning, for that matter.

Our agreement was, Father Bob would counsel me in exchange for money. It was practically prostitution if you think about it. I had him saying things like, "Make sure you don't give me a check. Only cash works for our church," and, "When can I expect to see some money?" I played it off like I just got paid and the money was gone for now. That bought me two weeks until my next check, plenty of time to record him pushing up on me for money.

Several thoughts occurred to me during our conversation. First of all, how many other people had the preacher duped? I was sure this wasn't the only time the pastor tried to screw someone out of money. Not for nothing, but this had probably happened hundreds of times. Secondly and more importantly, how much trouble could I get into for recording this guy? Since I wasn't a police officer or an undercover reporter, this whole scenario would be classified as vigilante justice. That sort of thing worked for Spiderman, but not for a school janitor. If this whole thing went down the wrong way, not only could I be fired, but I might also be held accountable legally.

Maybe the first recording was enough. If I went to the school board now with only a few lines of vague conversation, it might backfire. I mean, you could tell it was him talking, asking for money. Was this enough to bring down a well-respected reverend with lots of friends in high places? Ultimately, I decided to try for more incriminating evidence. I needed a grenade launcher to dismantle this guy. Anything short of him taking the money out of my wallet by force wasn't enough.

For the next two Sundays, I got minutes of voice recordings on the guy. This crook was a true con artist. I had him on record saying how he took money from the church and how my overtime money would benefit him and his congregation. Father Fuckface never spoke to me after the parishioners came in. I guess he didn't want to be seen talking with a degenerate, gambling janitor in front of his groupies.

For two weeks, he pestered me about the money. He offered to go to the ATM with me to make a withdrawal. I strung him along just enough to get him to say, "Look, I'll need the money by next week, or else I can't guarantee the Lord can save you." The last time I saw him, he gave me a warning: "You better have that money next time I see you. I don't want you pissing it away down in AC!"

Had I really needed help with my addiction, Father Bob would have been the very last person I would turn to. I truly believed he would have bashed me over the head with a Bible or one of those golden scepters if I didn't hand him a packed envelope. I didn't know what to expect when I brought the evidence to the board of education. They reviewed it, looked at one another, and then said they would have to have a meeting and get back to me. In the end, it was me who got fucked.

No, I didn't get fired or even any disciplinary action. I did, however, lose all my overtime for the remainder of the church project.

You see, the board of education let Father Bob off the hook. They had a meeting with him and his lawyer and told him to find another place to conduct his business. There was no lengthy court case and no newspaper inquisition. Nothing. The board covered their ass while covering Father Bob's ass as well. Those scumbags swept it under the rug.

The superintendent told his pal to use the Hospitality House on Main Street instead of the school. This way, he could avoid paying the school and got free usage of the center. In the bylaws of the town charter, it stated, "Any religious organization can use the Hospitality House for free on their holy days." Sundays were offered to the church for as long as the renovations lasted.

The board also sent me a nice letter, letting me know of another bylaw. Unfortunately, I didn't have permission to record Father Bob without prior approval of the board of ed. I needed a permit to use a recording device in a public school. Have you ever heard of such nonsense? It was a warning, as they put it, a warning in more than one way. They pretty much told me they would sue me if I took the evidence to the papers. No permit meant I was the one breaking the law. It was just a friendly reminder of how they got all the angles worked out. It was amazing how quick lawyers found loopholes in any paperwork. I guess that was why the board of ed had the best money could buy.

So let's recap. Father Bob saved a boatload of money for not paying overtime on a Sunday. The board of ed saved their friend's ass while covering up their own shady business deals. I lost all that overtime because I tried to bring a real criminal to justice. Do you know what the moral of the story is? Because I sure as hell don't. I guess it was legal to extort someone because you wore a long white robe. Maybe the lesson here was, the board of education always won in the end. Maybe my sin of greed, for all that precious overtime, came around to punish me. I learned a very valuable lesson: Don't trust the church or the board of education. That's a life lesson you can't put a price tag on.

CHAPTER 11

Brian the Birder

Did you know that bird-watching—or birding, as some people call it—is the number one outdoor activity in America? I didn't. That's a nugget of knowledge anyone outside of the birding community probably doesn't know. It blows away other sports, like basketball, baseball, football, etc. By the way, birding is considered a sport in some social circles. None of this made any sense to me until I met Brian Lenker, aka Brian the Birder.

A couple of years ago, one of my coworkers quit because he couldn't take the job anymore. This guy had been inches away from a mental breakdown for quite some time. He walked out one day, but not before he balled up his work shirt and threw it in the night boss's face. I was glad he left before he snapped, because he had a lot of pent-up aggression. Those were the ones who strapped a bomb to their janitor cart and drove it into a crowd of people. You think I'm kidding. Some dumbass will do it one day. You watch.

In stepped Brian with his Roy Orbison glasses and big Cheshire Cat smile. He filled the vacant spot at my school. He was tall with a medium build. I would say he was in his mid- to late forties, and he kind of bopped when he walked. The night boss brought this guy over to my post one evening and introduced us. All I remember seeing was this guy's toothy grin from down the hall. That's the first thing I remember about Brian, how his teeth were so white and straight. Anyone familiar with the Jersey Shore has seen Tillie on the side of buildings in Asbury Park. Think Tillie when picturing Brian. This guy had a set of choppers on him!

"Hey there! I'm Brian. Nice to meet ya."

"Hi," I said. "Nice to meet you."

"I'm kind of new to the area," he said. "I'm originally from Iowa. You sure do have a lot of trees around here!"

"I guess we do," I said. I never thought of starting a conversation with that line before, but to each their own.

"I bet this area has an abundant white-breasted nuthatch population," said Brian. He pulled away from me for an instant to look out one of the windows, searching for something.

"Excuse me?" I said.

"You know, white-breasted nuthatches? They're prevalent in this area according to the Audubon field guide for the state. Those trees out there are excellent hiding spaces for all species of nuthatch."

In all my years of pushing a broom, I never thought I would have someone say to me that the area outside my job looked like prime nuthatch habitat. Brian Lenker from Des Moines, Iowa, loved nature, particularly birds. From his hiking boots to his forest-green Subaru, Brian was the stereotypical environmental cornball. I would come to find out that a nuthatch was a species of bird known for its long beak, which it used to eat seeds, insects, and of course, nuts, hence the name. I could have gone my entire life without knowing that tidbit. The fact that I did not know what a nuthatch was seemed appalling to Brian.

"You're telling me you've never heard of a white-breasted nuthatch?" Brian asked.

"Nope," I said, "not until today."

"Oh man! Back home in Iowa, I've spotted numerous red-breasted nuthatches but never a white-breasted one. My field guide says they're migrating into this part of the state soon, so I'll be looking for them."

"All righty," I said. My enthusiasm was no match for Brian's. "I hope you get that white-breaster soon."

"Thanks! I'm counting on it!"

Brian's interest in birds was not the worst way to meet a new coworker. Maybe it was a little quirky, but it was certainly not the craziest first impression by far. One lady sneezed dead in my face while saying hello, right in my fucking face. As soon as I said hello, she sprayed me as if she was allergic to the word. I got the flu and was out a week thanks to Typhoid Mary. She never said sorry either. She just released a cloud of snot in my face and kept on trucking. Then one dude barked after saying hi. This guy straight up barked like a beagle after saying, "Hello there." I was familiar with Tourette's or talking to oneself, but not so much with animal sounds coming from people. That was a new one for me.

The man known as Brian the Birder gave me daily lessons on ornithology, the scientific study of birds. Not that I solicited any info. He gave it freely, because I guess that was what he liked to do. On his third day, Brian came to work covered in what appeared to be bird shit. He was wearing a camouflaged jumpsuit with a matching camo neck cover. "Hey there! You'll have to give me a few minutes. I'll just change out of my field gear and be ready to work in a jiff," he said.

Minutes later, Brian had his work shirt on, although he still smelled like citronella and deet. "Sorry about that," he said. "I was out in the woods, looking for those nuthatches. Turns out, I was right! I came across an entire colony of them nesting in the elms about three miles from here."

Brian informed me that the birds in question had made quite a home for themselves close to where we were standing. "Boy, I've never seen such tightly knit flying patterns on these nuthatches," he said. "I thought Iowa had dense woodland features. I sure am glad I left Des Moines. I haven't been this eager to go birding since I found a Bullock's oriole back in 2002!"

Some people got excited over winning fifty bucks on a scratch-off ticket. Brian got excited over spotting brightly colored birds in wooded areas. Personally, I would have taken the money over some bird any day, but Brian was different. He loved him some feathered friends. He felt the need to illuminate me on the flying patterns of several bird species that evening.

"I've seen a lot of birds turning in tight areas before," said Brian. "But these nuthatches have excellent flying maneuverability."

"You don't say," I said.

"Without a doubt!" said Brian. "I bet these nuthatches can give a golden-crowned sparrow a run for its money when it comes to tight-space flying."

"Oh, wow," I said. "Aren't all birds really good at flying? Isn't that their claim to fame?" When I got bored with someone, I tended to get sarcastic. It was what I did. Brian didn't pick up on my sarcasm, though. Instead of walking away, he dove into the conversation with excitement.

"Are you kidding? Some bird species are excellent fliers while others are better at coasting. Pelicans, for example, are highly skilled at long-distance coasting while smaller bird species, such as the barn swallow, are built for tight-turning radiuses."

"No shit," I said.

"Most definitely! You see, the shape of the bird's wing can dictate…"

I damn near fell asleep listening to the difference between soaring bird wings and fast takeoff wings. Twenty minutes this bro stood there explaining how the shape of a bird's wing ultimately dictated what kind of flying they excelled at. I had to stop him from talking because I had three sets of bathrooms to clean. Who got time to listen to some guy chat about birds all night?

"I'm sorry, Brian, but I've got bathrooms to scrub," I said. "I gotta go."

"Oh, sure thing!" he said. "Hey, maybe later, I'll tell you the major difference between tail feathers and wing feathers."

"Can't wait!" I said.

A lecture on birds joined a long list of topics explained to me against my will. Several occasions come to mind. One guy used to discuss his obsession with horror flicks. He would talk in bloody depth about his love of gory killer films. Then he would watch them on lunch break on his portable DVD player. He used to play the most terrifying movies while eating spaghetti. All this guy did was watch horror movies and eat pasta every single night on break. Experts say a criminal uses food and other items to get into character. Did he think the red sauce was blood or something? Maybe spaghetti was the closest thing to intestines he could think of.

It didn't bother me the first month, but hearing some poor victim screaming unmercifully got old quick. I complained to the night boss about this guy's slasher movie obsession. "I don't care what he watches, but enough with the sounds," I told the boss. "I'm starting to get nightmares over this shit." The boss finally told him to put on headphones so the rest of us could choke down our meals in peace.

I can't put a number on the times I've had uncomfortable conversations with coworkers. Some dummy used to complain about his hemorrhoids nonstop. He went on and on about his problem, which, in turn, became my problem, because I had to listen to him. Don't tell me your alignments in excruciating details. That's fucking rude! I get it. You can't sit down for too long. Your butthole bleeds on an hourly basis. Get a tube of Preparation H, for Christ's sake!

If pressed to choose between anal leakage, horror films, or bird-watching, I guess I would have to choose bird-watching. It's a tough call, I know. Besides, bird talk is far less horrific than listening to bones being sawed in half. Hearing Brian ramble on about his avian pals wasn't so much torture as it was annoying. If I don't know what you're talking about, how can I add to the conversation, especially if it's on a topic so mundane, like bird-watching?

After a few weeks, I got to realize that Brian wasn't so bad after all. He was very eccentric and smart as a whip too when it came to birds. Harmless was what I thought of Brian after we got to know each other during the first year. Brian and I talked often while working together. I wasn't completely sure what language he was speaking during our first months. He used words like *pelagic* and *endemic* when referring to bird migration, which coincidentally was happening at the same time he started working. He gave me one of the most compelling lessons I had ever had on the parts of a bird, and I spent years in college listening to professors squawk about a wide variety of topics.

"Hey, do you know all the parts of a bird?" asked Brian.

"Well, I know they have wings," I said.

"Of course, silly!" said Brian. "But do you know the proper names of all sections of a bird?"

"Not off the top of my head."

"Oh my!" said Brian. "I'll tell you what, I'll bring in one of my study guides tomorrow and go over the sections for you so you can identify them in the future."

"Um," I said, "I guess so. Sure. Why not?"

"Great! Make sure to bring a notepad and pen to take good notes. There may be a quiz at the end! Ha!"

The next day, I was expecting a small book on birds, which might have or might not have been covered in bird shit. What I got was a full biology lesson complete with a flip chart easel and expandable metal pointer. I kid you not. I can't make this shit up even if I tried. He brought in a massive diagram of a bird and began, in painstaking detail, to teach me bird anatomy.

"Here you'll find the crest of the bird, right above the crown," said Brian. He was using his extendable pointer as if he had taught this lesson a thousand times. "It's located on top of the bird's head, above the lore and the upper mandible."

"The what?" I asked.

"The crest," Brian said. "Think of it like a mohawk hairdo."

"Oh."

"The crest is normally prevalent in cardinal species but can be found in other species, such as the blue jay and the cockatoo."

"I see."

"Further down the body, you'll find the bill, which I believe to be the most important part of a bird—after the wings, of course." He let out a chuckle, thinking his little joke was a real hoot. Brian was extremely animated when he spoke. Think Bill Nye the Science Guy after a few hits of meth, but in a good way.

If any of you have read the first book, you know I spent a long time in college, taking way too many classes. Most science courses were boring to me. None of the science professors made their classes interesting at all. You would want to take a nap halfway through dissecting a frog. But I must say that I was very impressed with Brian's impromptu birding seminar. He had a knack for teaching. It showed when he spoke about birds.

He taught like most teachers should have taught, adding in real-world observations to keep the class from losing interest. Brian would use helpful analogies to help in remembering the topic. You can tell if a teacher is passionate by the way they instruct. Most teachers I've had simply phoned it in with the exception of a few. (You know who you are!) The way Brian taught made me want to learn even though my college days were far behind me.

After he finished discussing the rump and, ultimately, tail feathers, I thanked him for his class. "I have to hand it to you, Brian. I'm thoroughly impressed. You really know your stuff, man."

"Well, thank you!" said Brian. He was folding up the easel when his giant smile came out. "I hope you enjoyed the talk."

"You know what, I did. I didn't expect to have this good of a lesson. I've had plenty of college classes where the teacher didn't seem to care about the topic."

"I believe you have to love something wholeheartedly in order to instill the same love in someone else," said Brian. "That's what I really want to do in life. I want to show the world how much fun birding can be. We all have things we love and care deeply about, you know? Birding is my way of dealing with the stress of daily life while learning something interesting and important at the same time."

From that moment on, I dropped my sarcastic comments whenever Brian spoke about birds. Over the next year, Brian talked about his life in the Midwest and how he had wanted to move to the East Coast. Both his parents had passed away two years before, one right after the other. After living in Iowa for most of his life, Brian wanted a change of scenery. Or more importantly, he wanted to change his list of bird sightings to include more seabirds.

"Iowa has plenty of prairie species and some wetland bird species," Brian said to me one day. "I've got a lot of good birding memories from home. A person doesn't get to be president of the Quad Cities Birding Club without knowing a warbler from a woodpecker, you know?" I didn't have it in my heart to tell him I couldn't distinguish the difference between the two if my life depended on it. "I'm at the point in my life where I need to expand my birding horizons. A man cannot live a fruitful birding life unless he's observed a decent amount of shorebirds, and this state's got a slew of them! Am I right?"

"Go for it," I said. "If it's what you love, then you should do it."

"Exactly!" said Brian. "I'm trying to get all my ducks in a row so I can start taking people on birding tours. I think I can pull it off if I get enough experience in the field."

Over the next couple of months, I would get daily updates on what species of birds were migrating into the area. I would come to hear about how piping plovers migrated from the South in the spring to nest along the beach. Growing up along the Jersey Shore, I had always seen the roped-off areas on the beach each spring. I now knew what that was all about. Brian spoke often about the different types of jaybirds, like the Yucatan jay and the green jay in addition to the gray jay and pinyon jay back in Iowa.

"I've only heard of the blue jay," I said to Brian as we moved a load of heavy boxes to storage.

"Not many people know about the eighteen other species of jays in the world," he said. "You should see the Steller's jay. Talk about a truly striking bird!" I googled it later in the day. Brian wasn't lying.

When the topic of bird courtship came up, Brian was on point—a Stradivarius of the sparrow and a maestro of the marsh wren. He acted out these elaborate bird dances in the hallway, gyrating his neck and arms, imitating the bird as best he could. You have to imagine a guy with a mouthful of teeth prancing back and forth, trying to fluff out his make-believe feathers. It was a sight he replicated weekly depending on the bird in question. One night, the boss came by, responding to a call from a concerned teacher. She reported seeing some guy in the gym who might have been suffering from a seizure. Brian did his pantomime bird act in the seclusion of the break room from then on.

After months of repeatedly asking me to join him on a birding trip, I gave in. He planned an overnight trip to some forest in northern New Jersey to spot hawks on a mountaintop. He insisted on an overnight trip, saying the view would be worth the hike in the morning. I was intrigued by all his talk of being at one with yourself when you were in nature, peeking at birds through a set of binoculars. Reducing stress was something my doctor told me was imperative to my health, so I figured, against better judgment, why not? I agreed to spend a night in the woods with a man who valued birds over anything else in this world.

"Great!" said Brian. "Do you have your own tent, or do you need me to bring my big tent for us to share?"

"I got nothing in the way of camping gear," I said. "How about you bring the tent and I'll bring the snacks?"

"Sounds good! I'll pick you up on Saturday at 4:00 a.m. This is going to be an adventure for both of us. I can't wait to show you how to spot hawks at 1,500 feet!"

"4:00 a.m.?" I said. "Are you joking?"

"It's a three-hour drive up north," said Brian. "I'll drive. Don't worry about it. We'll be there at first light to greet the dawn!"

Let me explain something to you. I love to sleep in, so 4:00 a.m. on a weekend is about when I go to bed. I also hate bugs in general. I hate all bug species and subspecies. The few times I did go hiking, it didn't end so well. I fell into a wasp's nest more times than I would like to admit, and the goddamn mosquitos were savage. I must be made of the most delectable blood on the planet. It's for these reasons that I choose to stay indoors when the rest of the world is out enjoying nature.

As Brian's beat-up Subaru pulled into my driveway, I almost told him to go on without me. You could tell by the look on his face that he knew I was second-guessing the whole thing. "Don't worry," said Brian. "We'll be fine. I've been camping out in the wilderness for years. I've got some homemade bug spray that's guaranteed to keep them away. You'll be fine!" I figured, why not take a leap of faith? He was already in my driveway with his olive drab knee-high socks and a bucket hat most Army Rangers would have called sweet.

Brian persuaded me to come along for a quick hike, as he called it. A five-hour hike uphill most of the way was not what I would have called quick. Once we started hiking, I used some of his bootleg bug spray. I immediately broke out in hives.

"I've never seen anyone break out using hypoallergenic bug spray before!" said Brian as he reached for a small first aid kit.

"I told you I wasn't good at this outdoors thing," I said. My lips were starting to swell like one of the Kardashians's. I was scratching myself raw until Brian handed me two Benadryl pills.

"Here. Take these with plenty of water. We've got a few miles to go before we get past the really buggy areas."

By the time we had our first hiking break, I was out of Kind bars and iced tea. I pissed every twenty minutes like I was a pregnant woman. Thankfully, Brian brought extra everything. Out of his rucksack / mobile camper, he pulled Pop-Tarts and water. "You'd think Kind bars are the best for this, but you'd be wrong. Pop-Tarts are the best high-energy snack for the trail." He didn't say it in a pompous tone. He said it in more of a teaching manner, like he was shooting an infomercial for L.L.Bean.

I had never seen such an elaborate backpack before. He had pans, tent apparatuses, and refillable water bottles sticking out of every crevice. He looked like he was carrying everything he owned on his back. I, in contrast, had an old Jansport backpack that contained a pair of cracked binoculars, a bottle of Laird's Applejack, five cigars, and a half-frozen TombStone pizza. I had a whole box of Kind bars but had eaten them in the first hour. I didn't know what I had planned on doing with the frozen pizza. I didn't think that one out completely. I had plans for the booze and cigars, though. If I were to be stuck in the middle of nowhere, being eaten alive by mosquitos, I was going to dull my senses somehow.

Two hours into our journey, I started to panic. Since the homebrew bug juice didn't work, I tried a different spray. The Off! bug spray Brian gave me as a backup melted off as soon as it was applied. It must have been ninety degrees at the beginning of October. I was yearning for air-conditioning and a comfy recliner. Brian, constantly turning around to check on me, was fully aware of my inexperience. We made frequent stops to apply more bug spray while answering the call of nature on multiple occasions. I didn't know what it was about the woods, but I had to piss and shit no less than ten times that morning. It must have been all that fresh air or the ten thousand calories worth of Kind bars slowly working their way through my lower intestines.

Each stop was another chance for Brian to display his bird knowledge. "Look over there!" he said. "You see that pine grosbeak, the red-and-gray bird by the ponderosa pine tree?"

"I guess," I said.

"That's a male. The female has a mostly gray body while the male is red to get the attention of the female during the breeding season." Brian proceeded to make short chirping sounds, which the bird imitated. Good thing Brian was fluent in bird languages. At least if we got lost, he could tell his bird friends to go find help, just like Lassie.

Each time another bird came into view, Brian would point it out with enthusiastic vigor. "Wow, what a great dark-eyed junco! Look how it blends into its environment!" It took me a good five minutes to spot the bird, which looked like a speck in the tree. Brian was extremely jazzed about each new sighting. I, on the other hand, just wanted to crawl into a hole and avoid all nine hundred bugs buzzing around my head. I must have sounded like a little kid asking the forlorn question, "Are we there yet?" Checking his handheld GPS and the sun's placement in the sky, Brian would give me real-time distances without seeming pestered. "Just another hour until we reach the camping spot. It's a great location. You're not going to believe the view!"

Close to the end of our hike, I came to the realization that I was going to die in the forest, surrounded by birds I had never heard of. Cedar waxwings, northern flickers, and common yellowthroats—all their names would appear on my makeshift headstone, buried deep in the middle of fucking nowhere. Never in my life had I thought trekking would be how I would die. I pictured myself stroking out in an all-you-can-eat buffet or dropping dead in a dimly lit bar with an empty highball glass in front of me. Some mountaintop searching for hawks and covered in skeeters? Not a chance in hell. Brian reassured me we would make it out alive, seeing how he had done this type of trip many times before.

"Don't worry about it, buddy. I've got all the tools we need to survive in my day pack."

"You got a portable air-conditioning unit in your pack?" I asked in a whining tone. "If I sweat any more, my ass will start to float."

"I'll do you one better. How about a nice drink of filtered river water once we set up the tent? We're all out of the bottled water I brought. I'll use my filtering bottle to scoop up some river water. It's cold and refreshing, I promise!"

"Yeah, sure. That works," I said.

Apparently, the river water filtration system Brian used did not filter enough for my body. I got the Hershey Squirts immediately. They stayed with me until I vacated my colon of everything I had eaten since birth. I thought back to that time I had frozen margaritas in Cancun during spring break. I had never felt this kind of pain before. It was as if someone took a pool cue and tried to skewer all my organs for a barbecue. This was the end for me. I could see the light in the tunnel approaching at a rapid pace. Any minute now, I would poop out my liver, begging for Brian to cave my head in with his Fiat-sized backpack.

We reached the campsite minutes after sundown. A normal five-hour hike turned into an all-day affair on the account of my hives, explosive diarrhea, and swelled skin. My tour guide was very accommodating to my disposition, reassuring me the morning view would be well worth my struggle. We built a fire to roast the wild TombStone pizza I had hunted down from the grocery store. The thought of eating anything made me cringe.

"You have to eat, buddy," said Brian. "If you don't, you'll start cramping up, and it will hurt even more." He pulled two big Gatorade bottles from his pack, convincing me to drink them slowly. They were for emergencies, as he put it. I could not think of any more of an emergency than spending the night with the same bug-bourne virus that probably wiped out the dinosaurs.

Brian had a pan big enough for the pizza in his humongous rucksack. Who would bring that on a hike? A better question would be, who in their right mind brought a frozen pizza on a camping trip? I struggled to eat, which was something I never had trouble doing in the past. As the dark became darker, we ate our supreme pizza, along with some real camp food Brian brought. All we needed was to heat up some water and cook the food in its own packet. They were like the MREs the military used. It was a marvelous invention. I started to feel better within two hours, wondering how I was able to keep the food in without shitting it out.

As we digested, I busted out the cigars and liquor. If this was going to be my last meal, I wanted to go with a smile on my face. Brian didn't smoke or drink, but I insisted that if I was trying camping, he was to try something new as well. We talked by the fire after a few nips from the bottle. We both opened up, which normally happened when people shared a drink and a stogie near an open flame.

"So, Brian," I said, "what is it about birds that gets you so into them?"

"You know, I can't explain it. I've always had an interest since my dad took me out birding when I was seven years old. When I was really young, my dad took the whole family to the Iowa State Fair. It's what you do during the summer in Iowa. There, I saw a bird show with raptors—you know, hawks, eagles, etc. I'd never seen an eagle up close before. I was hooked right then and there." We passed the bottle back and forth as we talked.

"Wow, that's a young age to go out looking for birds, right?"

"Not necessarily. My grandfather took my dad out when he was young too," he said. "I guess we both took to it early on."

"I know what you mean," I said, but I really didn't. I thought back to my childhood without a dad, missing out on the chance to go to a state fair to see such a show. It was just me and my mother for a long part of my childhood. I remembered something we did together, much like Brian's family. "My mother took me to the library a lot," I said. "We didn't have a lot of money back then, so we went to the library because it was free. I read book after book, reading anything I could get my hands on."

Brian took another swig from the bottle, cringing after the sip. "You do read a lot at work. I always see you with a book in your hands. I guess you learned it from a young age, just like I did—you with reading and me with birds," he said. "My dad always showed me different birds when we went hiking. It's something I'll never forget."

"Yeah, me...me neither," I said.

As we took long drags from the cigars, Brian stared out into the darkness near our campsite. A high-pitched squeal came from the black. Slightly buzzed, I looked at Brian for his expertise. "Eastern screech owl!" he said.

"That's exactly what I was going to say," I said in my sarcastic, slightly buzzed tone. We shared a quick laugh while listening to the night coming alive with owl sounds. Brian seemed entranced by his surroundings; he closed his eyes, taking in the sounds blissfully. He looked at peace with himself and all that was around him. Leaning back in his fold-up chair, Brian was gleeful.

"I hope I can do this for the rest of my life one day," Brian said.

"What do you mean?"

"This," he said, "birding. I'm going for a grant to study birds in the wild down in Costa Rica. I applied for it through the Audubon Society last week."

"Really? A grant?" I asked, kind of dumbfounded. "You didn't go to college for it, did you? Will they give you money if you're not in college or have a degree?"

"I didn't go to college at all," he said. "My family couldn't afford it, so I went to work on farms near my house after high school. Plenty of farming work in Iowa for a young man trying to make some money."

"Wow. Hey, you gotta do what you gotta do," I said.

"This project is my chance to do something I've always wanted to do. The osprey project is a grant paid for by the state. I'd be working to band ospreys in Central America with a college. Once the ospreys migrate north for the spring, they come back to our area, so I'd like to see how long it takes for them to get here." Brian's face told me all I needed to know about how much he wanted this grant. "It's a nice, educational program," he said. "They'd pay all my expenses—lodging, flights, meals. If I get it, I'd even get new birding gear too!"

"Wow," I said. "I didn't know you were into something like that. Getting a new career, I mean."

"I've wanted to do it for a long time now. Birding has always been the one thing I've always come back to. I've tried other jobs here and there, but birding doesn't pay unless you have some academic backing. I wrote a short proposal to the board at the college. If I get the full grant, I'll be leaving in a few weeks."

"That's awesome. I hope you get it. I really do. I hope you get it," I said.

"Thank you," said Brian. "Can you do me a favor, please? Don't tell anyone at work yet. I don't want to put my two weeks in until I know I've got it. I'm kinda nervous. I've never taken a chance like this. If I don't get the grant, I'd be really bummed out. I've never wanted anything so much before."

"I'm sure you'll get it, Brian. You're a good guy. I mean that," I said. "You're practically a shoo-in with all your bird smarts. I'm sure you'll get it."

"Thanks, buddy. I hope I get it too."

We relaxed by the fire, contemplating the day's events. Most of my day was spent warding off bugs and hoping I didn't catch poison ivy while pissing. I hated being in the woods for the most part, but Brian was in his glory, surrounded by birds and nature. He was riding a wave so high I couldn't see him up there. Administering first aid to a tenderfoot like me didn't ruin his trip, because he loved every second of being outside with birds. He was happy, truly happy. It was a feeling I couldn't say I had had in a very long time, certainly not while working as a janitor.

We turned in for the night after the last ash fell off our cigars. I had a decent night's sleep regardless of the many, many bug bites all over my body. Three-quarters of a bottle of Applejack made any number of bug bites stop itching. When I awoke in the morning, Brian was already standing outside the tent, calling for me to come out and take a look. There, a few hundred feet from the tent, was a wide-open mountain view. The sun was casting light on hundreds of large birds flying in front of us, all coasting in the breeze.

"This was what I wanted you to see!" said Brian. He had his binoculars in his left hand, motioning for me to come closer with his right.

As I walked closer, I noticed that the wind was stronger at this elevation. It was a little too strong for me to be standing so close to the edge. I backed up a few steps. "That's all right," I said, gripping the blanket I had draped around me. "I'll...I'll stay here. I can see from here." Brian realized I wasn't too keen on coming any farther.

"It's so marvelous, isn't it?" said Brian. He was so happy to be standing there at that exact moment, watching birds fly. "This is where the migrating hawks come to catch the thermal winds from the valley below. They ride the wind upward, kind of like hang gliding. I found out about this place last year from one of the guidebooks. Take a look at how they seem to rise up without any effort."

I didn't know one bird from another, but it didn't matter in the least. Brian called them out as they came into view. For an hour, we stood there bird-watching, not thinking about anything else but birds. It was a tremendous view. The different shades of greens and yellows and browns of the fall change were very picturesque. Dragging my ass out into the unknown was worth it even if in my mind, I almost died of malaria and severe dehydration.

The hike back didn't seem so daunting as it was on the way up. I still got eaten up by no less than twenty thousand bugs, but the trail back was mainly downhill. We talked a little more on the way home, and by that evening, I was in my own bed, praying I would never see another mosquito in my life. I was covered head to toe in calamine lotion, and I was stuck to the bedsheets like a fly on flypaper.

A few weeks later, Brian put in his two-week notice. He got the grant due to his overwhelming knowledge of birds, of course. I was sure he knew a hell of a lot more than the professors he would be working under. Weeks passed into months before I heard from Brian again. He sent me a postcard from Costa Rica with a brightly colored bird on the front. He wrote about the bird in detail on most of the card space. He was doing great according to him. The birding was phenomenal with exotic species all within hiking distance from his village, which I was sure made him an even happier man.

The next time I heard from him, he was stateside, calling me to let me know he was home but only for a short time. The grant paid Brian all the way through spring, when he was able to monitor the return of the ospreys. Of the hundred or so birds he tagged down in Costa Rica, Brian said he saw seven birds return to the shore area. "I can't believe it!" he said. "To see the same bird I tagged thousands of miles away coming back to this area is crazy. Here they are. I've got their tag numbers in my notepad. This is amazing!"

I was guessing the level of excitement Brian had was equal to someone hitting the lottery. In a way, he did. Many colleges didn't give out grant money to people without advanced college degrees. Brian showed them he wanted it more than the other applicants, and he was ready to prove it. After the spring, he was offered a full-time position with a bird association out of state. He gladly took it, probably with the same eagerness as a football player getting drafted in the NFL. Mind you, he was pushing fifty when he got drafted. I guess your age doesn't matter in the world of birding.

Brian was able to quit his job to start working at one he loved. If that isn't the definition of hitting the lottery, I don't know what is. I miss Brian sometimes. I didn't like him when I first met him because he annoyed me. Did I give two shits about the migrating patterns of an osprey? Who gives a crap if they fly down to Costa Rica for the winter, then return in April? I would love to migrate from this shithole for the winter, but I can't. The more I thought about Brian living his dream, the more I started thinking. He made me want to pursue something I cared deeply about. I have a pretty good idea of where to start looking. There are a lot of books I haven't read yet in that library.

CHAPTER 12

An Evening with the Janitors

A camera pans in from the left to a wide-open area with seated audience clapping voraciously. It's a black-tie-clad audience, a very formal setting. The camera flies in above the crowd, moving toward the front of the stage. It stops briefly over the twenty-one-piece orchestra playing an upbeat song. The camera focuses on three empty seats with a glorious stage. It's like something you would see at the Oscars. A small table is set off to the side with engraved trophies. The awards are large; the cheap fiberboard table appears to be buckling under their weight.

The audience's applause grows as a man with a very bad toupee enters, waving to the crowd. He's wearing a tux from a few decades ago, which may or may not be a rental. His face is darkly tanned with way too much stage makeup. He looks like a circus clown with orange face paint smeared over his surgically enhanced face. Entering to his right is a blond bombshell with a fur coat—not faux fur but real fur. It's probably mink or arctic fox or some other endangered species. She, too, is waving. Her makeup is perfect, except for a small smudge of orange-colored makeup on her neck. The lanky man picks up a microphone and addresses the audience.

"Welcome, welcome, one and all, to the thirty-eighth annual An Evening with the Janitors! I'm your host, B. L. Tillingsworth, the four-time Emmy-nominated host and emcee extraordinaire. You may recognize me from my work on several high-profile events these past thirty years. Does fill-in host of the 1992 Democratic National Convention ring a bell? Ha! Perhaps you've seen me in my numerous television miniseries background roles on such channels as Hallmark and MeTV. Well, I'm here in the flesh, folks, along with my cohost, the lovely Kelli-Joe Rogers. Take a gander at the stupendous outfit she has on. Isn't it superb? Take a twirl, Kelli-Joe. Let the audience see that lovely outfit!"

Hostess twirls on cue, smiling and waving her perfectly manicured nails at camera in a coy manner.

"All righty, folks. Here we are, another year and another awards show. I don't think we can top the excitement from last season's event, but I'm sure we'll try our darndest! It doesn't feel like a year, though, does it? It feels like we were just here, on this very stage, giving out awards to well-deserving pillars of our community. Just the other day, I was talking to my publicist, saying how much I wanted to be back on this stage, in front of all you lovely people, to bestow these amazing awards."

The audience claps their approval at the nice comment the emcee has given them. Camera pans to a plump woman in the front row who's holding her hands to her open-chest dress.

"Speaking of awards, aren't these awards just grand? Catch a glimpse of them. They weigh close to five pounds each. These aren't your ordinary paperweights! These crystal-like trophies are made from the finest synthetic plastic material on the market. Each piece is handcrafted by a machine to resemble the natural rock formations you'd find hanging in a dark cave deep underground. What do you call them, stalactites or stalagmites, huh, Kelli-Joe?"

The hostess stands there with her hands on her hourglass hips, smiling without saying a word. She looks like a deer caught in the headlights on the interstate.

"That's okay, folks. She doesn't know. I don't know either, so I'll just call them marvelous! Aren't they marvelous?"

The audience whistles and claps.

"They are simply astonishing. Wow! I need a pair of sunglasses just to look at them!"

The emcee takes a pair of Dollar Store sunglasses from his chest pocket, puts them on, and basks in the glow from the awards. He revels for a few seconds, then puts the sunglasses back in his pocket. His fake spray tan face paint is smeared slightly around his eyes and ears. After a short applause, the demeanor in the room changes. It is now a serious moment. The emcee looks directly into the camera and goes into a speech.

"Tonight, we are here to honor and commemorate these fine individuals who've spent a lifetime working tirelessly for the public. It is because of their countless hours of service that we are gathered here this evening. Had it not been for the efforts of these three very special people, the world would be a less clean place. These three honorees embody the spirit of the hard work ethic. Just for the record, they've worked valiantly at their respected posts for well over one hundred years combined."

A hush comes over the audience. They are mystified by the mention of one hundred years.

"One hundred years plus of service, folks. That is a century of cleaning up after people. Can you imagine that? One hundred years! Let's give them a huge hand!"

The audience claps with vigor. A few "Bravos" echo throughout the amphitheater. It is an extended applause, well over ten seconds. Camera pans to a man toward the center of the audience who is clapping loudly and out of rhythm. He is trying to stand out by clapping his hands in an exaggerated gesture while mouthing the word wow. *Camera swings back to emcee, who is bowing his head to the audience like a Japanese businessman during a meeting.*

"It is, therefore, decreed that on this evening, we celebrate the careers of three remarkable janitors throughout our nation. They were selected out of hundreds of entries and reviewed by our dedicated field service representatives, whose job it was to narrow the selection to a trio of heroes. Let me remind you how hard these individuals worked to make this evening possible. I'm not talking about the honorees. I'm talking about the selection committee, who busted their humps to choose three very special janitors.

"The panel, consisting of several highly educated, multiversatile professionals, spent several minutes reviewing the submissions for this year's event. Despite heavy budget constraints, the panel was able to secure the necessary money to book this lavish concert hall and still have enough money to throw themselves a congratulatory after-party when this whole shindig wraps up. Don't worry, the shellfish towers are still on the menu!"

Hold for raucous applause from audience. Still holding.

"I'd also like to thank our sponsors, who made this night extra special. Had it not been for those amazing complimentary gift packages—or swag bags, as we call them in the business—the panel might have felt slighted for their efforts. I mean, it's already hard work to choose three random people, let alone do it without a gift bag to take home. I'm sure those spa certificates will help comfort the panel for undertaking such an arduous task.

"Also, before we begin our ceremony, the panel would like me to mention that if anyone in the audience or at home would like to donate to the Save the Panel Relief Fund, you can do so by texting #$$$$ to 61875. The panel had to endure hardships like sitting in leather office chairs for an undisclosed amount of time. Those poor souls suffered a great deal, and it's time we reward them. Every dollar donated will help go to comforting the panel in their time of need. Please find it in your heart to give them money to make them feel better."

There is a brief pause for a slow-motion montage of panel members sitting in captain's chairs. Camera filter switches to black-and-white. The orchestra plays "In the Arms of an Angel" by Sarah McLachlan. Camera pans to audience members crying, wiping tears from eyes. Short applause when montage ends.

"Now onto the show! Through the National Janitors of America, teamed with the Association for a Better Cleaner School Foundation and regional cable channel 88, we are proud to present this year's lucky winners!"

The orchestra plays a congratulatory song while camera pans to the big screen behind the stage. Three pictures are displayed on the screen: two men and one woman. The photos are blurry and appear to be taken with a broken cell phone. The audience stands for one of many ovations, clapping and cheering as photos are displayed. The emcee puts his hands up to quell the audience. His hands are motioning in a "Shut the hell up" gesture.

"All right now. Let's bring out our first honoree, shall we? His name is Luis Reyes, and he comes to us all the way from El Salvador. Mr. Reyes has worked for the city of West Palm Beach, Florida, for the past twenty-seven years as a public works janitor. Every day, Mr. Reyes empties garbage cans while scrubbing graffiti off the side of buildings. Talk about a dirty job!"

Audience laughs, as does emcee.

"Mr. Reyes came to this country in 1985, during the height of the Salvadoran Civil War. He was only a child when he landed on the shores of America, all of eleven years old. It's a good thing his family made it out when they did. The bloody civil war claimed the lives of approximately 75,000 people, many of whom were poor farmers in the countryside trying to stay neutral. Luis and his family were not members of the Salvadorian government, allegedly trained by the United States military, nor were they sympathizers with the FMLN, the so-called terrorist uprising of the common people.

Luis and his family were poor farmers caught in a tyrannical war. They chose to stay neutral, which almost cost them their lives. Luis lost several members of his immediate family, including an uncle who was captured by the military, tortured for three days straight, then disappeared like thousands of other Salvadorian citizens. Had his family stayed in El Salvador, Mr. Reyes would've surely been recruited into the military and been forced to kill prisoners of war. By escaping a resistance coup and surviving what can be referred to as a nasty conflict, Mr. Reyes showed courage in the face of danger. It's a quality he still carries with him today when going to work.

"A typical day for Mr. Reyes starts at 9:00 p.m. He works twelve hours a night, cleaning large metal garbage cans that line the sidewalks of Downtown West Palm Beach. With a view of high-rise buildings, designer boutique shopping, upscale restaurants, and palm tree-studded beaches, Mr. Reyes gets to work in paradise every night, although he wouldn't call it paradise."

There is a pause for dramatic appeal. A small hush comes over the audience.

"He works alone and has for almost twenty-five years. When he first started his career, Mr. Reyes had a partner to help share the workload. Unfortunately, his partner had to retire early due to a physical altercation. West Palm Beach looks glorious, but once you leave the downtown area, you risk confronting one of its many transient residents. Mr. Reyes's partner was assaulted one night near the train station by a gang of roving bums. This altercation left him badly injured, to the point of a near coma state."

Gasps arise from the audience.

"Without a partner to back him up, Mr. Reyes himself has been hospitalized on several occasions. I bet those hospital bills can add up quickly without proper medical coverage, which, I'm told, Mr. Reyes does not have. Self-defense is something Mr. Reyes practices every time he goes to work. He carries a sawed-off wooden baton when he works, which, he says, does the trick sometimes."

There is a pause for dramatic reaction. "Ohs" from audience. Pan camera to emcee and dumb blond hostess.

"Mr. Reyes says the hardest part of his job is working near the train station in the late evening / early morning hours. Although he has a walkie-talkie and a stubby club, it's no match against drunk vagrants who attack without remorse. If that isn't bad enough, Mr. Reyes also deals with a completely different set of danger: human trafficking. Yes, it appears the Brightline train system, which has a station in West Palm Beach, deals with a lot of unscrupulous characters who drag petrified people across state lines. It's modern-day slavery, which is very profitable for its purveyors, but not so much for the victims. Mr. Reyes has been confronted a few times in the past year alone with one set of traffickers lunging at him!"

Pause again for emphasis. Roll on dramatic music from orchestra.

"Don't worry, folks. He's okay! Remember that club? It saved his life!"

Audience has a big round of applause with many members standing in appreciation.

"Mr. Reyes is doing fine now, although he is a little beat up for this evening's interview. We promised to buy him a neck brace and provide a set of rental crutches so he can walk out here onstage tonight. So without further ado, let's bring him out! Welcome to the stage the first Janitor of the Year award recipient, Luis Reyes!"

There is a huge applause, and festive, upbeat music score is performed by orchestra. Mr. Reyes stumbles onto stage. He is sporting crutches, a neck brace, and several bandages near his eyes. He looks like hammered dog shit. Slowly, he walks out to greet the emcee and the ditzy hostess. The emcee offers a seat to Mr. Reyes, who gingerly takes it. He appears to be in excruciating pain. Dialogue starts onstage. Hostess says nothing; she's there as eye candy.

"All righty! Well, Mr. Reyes, I welcome you to this joyous event. How are you doing this evening?"

"Well, not too good," said Luis.

"Oh, I'm sorry to hear that. I see you're a little under the weather, even with the generously provided medical supplies. Tell me, what happened the night you almost got abducted? How did you get away from those human traffickers?"

"Okay. Well, I, ah, I was walking downtown by the train station around 3:00 a.m., and I saw three guys with backpacks walking toward me. They approached me and asked what time it was. Before I could answer, they sprayed me in the face with pepper spray. Then one guy swung a metal baton at me. It hit me hard above my eye. I fell to the ground badly."

"Ouch! Boy, I bet you didn't know what hit you, did you, Mr. Reyes?"

A slight laugh emanates from audience. The emcee smiles.

"Then what happened?"

"So the next thing I felt after being hit hard was being picked up in the air and carried toward the train waiting at the station. I...I was a little groggy. I knew I was off the ground. The lights from the train station were blurry due to my eyes swelling shut. I knew what they were trying to do to me. I grabbed my club in my pants pocket and started hitting the two men carrying me. I was up in the air, high above them. I hit them hard with my stick. It...it was the only thing I could do."

Mr. Reyes is tearing up. Audience is tearing up as well. Camera focuses on a lady in the audience, puffy-eyed. The emcee has rested a hand on his face, eagerly listening to Mr. Reyes.

"Oh dear, I'm so, so sorry that happened to you. Mr. Reyes, what happened next?"

"I don't remember. After I hit them on their heads, the two guys dropped me. I hit the ground. The third guy who was with them started kicking me in the groin. By that time, the train was making an announcement to depart. The men got up and hit me some more. They were still trying to pick me up when the train blew a horn. The men ran off to get on the train, leaving me on the ground. I was scared for my life."

"Wow. Just wow. I can't believe they tried to enslave you like that. It seems you were lucky, though, Mr. Reyes. Had they successfully gotten you on that train, you no doubt would've been knocked out or chemically sedated, then forced into slave labor in some faraway country. Perhaps you might have been taken back to El Salvador, where you're originally from."

"No, no, I don't want that."

"Yes, I see you most definitely don't ever want to go back to your country of origin ever again. Speaking of your hometown, Mr. Reyes, why don't you tell the audience about your time in El Salvador? Perhaps a riveting story about life before the military started rounding up your people like stray dogs?"

"I...I don't remember a lot about El Salvador. I was really young."

"Surely you must've seen the rebels defending their homeland or the police disemboweling citizens in the street."

Camera zooms in on Mr. Reyes's face. It's contorting, trying to hold back more tears. Judging by his reactions, he's surely seen his share of violence, both as a child and as an adult.

"Anything, Mr. Reyes? Any story you'd like to share with the audience here this evening?"

Mr. Reyes is crying now. Hostess gets Mr. Reyes a tissue from her bra.

"Okay, Luis. May I call you Luis? We all understand you've been under a staggering amount of stress recently, so we'll forgo inducing any more trauma. But before we let you go, we understand you lost something recently? Hmm? Maybe a defense weapon you've had for years? I heard the police took it for evidence, did they not?"

"Yes, they took my stick. The police thought I was a drunk on the train platform when I was beaten up. They locked me up. But after a few hours, they got a call from my boss, and they let me go. He wanted me to come back to work. But the police still kept my stick."

"Fear not, Luis Reyes, because we here at the committee panel chipped in to get you a present this evening. Consider it a small token of our appreciation for all you do!"

Hostess brings out a gift-wrapped box. Mr. Reyes opens the box to find a small bottle of pepper spray. He looks at the pepper spray. More tears develop.

"That's right, Mr. Reyes. We got you a key chain pepper spray canister for personal defense for when you go back to work! You can keep it on your set of keys, easily accessible if those terrible men ever come back to abduct you! Aren't we thoughtful, Mr. Reyes?"

Mr. Reyes looks up at the camera, wincing in pain as he does. He smiles. A few teeth are missing, no doubt due to his scuffle with his attackers.

"See that? Now you can fight back next time your abductors come. But use your pepper srpay spareingly. It's only the small key chain size. We here at the committee also got you this small flag of El Salvador so you can always remember the horrible events of your childhood. Make sure to keep it with you at all times. You might be able to jab a would-be attacker in the eye with the handle part when your spray runs out!"

Camera zooms in on meager gifts in Mr. Reyes's hands. The emcee instructs Mr. Reyes to wave the flag in front of camera. Audience claps with a standing ovation.

"Let's hear it for Mr. Luis Reyes, everyone!"

Orchestra is playing music in appreciation of Mr. Reyes. Camera pans back to the emcee, who has a massive smile on his face.

"Now that is what I call a heroic janitor, right? The personal struggles, the story of survival, it makes me proud to call Mr. Reyes a well-deserving winner—one of three winners tonight, I might add. Now let us take a minute to catch our breath to hear a word from our gracious sponsors."

Camera rolls on advertisements for random businesses in the community. Commercials play on-screen behind the emcee and the hostess—a fast-food joint, a local soccer team with its team stars talking into the camera, a family-owned funeral home. Stagehands usher Mr. Reyes off the stage, who is struggling to move in crutches. Back to applause and orchestra, and pan camera to the emcee. Hostess has changed outfits during break but still hasn't said a word.

"We're back! Let's talk about our next honoree. She hails from the faraway country of Croatia. Her name is Maria Tomic. Ms. Tomic immigrated to America with dreams of making it big on Broadway. Yes, Ms. Tomic had the voice of a songbird indeed. Too bad she had the bank account of a peasant girl from the Dark Ages. With only a smile and a beat, Ms. Tomic flew to the United States, hoping to land a spot in a new musical. But things took an ugly turn soon after her plane landed."

Ominous groans emanate from audience.

"Shortly upon arriving in New York, Ms. Tomic auditioned for plays. Unfortunately, so did about 25,000 other hopeful, young, aspiring actresses. The fact she didn't have a total command of the English language didn't help her cause. With her options looking bleak, Ms. Tomic decided to work with a tutor who said he could help her get into Broadway. Turns out, he charged a shitload of money, which Ms. Tomic didn't have. Instead of money, Ms. Tomic and the tutor worked out another deal, perhaps one of the oldest quid pro quos in history. Four months later, with no money and a human growing inside her, Maria gave up her dreams of ever becoming a Broadway star. Boy, that tutor gave her something, but it sure wasn't a musical career! Am I right, audience?"

Obnoxious laughter and applause rise from crowd.

"Well, now Maria had to decide and fast. Her visa only lasted for six months. With time ticking away, Ms. Tomic took the first job she could, as a public school janitor in New York City. The pay was horrible, and the back-cracking work was hell on her now pregnant body. The only good thing was, she was able to stay in the country to deliver her baby, a gorgeous girl named Petra."

"Aws" come from audience with a photo being displayed on large screen onstage.

"But she persevered. Maria may have not made it big on Broadway, but she made it to the big leagues of public school cleaning. With over 1,700 public schools in New York City, Maria was able to find plenty of work, scrubbing asbestos off the pipes and removing stains from years of uncleaned carpets. That's right, folks, Maria has been pounding away at her mopping job for all of thirty-three years now. Boy, that sure is a long time. I hear she spends most of her evening cleaning overcrowded, underfunded schools all over the city. It must be one of the most demanding janitor jobs in the country. I say we give her a humongous hand, shall we?"

Applause from captivated audience.

"So tonight, Maria Tomic, our little Croatian canary, we honor you as one of this year's most deserving janitors! Keep that applause going, audience!"

Forced applause from audience as camera pans to people in the seats who are clapping, sort of. Camera pans back to smiling emcee.

"Unfortunately, Ms. Tomic couldn't be here tonight due to her having two jobs. She is working her second job now, cleaning toilets in another school district in New York. That's a full sixteen hours a day working. I don't know how she sleeps. I really don't."

Murmurs come from visibly distraught audience.

"But fear not. We were able to get a camera crew out to the Big Apple and have Ms. Tomic on camera tonight during her lunch break. Yes, indeedy. Audience, give it up for the mop-swinging, show-tunes-singing Ms. Maria Tomic!"

Camera pans to the big screen onstage, where Ms. Tomic is sitting in a chair, staring at the camera. She looks deep into the camera, her mouth tight-lipped, her hands, arthritic and calloused, folded in her lap. She looks tired, very tired. Her eyes are half-open.

"Hello, Ms. Tomic! Can you hear me?" said the emcee.

"Yes, yes, I can hear…you well," said Maria.

Ms. Tomic is speaking in a thick, broken accent. The sign language interpreter off to the side of the stage is having a hell of a time trying to distinguish what's what. The emcee speaks to Ms. Tomic in an exaggerated tone. She's not deaf, but the emcee is speaking as if she is.

"Perfect! Okay, Ms. Tomic, I know you're pressed for time with your lunch break only fifteen minutes, so we'll make this quick. Tell me, Ms. Tomic, how did you feel coming to America to audition for Broadway?"

"Well, I…I wanted to…to be in plays in America. It…it was why I make trip to, ah, to the USA in first place. It was dream of mine. Always dream to do this."

"Yes, okay. And, Ms. Tomic, if you may, please tell me and the audience what it was like when your English tutor, the man who said he could make you a star on Broadway, took advantage of you."

Ms. Tomic looks confused. She stumbles over her words somewhat.

"I don't know…what you mean. Um…"

"I mean, Ms. Tomic, how did it feel to have your dreams dashed by your English tutor?" asked the emcee.

"I…I…don't know."

The emcee looks back to the audience with a devilish smirk.

"I guess he wasn't a very good English tutor. Jesus!"

Audience laughs nervously. The emcee adjusts his seat and looks back at the screen.

"Ms. Tomic, tell us how you feel about the guy who knocked you up and split."

Ms. Tomic's face changes. She understands the question now.

"Um, it was…very bad thing…to happen to me."

"Yes, I bet it was," said the emcee.

"He lie to me, and he hurt me bad with this…this leaving me and the baby alone," said Maria.

"Ms. Tomic, we understand you're very upset about the situation. Can you tell us what you've been doing at your job over these past thirty-three years?"

"Okay. I…I push broom in classroom. I pick up pile of dirt on floor. I…I go to throw out trash into dumpster. I get new bag for trash can. I…ah…um…"

MEMOIRS OF THE MOP

The emcee is nodding complacently. The audience and the camera crew are listening intently to Ms. Tomic discuss her daily duties at both her full-time jobs. She is taking a long time to enunciate the words.

"Wiping down the toilet bowls and toilet sinks. And…and…sometimes, I have to chase mouse in school with broom and hit mouse to kill mouse in school."

"Okay. Sounds good, Ms. Tomic. Sounds like you have your hands full at your jobs," said the emcee. He rolls his eyes at the audience and the camera in a joking manner. "So, Ms. Tomic, we wanted to say thank you for joining us tonight on our awards show. But before we let you go, we want to give you a little token of our appreciation for all the hardships you've had to endure. In addition to the standard presentation award we give to all our recipients, we wanted to give you something special to remember this evening."

An arm extends into the screen to hand Ms. Tomic a cheap plastic trophy and an envelope.

"We at the committee panel have decided to reward you for your merits. We've purchased you a ticket to an Off-Broadway musical during a weekday afternoon show!"

Audience applauds and shouts out cheers in recognition of the prize.

"That's right, Ms. Tomic, your dream of being on Broadway is complete, sort of. You'll be right there in the mezzanine, watching real Off-Broadway stars sing their lungs out. Yes, Ms. Tomic, we here at the panel want you to see what you almost got to do. Those wonderful visions of being under the lights, having eager faces watch you perform, will not be forgotten! Just imagine it, you sitting really far away from the stage, barely able to hear the songs being belted out on a Wednesday afternoon. You'll relive a devastating time of your life, wondering how close you came to greatness. How does that sound, Ms. Maria Tomic? Hello, Ms. Tomic?"

Camera shows Ms. Tomic on-screen, looking toward the floor. She seems to be daydreaming, no doubt of how her life could have been. With a single clap from the emcee onstage, Ms. Tomic is brought back to the present.

"Yes, yes, thank…thank you for ticket. I…I like the chance to see Broadway play."

"We here at the committee wanted to see your face when we told you about the ticket. Aren't you excited? Are you ready to see semiprofessionals doing the job you should be doing instead of mopping floors?"

Ms. Tomic smiles into the camera. She doesn't speak.

"All righty, then, Ms. Tomic. I hope you enjoy your day on Broadway. I hope you can get the day off from one of your jobs. Bye now! Thanks for coming on tonight!"

The emcee waves rather animatedly to Ms. Tomic. She is still sitting there, staring into the camera with a look of hopelessness. She claps half-heartedly with sorrow in her eyes. The audience claps a round of applause. Some are standing in the audience, but most of them are sitting down. The large screen onstage switches to infomercials while stagehands are trying to reset for the last presentation of the night.

The screen shows more advertisements from local business owners, who have paid lavish accommodations to the committee panel, the emcee, and useless hostess, who, at this point, still hasn't said a goddamned word. She smiles, changes outfits between presentations, and puffs out her tits. Surely the only reason she is there is to look pretty.

Many audience members are going to the lobby for refreshments. They check their phones, eagerly awaiting the after-party. The orchestra plays music to signal everyone to come back to their seats. The audience seems very antsy. They would like to wrap up the show and hit the after-party, which honorees are not allowed to attend.

"And we're back! Wow. Just wow, huh, folks? Wasn't that a touching story we heard from Ms. Tomic?"

Audience applauds, indicating it surely can't get any better than it already is.

"I think we can do you one better, my dear friends. We saved the most touching story for last. This man, whom we're about to bring out, is a true inspiration to us all, a real hero in the world of janitoring. He's been swinging a mop for over forty-five years."

The audience takes a deep breath in, shocked and excited. The camera pans to show various audience members holding their hands up to their mouths.

"By God, that's a miraculous feat, wouldn't you say? Forty-five years. Jesus, I didn't think anyone could do this wretched job for almost half a century without murdering someone in anger, but he did it. He surely did work that long, and tonight, we give the Lifetime Achievement Award to a janitor whom all other janitors should aspire to be. This story has many twists and turns, as do the other personal stories we've shared here tonight. I'm going to tell you the long story, but I warn you, it's a tale not for the faint of heart. Brace yourselves, dear audience, for a story you've likely never heard before. I give you the story of Ernesto Vasquez."

The camera pans up to the screen, which had a preloaded montage. Lights dim. The orchestra is silent. All eyes in the room are transfixed on the screen playing a slow-motion movie of the US-Mexico border. Images on-screen are of immigrant families making their way, or at least attempting, to cross into the United States. The screenshots are like old NFL Films movies—one clip after another with dramatic music in the background. The scene is very tense. Migrant families are separated at the border one by one with crying children filling many of the photos. Some are black-and-white. Some are in sepia tone. All are heart-wrenching.

The words Ernesto's Story: A Child Who Had to Become a Man appears. Movie goes on to tell the story of a little boy who came to America with his family at the age of six. He was the youngest of three. His mother, father, and two sisters all came to the border at the same time; but Ernesto's father was detained at the border. He had some bad gambling debts back in Guadalajara and was not allowed to finish the journey. Ernesto and his family were devastated. They were torn between a new life in America, filled with prosperity and new adventures, or staying in Mexico, living a life of despair and poverty. In the end, his family chose to leave the dad in Mexico.

The movie is ending. It is deliberately short. Lights come back up, and the screen goes dark. Camera pans to the emcee, who is holding his microphone. The hostess is sitting in the chair, crying, the most helpful thing she's done all night. The crowd is speechless. The emcee begins to speak.

"Terrible, isn't it? How can a family be put through this? Just picture the scene: your entire family, all the people in the world whom you love and care about, are all ready to start a new life in the Land of Dreams. At the last second, Papa Vasquez, the breadwinner of the family, is told he can't be with his family because he sucks at poker. Unbelievable. I mean, how much money could one person owe for five-card stud? How did he get the credit to keep playing poker?

"Well, audience, I'm told it was quite a lot of money, thousands of US dollars, which, I think, is, like, a million in their money, but still. The family made a game-time decision to leave their dad at the border so they could start a new life. It's a decision Ernesto and the rest of his nondegenerate, gambling family had to live with their entire lives."

The audience is crying. The orchestra is crying. The cameraman is crying. The hostess is still crying. The emcee is choking back tears to tell the remainder of the story.

"I tell you, folks, this is what makes my job harder than you can imagine. To tell this story is agony for me. I can't even imagine what it must've been like."

Pause for dramatic appeal. Sniffles arise from audience.

"But Ernesto struggled forward. He and his family established themselves in San Jose, California, and promised to pay the debts of their father so he could eventually make it to the United States. The Vasquez family all took jobs, anything they could to make money. At the age of six years old, Ernesto began shining shoes in a local office building. Instead of going to school or playing T-ball with other boys his age, Ernesto worked.

"His mother worked in one of the many fruit orchards in Southern California, picking oranges, apples, and eventually, grapes for wine. His two older sisters, not enrolled in school either, worked as a dishwasher and a waitress. Each week, they would put whatever extra money they had into an account to wire to the dad back in Mexico. Ernesto and his family did this for many years, working odd jobs to send money through Western Union to a welcoming father.

"There was a bright light at the end of the dark tunnel for Ernesto and his familia. Within ten years, their diligence had, by Ernesto's calculations, almost paid off their father's gambling debt. Within a few months, Ernesto's father would be able to pay back his accumulated debt and join the family in San Jose. But then the worst imaginable thing happened."

Audience gasps. Orchestra plays a short tune for emphasis.

"Ernesto's father told his family he had to pay off the interest on his gambling debt for the past decade. It came as a shock. Papa Vasquez was shocked most of all. I guess if you take a loan out from a cartel, they don't tell you the particulars of the deal. A poorly timed joke, I know, but one of sincerity, I assure you, audience."

A few boos arise from the audience.

"It was an astonishing number, almost equivalent to the amount of the original debt. Ernesto and his family were crushed, absolutely crushed. The hours spent buffing those office workers' shoes to a reflective sheen were all for naught. Ernesto was destroyed. He needed to make more money. At the tender age of sixteen, he needed a better job than buffing wing tip shoes.

"One day, while walking the halls at the office complex, Ernesto saw an ad. It was for a janitor position inside the office building he'd spent the last ten years working. He immediately contacted the number on the posting to inquire. The office manager was impressed with Ernesto's enthusiasm and offered him the job on the spot. The only problem was, Ernesto wasn't a legal citizen of the United States. Ernesto pleaded with the manager to please give him the job. He was desperate to free his father from the grip of his gambling debts. The office manager eventually broke down and gave Ernesto the job but with one caveat: he couldn't pay him on the books because he wasn't an American citizen. Ernesto took the job off the books and for a lot less than the average person.

"More years passed. Ernesto worked so hard for those years, as did his family. His mother, her body baking in the hot California sun, tried as best she could to reunite with her husband. The two sisters, now working at opposite ends of the state, had started families of their own. All their money went to paying for their own children to attend school and become legal citizens. Neither sister had money left to send back to Mexico. It was up to Ernesto and his *madre* to handle the burden of the father's wicked past.

"Twenty years is a long time to pay off a debt, am I right? It seems like a lifetime of money to fix a problem that most likely only took a few months to accrue. Just like the evil college loan departments, the cartel threatened bodily harm to Mr. Vasquez regularly. But after making constant monthly payments, Ernesto thought his father was in the clear. But it only got worse for poor Ernesto.

"Ernesto's father had to be the unluckiest man on the planet, because he was robbed on his way to pay off the debt. Yes, it's true. Mr. Vasquez, who for some reason kept all the money in a lump sum instead of making monthly payments, was relieved of all the cash on his way to make the final payment. In a stupendous turn of events, Mr. Vasquez phoned his son to tell him he was robbed at gunpoint and all the money his family had sent to pay the interest on the debt was gone."

More astonished gasps from the audience. Hostess puts her hands to her mouth in horror. The emcee gives a stern look into camera as it zooms in for a close-up. Camera picks up on all the lines in his spray-tanned face.

"One can imagine the shock Ernesto had when his father told him the news. All the money was gone. Ernesto was at his wit's end. A few days after the call from his father, Ernesto got more bad news. His mother was injured in the field by a harvester machine. She was picking black walnuts, and the machine operator didn't see her in the tree. I don't know if you've ever seen how they harvest walnuts, but let's just say the machine grabs the trunk of the tree and shakes the shit out of it. A lot of shaking, dear audience, so much so that Ernesto's mother was scrambled around like a paint can in one of those machines in Home Depot.

"Mrs. Vasquez was in bad shape, to put it bluntly. Not only did she have multiple broken bones, but she was also having night terrors about being shaken to hysteria. Each time Ernesto visited her, she would convulse violently like someone dislodging sediment from the bottom of a Snapple bottle. It killed Ernesto to see his once strong mama like this."

Audience lets out a huge huff in amazement.

"Can you imagine the stress Ernesto had in his life at that moment? A father who's stuck in another country with the cartel after him and a mother in traction in the hospital—I can only imagine what poor Ernesto was going through. Now that his mother was out of work with no money coming in, Ernesto made a life-altering choice. He decided to sneak back over the Mexican border. Once he got there, Ernesto thought he could sneak back over the border again with his father, and the family would be united once more. He needed to have his father be with his mother. It might bring her out of her shaking fits.

So Ernesto trekked his way back into Mexico, crossing the Rio Grande, and back to his old village to find his papa. He inquired about his father's whereabouts and located him in an all-too-familiar place. He found his father sitting at a blackjack table, drunkenly laughing with two Mexican prostitutes hanging all over him. He was gambling with towers of chips, pounding the table with glee as the two soiled doves pawed all over his sweaty, cheap suit-wearing body. Ernesto was in a rage. He leaped forward to confront his daddy. 'How could you, Papa? Mama and I have been sending you money for years, too many years now! How…how can you do this to us?'

"It was no use. Mr. Vasquez was super drunk with thoughts of winning in his head, nothing more. Mr. Vasquez screamed at his now-adult son. 'You and your mother left me in this shithole to die. Fuck you and America too! Leave me be. I'm on a roll here. I almost won all my money back from yesterday. Go. Go away now, *cabrón*.'"

Camera moves to show audience in tears. No one is talking. They are listening to Ernesto's tragic tale with anticipation. A few members of the audience scream inaudibly in anger.

"This was the last blow for Ernesto. He left his old village, saddened and angry, to trek home. He made it back across the border safely, then back home to check on his mother. He found that she had been committed to a psychiatric ward due to uncontrollable outbursts. She screamed unmercifully until the nurses pumped her full of pills. Then she lay in bed, vibrating in place as if she was still in the grips of the mechanical beast.

"With his family in shambles, Ernesto went back to his job, begging to be taken back. He had been gone for about three weeks at this point. His janitor job, the thing he did to win his father's freedom, gave him a hard time about being gone. Ernesto explained his situation to the office manager. He begged and begged, saying he'd do anything to keep his job, so the office manager told him he'd hire him back but at a lower pay, a lot lower than he ever made. Ernesto had to take it. I mean, it's not like he needed to send any more money back to Mexico now that his father spent it on cards and hookers. Ernesto agreed to the terms and went back to his old job with sadness in his heart. Just a mop and years of servitude to show for a now middle-aged man."

The emcee turns to wipe a single tear out of the corner of his eye. The audience is silent. All that the camera microphone picks up are the sniffles of the crowd holding back their crying. Camera pans back to the emcee.

"Twenty-five years later, Ernesto is still working at the same office building, cleaning the same hallways and toilets. For this, we at the committee panel have, therefore, nominated Ernesto Vasquez for not only the Lifetime Achievement Award but also the newly created award called the Platinum Plunger. Yes, yes, that's right, the panel has created a new award to be given out for the first time to such a deserving individual."

Whistles and loud claps erupt from the crowd.

"It is with humble regard that we honor Mr. Ernesto Vasquez here tonight. For the past forty-five years, Ernesto has been working to do a job not many people have the gumption to do. He is a trooper of the poopers, a hero of hallway mopping. We bestow the Platinum Plunger Award to a very deserving janitor. Let's bring him out! The man, Ernesto Vasquez!"

Ernesto enters the stage from the right side. He is very old looking although he is only in his early sixties. He is wearing a tan cowboy hat, old blue jeans from the 1980s, and a long sleeve blue plaid shirt. He waves to audience as he approaches the emcee. The two shake hands and sit down.

"Mr. Vasquez, thank you for coming tonight!" said the emcee.

"Thank you for having me, Mr. Emcee," said Ernesto.

"Please, call me B. L."

"Okay, B. L. Thank you for inviting me to the show."

"So, Ernesto, tell us, how in the wide world of sports have you kept your sanity over the last forty-five years?"

"Well. I…I don't know how, really," said Ernesto. "I had no other choice, I guess."

Ernesto is shy and sort of bashful. Audience picks up on his demeanor. The emcee adjusts himself in the seat.

"You'll have to excuse me, Mr. Vasquez. I'm simply in awe of all your determination for your family after all you've been through. It seems you've worked so hard to have it all crumble in front of your very eyes."

"Yes, it's…it's been a long road," said Ernesto.

Ernesto appears to be choking up while speaking. The emcee puts a comforting hand on his shoulder. The hostess hands Ernesto a tissue. Wow, she does something other than sit there. Camera zooms in on Ernesto patting his eyes with the tissue.

"I know, buddy. I know. You let it all out," said the emcee. "We've all been there before."

"Thank you. I try to move past it every day. It's hard to think about all those years working to save my papa. But I couldn't save him from his disease."

"Which disease: the gambling or the prostitutes?" said the emcee.

"Both, I…I guess," said Ernesto.

Ernesto is crying loudly now. His eyes are closed, and his shoulders are bouncing up and down. The audience is captured by the moment. There is not a dry eye in the theater.

"How is your mother, Ernesto? We hear she is doing much better than when she first had her tragic accident."

"She is doing well, B. L.," said Ernesto. "She hasn't worked since the machine almost killed her in that walnut tree, but she is stable. I've been trying to pay the medical bills, but it's hard."

"Very good! Has she been able to speak since the accident?" asked the emcee.

"No, no, she hasn't spoken since that day," said Ernesto. "She makes grunts to let me know she is happy or sad. But her violent shaking hasn't been a problem for many years now."

"Aws" and applause come from audience. Everyone is more upbeat now.

"Mr. Vasquez, if I may, do you think you could ever forgive your father for his sins?"

The audience is waiting. Camera slowly zooms in on Ernesto's face.

"He is my papa, and I still love him dearly. Maybe one day, perhaps," said Ernesto.

Audience claps in approval.

"I'm glad to hear that. Ernesto, I think it's time for you to have a little happiness in your life."

Ernesto looks puzzled. The audience is in a stupor. The ostess is dumbfounded, but what else is new?

"Mr. Vasquez, we here at the committee have thought long and hard about what to get you as a celebratory gesture. Including the Platinum Plunger Award and the Lifetime Achievement Award, we got you something you've always wanted. Through the efforts of some very able-bodied human smugglers, also known as coyotes, we were able to bring Papa Vasquez to the United States!"

The screen onstage turns on with a live video of Ernesto's father standing in front of a camera. He looks very old. He is wearing a similar type of cowboy hat as Ernesto. Vazquez Sr. is swaying a little and is not able to keep his focus on the camera. The audience is told through a voice over the live stream that the father only agreed to come to America if he had enough liquor to drown a pony. With one eye closed, it appears he got his request.

"Would you look at that! It's Ernesto's father, here in America, and I think he has something he wants to say."

Everyone focuses their attention to the screen, waiting for Mr. Vasquez to speak.

"Sank...sank you, Mr. Emcee and America, for bring...bring me to US." HE burps. "I want to say sank you for all you did." He burps again, swaying heavily now.

Ernesto seems happy but angry at the same time. He sits in his chair onstage with arms folded, nodding. The emcee begins to speak again.

"That's not all, Ernesto. Look in the background behind your father. Does the paint on the wall look familiar? I bet you've seen this location plenty of times, perhaps maybe while visiting another loved one?"

"No, no, please no. That's not where…where…"

"Right again, Ernesto! We brought your father to your mother's room at the sanatorium for a surprise visit! Ha! It's something I think you've been wanting for quite some time now, isn't it?"

The live video camera zooms out to show Mrs. Vasquez in her bed, eyes wide, making small grunting noises. She appears to be fearing for her life, like a Thomson's gazelle staring at a cheetah.

"Please, no! Mama is so good now. The doctors say she can't get too excited, or else she will get worse!"

"Oh, I'm sure the surprise of seeing her old husband after all these years of harsh times would be just the thing to cheer her up! Say, Mr. New American Visitor Vasquez, why don't you lean in and give your lovely wife a kiss?"

"Oh, okay!" said Mr. Vasquez drunkenly.

Mr. Vasquez bends down to kiss his wife. He is giving her more than a simple peck on the cheek. He is tongue-kissing her. His saliva-laced tongue is wiping across her mouth with little regard for her condition. Camera moves in to catch the action. Mrs. Vasquez makes loud, squealing grunts with her eyes closed. She is shaking more now as her drunken husband begins to climb on top of her in her hospital bed. Camera pulls away as scene escalates quickly. Attention comes back to the stage, where Ernesto is hiding his face in shame. He is sobbing. The emcee starts to talk again.

"Oh, wow, Mr. Vasquez, you little lovebug, you! I guess he missed his wife a lot! Just look at the happy couple, reunited!"

Camera shows a drunken man on top of an invalid woman, trying to force his tongue down her throat. A second camera shows Ernesto onstage, crying into his cupped hands, saying, "Why, why, why?" repeatedly. Then camera focuses back on the emcee.

"A very special thank-you goes out to the human smugglers along the California-Mexico border. It was their hard work of dodging border patrol agents who made this special moment happen. Let's leave the two lovebirds alone, shall we? All right, Mr. and Mrs. Vasquez, have fun catching up on old times!" He turned away from the large screen and directed his attention back to Ernesto.

"Well, Ernesto, I guess you got your wish after all. Your mama and papa are lost deep within each other's embrace, and now you don't have to pay back any more money to the cartel for the gambling debt! It's a win-win for you, my friend. Do you have any last words for the audience or the committee panel?"

Ernesto looks up from his bitter sobbing. He stares at the emcee with bloodshot eyes. He says nothing, but if looks could kill, the emcee would be dead ten times over.

"He's speechless, folks, at a total loss for words for this evening's events. Congratulations, Ernesto, on your Lifetime Achievement Award, your Platinum Plunger Award, and having your illegal immigrant family back together on non-native soil. Don't forget to take your trophies back home to show your family. Goodbye now!"

Audience sends Ernesto offstage with a mixed round of applause. The emcee tries to shake Ernesto's hand. Ernesto gets out of the chair with awards and walks offstage. Two loud bangs echo in the background where Ernesto has just exited. An educated guess would be that he has thrown his new awards at the wall behind the curtain.

"Well, that about does it for us here tonight. I'd like to thank my lovely hostess for all her outfit changes. Say goodnight, Ms. Rogers!"

The hostess waves to the camera with a stupefied smile.

"Before I sign off, I'd like to say a special thank-you to the people who made this evening happen. No, not the work-ravaged janitors who set up and will clean after this shiny massacre called an award show. I'm talking about the masters of the universe: the committee panel. They are the real winners tonight. They're the ones who organized this entire fiasco. Each year, they do a tremendous job of producing this evening's festivities. Only through their meticulous self-promotion and constant attention to themselves can this event be pulled off. I mean, who else but the committee panel has the audacity to throw an award show for so-called stars and give themselves all the credit?"

The audience laughs, and so do the camera crew and stagehands. Even the stupid hostess laughs, and she's a fucking moron.

"Yes, yes, it's the committee we're honoring here tonight and all subsequent nights from hereafter. They couldn't be here tonight because they've been at the after-party the entire time, drinking and eating like the self-absorbed assholes they are. So in their place, I'd like to say a few words of praise. Thank you, taxpayers, for funding this event and all their misguided endeavors.

"Thank you to the finance group for squeezing all the available money from other organizations, like charities and nonprofits. And a very, very special thank-you to the people who come to these types of events. It's your gullibility and blinded stumbling that promote these travesties in the first place. So long from the awards ceremony. Don't forget to take your swag bags, hop in your limos, and meet us at the after-party! See ya next year!"

The emcee waves to the audience as he gets up from his chair. He's smiling and waving. He may or may not be sprinkling a middle finger in between as he signs off. The orchestra is playing a rather festive tune for departure. As the audience exits the room, you can spot a crew of janitors off to the side collecting garbage bags and sweeping the floor, the all-inclusive sign that the evening's event has come to an end. Camera goes black.

CHAPTER 13

Summer Work

Do you know what pisses me off the most? When someone asks me what I did during the summer. I'm not sure if you're aware of this fact, but school janitors don't get summer off like the teachers do. Hell no, we don't go on safari in Botswana, photographing hippopotamus and leopards from a Land Cruiser. You won't find any mop jockeys ascending the mountains of Nepal, trying to achieve a bucket list climb. No, dear friends, we work, harder than you can imagine.

Once your children leave for summer break, the school janitors brace themselves for damnation. We take one last deep breath and let it out slowly, savoring the feeling of some downtime before the storm crashes onto our shores. You would think that having done this mind-crippling job for so long, I would be ready for summer work. Let me make this abundantly clear: Nothing can prepare you for summer work. No amount of cardio or dead weightlifting can help once summer cleaning commences. Forget about doing yoga. That shit won't help you now. Once the day summer work starts, it changes a person.

Cleaning a filthy school throughout the summer is a massive undertaking. Everything must be disinfected before your kids come back in the fall. Without proper staff or a battle plan, the entire operation turns into a boiling shit stampede quickly. Lucky for me, I know what to do. It took years of trial and error to get it right. Even now, with so many summers under my belt, I still get sideswiped when idiots try to take over. But now I take it easy, achieving a level of zen only seen by Buddhists. I have a preseaon ritual to help make the transition as smooth as possible.

All summer work starts with an offering to the gods. I perform a ceremony to the cleaning gods, asking for a safe summer clean. I start by burning incense or lighting candles while chanting spiritual phrases. "Please, oh gods of the summer work, please don't let some jackasses drop a desk on my head. Om. Most gracious Father, please keep me safe if the dreaded night foreman sticks his fucking nose in my business one more time. Om."

Next comes the performance of the haka. It's a traditional war dance used by the Maori in the face of their combatants. I'm not from Polynesia, nor do I have Pacific Islander blood surging through my veins, but any little bit helps. My haka starts by drawing black lines on my face with an erasable whiteboard marker. Then I stand in front of a bathroom mirror, stick out my tongue, stomp my feet, and pound on my chest while groaning aggressively. This display of power shows the evil summer work spirits that I am ready for battle and will fight to the death. I do this alone, because my coworkers will lock me in the loony bin if they see me gyrating in a bathroom with a broomstick held high above my head.

After that, I start tapping up like a UFC cage fighter. One must apply medical tape to one's wrists and mop handle to improve grip. You're going to need all the grip you can muster during the summer. Back braces don't do a thing. Don't even bother. If pressed to move heavy objects, which you will most certainly be asked, have the new guy do it. He can afford a hernia or two. You've already had yours and subsequent surgeries. Lastly, I put in a mouth guard. It's not for accidents. It's for fistfights. Summertime is the most brutal time of the year for a janitor. Tensions run high. Egos inflate. Chances are, you won't be in a fistfight, but it's good to be prepared. I've seen too many teeth on the ground to take any chances.

Here's the breakdown of summer work: We start with x number of workers. Smaller schools get a handful of workers if they're lucky. Middle schools and high schools get about double that number if they're lucky too. Don't pay attention to things like labor laws or proper workplace standards. The greedy board of education tries to cut staff so they can get a better raise for themselves come the following school year. School budgets get by with the least number of people as possible. This causes multiple issues down the line. Cutting corners I think they call it. Try driving a tow truck with one wheel missing and see what happens. That kind of corner-cutting gets people hurt, as you will see.

The general rule of thumb is to clean, move furniture, and wax the floors. That's the long and short of it. We clean everything with harsh chemicals, any surface the children touch. Their greasy little digits smear germs on everything. Desks, chairs, walls, lockers, ceiling tiles, and windows—anything you see in a school is contaminated. Don't let the EPA fool you. The stuff we use to clean is not green or safe for the environment. It's one step away from DDT. I recommend not eating off any surface we clean unless you hose it down with fresh water for an extended period. Hey, it's not my call. I won't use these cleaners unless I am forced to.

I worked with a lady years ago named Gina Rothbone, who got second-degree burns on her hands because she didn't wear gloves. It started as a slight burning sensation. She ran to the sink to wash her hands with soap and water. Big mistake. Adding water to this particular chemical only increased its potency. This poor lady's skin peeled off like a plastic wrapper on a DVD case. As she screamed in agony, trying to stop her skin from melting away, someone called 911. By the time EMTs got there, her hands looked like someone dipped them in battery acid. Essentially, they had been.

The chemicals they gave us years back were even worse. They worked really well. Just don't get it on your skin. Chemical engineers tuned the formula back somewhat in the last decade, but it was still harmful. On a side note, please tell your children to stop licking things in school unless you want their tongues to rot off.

If it were up to me, I would power-wash the entire school in bleach. Like a firefighter battling a four-alarm blaze, I would soak the place to the foundation. We can't do that anymore. It would cause too many floods. Instead, we wash down the furniture as best we can, then move it out of the room. This is where things get interesting. Most people I work with are not good in the coordination department. Accidents can and will happen when moving bulky, often still wet objects. I remind my coworkers to wait until the toxic chemicals are dry before picking up the three-hundred-pound teachers' desks. The smarter ones heed my warning. The dumb ones go in full steam. That's when the aahs and oohs start.

Organizing the furniture in the hallway is an operation reserved for the more intelligent worker. Anyone can drag shit out of a classroom, gauging divots on the tile floor in the process. We try to avoid collateral damage when moving furniture. Accidents do happen, though. I'm not saying we destroy things on purpose, but if you're a teacher and you've got a heavy antique cabinet you cherish, it's best to take it home with you when you leave for the summer. I've seen janitors go bowling with items not meant to be bowled with.

The lighter items, like student desks, teachers' boxes, stuffed animals, supplies, and toys, all get condensed into a high but manageable pile. It's like Tetris on expert level. It takes a genuinely smart person to stack things. One guy once insisted on stacking desks his way. He packed the stuff so high that it all came crashing down like an avalanche the minute someone touched it. He was not allowed to stack things anymore.

Approximately 90 percent of janitor accidents happen during the summer months. Things like not lifting on the count of three and underestimating the girth of a heavy table lead to bodily harm. I've been hurt before, I'll admit it. I was young and full of moxie back then, thinking I can lift a file cabinet by myself. I learned my lessons the hard way. After lifting an extremely heavy clay kiln the wrong way, I was laid up for two weeks. I never did it again. I can't say the same for my compadres. Some dummies love getting workman's comp even if they cripple themselves in the process.

One chap named Shawn Sikes broke his back trying to lift heavy things. The dumb shit always lifted stuff without help. Each time we had to move something, there came Shawn, barreling in. "I got it!" he would say. Little things, like a student desk, were easy enough and were usually a one-person job. He got cocky with the light items. When we told him we needed everything out of the room, he jumped at the task. Shawn grabbed ahold of a massive desk, something made entirely of metal from the 1960s. "I got it!" he yelled from across the room. I tried to yell back to him to grab the wheeled desk mover, but it was too late. "Oh! Shit!" screamed Shawn as he doubled over in pain.

It was four weeks of recovery for him.

Shawn came back a month later and did the same thing again, this time grabbing a file cabinet jam-packed with about two hundred pounds of paper. I turned my back for two minutes to grab a handcart. "I got it!" yelled Shawn. Two seconds later, I heard metal scrape the floor. "Oh! Shit!" All this idiot ever said were "I got it!" and "Oh! Shit!" Shawn reinjured his hernia the day he came back from recovery. It meant another four weeks out—paid time off, I might add. The following summer, he tried to lift a commercial refrigerator out of the school kitchen. That was the last day Shawn worked with us. It was probably the last day he ever walked without the help of arm braces, from what I heard.

There's a method to moving most janitors are oblivious to. A common sense rule is to move the heaviest items with either a handcart or a team lift. You move it the shortest distance from where it's coming from. There's no sense in moving a giant teacher's desk halfway across the school. You won't believe how many times I've seen people hauling stuff down long corridors instead of putting it next to the room it's coming out of.

Upon removing all the furniture from a room, it's time to strip—strip the floors, that is. The tile floor you walk on every day in schools, offices, the mall, etc. is coated with what's called floor finish. Some people call it wax or floor shine. Whatever the name or the molecular makeup, it's applied to the tile to protect it from damage. It's the same thing as carnauba wax on your hot rod or when the dentist cleans your teeth with bubble-gum-flavored stuff.

Floor stripping is one of the most dangerous jobs one can do during summer work, but not because it's hard. It's a relatively simple task. What makes it so dangerous are the dum-dums who don't respect the process. Floor stripping goes like this: A janitor will apply a water-based solution to the floor and use a floor-stripping machine to remove the wax. Sounds easy, right? You would be surprised by how many people get hurt each summer during this phase of the project.

I call it splashdown. The entire floor is covered in half an inch of viscous fluid with the same consistency as Astroglide. This fluid is extremely corrosive as well, burning anything it touches—skin, eyeballs, and genitals. Even the floor sometimes starts to smoke if the chemical concoction is too strong. Throw in an electric floor grinder with a high rate of speed while working in close proximity to klutzy half-wits. You've got the roundabout idea. What could possibly go wrong?

Floor stripping requires the use of protective gear with gloves and slip-resistant footwear being essential. A protective boot with a Brillo pad-like material on the sole is key to not going down like the *Titanic*. Three out of four janitors will wear regular tennis shoes or, even worse, slippers when stripping the floor. These are the ones who get concussions or broken hips from going ass overhead. Now you know why I call it splashdown.

Slips happen all the time. The problem is, some arrogant janitors try to mess around, sliding on the floor like a figure skater. That's when they bust their ass. You never forget your first time slipping. I remember it like it was yesterday. I went down like a sack of potatoes; wax clumps stuck to my uniform, the acidic floor stripper eating away my epidermis. Ah, memories! I've never been hurt (knock on wood), but some janitors get messed up pretty badly.

One guy went down so hard he cracked the tile. This poor man hit hard. It sounded like someone dropped a bowling ball off the roof. I'll never forget that sound. Blood gushed from his head like an oil derrick erupting in the middle of a barren field. As he tried to get up, the floor turned crimson instantly. I and another janitor waddled over to him, gingerly trying to tell him to stay down. He slipped again, planting his head on the tile once more, face-first this time. The floor looked like the sea after a great white bit into a Cape fur seal. He survived, barely, after being rushed to the hospital to stop the traumatic bleeding. Forty-three staples later, he came back, but he was never the same. He also lost vison in one eye when he face-planted the second time.

Some liquids can be very caustic depending on what manufacturer your company uses. Most are mild, causing skin burns or minor chemical scarring. More abrasive chemicals, the ones you need a filter mask to work with, are toxic. With names like Iron Fist Floor Stripper and Firestarter Floor Solution, it's best to take all precautions. Janitors often throw up bile or dry-heave when working with these chemicals. A well-ventilated area is recommended but not always available.

Two people I used to work with got sick as hell when my company switched over to a new brand. I'm talking emergency room visits. Upon learning the two janitors almost died, the boss came down and wrote them up for improper work procedures. I guess it was their fault they almost asphyxiated. Perhaps we shouldn't use chemicals traditionally used for stripping paint off the sides of oil tankers.

This next part of the chapter describes one of the deadliest machines a janitor uses during summer work. It's a lot like a venomous snake. When handled properly, it's a fine creature to marvel at. But when safety procedures are not followed, it can turn deadly.

The floor machine—or the stripper, as it is called in social circles—is a helpful yet harmful tool. It looks like a car tire on its side with a stick in the middle. It rotates at a high speed to agitate the wax from the surface of the tile. It consists of three parts: the stick, the brush, and the motor. You hold it like a big golf club, spacing your feet apart as if you're about to tee off. While resting the handle near or on your hip, you move it slowly across the wet floor.

The concept is not complex: sweep machine from side to side in an orderly fashion and it won't tear you apart. It's another easy yet remarkably hard idea to grasp for most. Please take this warning seriously: Never let the new guy or a mental case use this machine unless professionally trained. Even then, always keep your eyes on them. I've seen way too many avoidable accidents leaving people crippled or worse.

The top of the floor machine is where the motor is. It has a flat surface. The whole motor area kind of looks like a fancy top hat. It is not advisable to put anything heavy on it, especially a human. Two dudes tried to be funny one day, messing around with the machine.

One guy stood on top of the motor while the other held the handle upright. They faced each other as if dancing in a beautiful ballroom. As soon as they turned it on, they both spun around together. They thought they were cute, but they looked like two morons dancing in a circle. Once the machine gained high speed, the cord wrapped around them like a spider wrapping a web around a grasshopper. They stopped laughing after they hit the ground, crying for someone to cut them loose.

During one of my first years, I saw a guy get totally wrecked after grabbing the machine the wrong way. He was a muscleman, eager to put his pecs and deltoids to use. I told him to beware of the floor machine and to not use it until trained. "How hard can it be?" said Beefcake Man, who turned the machine on, all willy-nilly. Two seconds later, he was bucked off like a skinny cowboy from a wild bronco.

The stupid shit got thrown about six feet, crashing onto the terrazzo floor. I tried to get him up, but he was out cold. He hit so hard when he landed that it caused him to slide across the wet floor. I almost pissed myself because he kept sliding, like one of those stones curlers use in the Olympics.

Long story short, the brawny worker had his skin burned from lying in the liquid. His muscles were still buff, but the skin around them looked like someone took a cheese grater to it. He developed a head jerk too. Every twenty seconds, he would shake his head as if he got a chill. The guy looked like a rooster strutting across a henhouse. A few months later, the head bob became more frequent, causing him to go out on disability.

Horseplay is never encouraged when operating the floor machine. It can spin at six thousand rpms, more than capable of ripping flesh from bone. I won't lie to you, I've horsed around when I first started, trying to tame the monster known as the floor stripper. I was lucky. A few slips are nothing compared to the absolute destruction I've seen.

Even when not fucking around, the floor machine is dangerous at best. Most floor-cleaning solutions are slick to begin with. When you add in the extremely slippery liquid wax that you're stripping off the floor, you might as well be walking on a glacier. Even with protective shoes, you can still fall if you're not careful. If you step on the cord while moving the machine, you're going to slip. The trick is to glide as you step. Never tromp around like Godzilla crushing Tokyo.

Speaking of cords, always make sure they are in perfect working order, free from any damage. One of the worst accidents in the history of the custodial field happened when a crew of janitors were electrocuted. They were told to strip a floor that hadn't been cleaned in years. The wax buildup was so thick that they decided to flood the floor with a floor-stripping solution. They opted to use Old Gertie, an ancient floor machine that looked like it had been manufactured during the Civil War. Gertie was powerful, maybe a little too powerful. She was a gorgeous machine complete with an outdated 240 v power source. They don't make them anymore with 240 v because it draws too much electricity.

Old Gertie had a cracked old power cord in desperate need of replacing. When the cord split open, they were instantly turned into shish kebabs. Since they were standing in two inches of solution and not wearing insulated shoes, the three unlucky janitors cooked quicker than a three-minute egg. A coworker who wasn't with them called the medics, but it was way too late. The laws of electricity prohibited them from moving once they started to fry.

Those poor guys stood straight up, electrocuting in place, until the power company shut down the transformer outside the building. By that time, those three dudes looked like slabs of ribs someone forgot to take off the grill, cooking until charred. Imagine the excruciating pain with thousands of volts surging through your body until your brain steams itself inside your skull. I can still smell singed bodies during the summer when the room heats up.

Don't even think about using the larger, heavy-duty floor machines. They're powered by propane tanks with Kawasaki engines. We only had one of those machines many years ago, just before I started working. Some schmo placed quarters on the floor in the machine's path while he was dry buffing the tiles. When the pad touched the coins, they shot across the school like mini flying saucers.

The night boss at the time took the machine away after one of the quarters got embedded in a concrete wall. Imagine what that same coin could have done to someone's leg or forehead. Good thing we don't have the machine nowadays. I can see one of these cretins driving it full speed into a gas line, causing the whole school to go up like a Michael Bay explosion scene.

Summer work doesn't end with floor cleaning. You must reapply the wax you've taken off once the floor dries. I don't have any gross wax accident stories to tell you. I wish I did. Waxing is fail-safe. You just mop it on carefully in a slow, tai chi-like motion. It, too, is slippery, but we only let the most competent workers wax. We don't need any Andy Warhol artists creating designs on the floor. After a few coats of wax, we move all the furniture back into the rooms as neatly as when we took it out.

Then comes the fun work. Schools need all sorts of hazardous maintenance that can't be done when the children are present. Asbestos removal is at the top of the danger list. Any school built before July 1989 most definitely has asbestos in it. It's everywhere. Insulation on the pipes, certain sized floor tiles, and fire-resistant heating coils—you name it. This shit is beyond hazardous, requiring full spacewalk suits when removing. Once asbestos is broken apart, it's in the air like a microscopic virus. Only the most skilled and well-protected people should remove asbestos.

I know what you're thinking: "Is my little Trevor or Adeline safe in an older school?" The short answer is yes. The longer, more complicated answer is maybe. As long as your school district uses proper asbestos abatement procedures, your children will be safe. Just remember, you get what you pay for; and if your district loves to save money by cutting corners, you may want to consider pricing child-sized hazmat suits.

Less-lethal procedures, like rat termination and cockroach spraying, are just as toxic as a small nuclear reactor leaking. I've seen rats the size of sea otters scurrying in dimly lit storage rooms, not cute little field mice with adorable tiny faces and tiny paws. I'm talking Conan the Barbarian rats with beady red eyes and teeth capable of shearing tin, rats that can easily kick the ass of an alley cat when challenged. Traps don't work anymore; that just pisses them off. The beasts I'm talking about use rat traps for flip-flops. We've resorted to more chemically inclined options to dispose of our vermin. Have you ever seen a big black box outside a school, located near dumpsters? We call them the Hotel California for rats.

A rat will go into the hole of these devices, eat the tasty poison inside, and combust minutes later. Technically, it's not combusting; it is more like liquifying. The poison dissolves the rat from the inside out, leaving a soupy mess. When it rains, the now moist inards of said rat leech into the soil, eventually collecting in your reservoir or rainwater tanks. Roaches, on the other hand, are damn near indestructible. Cockroaches of all kinds are prevalent in any school. The same goes for bedbugs. Regardless of how many times you clean a school or how hard you scrub, the infestation will not be stopped.

On our honeymoon, my wife and I went to Bermuda. It was a gorgeous place, but the entire island was infested with cockroaches. We took a small boat from the nice side of the island to the extremely nice side of the island. When getting off the boat in Hamilton, we saw cockroaches stuck to the pier, hundreds of them. Our guide told us not to worry. "We've got six kinds of roaches in Bermuda. You'll find them in the cheap shacks all the way up to the million-dollar mansions. They're all over. Nothing can stop them."

There isn't a poison known to man that can kill a roach without risking potential birth defects. The stuff we're supposed to use has the same chemical makeup as orange juice. It may kill flies and worms, but roaches bathe in it, growing stronger with each spray. We break out the good stuff when faced with an outbreak, and by good stuff, I mean shit the EPA has outlawed. We keep it hidden, out of sight from the health inspectors when they make their semiannual visits. It's a catch-22, really. Either we kill the roaches, or we're swarmed with them.

The same goes for illnesses, like meningitis, the flu, or new respiratory diseases so prevalent in today's news cycle. To kill all these viruses and bacteria, we need to use the heavy shit. If not, they come back. Don't worry. By the time the little kiddies come back in the fall, most of the poisonous gases have evaporated. Most of it.

Other important jobs, like painting cubic yards of random surfaces, also happen during the summer. Do you know how many obscene, phallic pictures I've had to paint over in my career? A tremendous number. I see cartoon dicks in my dreams. Vaginas too. There are ridiculously illustrated genitals in all shapes, sizes, and intricacy. I've been doing this for so long I bet I've painted over artwork from multiple generations. Think about it. If a young boy has painted a dick in a school eighteen years ago and he grows up to have a kid who goes to the same school, there's a high probability I may paint over a penis his son draws. That's mind-boggling and depressing at the same time.

Summertime is, by far, when the most physical altercations take place among the custodial staff. For most of the year, janitors are by themselves, working in what are called sections. Basically, a janitor is given a specific area to clean on a nightly basis—their territory, if you will. Cleaning certain classrooms and bathrooms fall to one individual, so we know exactly who does what each night. Summer work is different. All the janitors work together in close proximity with a heavy workload and in hot conditions. This is when tempers flare. Beefs from throughout the year are brought up in front of everybody. If Janitor A thinks Janitor B stole his mop back in February, the entire group will hear about it. Minutes later, they face off like boxers.

I've witnessed several fights in my career and perhaps even participated in a few. Broken windows and disassembled tables—those can all be explained. If a coworker gets severely injured, we must call in a supervisor. Rules are, if you fight, you're fired. So most times, we settle it among ourselves, without union or administrator interference.

We had a few altercations where the boys in blue were dispatched. One such cataclysmic event topped them all. I'm referring to the Fat Guy Brawl of 2006. Jesus, the summer of '06 was particularly stifling. Average daily temperatures topped out at ninety-five degrees in July and August. These schools heat up fast without air-conditioning, like a brick pizza oven from Italy.

If I remember correctly, the two guys were named Joe and Derrick, and both were morbidly obese. They tipped the scales at nearly four hundred pounds each, true heavyweights. Well, these two did not like each other for whatever reason. They were always squabbling over something. I think it had to do with a certain lady friend, but I can't remember for the life of me. One very moist summer day, they started bickering. The next thing I knew, they dropped their cleaning buckets and charged each other like rhinos.

It was only myself and another janitor named Evan who saw the whole fracas from start to finish. Joe and Derrick clashed for a good five minutes, shoving and pushing like seasoned sumo wrestlers. Their grunts echoed in the small room, which, if I remember correctly, was a music room. The acoustics in the room really gave the fight a Dolby surround sound feel. They threw punches and snarled like possessed demons, bumping into walls and stacked furniture.

I figured, once they tuckered out, they would stop. They did not tucker out. These two behemoths raged onward, cursing each other out. Spit and blood exuded from their massive mouths like angry animals. Their destructive trajectory led them into the hallway and into the path of more stacked furntiture and, worse yet, more people.

Down the corridor they went, screeching with vile anger, smashing each other with whatever they laid hands on. Joe cracked Derrick over the head with a teacher's chair. Derrick came back with a fire extinguisher, hitting Joe across the back. It was chaos. They grappled with bloodied faces, busted noses, and slowly closing, swollen eyes. I had never seen such unbridled rage. Both men surged at the other with a ferocity only seen on the arid plains of the Serengeti.

A secretary from the front office heard the commotion and rushed out into the hall. She saw the blood-soaked fighters and screamed. "Someone stop them before they get hurt!" she said.

"Hell no, lady!" I said. "I ain't taking a fist to the mouth."

She ran back into the main office, locking the door, and called 911. A locked door didn't stop them from gaining access to the office. They broke through the all-glass door like two stuntmen. More screams bellowed from the office as the men tackled each other on her desk. By this point in the fight, both men had ripped each other's work shirt off. As they rolled around on her desk, the loose papers stuck to them like a dragonfly to a frog's tongue. When they fell onto the floor, they were covered with staples, sticky notes, and numerous fax transmission sheets.

When the police arrived, the two sweaty, office-supply-covered goliaths had made their way outside, to the front of the school. It took seven cops with pepper spray and multiple tasers deployed to stop them. Even then, they kept rolling around on top of each other like rabid gorillas. They should have sent out animal control to dart them. It would have been faster.

As they loaded the men into the back of the squad cars, I looked around to access the mess. You could plot the path where they started fighting from the music room all the way to the front entrance, a good sixty feet away. There were drops of blood, broken furniture, soiled papers, and bits of clothing. I had seen twisters leave less damage. Of course, Joe and Derrick were shit-canned while Evan and I, still shell-shocked from the event, had to clean up the mess.

This kind of hard labor is not for the weak. Each summer I hobble through, I add another stripe on my sleeve. All the summer work has to be done within two months. Mind you, that's not a lot of time to get these buildings back together from ten months of abuse. By the time August finally ends, we're exhausted beyond comprehension. Those of us who make it past August rejoice with cheers and congratulatory toasts. For those dear souls who don't make the cut, well, there's always Uber or Lyft.

I should start selling novelty items like they do at tourist traps. "I made it through summer work!" T-shirts would sell like hotcakes. Anyone care to buy an "I strip floors for minimum wage" shot glass? Nah, they wouldn't sell. Somehow, I don't think most of the public would get it. You gotta be here to see it for yourself. Instead of taking a cruise this summer, why not work as a janitor part-time to help clean these festering dumps? Each job comes with a complimentary psych evaluation once you quit!

CHAPTER 14

Tyrell Gets a Promotion

If you told me years ago when I first met Tyrell that he would be my boss one day, I would have busted my diaphragm laughing. Today, he walked into work wearing a suit. Commence organ rupturing. It happened on a Monday that was much like any other shitty Monday. I was pissed off because my weekend was over. Who likes coming to work on a Monday anyway? Let's be real here for a minute. Even though it was the middle of the afternoon, I was tired, mentally, physically, and emotionally tired.

In walked my pal Tyrell, fully clad in what could only be called a stellar three-piece suit. I hope you can visualize my face when Tyrell walked into the janitors' office. It wasn't the gaudy purple suit you would have expected he would wear but a dark-blue suit with a contemporary red tie, and he wasn't wearing a hat! I worked with this dude for years, and I had never seen him once without some form of head apparel. The only time he took off his hat was to wipe the sweat off his bald head.

I'll try to paint you an image, but there aren't enough words in a thesaurus to express my shock. *Stunned* is the best word I can think of. *Flabbergasted* may work. One doesn't come to work in the janitorial field wearing a suit unless it's one of those disposable white ones we use when swabbing out a sewer drain or the fluorescent-orange hazmat suit with a clear face shield for contamination sites. Janitors don't wear a traditional suit per se.

I was completely rocked when he stood in the doorway, staring at me. "Hey, man," I said. "You look like an usher at a funeral parlor." Tyrell said nothing. "Are you going to your own retirement party with that getup?" I asked with a giggle in my throat.

"Nope," said Tyrell, his face pointing down to the floor, "not today." His normal jovial tone was absent. He always followed up any conversation with "My brotha" or "No doubt, jack." Something was off about him.

"Where's your uniform?" I asked.

"You're looking at it," he said. He turned around to show off his bland suit, arms out. You can add confused to my feeling of being stunned.

"What do you mean?" I asked.

"Well," Tyrell said as he slowly walked into the office, "this is my uniform. I can't be wearing a jumpsuit or dingy shirt for my new position now, can I?"

"Huh?" I said. I was hungover a little, but things still weren't computing. I thought he was pulling a joke. Tyrell had always been a joker, finding ways to prank the people he felt cool with. Most of his hazings were stupid shit, like leaving pornographic printouts on coworkers' janitor cart. This didn't feel like a prank. Then I looked toward his feet. Tyrell was wearing plain black dress shoes. Footwear was something Tyrell never joked about. He once told me that if I ever caught him wearing shoes like this, I should bury him right there on the spot. "You ain't never gonna catch me wearing honky shoes unless I'm ready for the pine box," Tyrell had told me many times. Whatever this was, it was no joke. This was some serious business.

He stopped in front of where I was sitting and looked down at me. "You're looking at the new head supervisor of the department, my friend."

"Get the fuck outta here," I said. "Don't be joking like that."

"It's true," said Tyrell. "I interviewed last week. They said they was extremely impressed with my work as of late and said, with my longevity and new positive attitude, I'd be perfect for the job."

"Whose job? Genger's job?" I asked.

"That's the one," Tyrell said.

"Yeah, okay!" I said. "You, the same guy who said this job was a waste of fucking time and told the last boss to suck your bulbous black dick on numerous occasions? Is that the positive attitude you speak of, Tyrell?" He smiled at me, then pulled out his new ID badge with a lanyard attached. It read, "Tyrell Jones, Supervisor of School Service Workers."

"I decided to take this job more seriously," said Tyrell, "which is something I suggest you try. Your attitude will prevent you from achieving your best abilities. You should try a change sometime."

"Change? That's all I got in my pocket, change," I said jokingly. Tyrell didn't blink. That line always brought a smile to his face. Tyrell said it anytime someone mentioned the word *change*. Today, the joke fell on deaf ears.

"Not everyone can say they've changed for the better," said Tyrell. His smile turned into a smirk as he walked toward the doorway of the office. His typical swagger was gone, replaced with the stiff, rigid walk one found on any company man. His right hand was in his pocket with his left holding his ID. Tyrell stopped at the doorway, looked down at his watch, and turned back to address me. "It's past three o'clock. Shouldn't you be working by now?" He smirked, then walked away, his Buxton shoes clip-clopping on the terrazzo floor.

What the fuck just happened? I said in my mind. *Tell me this guy didn't say that.* This betrayal was by far the worst I had ever dealt with. Not him, not my Tyrell! The man whom I had considered a close friend pulled a 180. There he was, checking his watch and shit, telling me it was time to go to work. Tyrell always treated me right. Now this.

After the shock set in, I made my way down to my janitors' closet to start my shift. Things were fuzzy for a bit. My mouth was dry. I had a quick cooling sensation run across my body. Was it nerves, anger? A feeling of unknowing drifted into me. It was kind of like how a person who got out of a car crash was shaken, yet they knew they just got out of a wrecked car.

As I reached the door to my janitors' closet, I heard Tyrell's voice down a corridor. He came into view, speaking to Juan, a part-time janitor at my post. "Hello there," he said. "How are you today? Working along, I see. Very good, very good. Just coming to say hi as the new head supervisor. You'll be seeing a lot more of me in the coming weeks. I'll be here to monitor your work performance. Just act natural. Work like you normally do. Nothing has changed except my job title. Okay, then. I'll be around. Have a good day!"

As Tyrell made his way toward me, the cooling sensation overcame me once again. He looked like a cracked-out Steve Harvey hosting the new *Family Feud*. What the hell was he doing wearing a frigging suit? I didn't know how to go forward. The feeling was unnatural, weird, and unknown to me. He was looking toward the ground while opening a leather padfolio, glancing at the pages inside. Briefly, from behind Tyrell, I saw Juan walk into view. He looked to me for an explanation. I sure as shit didn't have one. Tyrell came to a halt in front of me, looking indignant. "Well now," said Tyrell, "I hope my promotion won't affect our working relationship as we move forward. I plan on evaluating everyone equally, including you."

This motherfucker. "Cut the shit," I said. "Don't you give me that speech, man. I've known you too long to be talked to like some serf. How in the fuck did you get Genger's job? And why are you talking like this? This ain't you."

Tyrell closed his padfolio, looking perplexed. He hadn't made good eye contact with me since he walked in. "Well," said Tyrell, "it seems Mr. Genger wasn't the right man for the job. He didn't have the same passion for it. You and I both know he wasn't a people person, which I believe this job requires."

"Really? You're telling me you're a more capable boss, the same guy who used a total of 116 sick days last year?"

Tyrell shrugged his shoulders, relaxing his posture. He placed the padfolio in front of his crotch, holding it with both hands. "Tell me," he said as he tilted his head to one side, "do you think questioning a boss about his new position is the best way to move forward?" Tyrell looked as if he really wanted an answer to his question.

"Do you think anyone is believing this bullshit charade?" I asked. "Your new position, what does that mean? You gonna drop me like that after all the stuff we've been through?"

"I'd like to start off on the right foot with you, one of professionalism, one without hostility." Tyrell cocked his head back to center. "But you don't seem to want to do that, do you?" He shook his head tirelessly as if he was ashamed for me.

"Tyrell," I said almost exhaustedly, "this ain't you. This ain't the same guy who walked out of this building Friday night talking about how he was going to party his ass off with 'two fine honeys.'"

"Perhaps I was celebrating my new promotion," he said.

"Bullshit!" I yelled. "Don't think for a second you're fooling me or anyone else with this new persona. I know you. I've been around longer than you by now and know a fake person when I see one. Hell, you never used to pronounce words fully. Yet here you are, annunciating as if you were schooled at Oxford."

"Now that I'm your boss, I expect your behavior to be courteous. This is a professional work environment in case you don't know. It's my job to make sure you take this job seriously," said Tyrell as he adjusted his tie, straightenting it out.

"Don't fucking play me like this," I said, "not you."

Tyrell shook his head again, a frowning, disappointed look on his face. He was a changed man all right. A total and completely fake person stood in front of me now. *What's with this suit?* I thought. Tyrell wouldn't have been caught dead in a suit like that. I had expected him to wear a clan robe before this generic, off-the-rack ensemble. I stood in front of him, not knowing how to act. Most days, we would laugh and kid, but it was all different now.

"Fuck that," I shouted. "Now you're being a hypocrite. After all the stunts you pulled, all the write-ups you got, and all the harassment charges you filed against this place, now here you are, selling out?"

"If you continue to curse, I'll be forced to write you up. This work environment does not tolerate hostile speech," said Tyrell.

"The last thing you said to me on Friday night was, 'I'll see your goofy white ass on Monday, mothafucka! I'm off to go slay these hoes all fucking weekend long!' Is that acceptable workplace speech, Tyrell?"

"Things have changed," said Tyrell. His tone was absent of feeling, almost lifeless.

"No, you've changed, boss man," I said. My voice carried down the hall. "Don't kid yourself now that you've got a little power. This ain't you. This ain't even close to you."

"I understand your frustration. This is new to all of us," Tyrell said in a mocking tone. "We used to work as equals before, but that is no longer the case. I hope we can move forward in a new, more positive direction. I will ignore your tone and attitude this time, but I hope during our next meeting, you will give me the courtesy my new title dictates." He smiled one of those fake corporate smiles, then he turned to walk away, strolling down the hallway with his head held high.

I, still stunned, confused, and now mortified, stood there alone, getting angrier the farther he got from me. "Unfucking real," I said loudly. It was loud enough for him to hear.

Tyrell stopped walking and turned around abruptly. "Don't mistake my kindness for weakness," he said, pointing at me, then he swiveled back around and left. This last tone was quite different from the fake one he had been giving me since he came in. Tyrell spoke at me like I was some yahoo on the street who owed him money. I had never heard this from him ever. I got a little worried as he walked away. Even though we had been cool for a lot of years, I remembered what Tyrell used to be back when he was running the streets. The thug came out in his voice.

I got back to work, doing the damn thing I always did. The more I worked, the more my mind started to roll. This whole thing didn't add up. Something was very off with the entire situation. Who in their right fucking mind would give Tyrell Mr. Genger's job? Tyrell didn't even have a diploma, let alone a college degree. Mr. Genger's job was technically a supervisory position; it required at least a four-year degree and experience. This didn't make sense on so many levels.

Having Tyrell as the big boss, the head cheese of all of us service workers, seemed surreal. I'm not going to lie, I had dreamed about him doing Genger's job on more than one occasion. The old Tyrell performing Mr. Genger's job would have looked like a scene out of the movie *Soul Plane*. I could envision it now, Tyrell cruising into the parking lot, blasting Biggie with the absolute largest rims money could buy. He would step out of his Lincoln Town Car wearing a red top hat and a white pimp coat with smoke billowing out from the car. That son of a bitch would be carrying a cane too. I just knew it! There would be something tacky on the head of the cane, like a gold panther or a rhinestone-covered cobra.

Then after being about two hours late already, he would pull out his phone to start up a conversation with a random skank. I hoped that with his newfound success, Tyrell's taste in women would improve, but I doubted it. Instead of a higher class of women, Tyrell would still run around with gutter chicks, just a lot more of them. He would hire a smoking-hot secretary, maybe even two secretaries. He always said that if he ever got to be a big shot, he would have two secretaries fulfilling all these dirty fantasies he had.

Office meetings would revolve around what Tyrell referred to as hood business—him and three of his homeboys smoking Macanudo Cigars, drinking Courvoisier, and watching a Knicks game. They would shoot dice all morning instead of doing paperwork. Lunch hour would be held at the local titty bar with tiny hotdogs on toothpicks for appetizers. No real work would ever get done, just Tyrell screwing around on a grander scale. But I didn't see any gangster activity in the foreseeable future now that Tyrell the Tyrant was boss.

Knowing Tyrell had left the building, Juan came to find me. He was upset and just as confused as I was. "What's he doing?" he asked. "Why Tyrell do this to me? He say he is the boss now. How he get that job?"

"I don't know, Juan," I said. "Tyrell sold out, I guess." I shook my head to Juan, who was shaking his head as well but faster.

"Is Tyrell mad at me?" asked Juan. He looked scared. "He always say he going to deport me if he was boss. We always joke like this. All of us laugh, remember? Can he do this now?"

I shrugged my shoulders, trying to play it off. "He can't do that, Juan. Don't worry about it. Tyrell can't deport you. He doesn't have that kind of power."

"What he going to do to us? He can't fire me and you, can he?"

"He wouldn't dare fire us," I said. "Let me make a few calls and see what this is all about."

Juan sprinted out of the room, flustered. I made some calls to a couple of known rumor starters and gossip hounds. None of them knew about Tyrell's new position. No one heard of it until I reached Rodney, a union rep. He said he just got an email stating Tyrell was the new head guy for the department.

"I thought it was spam," said Rodney. "I almost dropped my coffee when I read it!"

"Yeah, but how can they do that? How can they give Tyrell that job?"

"Beats me," he said.

"So they can ignore the job requirements and hire whoever the hell they want?" I said. "Who even hired him?"

"Sanders gets the final say on who gets what job. We've tried plenty of times to push back against him, but the bastard has all the power on the school board. It's his world. We're just living in it."

Fucking Sanders. Satan's spawn himself must have hired Tyrell. Now things were getting even weirder. We all knew Sanders was a wild card, but hiring Tyrell for the head position was plain loco. The Gray Viper had complete control over hiring and firing within the board of education. Most school districts had a committee or school board to evaluate employee affairs, but Rodney told me about Sanders's new contract, which he had inked a few weeks ago. Through some kind of black magic, Sanders got a clause put into his contract that declared him the hiring czar. He had the final say over all matters. Having an ironclad contract gave him the power to get around loopholes, like hiring someone who had absolutely no experience for any posted job. I knew this place was crooked, but even this was pushing it.

If you learn one thing at all from any of my books, let it be this: The Gray Viper didn't do a thing unless it benefited him in some way. It could be a hefty construction contract with hidden kickbacks or a revenge firing of an employee who wronged him somehow. Sanders always did things in his favor. He was a weak, jealous sycophant who didn't trust anybody. This was why he hired thugs to take the fall for him. He liked to set up cronies all around him, doing his dirty work. Most of the time, the cockeyed cocksucker came out squeaky-clean.

Call me paranoid, but I thought Tyrell's new promotion was all part of a larger, sinister plan. It was no secret that I had had beef with Sanders for a long time. He had been gunning for me ever since I started working. I mean, the scoundrel hired a former IRA operative to try to exterminate me. How much more evidence do I need to give? For some reason, he had always come up short. His plans to get rid of me never panned out.

I figured Sanders would make his final move with a hit man, like, an actual hired professional killer. I would be sitting outside a café in Italy on my fortieth birthday, finally taking a trip to Rome to take in the sights. The last image I would ever see would be a silenced pistol before everything went black. It never crossed my mind that Tyrell could be the triggerman. Turning my closest ally against me? That was some next-level shit. I didn't know how he did it, but Sanders had infected my best buddy Tyrell, poisoning his mind with notions of a quick paycheck.

Once I figured out Sanders's dirty scheme, I got to work in trying to formulate a defense. Years of constantly looking over my shoulder had prepared me for this. Anyone who had ever worked a state job knew about the paranoia effect. It must have been something about the environment we worked in. I don't know. You got this feeling like someone's lurking behind you 24-7, holding a knife high above your head.

Now that Tyrell was holding the knife, I had to be even more careful. This man knew me better than anyone in the district. He knew my faults, my weaknesses, and all my tricks. Hell, he was the guy who showed me most of those tricks! Tyrell trained me in the art of fuckery—how to do as little as humanly possible and still have a job. Tyrell called it freaking it. Let me explain.

Say you're having a bad day. You come to work maybe a little tired from partying with loose women all night. You've got a full workload, lots of toilets to clean and so forth. "Just freak it" were the everlasting words of Tyrell. He made a career out of half-assing everything he did. He knew how to make an hour of work look like a full day—things like sweeping piles of dirt under a carpet, for instance.

"As long as you don't have big clumps under the rug, it's fine, baby!" said Tyrell. Got a dirty, stinking bathroom? Let Tyrell handle it. He simply doused cleaner all over the place, then let it air-dry. "As long as you get a little cleaner in the bowl, it's fine. When people see that blue water, they think it's clean!" he had said on more nights than I would like to admit. "All you gots to do is freak it, my brotha!"

We had a system for all situations. In shorthand, "No problem!" Just pick up the big pieces of paper and throw out the trash, then flush the toilets twice, and you were done. If we felt like taking it super easy, we would have the new guy do our work while we take a snooze in an undisclosed location. We told all new workers this was the way it went, that they picked up our work and we would pick up theirs next time. Chances were, the new guy would quit or get fired within a few weeks anyway. If one of us wanted to leave early or not show up at all, we had a system set in place for that too.

We even had lookouts at other schools to keep us in the loop—texts, phone calls, code words over the radios, etc. I liked to think of us as the new Navajo code talkers from back in World War II. "Snakes on a plane!" was the text for whenever a worker spotted Sanders in the building. "The walrus is in the pond" was another code for some dipshit boss we had years back. You name it, we had planned for it. You gotta remember this. We had a good ten years when the district's budget was cut so thin that we didn't even have a night supervisor. The psychos were running the lunatic asylum, and we loved every minute of it. There were tons more short cuts Tyrell showed me, but I won't divulge all our secrets here. Let's just say we didn't do a lot of work back then.

I devised a whole new system to tackle this new threat. I launched a preemptive plan with new code words. I cleaned my whole area too in case that turncoat wanted to inspect my work. All the half-assed work we used to do was no more, because this motherfucker was sure to check all the hiding spots. Dirt under rugs, windowsill dusting, or workers leaving early—all that shit stopped overnight. I taught Juan and Julian, Tyrell's replacement, new code words for texts in case they saw him in the building.

Sure enough, that same week, Big Boss Tyrell was back, looking to bust me up. I got a text from Juan on Thursday of that week around 6:00 p.m. saying, "Your eggs Benedict is ready." I had a hell of a time explaining who Benedict Arnold was to two Mexican guys, but they figured it out eventually. Tyrell headed right to my area, sneaking in quietly. When he popped up behind me in a classroom, I was working away without skipping a beat. Tyrell had on a different suit. It was blue tie and pinstriped blue suit this time. In a matter of days, he obtained the silent steps most vindictive bosses had. The fucker was like a ghost; I didn't even hear him.

"Good evening," he said in a booming voice. He thought I didn't hear him walking up behind me.

"Nice suit," I said, looking at him. I was washing down a blackboard.

Tyrell looked dismayed when he found me. "Working diligently, I see," he said. His tone was rife with sarcasm.

"As always," I declared. I didn't turn around to look at him. His face disgusted me now.

"Hmm," said Tyrell. He walked into the room, looking for signs of disarray. "That's not always been the case, has it? I seem to recall your cleaning methods as being subpar." He stopped to pick up the small rug in the classroom, checking under it for sand and dirt.

"I learned from the best," I said curtly, trying to keep my cool as Tyrell scrutinized my work.

"Well, I don't know about the best," Tyrell said. I turned to look at him. A smile came across his lips. "But I did get promoted, so maybe I was the best." He looked back at me as I rang a sponge out into a wash bucket. He strolled over to where I was standing and looked in the bucket. "Water looks a little dirty," he said, pointing at it.

"There's a lot of things here that are dirty," I said. We exchanged looks.

Tyrell spoke again. "Maybe that's why the supervisors gave me the promotion, to clean things up around here." He didn't show any of our previous rapport. He was looking to get a rise out of me.

"Yeah, maybe," I said. I grabbed the bucket and walked away to change the water.

This guy had flipped the switch overnight. He was anonymous to me now. He was a plain turncoat, simple as that. He followed behind, evaluating from afar, judging me with his little clipboard clenched in his hands. I hated Captain Clipboards. They infuriated me. I reached the janitors' closet and dumped my bucket with a hefty splash into the sink. *He better not follow me like a fucking shadow all night. I ain't having this,* I thought. After filling the bucket, I turned around to leave the closet. There he was, staring at me, checking the time on his watch.

"I've been checking out your work these past few days," said Tyrell. He fell silent after the last remark, waiting for my retort.

"Yeah?" I said. So he was here. I must have missed him. Checking up on me without being seen was another sneaky trait I assumed he learned from his mentor Sanders.

"To be honest, it doesn't seem up to the standards of the district," Tyrell said. He flipped a few pages on his clipboard, searching for notes. "To me, your work isn't what the district expects of its employees."

"What does that mean, boss?" I asked.

"Well, it means we expect more out of someone who's been with us for over twenty years," he said. As he flipped through his notes, Tyrell had short pauses. He was waiting for me to blow my top like he had seen me do countless times.

"Gee, I thought I was doing a great job all this time," I said. "Who's the 'we' you're talking about, huh?"

"Me and the other bosses in charge here," said Tyrell. "It seems like your work quality just…just isn't acceptable." He went in deeper, trying to fuck with me even more. "In our observations, we can see you may not have what it takes to work here going forward." Tyrell stopped flipping aimlessly through the clipboard. Now he wrote something down.

Oh, that bastard knew where my buttons were and how hard to press. But like all the times I was provoked, I used a little sarcasm and wit, seeing how far his buttons could be pushed. "Well, since you're new here and all and I know you've never had any real training, how can you be in a position to correctly evaluate me?" I paused a few seconds before I went on. "I mean, maybe you're not qualified to do your job."

Tyrell clicked his pen a few times out of anger. We stared back and forth at each other like two alley cats hissing. He put his pen away with a tsk. "You know, it didn't have to go like this," he said.

"Oh, like how?" I said back. "Like being treated like shit?"

"You disappoint me," said Tyrell.

"Me? Disappoint you? Oh, that's rich!" *No more games,* I thought.

"This whole attitude of yours," said Tyrell, "it's always been your biggest problem."

"My problem is you!" I yelled. "You're stabbing me in the goddamn back!"

"Watch your language," said Tyrell. "I won't tell you again."

"Oh, fuck off with the language trick, Tyrell. I'm so sick of this new promotion of yours. Who are you trying to impress, huh, Sanders? That's the thing, isn't it?"

"I'm warning you, mister," said Tyrell as he pointed his finger at me. "Watch your language."

"You think that demon cares about hiring you? You think Sanders respects you in the least bit?" I was losing it; the whole thing was coming undone. Goodbye, Tyrell. Our friendship was ending within seconds.

"Easy now. You freak out and I'll be forced to—"

"Forced to what, fire me? That's what that scumbag wants, your new pal Sanders the snake, the guy who took you under his devil wings, that piece of absolute monkey shit? He offered you a little extra money, and you fell for it. Why would you do that to me?"

"You keep cursing and I'm writing you up for slander and insubordination!" said Tyrell. We were centimeters apart now, going at it in the hallway—angry faces, bitter resentment for betrayals, and yelling words that couldn't be unsaid. Juan and Julian came into view from the end of the hallway, but I didn't give a rat's ass at that point.

"Tell me this, oh buddy of mine. Are you and Sanders best friends now or just until I'm fired?"

"You don't know what you're talking about," said Tyrell. His eyes narrowed. He was getting as worked up as I was.

"Oh, wait a minute! I get it now," I said. I put my finger against my temple. "I seem to recall you have a lawsuit against the board. Remember? That's it! Sanders the omnipotent gave you a raise so you'd drop the case! Right?"

Tyrell was seething where he was standing in front of me. The anger in him was red-hot, burning through his skin. "I told you to watch your tone!" he shouted. "Keep it up, man. Just keep it up!"

"Oh, fuck you, fuck this bullshit job, and especially, fuck that motherfucking Sanders!" I screamed. Tyrell backed away suddenly. Maybe he thought I was going to swing at him. I certainly had the adrenaline pumping. I was revved up. I was supercharged and gaining rpms as seconds ticked by.

"That's it! You're done!" said Tyrell. "I warned you about your attitude and your language. Consider yourself written up!" He turned to walk away, quickly writing something down.

"Oh, blow me, will ya?" I yelled at him. Tyrell swiftly jogged past the two men standing at the end of the hallway, their mouths open. I started to walk toward them, yelling from a distance. "Make sure you run to tell your new hero Sanders about this!" I yelled. "Can't wait to see his face when he gets what he wants!"

Tyrell ran out of the building. He must have called Sanders as soon as he got outside. Sanders, not surprisingly, sent me an official letter the next day detailing the charges against me. Not only was I being charged with "causing a scene in the workplace," but I was also hit with insubordination for "using foul language and unprofessionalism in a school setting." I was placed on unpaid administrative leave starting that day. It was my second offense.

It finally caught up with me. My damned mouth wrote a big, sloppy, fat check, and it was bouncing right in front of my face. I cursed out a superior, a huge no-no. After the whole HR scandal, where I supposedly threw a chair, and the subsequent sensitivity training fiasco, I knew this was it. There were no last-minute Hail Marys or union reps to save my cooked ass. I was done, and deservedly so, I might add. Losing this job, which had been a dream for quite some time, was quickly becoming a reality.

It didn't bother me so much that I would lose it as how I would lose it. My friend turned on me. He was a good friend too. Sanders played the game perfectly by using Tyrell. I lost it, or maybe it lost me. Who knew anymore? I ran out of people to blame when I saw the letter.

I sat at home, sadly getting my stuff in order. I knew Sanders would act fast with this one. He would probably bring in the good lawyer from the board of education, the one they paid an unholy amount of money per hour. They only brought that guy in when they knew it was a done deal. I was on unpaid leave "until further notice." I had maybe a few days until the job called me in for a meeting, most likely my last.

CHAPTER 15

There's No Hope for Hope

Now that I had some time on my hands, stuck home all day, I might as well blow off some steam. The best way I knew how to do that, other than getting loaded and gorging myself on fancy food, was to write funny little stories. If I let Sanders get to me while waiting for this stupid meeting, I would go completely batty. It was time for a trip down moron lane!

My situation looked bad and all, but at least I would never be as bad as Hope was. Hope Ridgewell, a twenty-six-year dingbat from Surf City, New Jersey, was a train wreck. She was like a derailed commuter train scattered across two miles of urban wasteland with no sign of survivors. I had never met someone so disorganized and so completely clueless as to how life operated.

Records showed that Hope was employed for almost two years, but she wasn't physically at work for two whole years. I estimated that her actual number of days of being physically at work was closer to a year. She spent half those days being late, calling in sick, and on occasion, not showing up at all. She started working during the first week of September about ten years ago. The district had a hiring influx after the brutal summer work killed off the undesirables. Okay, so most of them didn't die, but a good number quit or got shitcanned with maybe one or two dying on average. Hope was hired to replace one of the casualties.

When Hope walked into the janitors' office on her first day, I thought she was a lost soccer mom looking for her kid. She had this face on her, sort of confused, kind of lost. A lot of parents walked into the janitors' office, believe it or not, looking for directions to their kids' classroom. It was Dean Smiley, the night head janitor at the time, and I who were sitting in the office, waiting for our new worker to arrive. I was reading a book while Dean skimmed his newspaper.

"Hello," I said to her. "Can I help you?"

"Um," she said, "I'm looking for the janitors' office. Can you help me find it?"

"You're standing in it," said Dean. "Didn't you see the big yellow sign outside of the door?" Dean wasn't a nice man. Let me just preface that right away. It was one of the many reasons he was no longer here.

"Oh," said Hope. She looked around inside the room, searching for something. Her head turned from side to side slowly as if she was scanning the walls for a secret lever. She stood there for a few seconds, lost in contemplation, which I came to realize later was her regular pose. Picture someone looking out into a wide-open field on a bright, sunny day.

After a few moments of blank staring, Dean chimed in. "Can we help you with something, sweetheart?"

"Yeah, um…um, I'm here to work," Hope said. She didn't say anything else, no, "Hi. My name is…," or, "Sorry I'm an idiot. Show me where the brooms are at."

Dean and I exchanged brief glances. "Christ, not another one!" said Dean. He slammed his newspaper down. "Is your name Hope?"

"Yes," she said, but she didn't seem 100 percent sure it was her name by the way she said it.

"Are you sure?" Dean asked. I could hear the sarcasm in his voice.

"Um, yeah."

"Welcome aboard, missy. I'm Dean. Let me show you around."

Dean and I extended our hands. Hope, either because of reluctance or a slowed intellect, eventually put her hands out to reciprocate. Dean shot me another look before he led her down the hallway to give her the tour. It was the "Here we go again" look. I'm sure you have a similar look when dealing with a not all there kind of new coworker. Hope followed me and Dean out of the office to start her career. Besides the confused introduction, she was off to a bad start.

"Where's your uniform?" asked Dean. "Didn't the office give you a work shirt to wear?"

"Oh yeah, that," she said. "I don't know."

"What do you mean?" asked Dean. "Did you bring a shirt or not? Are you wearing it under your jacket?"

"I guess I forgot it. I don't know."

She didn't seem sure of her answer. Dean and I continued to exchange looks as the three of us walked. It seemed the bosses outdid themselves with this new hire. Once in a blue moon, admin hired an exceptionally stupid worker, one who baffled the mind on so many levels.

Dean couldn't help himself with his new employee. "Wait a minute," he said. He stopped walking, putting his hands up in a "Don't shoot" manner, causing both me and Hope to stop. "You're telling me you don't know if you brought the shirt with you?" Dean looked at Hope, perplexed. "How do you not know? I mean, you're not wearing it, so you must've left it home, right?"

"Do you have it in your car maybe?" I asked. I was trying to give her the benefit of the doubt.

"Jeez," said Hope. Her face was stoic and blank. "I don't know. I think I forgot it at home."

Both Dean and I were stuck in place, almost glued to the floor in amazement. Hope looked at us as if nothing was wrong. "Are you kidding me with this?" Dean said to me like it was my fault. "This is what they give us? This is who I'm supposed to work with?" He never beat around the bush, I'd give him that. Dean continued to talk about Hope in front of her as if she wasn't standing a few feet away. "What kind of dumb shit did they send us?" he said.

I tried not to laugh, but looking at Hope's oblivious face did not help. Hope, still not grasping the situation completely, stood there like a cardboard cutout. Her face was motionless. Dean rolled his eyes. "All right," he said. "Let's go. Keep walking straight ahead, honey." He pointed to the direction he wanted Hope to walk. "We'll get through this somehow. Come on."

We parted ways at the end of the corridor—me to the left, to my janitors' closet, and Dean to the right to train our new worker. It took all of five minutes for Dean to lose his patience. "What do you mean you've never used a broom before? How do you not know how to use a fucking broom? Monkeys know how to use a broom, for Christ's sake!"

I heard pieces of their conversation as I moved my cart down the hall, trying not to blatantly eavesdrop. Within minutes, I gave up trying to avoid their conversation and instead focused solely on it. Dean's voice soon overwhelmed Hope's. "You start by picking it up with two hands, like this. Do you see? It's not difficult, sweetheart. Just pick up the broom and start pushing it."

By the sound of Dean's questioning voice, training was not going so well. The clink of a metal pole hitting the floor led me to believe pushing a broom was an exercise Hope was not accustomed to. "Wrong!" came from Dean after each clanking. "This isn't brain surgery here, girly," he said. "What, you got crippled hands or something? Why can't you hold the broom straight?"

An hour into the training seminar, it seemed Hope still had zero manual labor skills. I couldn't see exactly what Dean was training her on; they were in a classroom, and I was walking back and forth near the area. From the sound of it, Hope was hopeless at best. Things like how to empty a garbage can, push a broom, and hold a dust rag, all these things appeared to be absent from Hope's repertoire. After an hour of not getting it, Dean resorted to whistling and snapping his fingers above her head, trying to get her attention like a dog trainer to an unruly puppy.

"Watch me closely. Then you try. You put the rag in the bucket like so, then you wring it dry. See?" Hope tried but failed. "No, don't do that! That's not how to do it," Dean said. "Wring it like this. Oh, for the love of God, how are you not getting this?" Sounds of water splashing in a bucket as if it contained a live largemouth bass filled the air.

I heard Dean's regular rhetorical phrases, such as, "You gotta be kidding me!" and "Why do they keep sending me these kinds of people?" after each instruction. The only thing I heard Hope say was,

"I don't get it." Occasionally, she would say, "Oh, okay," but I highly doubted she fully comprehended what she was being shown. Finally, Dean broke, not only berating her but also doing it with such anger that he seemed genuinely confused himself.

He gave her a simple task, trying to get her out of his sight for a few minutes. "You think you can fill a mop bucket with water? Can you handle that? Wait, wait, wait. Tell me you know what a yellow mop bucket is. Okay, good. Go find one and fill it with water, all right?" Hope left the classroom, walking to the end of the hallway, where I stood. As she passed me, she smiled, saying, "Hello." She wasn't crying or mad with anger, just walking aimlessly down the hall.

I started to walk toward the classroom where Dean was, but he walked out, meeting me in the hallway. His face was red and full of sweat. "That girl is a fucking moron," he yelled as he pointed in her direction. "I ain't never met anyone so dumb before!" He said it so loudly. It was like someone screaming from the witness stand in a murder trial.

"Take it easy, Dean," I said. "She's probably just overwhelmed on her first day."

"No, I'm positive she's like this all the time," said Dean. "There's something really wrong with her. She doesn't understand shit."

I had seen him flustered before, but this time, Dean was pretty worked up. His eyes were darting back and forth. He wiped sweat from his head with a red bandanna from his back pocket. "Maybe she has a handicap or a learning disability," I said. "You have to be patient with her. Try to say things without frothing from the mouth so much."

"It's like she's an alien who landed in the cornfield last night," Dean said. "And this is the first stop she's made." He paced back and forth, waiting for Hope to return with a mop bucket of water. As the minutes passed, he tried to elaborate on Hope's lack of training. "She doesn't even know how to hold a broom! Even if she's never done this kind of job before, she has to have used a mop or broom before in her own house."

I was trying to find a reason for her ignorance. Maybe she had a maid who did all the cleaning. Perhaps she lived a sheltered life. As Dean and I chatted away, we heard a low squealing sound coming down the hall closest to us. Both of us recognized the familiar sound as the rusty wheels of a mop bucket. "At least she found the mop bucket," I said.

Dean and I waited as Hope rounded the corner. As she came into view, I realized perhaps Dean was onto something with his assessment. You've seen a janitor push a bucket before, right? They normally have a mop in it and are walking upright. Hope opted for a different route of motion. She was doubled over the bucket, hands around each side, pushing it forward. Each time she pushed the bucket, water came sloshing out of the sides like a tidal wave in a kiddie pool. Most of the water spilled onto the floor, leaving small ponds as she walked.

"You seeing this?" said Dean. "This was what I meant when I said there's something wrong with her." He pulled out his flip phone to take a video. "I'm showing this to the boss," he said. By the time Hope reached where we stood, she was out of breath and water. The bucket was nearly empty from her awkward pushing method. Dean filmed away on his old-school flip phone, documenting with audible commentary. "Take a look, world," he said. "The elusive Stupidous Moronous in its natural habitat!"

Hope came to a stop in front of us, looking confused yet again. "I did like you told me," she said in between breaths. She looked inside the bucket, oblivious to where the water had gone. "I had it filled up a minute ago." Hope turned around to look down the hall. She had no idea how the water got out of the bucket even though she was indeed pushing it while getting soaking wet. "Must be a hole in the bottom of this mop bucket."

"And cut!" said Dean. He stopped the video, putting his phone back into its clip holster. "I'll tell you what," he said, "why don't you go take a break?" Dean moved his hands in a shooing motion. "Go eat your lunch in the break room, sweetie. Try not to choke on your food, okay?" He spoke to her in an almost baby voice.

"Okay," Hope said. She left the bucket in the middle of the floor, the water stagnating in pools as she walked back down the same hall she had just come from.

"Look at her. She's walking through the puddles. She's gonna slip and crack her head open!" said Dean. "That girl's missing a few million brain cells, I tell ya." He went to call the boss while I stood there.

Back then, I was a vastly different person. The years of abuse from this job hadn't worn me down to the vile, sarcastic bastard you see today. Had I met Hope a few months ago, I might have agreed with Dean, and I would have filmed away with my phone or laughed hysterically as the water lapped over the sides of the bucket. But at the time, I tried to help her somewhat.

I went down to the break room to see if Hope was sobbing uncontrollably or lashing out at the wall. Alas, she was not. She was sitting quietly and eating part of a Twix bar, humming a tune and looking down at a magazine. Had I been in her shoes with a new boss recording me and calling me an oaf, I might have quit.

As I entered the room, Hope looked up at me, again saying, "Hello."

"Hey," I said. "Are you all right?"

"Yes," she said. "Sitting down, having a break. This Twix bar is tasty."

"Oh," I said. I walked over to the table, trying to talk to her a little. "Don't worry about Dean," I said. "He's just…just an asshole sometimes."

"About what?" Hope asked. She was looking at me, confused, seemingly unaware of Dean's treatment.

"He's fooling around. I'm sure he doesn't mean half the stuff he says. He's a little paranoid and yells a lot."

"What stuff?" asked Hope. "He was yelling at me?"

"Yeah," I said. "I'm sure you heard him calling you stupid. Didn't you?"

Hope's face was as still as a painting. "Oh, okay." She looked back at her magazine again, licking chocolate off her fingers. She continued to read through the periodical without pause, eyes focused on the pages, humming away in her little world.

Either Hope had no emotions, or she was the most carefree person I had ever met. I figured I would talk with her a little more, mainly to see what kind of person she was. "Have you ever done this kind of work before? You seem a little new to the janitor field."

"No, not really," said Hope. "I mean, I've cleaned my room and my bathroom a few times, but nothing like this." She looked back at her magazine, unfazed by the level of alertness in my voice.

"Is this your first job?" I asked.

"No. I worked at a pet store for a few months before," said Hope. "I love animals. I have a lot of pets myself."

"Oh, that's nice."

"I wish I still had that job," she said.

I was reluctant to ask why she no longer worked at the pet store. I couldn't picture her having enough common sense to raise a parakeet, let alone a whole store full of animals. "What…what happened at the other job?" I asked, expecting a gruesome response.

"They closed," said Hope. "I think the owner had to file bankruptcy or something."

"Oh, good," I said, relieved. "That sucks. Sorry to hear that."

"Yeah, me too. I wish he didn't have to close. I'd still be able to get a discount on all my pet food."

We sat together for a few moments in the break room, silent except for a little humming. Hope seemed joyful to be perusing a magazine. I studied her, watching her body language. She seemed incredibly young for her age. Other than the humming and the mindless flipping through a magazine, Hope didn't exhibit any signs of adulthood. She had no engagement or wedding ring and no jewelry or makeup. She didn't even have a purse or a clutch of any kind. Most women needed access to a purse crammed with adult things, like a checkbook, a wallet, or a calendar of some kind. From what I could see, Hope didn't need things other women her age used frequently. Where did she keep her money or tampons or other adult shit?

As I pondered her lack of stuff, I began to check her out. Yes, I'll admit it, Hope was an attractive woman. Ever since she walked in, I had taken note of her body. I wished she wore something other than a baggy fleece sweater and loose-fitting pants. I could tell she had a nice body under the hobo clothing she had on. We were only a few years apart in age, as I came to find out, so of course, I gave her a look. She had light-blue eyes and medium-length blond hair with curls. Hope was thin, and her face had a few freckles, but there was not a single aging line or crack. She was a typical Irish or Scandinavian woman in outward appearance.

A few minutes into the break, Dean walked in. He was on his phone, talking loudly. I heard the standard lines one used when they wanted to end the phone call, no doubt pissed off at the person on the other end, such as the *yeps* and *yeahs* and *uh-huhs* you said when you knew your call was falling on deaf ears. Dean closed his phone, then addressed us. "Okay, well, that was fucking pointless," he said. "I tried to tell that son of a bitch about how stupid this one is, but he ain't gonna send us a new worker. He won't even look at the video showing how useless she is!"

Dean had spoken as if Hope had noise-canceling headphones for blocking out his conversation. She was still oblivious. She watched Dean closely but didn't quite understand him. I looked at Dean with embarrassment in my eyes, pleading with him not to talk about Hope while she was in the room. "What?" he said, addressing me. "Oh, her? She's clueless." Dean was looking at me, never making eye contact with Hope. "She doesn't understand a word I'm saying right now." He sat down at the end of the table, then made eye contact with Hope. "You still with us, honey?" He waved his right hand in front of her face as if she was blind.

"Um, yeah, I' still here," said Hope. "Where would I go?"

Dean looked back at me. "Told you she was dumb." He continued to shake his head, disappointed, letting out a huff. "Well, we're stuck with her," he said. I didn't speak immediately, not sure what to say. Dean spoke again. "The little dick boss said to train her 'cause she ain't going nowhere. I said, 'What the fuck am I supposed to do with a wet brain like her?'" He shook his head, looked down at the table, and pulled out his phone. "I even tried to text him the video of her pushing the goddamn bucket with all the water spilling out. Fucker didn't even want to look at it."

Dean waved his phone in the air, angrily trying to replay the video. I told him shaking it wouldn't make it go any faster. He called me a dick. Our little human moment didn't seem to have any effect on our new coworker. Hope, absent of any feelings or thoughts, sat there like a scarecrow. I was beginning to think maybe there was something wrong with her, some kind of undiagnosed mental health issue. I looked at Hope to see if anything we were saying was sinking in. Sadly, none of it was.

The video finally started to play. "Look at this shit! You ever seen anyone so stupid before, pushing a bucket like that?" Dean had the phone facing my direction, letting the video speak for itself.

"All right, man. Enough already," I said.

"Look at her. She looks like a fucking ape pushing a wheelbarrow. Look at her! What a dumb broad. What kind of stupid asshole pushes a mop bucket like that?"

"I get it. Just let it go."

Dean wouldn't. He was always a mean prick, but he was excessively mean that day. Behavior like this, replaying the video and pointing directly at Hope while laughing, was something you would get fired for at any reasonable job. There, the environment almost encouraged it. As Dean tried to play the video for a third time, he laughed hysterically.

"What?" I asked.

"Check this out." Dean pointed at Hope as she looked back at the two of us. "Now look at the video. Wide eyes and scraggly limbs—she looks like a lemur." Now that he mentioned it, Hope did, in fact, resemble a lemur, especially when she was bent over, pushing the bucket. The only thing she was missing was a prehensile tail and fluffy ears. "They sent us a friggin' lemur! Ha ha!"

"Enough already, dude!" I said. "You have to be an asshole all the time?"

"What?" said Dean in between fits of laughter. "You know you're thinking the same thing."

"No, I'm not." I was starting to walk out of the room when Dean stopped me.

"Hold up there, chief. You're taking her for the rest of the week. I'm done training the blond lemur."

"But that's your job. You're supposed to train the new workers."

"Not this one. I've tried to get through to her. She's a lost cause. I've got a better chance showing a bowl of oatmeal how to clean the floor." Dean got up to grab his lunch sack from the fridge. "When you go back to work, just walk her around a little. Try to get her to hold a broom without impaling herself while pushing it."

Had it been me Dean was talking about, he would have already been in the back of an ambulance, being rushed to the hospital. "All right, Hope," I said as I walked out of the room. "Let's go."

"Okay," she said. She stood up, closed her magazine politely, and then shadowed me for the rest of the night.

Training Hope to do the most basic of things would be my burden for the remainder of her stay with us. Dean washed his hands completely, stating he would rather smear peanut butter on his naked body and walk through grizzly bear country. I didn't mind working with her at first, but she tended to be absentminded and completely devoid of any life skills any twenty-six-year-old should have possessed. I had worked with less-intelligent people before, but never had I ever worked with a person so unprepared for life.

Since Hope was my burden now, I tried to talk with her and perhaps tried to show her some compassion. Maybe something would sink in. I started out simple: "Where are you from? Do you have any family?" Of course, I asked her about any possible husband or boyfriend just because. Why the hell not? She was still a good-looking girl regardless of her uncanny resemblance to a primate from the island of Madagascar. What I got was a glimpse into the world of an unprepared child.

Hope didn't have any brothers or sisters. She was an only child born to Maye and Thomas Ridgewell. Her father was a top executive at the TSA while her mother was a teacher in another school district. She must have come from money because the trio lived on Long Beach Island. It was a quaint summer destination along the Jersey

Shore. Lots of people lived along the Jersey Shore, but Hope and her parents were from the nice part.

I can't stress this concept enough, people. There are two kinds of Jersey Shore: (1) the rowdy, fist-pumping beach bunnies who live most of the year in hellholes like Staten Island and (2) the sweet, innocent year-round residents who don't treat New Jersey beaches like a porta-potty.

Hope came from the really nice part of the island, where houses started out at more than $1 million. She came from money, a decent amount, from what I could tell. What the hell was she doing working there? In my talks with Hope, I came to discover that her dad died a little over two years ago from lymph node cancer. He had a large life insurance policy, leaving his wife and only daughter in good standing for the remainder of their lives. According to Hope, their house was paid off, which meant her pops took out the best life insurance policy going. Smart guy. Then again, he worked for the TSA, so it was a no-brainer that he had some intelligence. Too bad some of it didn't rub off on his daughter.

Hope's mother died a year ago from a heart attack. I was sure losing her husband contributed to her demise. Hope had no other family, so the estate went to her and her alone. Her parents must have severely sheltered her to keep her safe knowing she wasn't prepared for the real world. *Sheltered* might not be the best choice of word. Locked in a hermetically sealed bomb shelter buried sixty feet in the earth's crust might be a better description.

In truth, Hope appeared to have the same skill set as a junior in high school. She had a driver's license. She had a car. Feeding, bathing, and clothing herself appeared to be the extent of her mechanisms. The clothing part was debatable. Hope looked as if she picked up clothes left in a wrinkled pile each day.

She was always late. I didn't think she ever showed up on time, which was apparently perfectly acceptable for everyone but me. Some days, Hope rolled into work two or three hours late without the slightest notion of any wrongdoing. Under standard work regulations, Hope should have been fired on day 2, but the bosses simply did not care how late she showed up. They all felt sorry for her because she lost her family.

She made childish excuses as to why she couldn't make it on time. "My alarm didn't go off" was used on average about twice a week. I mentioned numerous times how she could maybe get a new alarm clock with all the money she had. "Why would I buy a new alarm clock when I have one already?" was her usual response. "The one I have is in the shape of an elephant, and they're my favorite animal!"

Hope was out one day each week, and she would claim she got lost. I could possibly buy getting lost a couple of times during the first month. Maybe she was new to the area, or maybe her GPS was as busted as her alarm clock. But she used the lost excuse all the time. How the fuck did someone get lost driving to work and still have a job for almost two years? I mean, it was not like she was long-hauling it out of state to an unfamiliar location.

Now let's talk about her actual work habits. In full disclosure, I will reveal that Hope had no abnormalities prohibiting her from physical labor. Her hands were of the proper dimensions, and there were no missing digits or skin grafts. Hope walked fine and without any ailments or otherwise limiting restrictions. She wasn't blind or deaf or clubfooted. But she couldn't do a lick of work to save her hide. The mop bucket incident was just the beginning.

It was like she had never had to do any form of physical labor before. I was sure her parents had made her clean her room, and if they hadn't, then shame on them. She kept screwing everything up each time I told her to do something. She dropped anything she laid her hands on as if her fingers were smeared with olive oil. From brooms, to mops, and to trash bags—anything she touched ended up on the floor like she was a little kid.

After attempting to train her for an entire week, I sided with Dean on her abilities. Had she been born any species other than human, Hope would've succumbed to Darwin's rules of natural selection within the first week of her existence. I pictured her as a ring-tailed lemur waving from the top of a tree line to a harpy eagle. I could imagine her saying, "You look hungry, Mr. Eagle. Why not pick me up with your sharp claws and take me to a mountaintop for a quiet picnic?" Had she been born a seal in Southeast Alaska, Hope would have tried to hug the killer whale before it devoured her whole. I had seen squirrels with more life skills than her.

I don't want you to get the wrong idea about Hope. She wasn't a bad person or even stupid. She just wasn't given the proper skills to survive in the real world. True, she was brain-dead in terms of normal, day-to-day operations. If she hadn't been coddled, she might have led a so-called normal life. When her parents learned she was less than stellar in the common sense department, they should've helped her instead of placing her in a bubble. Once her parents died, the bubble popped, leaving her exposed and unprepared for the future.

After working with her for about two weeks, I gave up on training her. Besides, Dean was supposed to train her. Why was I worried? Her lack of cleaning skills would become evident within days. Her work was abysmal, if I must say. The teachers complained, but once they found out she was an adult orphan, they felt sorry for her. Everyone left her alone to do whatever work she produced. It was kind of like giving a gold star to the kid in class who clearly didn't know their ABCs, but the teacher wanted them to feel special anyway.

I would say that was the perfect analogy for Hope Ridgewell's time as a janitor. This person should've been clubbed to death long ago by the hand of evolution, but she still managed to skimp by. People felt sorry for her, and to be honest, what happened to her did suck. For two years, Hope came to work and was given a pass because people felt sorry for her. Then one day, she stopped showing up completely. She was in on a Tuesday night, then never came back. There was no call, and she was a no-show for the rest of the week. Two weeks later, the board of education was forced to terminate her because they couldn't get ahold of her. She simply vanished.

Nobody knew what happened to Hope. One of the bosses said she never returned any phone calls, so they paid her for her last few days, and that was it. I checked the local paper for any info on car crashes or weird accidents and found nothing. There was no obituary or headline detailing a sloppily dressed woman driving around in a daze. It was like she disappeared. Not that anyone missed her. She had no one looking out for her. She was ultimately alone in the world.

My imagination ran wild with possible end case scenarios for Hope. Maybe she was abducted by aliens, but they couldn't figure her out, so they dropped her off on the closest planet. Perhaps Hope fell in love with a gas station attendant named Spike when she stopped to ask for directions, and they raised a family of petrol-smelling, dim-witted children.

Unfortunately, something bad probably happened to her; and since she didn't have any family, the state got all her money. That was what happened to people who were alone in the world, unfortunately. It was an unthinkable end, but it did happen. You would read about it in the newspaper from time to time. Old or young, it didn't matter. The house ended up in auction, and the pets, left alone without someone to feed them, ended up dying. It was sad. It truly was.

The optimist in me had hope for Hope, but the pessimist in me was a more reasonable person, and he believed that bad things happened and that there was nothing I could do about it. I was sure the job had her address and banking info. Someone from HR could've driven over to her house to see if there was a For Sale sign on the lawn.

Whatever happened to her was a mystery, but then again, so were a lot of things in life. It was just the way it went sometimes. I was sorry things didn't work out for Hope. This place was full of sob stories from workers who left without so much as a phone call, but life always pushed on with or without you in it.

CHAPTER 16

Chicken Neck

In the public school system, there were three areas considered as environmental services. There was the broom pushers, the grass cutters, and the wrench turners. I fell into the broom pushers subdivision. There, you would find the rusty, shabbily dressed individuals who possessed a massive key ring.

Most janitors are nice people as long as you don't change our routine. Never change a janitor's routine without first consulting them. Detrimental things happen if you alter their day unannounced. We're nice people. Really, we are. Just don't mess with our routine.

Grass cutters did what their title claimed they did. These people achieved Mach 4 speeds on tanklike mowers with deep tans and Oakley shades from the 1990s. They were usually wearing earbuds, playing Nickelback or some other crappy band. They, too, were nice enough people once you got past the dried grass, sweat stains, and faint aroma of Roundup Weed and Grass Killer. I've known quite a few grass cutters in my day. They were a little pretentious, but that came with mowing down acres of Kentucky bluegrass in more than ninety degrees heat. You wouldn't catch me on a mower, doing that job. It was too fucking hot out there.

Finally, we had the wrench turners. We didn't associate with the wrench turners. Only under dire circumstances did the broom pushers and grass cutters speak to the wrench turners. There are some rules of environmental services you won't understand, and I'm fine with that. Just know that the wrench turners thought their shit didn't stink. Some of them anyway.

Most wrench turners were very skilled at their trade. I would have been lost if you had told me to rebuild a boiler or solder miles of copper tubing. The issue was, most of them were snobs because they went to a trade school or had a locksmith license. That was the shit that drove me insane about this job. We were all subdivided into different classifications and, ultimately, different pay scales. This ruined jobs because no one ventured outside of their rank. No one wanted to break down class barriers and storm the Bastille.

But I was sure most wrench turners were solid dudes and dudettes, except for one guy. He made the hall of fame for professional fuckups on the first ballot. This guy would forever be known as the Hillbilly Handyman. I give you Chicken Neck. Hank Jefferson Davis, otherwise known as Chicken Neck, was a rebel in more ways than one. I say this with all sincerity. Chicken Neck was a good old boy. He was the redneck with a wrench, as one coworker called him. He claimed he could fix anything, a claim which was later debunked. It turned out he was one of the worst wrench turners who ever turned a wrench. Everything he touched, he destroyed. I'm not talking about a little collateral damage. Think of condemned areas like the abandoned fields surrounding Chernobyl.

Chicken Neck came to us from the deep South, and I mean deep South. I can't remember the name of his hometown in Tennessee, but it sounded quite rural. It was a place where they didn't have running water, but they did have a Walmart and a Stuckey's. Without such luxuries as indoor plumbing, a person must rely on their hands to perform daily necessities. Instead of roofing shingles, the town's inhabitants used an oversized blue tarp. It did the same thing, as Chicken Neck used to say. If they had no money to fix a woodburning stove, why not use an old oil drum to cook the local game you shot a few hours ago? It was not like motor oil had harmful chemicals in it.

Chicken Neck moved up north a few years ago after a bitter divorce. "She was smothering me too dang much," he said one day as he stuck an entire can of Skoal Wintergreen in his bottom lip. "I'll never be with a woman who says I can't go skeet shootin' every weekend. That's crossing a line, if you ask me." He usually ended every conversation with the line, "If you ask me." Chicken Neck found ways to bring up his hometown in daily conversation. "You know, back where I'm from, we don't have cellular devices. Ain't no dang cell phone towers in the mountains. We'd just holler out the front door down to Meryl's or Bongo's trailer to see what's happenin'."

Once a year, we had a new employee orientation, usually during Christmas break. Management mixed the orientations with basic safety classes, which was a smart move given the caliber of employees the management tended to hire. We're not talking about intelligent life-forms here. Think single-celled amoebas with brooms and hammers. I attended a gaggle of these seminars, and not once did I learn a goddamn thing worth writing about. How many times can one be taught the same thing before they're legally permitted to go on a rampage? We were told it was mandatory to attend, yet half the employees called in sick. I had to start saving some sick days for the end of the year because I couldn't do it anymore.

Each new employee was far worse than the last. I didn't know how they topped themselves each year; but management dug these losers out of the trash pile, dusted them off, and handed them a uniform. The old-timers, such as myself, listened to the bosses rave about the new guy as we giggled with glee. "I'm telling you, this new guy is great. I've never seen such ambition and skill all in one person! You watch. This new guy will be a boss one day." The sad truth was, the new guy they were raving about would get fired a month later because they caught him stealing tools.

So back to Chicken Neck. One year, we gathered at one of the high school's auditoriums to meet the new workers. Mind you, this department had three work assignments who wore three different-colored work shirts. If you stood in front of the congregation, you would witness a sea of red shirts, purple shirts, and brown shirts all neatly divided. Not a single shirt color was out of place. All the grass cutters were on one side, the broom pushers on the other side, and the wrench turners in the middle.

When Chicken Neck made his grand entrance, he shocked the shit out of everyone. He came flying into the room with a spit bottle in one hand and a Dr Pepper bottle in the other, saying, "Hey, everybody! How y'all doin'?" The whole room took notice of this new face, complete with cutoff jeans and cutoff sleeves. It was the end of December. I didn't know how he wasn't freezing his balls off.

There stood Chicken Neck, a gangly man with a soda bottle in each hand. My first impression of him was, where the hell were his teeth? He was missing quite a few of them. The man in front of us did not have dental insurance in whatever backwoods community he migrated from. His chin protruded, giving him the look of Popeye the Sailor Man, only lacking the spinach-charged muscles. "My name's Hank, but most folks call me Chicken Neck. Feel free to call me Chicken Neck if y'all like!"

Chicken Neck had sped into the auditorium so fast he stopped the room's many conversations. The crowd eagerly awaited his next move. Would he start whistling "Dixie" as he stood there gawking at us? Did his next sentence involve asking a pretty lady if she would like to square dance? Chicken Neck proceeded to walk toward the bosses lined up on the side of the auditorium to shake their hands. Great, he was an ass-kisser too. Like we didn't have enough of those collecting a pension around here.

Not to be gross, but have you ever wondered if someone who holds a tobacco spit bottle in one hand and a soda in the other ever mixes up the order? You know, the bottle collecting used chewing tobacco spittle has been mistaken for an ice-cold soda at least once. It's bound to happen. That was all that my mind kept playing on repeat upon watching him.

Although he looked and acted like the fifth member of the Blue Collar Comedy Tour, Chicken Neck was not like most new hires. He had manners. I had seen hundreds of employees come to these meetings with maybe only 5 percent introducing themselves. Most dummies walked in, sat down, and buried their faces in a phone until it was time to leave. Chicken Neck walked the perimeter and shook all available hands in his path. Mind you, he shifted his spit cup to the same hand as the Dr Pepper bottle, but at least he was a gentleman. He dug into everyone's conversations as he made the rounds: "Hi there! I'm Hank, but you just call me Chicken Neck. Everyone I know does!" or "Hey! My name's Chicken Neck! What's yours? You look like a Steve to me. Is your name Steve?"

I was already casting judgment before I was introduced. Every stereotypical redneck joke I had ever heard popped into my head while watching Chicken Neck work the room. Any minute now, I was expecting to see a three-hundred-pound hog dash across the room with the Dukes of Hazzard doing burnouts behind it. An entire tribe of Hatfields and McCoys would start shooting muzzleloaders at one another from behind massive copper moonshine stills.

Before long, Hank ventured over to my seat. "How's it goin', man? I'm Chicken Neck, if you haven't heard by now. And your name is?" I told him my name as he shook my hand up and down with such force. It was as if he was using my arm to pump water from a cistern buried deep underground. He damn near pulled my shoulder out of the socket. I figured he would move along after saying hello, but he hung around for a few a seconds. "Hey, where you from? You look familiar to me. I can't place it, but you dang sure look like someone I went to school wit'."

"I'm sorry," I said. "We've never met before."

"You sure 'bout that?" said Chicken Neck. "You got one of them faces to me, like I've seen you before." He stood there with a tilted head, searching his memory. He wouldn't leave until I gave him a full bio sheet, underlining my credentials. He was sure we had been in contact with each other at some point in time. "Damn," said Chicken Neck. "You look so dang familiar." He stood there, perplexed beyond belief. It was a good thirty seconds before he broke off his bewilderment. He just stood there, holding two plastic bottles in his left hand, with his weight shifted to one side, staring at me in disbelief.

"Oh well!" said Chicken Neck. He threw his right hand up toward the ceiling, then let it fall to his side. "Dadgum it if you don't look like someone I used to hang 'round wit'! I for sure thought you was in my life at one point or another before today. Never mind, bro.

I'll catch up wit' cha later. Bye now!" Off he went to shake the hand of another new coworker with excitement.

Let me state just for the record that I didn't trust new jacks. A new jack, as told to me by Tyrell Jones, was a new coworker whom you did not associate with until you knew for sure they were not a rat. Only after a long, investigative inquiry into their work behavior could one fully trust a new hire. If past practice held true, you must perform a full-body pat-down and x-ray scan before trusting anyone. Hell, I had been screwed by people I had known for years, people I had been to the house of for barbecues and the like. It took a good four months of constant monitoring for me to determine one's trustworthiness. In other words, this place fucked me up so much that I didn't trust anyone.

Chicken Neck could've been a mole, a Southern fried catfish mole wearing a wire under his way too short shorts. Bosses loved to hide secret double agents on a crew. Maybe Chicken Neck was a rat fink, a narc sent to spill his guts to an eager overlord. One dude whom I spent an entire school year with turned canary on me for using the school's Wi-Fi during a break. (Why should I have burned my data when I could stream YouTube for free?)

Having a coworker whom you could trust in this cutthroat business was a rarity. DTA meant don't trust anyone, and I was wary of any unsanctioned new jack, especially if that coworker was overly nice. Call me paranoid if you like, but if a person was too friendly too quick, it was time to put up the guard position.

Whenever I met a new coworker, I evaluated their appearance to solidify my assumptions. Don't give me the judging a book by its cover routine. This was the real world. You mean to tell me you've never looked at someone and said, "Man, that guy looks like a sneaky fuck," or, "Jesus, look at that outfit. I'll bet she's a real whore!" Chicken Neck looked like a deluxe model country boy who had relations with his sister. His mullet was sprinkled with just the right amount of dandruff. His tanned skin had the same color as his tool belt, which signified that he had spent many years fishing by a muddy lake.

Speaking of his tool belt, it held an unholy amount of duct tape. One roll would have sufficed, but not for Mr. Fix It. He had tape for days in all sizes, colors, and textures. Instead of tools per se, I saw cable ties, wood glue, and a dip cup in his tool belt. At no time did I see things like a screwdriver or even a wrench in there. The name Half-Assed Hank stuck to him like a thick, seasoned musk.

Let's talk about Chicken Neck's clothing, or lack thereof. The only place I had seen shorter shorts was at a strip club, and not a good strip club either. Think glory hole in the bathroom kind of joint with bullet holes in the marquee. Nut huggers were what one would call them. His work shirt, which was new when he received it, was already tattered with the sleeves cut off. This seemed impossible given the fact that Chicken Neck had only started working a week before I met him. How did one achieve a weathered shirt in less time than it took God to create the heavens and the earth?

If we made our way down to his feet, we would see a very broken-in pair of brown work boots with ominous stains. Those stains might have been dip cup spits that never made it to the bottle. I noticed more duct tape strapped around the left boot, holding the sole in place.

I was no tattoo aficionado, but I knew prison ink when I saw it. Chicken Neck had multiple faded tattoos on his oak-colored skin. I couldn't decipher them all, but I did notice the appearance of several women's names on both upper biceps. Beverly looked to be the newest, followed by Joyce, then Beth. This indicated that Beverly was the most current love interest in Chicken Neck's life. Then I noticed a fourth word: *sticky*. Why anyone would have the word *sticky* tattooed on them was beyond my comprehension, but I was guessing it was a really faded Stacey. I hoped it was a well-faded Stacey. If not, I didn't think I wanted to know who Sticky was or how she earned her nickname.

Other classy tattoos included cartoon characters engaged in shall we say reckless activity. I didn't think Mr. Disney ever imagined a time when Minnie would be involved in a three-way with Donald Duck and Daisy Duck. The Tasmanian Devil was a violent character for sure, but to see him holding Bugs Bunny's severed, bloody head was something that still haunted my dreams. Don't even ask what

Elmer Fudd was doing to Tweety Bird. I can't repeat it without blessing myself three times.

Chicken Neck also had a perforated line tattooed around the circumference of his neck with the words, "Cut here," written above it. There was not much I could say about this tattoo other than the fact that it looked very old. Why anyone hadn't taken him up on the offer yet was puzzling.

I observed the new wrench turner known as Chicken Neck for several weeks. He gave me the heebie-jeebies from the start. First off, most Southerners didn't like Yankees to begin with. Every true Southern boy had a gripe with the North ever since the Appomattox Court House. Take a trip down I-95 through the Carolinas and Georgia. If you've got a New York or New Jersey license plate, you can expect to be harassed nonstop. Yet Chicken Neck held no grudges. Not once did he slap me in the face with a leather glove, challenging me to a duel. He did, however, still insist he knew me from somewhere.

The next time I saw Hank after orientation, he stopped me in the hallway to ask a dire question: "Hey, buddy! You sure you and me never met before?" He took a fresh tin of Skoal Long Cut from his belt, slicing the wrapped sides with a pocketknife as he awaited my response.

"I don't think so," I said. "Never seen you before."

"Huh," said Chicken Neck. He systematically opened the tobacco container while in critical thought. "I could'a sweared you and me was on a double date years back in Johnson City, TN. You ever been to Johnson City? Nice little place. Big meth problem, though. Never touched the stuff myself. Always been a PBR and spittin' kinda man! You catchin' my drift?" I was in the middle of explaining how I had never been to Tennessee when he interrupted me to continue his speech. "'Course, I have smoked a li'l ragweed pot now and again," said Chicken Neck. He laughed audibly while packing a wad of spearmint-flavored brown tobacco.

"Nope," I said. "Never been to that town ever."

"Man, you done look just like this guy who played my wingman on a double date." Chicken Neck was struggling to speak with the golf-ball-sized tobacco plug settling into his bottom lip. It didn't take long for it to get snug since his bottom teeth were missing. After a few seconds of tobacco juice gathering, Chicken Neck spoke again. "I know! You used to work at the Piggly Wiggly in Pikesville. You was down there years ago, working the seafood counter, right?"

I denied working at any Piggly Wiggly regardless of its location. Chicken Neck was not convinced. "That's it, man! I knowed it was you. Dang. It's been damn near eight years since I been to Pikesville. They got this little burger shack called Sebastian's, and they sell these french fried potato skins with mayo and sea salt mixed together. Boy, you ever eaten at Sebastian's with them french fries?" I was beginning to wonder if Chicken Neck's brain stem was connected to his spinal cord. He finally ventured off, leaving me to wonder how many more times I would be approached in the future.

I never felt threatened in any way by Chicken Neck. More like hassled. Any time I saw him working on a repair, he would stop tinkering and would make his way over to me. I saw him on the roof of my building one day as he waved aggressively to me from high above. A minute later, he shimmed down the ladder, practically falling to his death in the process. Chicken Neck followed me into the building, yelling at me to stop so he could catch up. He stopped working on a roof leak to ask me a serious question about soft drinks: "Are you hip to Yoo-hoo?" he asked. "I can't drink the stuff if it's a hot day, but I'll swallow down some if it ain't too hot out. Dr Pepper, though, now that's the stuff I can't get enough of. I can do without Sunkist or A&W, but dang it, I need my Dr Pepper!"

I said I didn't drink soda, to which he replied, "Are you crazy? You don't know what you're missin'! I grew up on soda pop. My mama used to put it in my sippy cup when I was a little baby." That explained a lot regarding the missing molars. The topic quickly turned to one's favorite salty snacks, which Chicken Neck was equally well-versed in. "Slim Jims are my favorite of all time. I don't like them new ones with the cheese in 'em. Have you ever had pork rinds with cheese dust on them? Combine them with a few hard-boiled eggs and you got yourself a meal and a half!"

The entire time he was rattling off snack foods, I saw a stream of water dripping from the ceiling. Whatever he was doing to repair the roof was not working in the least bit. In fact, I noted that the leak was minor before he got his hands on it. Now you could have taken a shower under the stream. I pointed it out to Chicken Neck before he started listing his favorite candy bars in order of the most to least chocolaty. "Oh, that?" he said, glancing over his shoulder to the torrent of water coming from the ceiling. "That's nothin'. I'll get that taken care of faster than a jackrabbit eats a carrot." Off he went.

I walked away not so much angry but astonished on how this guy got the job in the first place. Most handyman jobs required you to fix something in front of a boss before getting the job. You know, so they would know you could do the job before they started paying you. Maybe Chicken Neck embellished his mechanical skills a smidge on the interview. Over the next few months, I would learn that Chicken Neck was only skilled in the art of conversation, not building maintenance. The roof, by the way, was never fixed. The leak got significantly worse the next day, turning the hallway into a class III rapids.

I can't tell you the number of times I saw Chicken Neck half-assing something instead of fixing it properly. A hole in the wall caused by a disgruntled high schooler usually required screen mesh and Sheetrock and perhaps a little matching paint to make it look nice. Chicken Neck thought it wise to smear wet newspaper and glue in the hole, kind of like a paper-mache. It lasted two days. Replacing a broken pencil sharpener on a countertop usually required screws. Chicken Neck used duct tape from his collection. He used the camo duct tape in an attempt to disguise his short cut, thinking maybe nobody would notice. In his defense, the pencil sharpener stayed upright for a good four days before coming undone.

Over the course of six months, I saw Chicken Neck almost weekly at my post. Eventually, he stopped asking if we had ever met before. His new round of questioning was based primarily on vehicles. "I noticed you drive a four-wheel truck," he said one day. "Tell me somethin'. You ever take that puppy off roadin' out by the Sarco pits?" He was holding a small motor in his hand, which was possibly from some larger machine he wrecked while trying to repair.

"No, I don't do that kind of thing," I said. "It's too expensive to fix if I break something."

"Well, that's half the fun of wheelin', dude!" Chicken Neck's eyes opened like a boy who had found his dad's porno stash. "You ramp that sucker up over a hill and crash her down onto a pile of rocks. Best thing ever!"

"But I need my truck to get to work," I said. "I can't break it like that. I'll never be able to get it fixed."

Chicken Neck, still holding the dilapidated motor, smiled wide with his eyes closed. He placed his grease-covered hand on my left shoulder and leaned in close. "Listen. If you ever need someone to work on your vehicle, don't hesitate to ask. I can fix anything with wheels, especially trucks." He pointed to his truck, which was parked outside the window, smiling affectionately. "Ya see that glorious pick 'em up out there? She's my pride and joy. I've had her since senior year of high skool. I fix her all the time. You jus' tell what you need fixin' on your rig, and I'll set ya straight. No charge neither."

I looked out the window to a helpless pile of metal shit, counting no less than seven spray-painted colors. It looked like it had been hit by a land mine, then was fused back together with the aid of rebel flag bumper stickers. I thanked Chicken Neck for his offer, saying I would consider it next time I took my truck out swamping.

I might have been giving Chicken Neck the business here, but I felt it was warranted. If you worked in a place where safety was paramount, say, a school with hundreds of children, nothing should have been jerry-rigged. Duct tape was not a suitable replacement for screws and nails. The last thing a parent needed to hear was that their child was burned alive because someone didn't install the fire alarm correctly. Can you imagine some dude who looked like a methed-out Ernest P. Worrell fucking up a simple repair, causing massive casualties?

It might not have sounded like it, but I took my job seriously. I didn't want your kid getting sick. If the janitor didn't clean the bathrooms properly, it could lead to the development of a norovirus. That was why we used bleach. Same went for mopping all the time. Germs were everywhere in a public school. If you had several hundred people using the same area, it needed to be cleaned right. Cruise ships got norovirus outbreaks all the time. That was what happened when a thousand people charged the buffet line, sneezing and burping all over the Caesar salad tongs. I didn't want that to happen to your kids. I might have been a sarcastic prick, but I was no monster.

But people like Chicken Neck gave people like me a bad name. Instead of fixing something right, he would rather walk around for an hour, asking people who their favorite NASCAR driver was. The bosses thought Chicken Neck was the greatest thing since Cheerios. They saw past the lewd tattoos and spit cup, mesmerized by his gift of gab. What Chicken Neck lacked in basic handyman skills he more than made up for in jibber-jabber. He could talk his way out of anything by diverting attention away from the topic.

You would think the bosses saw that everything he did was a complete disaster, but nope. Chicken Neck schmoozed his way out of trouble by deflecting the conversation. "Hey, man. I'm sorry for not fixin' that machine. Ya see, my dang girlfriend keeps calling me, bothering me all the time. You ever get that? You ever have some woman calling you, pissin' in your ear all day long?" Once Chicken Neck diverted the boss's attention, he ran with it. "Speaking of women, you check out that new teacher in room 133? Whoo, doggie! Is she a fox or what? If you ask me, I'd stay for detention any day of the week! You feel me?" The bosses were like energetic kittens transfixed by a red laser pointer.

Chicken Neck could do no wrong regardless of his work record. Several children were burned from a water fountain when he replaced the cold water valve with a hot one. Instead of a crisp, cool drink, the kids got a mouthful of scalding H_2O. Chicken Neck claimed the manufacturer put the wrong part in the box. "Ya know what, that pipe looked funky to me. I didn't want to say nuthin', but that part sure did look like a hot water pipe. I bet some dope in the assembly plant put a hot water pipe in the box instead of a cold water pipe. Yep, must've been what happened all right."

Were the bosses too stupid to know that was not how general plumbing worked? You bet they were. They believed Chicken Neck even though you had to be a complete moron to think pipes were made that way. What really happened was, Chicken Neck took out the faulty pipe and uncapped a hot water line that was installed years ago, when the school was first built. The original engineers installed hot and cold water lines on every water source. Chicken Neck attached a new pipe to the hot water instead of the cold. The only thing he did right was install a new pipe, which I would bet my life on was secured with duct tape. Too bad it was pumping out water hot enough to brew cappuccinos.

Then came the ladder incident. A simple repair of a light fixture turned into a lesson in human anatomy. This was a different kind of faux pas, one Chicken Neck didn't plan on having in front of thirty youngsters. While dangling precariously seven feet in the air, Chicken Neck's manhood slipped out. That's right, a set of hairy testicles obeyed the laws of physics, swinging pendulum-like above a group of unsuspecting kindergarteners.

Those poor children got a view of Chicken Neck's balls while he crimped wires on a broken ceiling light. He had to fix the light in the middle of the room above the show-and-tell rug during storytime. Why he couldn't wait until they went to lunch was beyond me. What began as a book reading turned into a puppet show starring the carefree Chicken Neck, who told the kids, "Whoops! Don't mind my yam bag, boys and girls. It won't hurt ya none!"

Needless to say, it's extremely hard to keep your job when you flash your genitals to minors. All thirty kindergarteners went home to ask their mommies and daddies what a yam bag was. The administrators immediately ran damage control, saying the worker in question suffered from a medical condition. Chicken Neck was placed on suspension shortly after the debacle made the rounds on social media groups. The parents of those terrified youngsters started a conversation on the school's Facebook page, calling for his dismissal. He was officially fired two weeks later.

I don't have much else to say about Chicken Neck. Had his shorts been two inches longer, he might still be employed. Or maybe if he had worn underwear that day, none of this would have happened. Who knows how many more projects Chicken Neck would have botched before he got booted? At least no one got killed from one of his shoddy repairs, not yet anyway. I still find ripped, worn-out camo-colored duct tape on broken faucets from time to time. If I ever start chewing tobacco or dipping chaw, I'll raise my spit cup to toast a man who still thinks we met years ago in the great state of Tennessee. Goodbye, Chicken Neck. May your dip cup never run over.

CHAPTER 17

Ms. Francesca

The relationship between a school janitor and the rest of the staff was a delicate affiliation. It was a bond that relied heavily on trust, honesty, and above all, respect. Respect was something you needed at any job. Most teachers respected janitors, and we, the cleaners of the night, passed the same respect back to them. As an evening janitor, I worked when most of the staff had left for the day. Like two trains passing in the night, we saw one another on our journey, exchanging waves silently in the hall. Just imagine a scene from a factory where one crew clocked in and a separate crew clocked out. But some people were just plain cunts, and they fucked with the delicate spiderweb that was the public school system.

Let's have a biology lesson, shall we? Think of the public school system as a model of the human body. Different parts have different tasks. The backbone, or spine, of any school are the janitors. We do the heavy lifting in more ways than one. Without a spine, a body can't stand up. As a support beam, the janitors are critical to the overall system. They keep things upright.

Think of bus drivers as the legs who move the body forward. They take the students where they need to go. The stomach is a euphemism for the cafeteria and school lunches, which constantly provide food to the body so it can grow up big and strong. A school nurse is a liver, healing the aches and pains. I would rather not say what department is considered the anus of the public school body. Use your imagination for that part of the lesson.

Teachers, however, are the heart of any school system. They are the beat that give lifeblood to the rest of the body. Without a heart, the body will not survive, and I truly believe teachers are the core of any successful public school. It takes love to be a teacher nowadays with all the budget cutbacks. They do it because they care, not for the paycheck.

But sometimes, an organ could go bad; and if teachers were the heart of a school, then Ms. Francesca would be the diseased, rotting black heart in need of a transplant. Gianna Francesca, a twenty-four-year-old art teacher, was a stone-cold bitch. There's no sugarcoating this one, my dear reader. Have you ever seen someone with a resting bitch face? That was Ms. Francesca. Not that she was ugly or morbidly deformed, but she always had the look of someone who would ask for a manager anytime she had a meal out. She was the kind of person who thought their shit didn't stink. Pardon my improper speech.

I'm sure you have the same person at your job. Every job has at least one. They are haughty to the tenth power of haughty! Designer clothes and perfectly manicured nails—they have the whole nine yards with the attitude of a chronically pissed off old lady hellbent on ruining everyone's day around her.

I met Ms. Francesca while working many years ago. The day shift janitor called in sick, so I had to fill in. The day janitor opened the school for the rest of the staff, turning off the alarm while turning on the lights. So there I was, pulling into an empty parking lot about twenty minutes ahead of my shift. I parked in a spot away from the main parking row. The parking lot was desolate, not a soul in sight. As I got out of my truck, I saw a black BMW flying into the parking lot, hauling ass. It was an M3 series too with tinted windows and nice rims. The car's tires squealed as it screamed into the lot, stopping a few feet from my bumper. I jumped back a little, thinking this car was going to mow me down.

The driver's tinted window rolled down. "You're in my spot," said the woman. Her dark sunglasses covered her eyes, but I could tell she was mad as hell.

"Huh?" I said.

"You're parked in my spot!" she yelled. "That's where I park. Get out of my spot!"

"Excuse me?" I said. I was holding my lunch in my hands, trying to regrip it. "There are no assigned spots here. What…what are you talking about?"

"I'm the goddamned art teacher. I always park there. This is where I've parked for months! Move that hunk of shit out of my spot now!"

She could've been the queen of England for all I cared. I fired back my response while pointing to the remaining hundred or so empty spaces. "And I'm the janitor. So what? There's plenty of spaces around. Back up into another one."

She pulled her Christian Dior sunglasses down, revealing narrow, sinister eyes. "How dare you speak to me like that?" I got my first glimpse of her resting bitch face, one I would come to see each time I saw her from then on out. "I'm a teacher at this school. I said move your truck, or else!"

"Or else what, you'll paint me a sad picture? Don't yell at me!" I was taking a wild guess here, but the painting a picture line only enraged her more.

"Ugh!" she said. "Fuck you, you stupid janitor!" She immediately threw her car into reverse, burning rubber as she jammed on the gas. Off she went to park in one of the numerous other spots. Heavens to Betsy, she parked a $67,000 brand-new car near my reasonably priced, well-used work truck.

I entered the building, turned off the alarm, and started to walk the mile, as janitors called it. It was the act of turning all the lights on while checking out the building. I was steaming inside while flipping light switches. Who the fuck did she think she was? It was not like I took the only available handicapped spot or blocked a fire hydrant. I was alone at this point, opening the building without anyone else inside yet. I heard the front door close, and there she was. As I came around the back hallway, I heard someone mumbling. "Stupid fucking janitor. Fuck him." A pair of stiletto heels clicked on the terrazzo floor. It was a fast-paced clicking. "The goddamn lights aren't even on yet!"

All I could hear was this tiny, mouselike voice mumbling obscenities. She sounded like a high-pitched Eminem cursing in anger. As she turned the corner, I saw what most people would refer to as a Real Housewives of Beverly Hills wannabe. Matching her domino-patterned designer handbag was a long black quarter coat. Then those wretched heels, about six inches in height, screeched to a halt as she noticed me.

"Excuse me, janitor! How come the lights aren't on? The other janitor has them on by now."

"I have a name. Don't call me janitor, okay?"

"I don't give a fuck what your name is!" she said. "Turn the fucking lights on! I'm not tripping because you're too stupid and don't know how to turn lights on."

"I'm going as fast as I can, lady." Mind you, only half the lights were off in the hallway. Schools always kept half a set on in case of emergencies, so it was not like she was stumbling down a pitch-black corridor. She sped past me as if I had some contagious airborne virus and was wheezing all over her. As she passed, I heard her expensive heels click on the tile at a rapid pace. I tried to be nice by warning her of the danger. "You shouldn't be wearing heels on this floor," I said.

"What?" Again, with a befuddled tone, she spoke. "What did you say to me?"

"I said you shouldn't wear stiletto heels on this kind of floor. You're going to slip and fall. Terrazzo floors are notoriously slippery if you wear a high-arched, off-balance kind of shoe."

"The day I need fashion advice from a scummy janitor is the day I throw myself off this fucking building," she said. Little Ms. Devil Wears Prada took off down the hall, almost sprinting.

"Suit yourself, lady."

Ten paces down the hall, her feet gave way. She collapsed like a baby giraffe taking its first steps. Ms. Francesca let out a shocked cry as she tumbled to the ground. She hit hard too. "Told ya," I said. She struggled to get vertical again, her arms and legs jutting in all directions. I started to walk toward her, feeling slightly sorry for my remark, but she let out a banshee scream.

"Get the fuck away from me, you stupid…stupid—"

"Stupid janitor?" I said. "Is that the word you're looking for?"

"Turn the goddamn lights on, asshole! I fell because I can't see in this dark-ass hallway!"

"No, you fell because you were jogging in stilettos."

"Whatever! It's all your fault. I tripped, getting my new Christian Dior coat all filthy, and it's all because you're too stupid and don't know how to turn the fucking lights on!"

In my line of work, being yelled at was something you came to accept. People in the service industry shared my pain. What this broad did to me was completely uncalled for, and I wasn't going to take it. First, the parking lot, and now this?

"Eat shit, lady! How's that?" I said, then turned around to walk away. An audible grunt flew out as she finally made it to her feet.

"Argh! I'm reporting you to the superintendent for this!" Ms. Francesca did an about-face, her expensive heels clacking as she trotted away. She walked slower now, trying not to face-plant once more. Now you know why I called her a cunt a few paragraphs before.

As the day progressed, the daily routine started to flow. The rest of the staff began coming in. The time before the busses arrived was precious to people who worked in a school. It was the calm before the storm, an hour or so of downtime ahead of the noise. I knew a few of the teachers at my post, and we normally talked before the kids came in. Most of the teaching staff were not like Ms. Francesca at all. You could talk to them without fear of being screamed at. While consulting them, I had concluded that Ms. Gianna Francesca was hated by all.

I spoke with three teachers whom I usually saw when I covered the day shift. We got on the topic of Ms. Prissy, a topic of much discussion in the teachers' social circle. They couldn't stand her either. While I was speaking to them in the hall, one of them called out to another teacher in her classroom across the way. "Hey, Tammy, he met Gianna today!" I heard a laugh from inside the classroom.

"Ha! How'd that go, huh?" All three of them cackled with glee.

"That bitch told me I wasn't a good teacher," said Mrs. Rouple. "She questioned my grading scale at a faculty meeting last year. I pulled her aside after the meeting and said, 'What the hell do you know about grading? You're an art teacher.'" All three teachers let out a giggle.

Not being a teacher, I was left out of their joke. It seemed there was a hierarchy among the teaching staff, a pecking order among the pack. Core curriculum teachers, such as math, English language arts, science, and social studies, had beef with elective teachers. Things like music, art, computers, etc. weren't as important as the big four classes in the eyes of some teachers. See? Even in the world of teaching, there was a cool kids table in the lunchroom.

I decided to pump other teachers for info on Ms. Francesca. If she was such a bitch, I was sure others had more info about her. It turned out that she made enemies right from the start. She pissed everyone off a year ago when she first got hired. She was the type of uppity teacher who criticized her colleagues' teaching style. If you were the new girl at work, you didn't make waves, acting like you were hot shit. Ms. Francesca opened her mouth on numerous occasions, claiming she was better than everyone else. That was a no-no in a profession where word traveled fast.

It didn't help that she came to work dressed like she robbed Barneys on Madison Avenue. "What kind of teacher dresses in Prada," said Ms. Rouple, "especially an art teacher? Aren't they supposed to wear smocks and get paint on their outfits? I look at her and I don't see a spot on her!" Ms. Rouple had a good point. Most art teachers got down and dirty when they taught. I doubted Ms. Francesca ever had clay under her perfectly manicured nails. Other teachers I spoke with talked about her wardrobe constantly. "I've never seen her in the same outfit twice," said the gym teacher. "Who does she think she is, Vanna White?"

Several teachers talked about her black BMW with envy in their eyes. It was a sweet-ass ride, no doubt, but an entry-level salary for a teacher could hardly afford a BMW car note and expensive clothes. I ran into a math teacher during the lunch period, and she talked about her first few years of teaching. "I sure as hell couldn't afford a Beamer my first year on the job," she said. "I've been here nine years, and I still drive a seventeen-year-old Honda Civic. I can't afford a BMW, even a used one. Where does she get the money for this stuff?"

By the end of the day, I had made the rounds to get the gossip on the very hated Ms. Francesca. I needed more info, though. How did she get the bankroll to afford all these flashy things? I knew where I had to go to get my answers: the front office. If you ever wanted to get dirt on someone in a school system, you went to the secretaries. These ladies knew everyone's business. I chatted up the topic to Gladys McKinney, the head office secretary. She dished almost immediately.

"You know her dad owns a marina in Sandy Hook, right?" she said to me. Her eyes were lit up. "That's where she gets all her money. Daddy pays for everything."

"Yeah, but how much money are we talking?" I asked.

"Honey, have you ever seen the marina? Do you know how much money's in boats?" She snorted. "We're talking millions here, sugar."

"Get the hell outta here!"

"It's true. Pretty girl Gianna's got plenty more where that came from. Her fiancé works at the Bank of New York in Manhattan. He's loaded too."

"Unreal," I said. "Then what the hell is she doing working if her dad and her fiancé have money?"

"Beats me. Once you got money like that, you can never have enough. You always want more," said Gladys.

So Daddy's little girl was rich. That explained the wardrobe that would make Donna Karan jealous. Figures, you know? There I was, rubbing two nickels together, while the princess had a banker and a boatyard owner shoving money down her throat. We were probably the same age at that time, Ms. Francesca and I. I was working two jobs just to eat while she worked to get a summer home in Tuscany.

I went home that night angrier than normal. I usually went home angry, but that day, I was a different kind of angry. Life was not fair, brother. I was well-versed on the subject of unfairness. You could drive yourself mad thinking about why you were poor and others were rich. It still pissed me off how she screamed at me twice, being an asshole, just because she could. Those people were the same ones who thought money made them better, giving them the right to treat others like garbage because they got lots of cash.

My deck wasn't stacked like Ms. Francesca's. She was in a different world from most around her. Fancy car, luxury clothes, and the ability to buy a large Starbucks specialty coffee every day—that was wealth I didn't think I would ever achieve.

I had put her out of my mind until late one night, weeks after our first meeting. While closing down the school for the evening, I noticed a light on in one of the classrooms. It was late, like, really late. All the lights should have been off. One of the other janitors must have forgotten to turn it off. As I walked into the classroom, I was met by the resting bitch face herself.

"What the hell do you want?" said Ms. Francesca. She had her hand on her temple, looking up at me. Usually, I gave teachers all the time they wanted to stay in the building. Some of them stayed late, but most of the staff were gone once the bell rang for the day. I informed her it was time to leave.

"Sorry, but you have to go," I said. "We're closing the school down for the night."

"So? What's that got to do with me?" she asked.

"It means you gotta go," I said sternly. "Doors are getting chained, and the alarm's getting turned on." Ms. Francesca didn't seem to grasp the concept of closing time. She sat in her chair with her mouth wide open.

"I have work I need to get done. You can't kick me out."

"Sorry," I said. "I'm locking up the building, so you have to leave. My shift is over."

"I'm not leaving. I've got projects to grade. Get the hell out of my classroom!" She went back to looking at something on her desk, ignoring me as if I wasn't standing in the doorway.

"Sure thing," I said. I walked around the school one last time, checking the doors and windows, before telling the rest of the janitors to leave. With five minutes left before the end of my shift, I walked into her highness's room and started to flip the light switch on and off rapidly.

"Let's go. It's closing time. Time to vacate the premises."

"What the fuck do you think you're doing?" she said. "I told you to get out of here. I'm not going anywhere."

"Alarm's going on in five minutes. You need to leave now, or else you'll be locked in here for the night." I shook my key ring in front of her, hoping she would get the hint.

"Get the fuck out of my room," she said. "I've told you before. I'm not ready to leave. What are you, deaf too, you stupid fucking janitor?"

"I'm in charge of the building at night. I don't get paid overtime just because you wanna stay late. You need to go now."

"Fuck you."

She turned her face back toward her desk, and I saw a smug smirk on her lips as she looked downward. *What a defiant little bitch,* I thought. *Someone should teach her a lesson on knowing her place in this world.* I left without saying another word. I clocked out for the night and set the school alarm like usual. You typically had about thirty seconds to leave the building after you hit the alarm button. Any movement in the building triggered a silent alarm, which, in turn, dispatched the police. I would say Ms. Francesca got quite the surprise when she finally did leave for the night. She probably looked like a deer caught in the headlights standing inside the school when the cops pulled up.

My night boss came to the school the next day to give me a ration of shit over the alarm business. It was worth it. "I'm sorry," I said to my dim-witted boss. "I thought she had left already."

"Oh man," said the boss. "She was really scared when the police came to the door."

"Wow. Sorry that happened," I said.

"Yeah. She was pretty shaken up when the cops pulled their guns on her, thinking she was an intruder."

"Jesus," I said. "Boy, I hope she's all right."

"Oh yeah, she'll be fine, just a little shaken up. But make sure you check the rooms each and every night."

"Got it." I gave him a thumbs-up.

Ms. Francesca stayed late every night for the next two weeks, defiantly asking me why she had to leave. She complained and yelled at me repeatedly about how she was a teacher and how janitors were stupid and so on. I would brush it off, reminding her she had to go. When she finally did leave, she would take her time, and she would leave a mess in her room, causing me to stay late in order to clean it up. "Make sure the floors are spotless, or else I'll have you written up!" she would say as she waltzed out the door exactly one minute before the end of my shift.

Come Friday of the second week, I was done taking her shit. With ten minutes until I had to go home, I went down to her room to kick her prissy little ass out.

"Closing time. Let's go," I said. I knocked on the door loudly to get her attention.

"I still have ten minutes, janitor," she said. She didn't look up from her desk.

"No, you don't. I have to clean this room before the end of my shift. I'm tired of you making me late."

"I'm busy grading the students' work," she said. "Get lost, dummy."

Enough was enough. I didn't give a shit if the boss fired me at this point. "How hard is it to grade artwork?" I said. "It shouldn't take all night to determine if a picture looks like a flower vase."

"Excuse me?" Her voice was the loudest I had ever heard it. "How dare you insult my work like that."

"I'm not insulting you. I'm simply making a statement. How hard can it be to be an art teacher?"

Ms. Francesca pushed herself away from her desk with force, obviously disturbed by my comment. "You don't know shit about teaching! All you know is how to swing a fucking broom across the floor. You're not smart enough to be a teacher. You're just a dumb janitor who cleans up shit all day!"

"I bet I can do your job," I said. "Throwing some paint on canvas isn't exactly quantum physics."

Ms. Francesca was stunned. She stood up to grab her things in a hurried state. "Do you know how hard it is to be a teacher? Huh? Do you?"

"Actually, yes, I do," I said.

"Really? Yeah, okay. They don't teach Mopping 101 in college. You didn't go to college."

"I sure did. Graduated a few years ago."

"Bullshit!" she said.

"It's true," I said smugly. Ms. Francesca had her bag in her hands as she made her way to the door.

"What degree do you have, huh? I bet you're not smart enough to even know what the degrees are!"

"I have a BA in English," I said. She stopped dead in her tracks.

"No...no, you don't!"

"I sure do," I said. "I'm going for my master's now." Ms. Francesca stopped walking to let the news sink in. Personally, I thought she short-circuited right there, unable to think and walk at the same time.

"That's impossible."

"No, it's not," I said. "What, you think because I clean up vomit, I'm not intelligent enough to pass exams? How could a person dump garbage cans and obtain multiple higher learning degrees at the same time?" I walked around the entrance of her classroom a little, surveying the desks, keeping my eyes fixed on hers. "I'm more than halfway there already. Might get my degree in less than a year if I double up on classes. Then again, I might go for my doctorate while I'm at it. I mean, I've essentially gotten my master's, so I might as well go all the way for a PhD." I folded my arms, letting my speech take hold of her.

"You're...you're lying. You're a janitor. You're not smart enough to get a master's degree. I don't even have a master's degree." It slowly began to register to her. The thought of a janitor being able to attend college and obtain more degrees than she had was out of her range of comprehension. "I don't believe you! You...you're not serious."

"Oh, but I am. I'm almost done with my master's in English. You don't have a master's, do you? That's a shame." Ms. Francesca was in a trance, realizing the person she was undermining was further along in college than she was.

"What are you doing working as a janitor if you've got a degree, huh?"

"How else can I afford to pay for college?" I said. "It's not like I've got someone handing me money. I guess you don't have to worry about money like I do." She was silent. Not even her heels made a sound. "I clean toilets because I wasn't born into money, and I earned my degrees, all of them. Pretty good for a stupid janitor, eh?" I said.

Ms. Francesca, standing there with her bag in hand, didn't believe a word I said. Or perhaps she didn't want to believe me. In her mind, I was beneath her in every aspect of life—money, social status, and wardrobe. To be further along in education than she was, was an abomination to her. She got herself together, walking past me with disbelief in her posture. She didn't mumble or curse this time. That Friday was the last night she stayed late. Never again did she call me a dummy—not to my face anyway.

A month later, I had to come in for the day shift again. I feared being run over by a tinted European sports car before getting into the building. Alas, no such car rolled into the lot. I ran into a few familiar faces in the hall later that morning. They were laughing it up like someone they hated just died.

"Did you hear what happened to Ms. Francesca?" asked Ms. Rouple. "She got fired last week!"

"No shit," I said. "What happened?"

"Princess mouthed off to the principal during her classroom evaluation. You never raise your voice to the principal of the school. What a dumbass!"

"Good Lord!" I said.

"Yep! No more Ms. Prissy!"

Upon further investigation, we found out that it seemed Ms. Francesca's world was crashing down on her. The teachers heard a rumor about how she wasn't as loaded as she originally made it out to be, not anymore. Papa's marina was going under. The recession had hit the luxury markets the hardest. No one was buying a brand-new yacht when they could barely afford gas in their car. Pops had to sell it for pennies on the dollar just to break even.

The same went for her fiancé. Banks were laying people off left and right after they fucked up the hedge fund game in 2008. He was downsized. He now worked as an assistant manager in some grocery store, a far cry from his massive six-figure-plus salary in New York. I guessed Ms. Francesca was staying late to avoid the catastrophes at home, in her personal life. Whoops, tough break, as they say. It coudn't have happened to a nicer person.

There's nothing wrong with working for a living. If you get everything handed to you in life, you can't appreciate the things you do earn. Money doesn't make you a better person. It just means you've got more money to lose if tragedy strikes. I'm glad I'm poor. It keeps me honest. Ms. Francesca, on the other hand, will never know what it feels like to be hungry. I'm sure she's fine wherever she has ended up. People like her always come out ahead. That's just the way life works.

CHAPTER 18

That Time the Pony Got Loose

I didn't remember much from my childhood, but I did remember going to the circus when I was seven years old. On one of the last days of first grade, my teacher handed me a pamphlet with an advertisement for the circus. I was ecstatic. I absolutely loved animals. What small child wasn't astonished in the presence of a majestic animal? Maybe a kid who got bitten by a rabbit his last time at the petting zoo. Not me, though. I had always been fascinated by animals.

My mother took me to the circus after she was done working one weekday. She had been busting her back all day. I was sure the last thing she wanted to do was take a pleading child to a hot, crowded tent to watch smelly mammals perform tricks for snotty-nosed little children, but we went anyway. I got my way, as I often did.

Certain things, like a trip to the circus, couldn't be forgotten. You would have to assault me with a tack hammer several times over to get me to forget the smell of wild animal sweat and freshly popped popcorn, hissing tigers, and other families clapping and pointing euphorically at the elephants walking in a line and tethered trunk to tail. I had a rainbow snow cone, which since it was about one hundred degrees in the tent melted soon after purchase. It was a race against gravity—me versus the dripping iced treat. I would have you know that I won that race, although I got purple lips and a stained shirt for my efforts. I got to see those elephants and tigers and was overwhelmed by it all.

This was at the height of the traveling circus era across the Northeast. It seemed like everyone and their brother had a circus company who rolled into town during the summer. They had colorful posters and flashy art of trapeze artists gliding through air like astronauts in weightlessness. Those were memories even my twisted sense of humor couldn't make fun of no matter how much I wanted to, though I couldn't say the same for those children who attended the Colati Family Traveling Circus Show one frightful evening.

This was years ago, when circuses actually came to schools. Now since society became a bunch of candy-asses, circuses and the animals they kept were pretty much all out of business. But back in the day, anything was fair game, especially for schools who would do just about anything to make money. If that meant housing a traveling act in a crammed school for a profit, the board of education allowed it even if that circus group had untamed, slightly agitated animals being prodded by hundreds of loud children in a confined area. When I found out my job was to host the circus in the school's cafeteria, I wasn't the least bit shocked. Sure, bring in a whole pack of malnourished barnyard animals and let them shit all over the floor. The janitors would clean it up as well as the rest of the debris left by hundreds of people.

I almost called in sick on the day in question, but a lot of reasons stopped me from doing so. One, I was out of sick days, which was a regular occurrence for me. Two, it was a Friday. Who in their right mind wanted to work when they could bang out and make it a three-day weekend? Three, I would be working with Tyrell, and I would give my left nut to see him ride an elephant across the school. And four, I kinda wanted to relive a little of my own childhood with the wonderment I experienced when I was a tiny tot.

As I got older, I realized what it meant to be young and full of joy. Animals gave me that feeling no matter when I saw them. You couldn't pull me away from a good *National Geographic* show. So I went to work knowing I would be shoveling poop from all kinds of quadrupeds, but at least I would get to see some animals.

That night, the Colati Family Traveling Circus Show pulled into the parking lot just after 4:00 p.m. I texted Tyrell to come outside with me to greet the circus people. Maybe we would get some free tickets to the show or perhaps get to feed one of their majestic furry performers.

Instead of a long motorcade of tractor trailers with advertisements painted on the side, there were three hillbillies driving a rusty dually. The brakes squealed as they ground the truck to a stop. They had one beat-up trailer with hay sticking out of the sides. I waited for more vehicles to pull in, but no such vehicles arrived. There were no glamourous tumbling clowns honking horns or juggling bowling pins and no high-flying gymnasts swinging from ring to ring. There were just three hicks and a shitty trailer with the words Colati Family Traveling Circus Show spray-painted on the side.

"What the fuck is that?" asked Tyrell as we stood outside the café doors. We waited for one of the circus folks to come introduce themselves. "That ain't no damn circus!"

"I don't know, man," I said. "Boss man said the circus was coming tonight." I looked at a flyer I printed off the Internet. It was a big, showy poster complete with realistic animals jumping through hoops ablaze. Nowhere on their website did it mention the redneck Ringling Brothers before me.

"This better be good," said Tyrell. "I almost called out today. They better have an elephant in their trailer or something big I can ride!"

Tyrell and I stood on the sidewalk, waiting for someone to exit the truck. We could hear a horse or two hee-hawing in the trailer, causing more hay flecks to fly out of the sides. We stood there for, like, ten minutes, looking all stupid while waiting for something to happen. The truck doors finally opened, and three scrubby-looking men got out, hocking spit and coughing as they climbed out of the cab. These men sounded like they had malaria or tuberculosis. They dusted themselves off while talking in a deep Southern twang accent to one another. It felt as if I was watching disgruntled stagecoach travelers disembarking from a particularly long journey through the desert.

From what I could make out, there seemed to be some sort of disagreement as to who would feed the animals before the show.

None of the three workers appeared to want to get whatever beasts they had out of the trailer. After an argument, one of the men came over to us.

"You da janitor?" asked a scruffy, thin man. He spit a hock of chaw out onto the sidewalk, then coughed.

"Yep, that's me," I said. "Are you the circus act?"

"Well, I ain't towing live animals for my health now, is I?" he said. "Where can I load at?"

"Load what?" asked Tyrell. "Whatchu got back there?" He looked at the man with disbelief.

"Animals," the man said dryly.

"What kind of animals you got?" Tyrell asked.

"Circus animals." The man coughed again, this time hacking up phlegm.

"Bullshit," said Tyrell. He was genuinely upset, questioning the assortment of animals this man was pedaling. "I don't see nothing but horses in that trailer. I damn sure know you ain't got no giraffes or elephants in that hunk of shit you towed here. How you gonna call yourself a circus if you ain't got not circus animals?"

"Got a monkey. Just one. He's real old. Don't move around too much anymore."

"Now we gettin' somewhere," said Tyrell, his interest piqued. "What else?"

"That's it. Where am I loading them?"

Tyrell sucked his teeth, shaking his head in disapproval. "Ah, right here," I said. "Bring them in through these two double doors."

"All right," said Mr. Pleasant Man. He walked away, yelling something to the other two circus wranglers. They were grappling with lead ropes, trying to pull a horse out of the trailer. All three men yelled back and forth, constantly coughing as they dragged ornery animals out of their confinement.

Tyrell continued to suck his teeth, restless at best. "This some country-ass bullshit!" he said. "How you gonna call yourself a circus if all you got is some horses and a half-dead monkey?"

"You're telling me," I said. "We should've called in sick. I knew this was going to be stupid."

Tyrell and I watched the men bring a total of four animals into the school—one brown horse, one black-and-white pony, a one-eyed goat, and a geriatric chimpanzee. As the men gathered their animal crew in the cafeteria, Tyrell and I asked a few basic questions.

"Do you guys need anything for a setup?" I asked.

"Just a hose for water," said the skinny man from earlier. "We got buckets."

"Okay. Sure," I said.

Tyrell inquired about the chimpanzee. He asked one of the other men about it. "Hey. Ah…ah, excuse me, sir," he said, pointing at the cage. "That's a chimpanzee, right?"

"Um, yeah, I think so." The man was placing the cage down on the floor with a wheeled pallet jack.

"Whatchu mean, 'I think so'?" asked Tyrell. "Don't you know what kind of animal this is?"

"I just wheel it in," said the worker. He left out a snort like what a wild hog made when it was digging around in the dirt.

Tyrell looked at me with his mouth open. I could read his mind already: "What kind of dumbass honkies they got working at this rinky-dink circus?"

"This the only animals you got? You don't got any other animals coming in another trailer or something?"

"Nope."

"Well, damn, man!" Tyrell said loudly. "You ain't a fucking circus! A baby-sized petting zoo is what you got here, Jack!"

The ringleader walked over to confront Tyrell. "This all we got, dude. They told us to bring this trailer here, so that's what we did."

"Yeah, but you can't be calling yoself a circus if you don't got any circus animals!"

"The Colati Circus filed for bankruptcy two years ago," said the ringleader. "They sold all the bigger animals to other circuses. This all they got left." He spit a load of chewing tobacco liquid on the ground as the third man started to drop straw flakes all over the café floor.

Tyrell watched the spit leave the man's mouth, then followed it to the floor with the rest of the straw. "Ain't this a bitch!" he said. He walked back over to me with his eyes and mouth wide open. "Not only do we get screwed out of real circus animals, but now we got to sweep up fucking straw, spit, and shit all night long!"

"That's the way it goes, pal. You know as well as I do we're the cleaning crew here. Nobody gives a crap about us."

"Yeah, but did you hear what that redneck mothafucka said when I asked if that was a chimpanzee? He didn't know what the fuck it was! That first weirdo said they had a monkey. Chimpanzees ain't monkeys. They apes! Even I know that. How you work for a so-called circus and not know what animal you working with?"

"You know why, Tyrell. Because they don't care. These companies hire these momos for minimum wage. We're lucky they got them here in one piece," I said.

Tyrell let out a loud "Pfft" to show his displeasure. He looked down at the floor covered in straw, then looked back up as the men brought in the last animal: a rowdy pint-sized pony with an attitude problem. Two men were dragging the mini horse in by its bridle and lead rope as the tiny horse bucked profusely. It kicked its back legs wildly when they pulled its rope.

"Damn!" said Tyrell. "That little mothafucka is pissed off!"

"He sure is," I said.

"Hey, my man!" said Tyrell. "What's the pony's name?"

"This here is Samson," said the worker. "He's a pistol. Angry little bastard." As he said the pony's name, it reared up, pulling the rope out of the workers' hands. The pony tried to run for the door, but the slippery straw gave way under his hooves. He fell just long enough for one of the workers to grab the line, tugging him back into place.

"Woah! Woah!" yelled the ringleader. "Get ahold of his bridle! Get ahold of the rope!" All three workers held the small pony's line, yanking it back under control.

Tyrell stepped back a few feet, laughing hysterically. "Look at 'em! Look at that little sonabitch pull those guys!" If Tyrell got to laughing, there wasn't a lot you could do to stop him. "Hey, man, make sure that tiny horsey don't bite you!"

"You think this is funny?" said the ringleader. "This ain't funny. This is the most dangerous animal I've ever worked with."

"Dangerous?" Tyrell said in between laughs. "He's the size of a large Saint Bernard. How dangerous can he be?"

"He's bitten off fingers, toes, and a piece of some woman's scalp at a show two weeks ago," said the third worker. All three men struggled to hold down the pony.

"Then why'd you bring him for children to touch?" I asked. "You're gonna let kids ride him?"

"'Cause the boss told us to," the ringleader said. "We can manage him once we give him a shot." With that, the second worker pulled a leather pouch out from his back pocket. He brought out a prefilled syringe and instructed the other two men to hold the pony still. With great efforts, the workers got the pony still long enough for him to deliver the needle. Almost immediately, the pony stopped rearing back—standing still, at least. His pupils were dilated.

"Damn, that must be some good shit," said Tyrell.

"It's the strongest we can get without going to the black market," said the ringleader. "One shot per show is all we're allowed to give him, or else he'll start seizuring."

"You tranq him like this all the time?" I asked.

"Have to. If not, he goes berserk."

I tried to process this information without success. The thought of drugging an animal to the point of a near-comatose state just so kids could take a picture on its back appalled me. It didn't seem safe either—not for the kids and the handlers and certainly not for the pony. What kind of life was this for Samson? I was sure his outbursts ramped up with each show. Another town meant another needle to numb his obvious distress.

When you were young and oblivious to such things, you never had these thoughts. I could never have dreamed that the animals I was watching at the circus might have been slipped a Mickey. It was my naive belief that those elephants and tigers wanted to do tricks. They seemed happy when they sat up, roared for the crowd, or bowed their trunks. Then again, that was something your parents never told you when you begged them mercilessly to go to the circus. If I had known the animals were given sedatives for my enjoyment, I would've asked to be taken to the public library instead. I felt queasy now watching this hick shoot up a pony so it didn't chomp someone's finger off.

"Come on, Tyrell. Let's get out of here," I said.

"Yeah, man," said Tyrell. "Maybe I'll come down later and talk to that chimpanzee."

"What?" I asked. "What do you mean talk?"

"Just like I said. I might come down and rap with him for a few minutes. Might get me some popcorn too."

I wasn't sure if Tyrell was being serious, or maybe he was trying to get me to lighten up a bit. We left to go do our jobs for the evening. We would wait for a chance to slip down to the cafeteria later.

*****

A couple of hours later, before the dinner break, I ventured down to check on the festivities. The cafeteria was a sea of people and was smelling like a barn stall on a hot summer day. The three circus hicks were busy loading and off-loading children onto the backs of the horse and pony while the other side of the café housed the goat and chimpanzee. The school's PTA was set up on the side of the café, selling prepackaged popsicles on a stick and red-and-white boxes of popcorn.

The place was packed to the ceiling with happy-faced families. Children ran around the floor, throwing popcorn at one another and screaming nonsense. I looked around at each station, checking them out to see if everything was okay. The one-eyed goat drew a big crowd due to its cyclopean appearance. The kids were grossed out yet intrigued. The horse and the pony had equally long lines, each child wanting to get a selfie with them. Then there was the chimpanzee cage. There was not much activity there. A few parents had parked strollers around it like it was a receptacle for out-of-commission bumper cars.

I locked eyes with Tyrell as he waved at me with a smile. He motioned for me to come over. As I approached the cage, I got a good look at the chimpanzee. It surely was old. It sat in the corner, on a fake log, not moving. It had wrapped its arms around its legs, pulling them close to its body. Its food bowl had half-eaten apples and what looked like lettuce. The water dish was knocked over, empty.

"His name's Bobo," said Tyrell. He had a mouthful of popcorn. "That's what the sign says. But I call him Jeremy."

"Jeremy?" I said questioningly. "Why do you call him that?"

"'Cause he looks like a Jeremy," said Tyrell. He reached into his popcorn box, digging toward the bottom, gathering unpopped kernels.

"You're going to crack your teeth," I said.

"Nah. My teeth are in great shape, baby. Besides, I ain't chewing on 'em, just sucking the salt off 'em."

We watched the chimpanzee together, not saying much. Scientists said you were not supposed to anthropomorphize animals, but how could you not? Bobo, or Jeremy, had sadness in his eyes. Most circus animals had been captured since they were babies and forced to learn tricks from a young age. They were often beaten if they failed to comprehend early on. It was all most of them had ever known—pain and imprisonment. The average life span of a chimpanzee in the wild was forty to fifty years, but it was up to sixty years in captivity according to some sources. Imagine sitting on a plastic log in a cage for most of your life while strangers ogled you for hours on end.

"Whatchu think he's thinking about?" said Tyrell.

"Probably getting the fuck out of here," I said. "He looks sad as hell sitting in the corner."

"I believe you're right," Tyrell said. "I gave him a snack, but he wasn't having it."

"What do you mean a snack?" I asked. "The sign says not to feed the animal, Tyrell."

"Yeah, but Jeremy looked hungry, so I gave him some Fritos."

"Fritos? His name isn't Jeremy," I exclaimed.

"Yeah? Why not? I got 'em from the vending machine over there. It don't look like he likes what's in his dish. And I'm sure he's eaten more popcorn than any chimpanzee should ever eat, being that these kids throw popcorn at him all day long, so I got him some Fritos."

"Tyrell, you can't feed a chimpanzee Fritos!" My voice cracked a little. "Their diet consists of fruits and nuts. Fritos is junk food!"

Tyrell looked at me with his mouth open, sort of laughing, trying to keep it together. "Well, shit! I know it's junk food, but Jeremy looked like he was yearning for something a little salty."

As I argued with Tyrell over what a balanced primate diet should and should not contain, there was a loud screech from behind us. I turned to see a crowd around the pony pen all backing away quickly. When a hole in the mass of people came into view, I saw one very pissed off pony rearing up, shaking its head. He had a small child on his back in a tiny saddle. The boy was crying, shrieking with fear.

One of the hillbilly trainers ran into the circle, calling for help, trying to secure the pony's lead line. A second handler grabbed the small child a few moments before Samson the pony broke free from his tether. People screamed, running for cover, grabbing their children as they fled.

"Look out!" Tyrell said as he ducked for cover behind the chimpanzee cage. "Jeremy, get down!"

I ran around to join Tyrell. I still didn't know why he yelled for Jeremy to take cover; the damn chimp was already safe behind his bars. The handlers tried to surround the pony, but each man was scared to grab him. Perhaps they had already tangled with Samson before and got hurt for their efforts. The crowd's screams caused the pony to become more agitated. Someone ran out the side fire doors, triggering the alarm. The bells echoed throughout the café, mixing with the screams, turning into a symphony of sirens.

Samson did not like this sound whatsoever. He lunged up, neighing loudly, kicked his two front legs, and made a beeline for the ramp that led to the rest of the school. From a prone position, I saw Samson book it up the ramp, hauling ass out the double doors and into the open hallway with the three circus jerks running after him.

"Oh, fuck, there he goes!" said Tyrell. "He gone now!"

"Shit!" I said. "What do we do?"

"We stay here to protect Jeremy. That's what I'mma do," Tyrell said.

"Jeremy's fine. He's in a cage! We gotta try to help them catch that pony."

"What?" Tyrell yelled. "I ain't catchin' no damn angry horse. Are you crazy?"

"Come on, dude. You know we're gonna catch hell for this anyway. If that pony gets hurt in the school, that's more of a mess we have to clean up."

"Ain't this some bullshit," said Tyrell. "All I wanted to do was talk to my new buddy Jeremy, see how he doin', and now you got me playing Rudy the Rodeo Wrangler. This some fucked up shit, man. I ain't no damn cowboy! Let them crackers catch it!"

I reached for my phone. Seeing a few parents on their phones already on the line with police, I looked up the number for animal control. I told them who I was and what was running loose in the school and to send someone over as quickly as possible. Then I called Mr. Polotski, which went over extremely well.

"A what?" he said. "A pony is running around the high school? Just…just go make sure it doesn't kill itself on something!" Mr. Polotski was usually never any help. I could see we were all alone on this one. Tyrell and I left the cafeteria, crusading into the hallway in search of Samson and the hillbillies.

You would think tracking a five-hundred-pound pony in an empty high school wouldn't be so hard. It was much harder than it sounded. This joint was full of places to hide. Fifty-some classrooms, storage closets, and big, open band rooms—all these areas had their doors open because the rest of the janitors cleaned at night. If the pony got into an open area, we might not find him for hours. As we came around the first corner, we still hadn't seen a thing.

"Maybe he broke out a window and ran for the highway," said Tyrell.

"I'm sure we'd have heard the glass break or seen a busted door if he did," I said.

"Shit, if I were him, I'd run as fast as I could for as long as I could. You'd never catch me," Tyrell said. He walked slower than I did, looking over his shoulder nervously, expecting Samson to plow us down on his route to freedom.

"If I were Samson," I said, "I'd probably be eating or hiding. I'd be hunkered down someplace quiet."

"Not with them idiot circus morons chasing behind you," said Tyrell. "Where the fuck did they go?"

"Follow the screams," I said. "I'm sure we'll run into them sooner or later."

We passed the second hallway to the right, and Tyrell and I ran into Jane, one of the other janitors in the school. She was hiding in the teachers' lounge, holding her broom in front of her like a spear. She yelled as we stumbled on her, causing us to yell too.

"Easy, easy, Jane. It's just us," I said.

"Why is there a horse running down the hall?" she asked, still holding the broom in front of her like she was a gladiator. She was out of breath.

"One of the circus animals got loose," I said. "We're trying to find it and the circus guys who ran after it."

"You see the pony yet, Jane?" asked Tyrell.

"Of course I've seen it!" she said. "Why do you think I'm hiding here, holding my broom like this?"

"I see. I see. My bad, Jane."

"Which way did it go?" I asked.

"That way," said Jane. She pointed to the right, our left, down a long corridor. "It was snorting a lot. Looked like it was foaming from the mouth." She put down her broom, easing her standoff position. "Do you think it has rabies?"

"No. It's just scared," I said.

As the three of us stood there, a yell came from the direction Jane pointed. Our heads darted toward the sound. It was a man's voice, a bloodcurdling scream of agony. Seconds later, two of the handlers turned the corner and came barreling toward us, running at full steam. The three of us stepped into the teachers' lounge doorway, letting them pass. They both looked roughed up. One had blood coming down from his head. His shirt was ripped, and a sleeve dangled in the wind behind him. I saw their eyes for a moment as they jogged past us. They were petrified. They passed without saying a word, fleeing back down the hall we came from.

"Screw this! I'm fucking outta here! No, no, no!" said Tyrell. He started to follow the guys, but I stopped him.

"Come on. Don't leave me to face this alone," I said. "I need your help."

Tyrell whirled around to look me in the eyes. He shook his head. "What you need, my brotha, is the mothafucking SWAT team," he said. "You not gonna get my ass chewed the fuck up."

"Oh, so you'd let me get the shit kicked out of me by some mini horse by myself?"

"Hey," said Tyrell. He shrugged with his hands up in the air. "Thems the brakes."

"That's messed up, dude. After all these years? I saved your ass how many times? You remember when I drove your drunk ass home two months ago because you drank a fifth of Hennessy on dinner break? How soon we forget."

"All right, all right, all right!" Tyrell said. "I'll help you, but if that sonabitch charges, I'm pulling you in front of me." He walked back toward me, passing Jane. "Gimme this!" He grabbed the broom from her hands and followed me. "Ain't this some bullshit."

Tyrell and I journeyed down the hallway until we came to the science labs. My school had three large classrooms dedicated to science-based learning. I always liked the sciences, but my math was abysmal. I never took it up in college because I couldn't hack four years of advanced algebra and trigonometry, but I used to love dissecting skates and baby sharks in marine bio. Venturing into this area brought me back to the old days of my high school.

As we passed a classroom with fish tanks, it reminded me of a horror movie where the mad scientist conducted experiments on unsuspecting civilians. Lights from the tanks looked ominous with their different-colored lamps. I saw blue, red, and yellow lights. The air bubbles inside the tanks from the air stones rose to the top eerily. I flicked on the light in the classroom and found shattered glass all over the floor. There was liquid on the floor too. It was kind of like oil or some sort of slime.

"These look like beakers or broken test tubes," I said out loud to Tyrell. He was still carrying the broom.

"Yeah, man. Looks like he's been through here, don't it?" he said. "You think he ate some chemicals or something in these tubes?"

"Nah, probably not. He might've knocked them over when passing through."

Suddenly, we heard a loud bang come from inside the storage room next to another science lab. A muffled voice and what sounded like items hitting the floor came from the room. Tyrell and I stepped back, waiting for someone or something to rush out at us. A massive crashing sound rang out from within, causing us to run out of the room. We stood in the hallway for a few seconds until a grunting snarl erupted. Samson emerged from the next door down, running as fast as he could into the open corridor with a bag in his mouth.

"There he go!" yelled Tyrell, holding the broom like he was a Shaolin monk. Samson jetted away with pieces of something flying out of the bag. Just then, a short, medium-sized man dressed in a brown khaki outfit ran into the hallway with a rifle in hand. He wore a floppy hat and black boots laced up to his knees. He was aiming at Samson as he ran away, trying to get a bead on him.

"Shit!" the man yelled as Samson turned the corner into another hallway. Then he turned around to face me and Tyrell, about forty feet from us. Tyrell dropped his broom and reached around to this back pocket. "Who are you?" yelled the man, still aiming the gun at us.

"Woah, woah, buddy!" I said. I stuck my hands in the air. "We're the janitors. Put the gun down!"

"Drop your gun, sucka, or i'mma blast you!" said Tyrell as he pretended to reach for a gun.

"Jesus Christ, I almost plugged you." The man dropped his stance, relaxing the gun at his hips, relieved somewhat. He walked toward me and Tyrell, switching the rifle to his right hand and putting his left hand up in an easing motion. "I'm so sorry about that."

"Who is you?" asked Tyrell. "And where the fuck you come from, Jumanji?"

"I'm Jarod Miles. I'm from animal control."

"Yeah, and what's with the gun, Jack? You lucky I didn't have that thing on me, or else I'd have smoked your ass," said Tyrell, looking suspiciously at the intruder.

"It's a tranquilizer gun," he said. "I got a call from dispatch telling me you had a wild animal loose in the school."

"It's a pony from the circus down in the café," I said. "He's been loose for about fifteen minutes now."

"You're gonna need something bigger than a dart gun, Jarod," Tyrell said. "That little bastard is vicious, you hear me?"

"Oh, I know. That horse is out of control. I haven't seen anything this violent since I had to shoot a black bear my first year on the job." The three of us shook hands briefly before starting to walk again. Jarod held the gun at the ready as we walked, trying to follow Samson's trail.

"Do you know if the cops got here yet?" I asked.

"Beats me," said Jarod. "Dispatch told me to go to the front of the building. I came in and followed the sounds until I got here. I figured he'd come to this area, looking for something to eat." I shot a look at Tyrell, telling him telepathically I was right about the pony looking for food. Jarod went on with his story. "I heard a noise in the small room over there. I found it eating from a hamster or gerbil food bag. I had him cornered. As I raised the gun to fire, the bastard charged me, knocking me down."

"See? I told you that little mofucker would charge," said Tyrell.

"Did you shoot?" I asked.

"Couldn't get a shot off in time. He came at me hard. In the seventeen years I've been with animal control, I've never had an animal charge me like that. It's like he was on a mission." Jarod looked down the hallway, listening for pony noises. "There's something wrong with him."

"Maybe he felt threatened and did the whole fight or flight thing."

"No. Something is different about this animal," said Jarod. "He's on something, some kind of drug or narcotic."

"Them hillbilly circus folks gave him a needle a couple of hours ago," said Tyrell.

"Hmm, that's strange," said Jarod. "Any sedative they had given him shouldn't have made him charge like he did."

"Do you think he had an adverse reaction to the needle?" I asked. "Those handlers said they give him a shot before each show to keep him from going insane."

"Could be," said Jarod. He reached for his walkie-talkie to call his dispatch, telling them about his location in the school.

"I'd like to speak to one of those handlers. See what they injected this animal with."

The three of us started to walk down the hallway, searching for Samson. We chatted about the pony and what could be wrong with it. I suggested that years of torment and drugging most likely caused Samson to snap. Jarod agreed but went into detail about the adverse effects of consistent drugging of circus animals in Malaysia and India. Jarod spoke of studies stating the chemical toll sedatives had on the cerebral cortex and thalamus of the brain. It had been years since I studied marine and environmental science, but the terms were relevant to me. Tyrell, oblivious to our science talk, suggested that Samson was rabid and needed to be put down as soon as possible.

Down the empty, silent hallway we walked. Jarod, with his tranquilizer gun, led the way. Tyrell, with his lethal broomstick, walked directly behind him, turning his head side to side, looking around each corner cautiously. Then came me, bringing up the rear, with a small cellphone light for defense. We journeyed down the locker-filled hallways in semidarkness. By this time of the night, most of the other janitors had finished cleaning their areas and were relaxing in various break rooms throughout the huge high school.

Most of the doors were closed in this part of the school. *Fewer places for Samson to hide,* I thought. Only the emergency lights were on in the hallway, giving us an ominously lit environment. These schools might not look like it, but they were massive inside. You wouldn't realize how long the hallways were until you were stalking an irate animal across a ten-thousand-square-foot building. Any sound echoed from either end of the hallway, making it extremely hard to judge where the sound came from.

I didn't know this guy Jarod in the least, but he looked exactly like a stereotypical animal control guy. Don't get me wrong. He was cool and all, but he took his job a little too seriously. His bucket hat and knee-length snake-proof boots were overkill if you asked me. I was not sure how many venomous snakes this guy had come across during his career, but he would be prepared if the situation arose. Had we been trekking through Borneo or the high grasses of the savana, perhaps the boots might have been appropriate. Except for his name badge and walkie-talkie, he looked like a character from Hemingway's many African safari stories.

Jarod walked low to the ground, assessing the environment with each step. He played the part of an expert tracker, stopping at each piece of debris to check it out. "This looks like gerbil food all right," he said. "He must've gone this way."

"Ya think?" said Tyrell sarcastically.

"Oh, definitely," said Jarod. "Judging by the sporadic placement of these kernels, it looks like he's trotting. We should be seeing scat anytime now."

"Yeah, okay, buddy," said Tyrell, looking at me for input.

"Keep on eye out for poop, Tyrell," I said, looking down. I smiled at him.

"Great. If I fuck my shoes up, this school gonna pay for a new pair! I'll be sending over an invoice. These are my best pair of Jordans too!"

Two more hallways were empty as we traveled, then came the piles. I counted about twenty piles of horseshit in the next corridor as we passed. They looked like unburied land mines without the trip wire.

"Bingo!" shouted Jarod. He shuffled over to the first heap, surveying the surroundings. "This pile of manure is fresh," he said, touching it to test its heat level. "He's close." Jarod crouched low to the floor, turning to look at me.

"Ew," said Tyrell. "Don't touch it! Why you gotta touch it for?"

"To see how far off he might be. I'd say he's about five minutes away at most," said Jarod. He called over his radio to dispatch, giving updates on the hunt.

Tyrell looked at me funny as Jarod stooped over the dung to inspect it. "I think we're on the right track, Steve Irwin," he said.

"Just keep that gun at the ready to shoot that mothafucker if he pops out in front of us."

"He left these here to slow us down," declared Jarod. He slowly rose from the pile, staring into the dark, searching. "Come on. Let's go! We're close!"

Tyrell spun around as Jarod sprinted down the hallway like a soldier to the front lines. "Does this asshole think he's in Jurassic Park?" Tyrell said to me. He hooked his thumb out in Jarod's direction.

"He's very passionate," I said. "Come on. Let's keep up."

Tyrell and I hoofed it for thirty seconds to try to catch up with Jarod. In between piles of horseshit and loose gerbil food, we shouted for him to slow down. He shouted back, "I see something in the distance, at the end of the other hallway!"

As we turned the corner to the left, we spotted a figure on the ground. Jarod already had his gun aimed, about twenty feet away, ready to fire. In the dim light, we could make out a silhouette. Jarod was already engaging the subject as we moved in closer. It was the circus ringleader. He had his back to the wall, and his legs were splayed out in front of him. I shone my cellphone light on him. He had a few cuts on his face, and two large hoof-shaped welts were turning black-and-blue already.

Jarod led the rounds of questions, crouching in front of the man with his hand on his shoulder. "My name is Jarod Miles. I'm with animal control. Are you all right, friend?" he asked.

"Oh," moaned the handler, his eyes closed. "Oh, I'm okay."

"Is anything broken?" asked Jarod. "Can you speak?"

"No. I think I'm just beat up a little."

"Damn, you got messed up, buddy," said Tyrell. The two of us kept our distance, letting Jarod handle it.

"Tell me, friend. What happened? Did you engage the culprit?"

"Yes. I...I tried to grab the halter around its mouth," said the handler. "He's out of control."

"No shit!" said Tyrell, leaning on his broomstick like it was a wizard's staff. "What made you think that?"

"I'm calling for a medic now," said Jarod. "Hold tight, dear friend. We'll get you help." He placed the gun on the ground, grabbing his radio. "We got a man down in the..." He looked at me for guidance.

"Ah, this is the south-end corridor," I said quickly.

"We got a man down in the south-end corridor," said Jarod. "I repeat, a man is down and in need of medical assistance!"

"Stand by, Unit Seven. Await instructions from police and fire."

"Negative, dispatch. There's no time," Jarod shot back into the walkie-talkie. "I'm pursuing the suspect on foot now! Over and out." He placed his walkie back in its holster, then reached for his gun. "You two stay with this man until help arrives," he said. "I'll track this pony down." He straightened up and cocked his rifle.

"Wait. Don't leave us here," I said. "You're going to need backup from the police."

"You're gonna get hurt, Jack!" said Tyrell.

"There's no time to waste," said Jarod. "I've got to catch him before he does any more harm."

Just then, the sound of neighing came from down the corridor. It was a high-pitched call, echoing down from the last part of the school. All of us froze in place, not moving, trying to pinpoint its location. The sounds got louder and longer. Then metallic sounds bellowed as they got the loudest yet. They were horseshoes. Samson appeared from around the corner, halting to a stop. He was about a hundred feet away now, locked in place in the middle of the hallway. Samson kicked his front right foot down, dragging it back and forth the same way a bull dragged its hoof. He lowered his neck, sniffing the ground.

"Oh, fuck, there he is!" said Tyrell. He whirled his broom in his hands defensively. "Back up, mothafucka! Stay back, you wild-ass bitch!"

Jarod got down on one knee, aimed hastily, and pulled the trigger. The dart rang out, whizzing down the hallway, missing by a country mile. "Shit!" he yelled out. "Shit!"

As Jarod reached down into his front pocket to grab another dart, Samson reared up at us. He was still over one hundred feet away, but his defiance was clear. His neighs reeked of mockery, taunting us with each snort. Samson reared back down, dancing in place.

He kept neighing at us, faking a charge, then dancing back to his original spot. Jarod fumbled nervously with the dart, trying to load it under duress.

"He's trying to display dominance," said Jarod. He finally locked the dart into place, aiming again.

"Mission accomplished!" declared Tyrell. "Shoot him! Shoot that mothafucka!"

Jarod composed himself from a prone position. He let out a breath, then squeezed the trigger. Another dart missed its mark, striking the wall behind the pony. "Goddamn it!" he said. "He keeps moving around." Jarod reached for a third dart, loading it faster than the last dart.

"Gimme the gun," said Tyrell. "I'll get his ass." He dropped his broom, running over to Jarod's position. They jostled around with the tranquilizer gun, both men cursing each other out, staging a mini tug-of-war. Jarod stood up, trying to keep Tyrell from obtaining the gun. It was like watching two infants fight over a bottle. They argued for a few seconds, declaring why they should have the gun instead of the other.

"I'm a state-hired official! It's my gun!" said Jarod.

Tyrell retorted. "I got better aim! I shot thugs before! Gimme that shit!"

I was still standing like an idiot in the hallway, halfway between the circus wrangler and the squabbling. What the hell else could I have done? I didn't have a gun or a broomstick. I was yelling at Tyrell to stop lunging for the gun when Samson interrupted us. The pony screamed one last time before turning to run back down the hallway it came from. With his departure, Jarod wrestled the gun free from Tyrell.

"Stay here! I'm going after it!"

"Wait! Don't be a fool!" I said.

"Nah, nah, let him go," said Tyrell as he ran back to grab his broomstick from the ground. "That pony gonna flatten his ass."

As Jarod ran down the hallway, pursuing his prey, Tyrell and I came back to sit near the wounded man. He was beaten up, but there were no life-threatening injuries to speak of. That little horse must have cracked him good with two hooves. I reached in my back pocket to get a handkerchief. I started to wipe the now drying blood from the handler's face while Tyrell stood guard over us with his trusty stick. The redneck wrangler was moaning in pain.

"Hey, what'd you give him in the needle?" I asked.

"We thought we gave him a tranquilizer," he said. He cleared his throat. "The first needle worked, but it started to wear off an hour in. The other guy who handles all the needle stuff gave him a second dose after Samson started to buck a little."

The handler started to cough up. Tyrell reached into his pocket and brought out an airplane bottle of Bacardi O, cracking the top. I looked at him disapprovingly. "What?" asked Tyrell. "It's for the pain, my brotha." He handed the bottle to the wrangler, who downed it.

The wrangler cleared his throat again, nodding in appreciation. "I don't know what happened. I think the second needle maybe wasn't a tranq," he said.

"What was it, then?" I asked.

The handler waited a few seconds before answering. "It might have been a dose of steroids," he said.

"Jesus Christ!" I said.

"I think so. It was a double dose too."

"Huh?" said Tyrell. He threw his hands up quickly, then let them fall to his waist. "Ain't this about a bitch! You mean to tell me you gave that monster a shot of roids?" Tyrell closed his eyes and stood up. "No wonder that horse is goin' buck."

"How do we stop it?" I asked. "Is a dart going to work?"

"I doubt it. All those hormones need to be worked out before it stops going berserk. A dart will only piss it off even more," said the handler.

We heard more echoes of horse neighs and a tranquilizer gun firing. It didn't sound as though Jarod was a very good shot. I looked at Tyrell, who had his mouth open with his tongue half out, sort of laughing. Tyrell asked the handler what he meant by all those hormones needing to be worked out. Without going into too much detail, the handler compared Samson to a frustrated teenager who took too many Viagra pills and was looking for relief.

"Oh, I get it," said Tyrell with a devilish smile across his lips. "You mean that little pony gonna release the Kraken, so to speak."

"I guess that's what you'd call it," said the bruised-up handler.

"Ha ha!" Tyrell's face lit up. "Yeah, man, Samson needs to get himself some!"

"Goddamn it," I said. Tyrell was giggling something fierce. He kept thrusting his arm up in the air, his fist clenched tightly, and making a springing sound. "We gotta let Jarod know about the steroids before—"

"Before he gets mounted!" Tyrell said, interrupting me.

"Yeah, that."

"Dig this, man. You on your own with that one. I ain't going anywhere near Mr. Twister until he's worked himself out."

"Come on, Tyrell. I need—"

"Hell no! Tyrell don't need no horse ding-a-ling tryin' to penetrate me!" said Tyrell. He dismissed me with his hands, shooing me away. I stood up. I needed to get to Jarod, and fast, before he took his shot. If he hit Samson with a dart, he might awaken a whole new level of anger. As I jogged away, Tyrell yelled out a last-minute encouragement to bolster my confidence. "Watch out for Samson's tallywhacker, Jack! Neigh!"

Rounding the corner of the last hallway, I found myself staring down the entrance to the gymnasium. This was the only place Samson and Jarod could be. The hallway emptied into the gym with the side doors closed and locked. I proceeded forward. The doors leading into the gym looked to be kicked in. Bits of wood and glass lay on the ground near two small piles of horse flop. I approached the doors cautiously, tiptoeing softly. The gym hallway was surrounded by a glass corridor on either side. I had the feeling I was walking into a greenhouse.

Looking out a side window, I saw some hope. In the darkness, I made out flashing red-and-blue lights in the faint distance. It was coming from the parking lot near the cafeteria. Where the hell was the damn police or fire department? Where was everybody? I was doing this alone. Somewhere in this huge, cavernous gymnasium was one horny pony and possibly a dead animal control officer.

I avoided the horse crap piles that I saw in the shadows. The same went for the glass shards and wooden pieces littering the floor. They were easy to avoid. Five feet from the entrance to the gym, I hit a wet patch. Below my right boot was a small puddle of slippery, clear fluid. I didn't need a degree in biology to know what I was stepping in. I let out an audible "Ick!" and "Tsk." Of course, with my luck, I would be the one to step in pony juices. It wasn't the worst fluid I had ever stepped in on the job, but still. Now that Samson's pump was primed, he was surely more dangerous than before.

I heard a grumble come from the far end of the gym. It was either the dying sounds of a worked-over Jarod or Samson satisfying his urges. I feared it was both happening at the same time. Exploring the gym after hours was normally not a difficult task. Most scenarios were rather uneventful. One could potentially trip over a set of workout weights or tangle their feet in a thoughtlessly left out jump rope. Never once had I ever feared being anally invaded by a revved-up circus animal.

I took my time scanning the hangar-like area, listening for any sounds. The grumbling I heard moments ago was long gone, as were any sounds, for that matter. With gentle steps, I proceeded further, allowing my eyes to adjust to the blackness of my surroundings. I got down low to the ground, praying for vibrations or a signal. Two minutes into my quest, I heard noises coming from the far end.

The back half of the gym had a divider curtain drawn across the center. Gym teachers pulled these large vinyl curtains out to segment portions of the gym. The far end was reserved for the gymnastics team for daily after-school practice. Things like a huge floor mat for tumbling and parallel bars were set up in this area permanently. The back half of the gym was where the folding bleachers were housed as well.

Suddenly, something behind the curtain made a knocking sound. Looking around on the floor, I found a hockey stick used for floor hockey games. I knelt to grab it. Next to it was a Jason-style white goalie mask. I grabbed them both for some kind of defense. As I stood up with the Mylec stick in hand and a hockey mask over my face, the knocking sound grew. A continuous, deep racking thud got louder and louder.

Upon obtaining the stick and mask, my conscience got bolder. I wasn't bulletproof, but I knew how to wield a hockey stick with the best of them. Back in the day, I was quite the hockey player myself. Not professionally, of course, but I could hang. I walked closer to the curtain, easing into the act of confrontation if need be. With one last breath, I found the center opening of the curtain, drew it apart with the hockey stick, and let out a roar of my own, running into the void of the gymnastics area without fear.

What I saw on the other side of the curtain was ghastly amusing. There in the corner of the gym, near the bleachers, was Samson mounting the stationary pommel horse, rhythmically rubbing his manhood onto the leather-covered apparatus. The pommel horse was too high for him to get a good grip, but he gave it his best effort. Poor Samson. He was a foot too short. The fully aroused pony was so focused on the activity that he didn't hear my battle screech, or maybe he was too busy air-humping the shit out of his companion to care. His thunderous thrusting was compulsive. It was like he knew he had to work himself down before his heart exploded.

I relaxed a bit, dropping my charging stance, but I was still holding the hockey stick. I shifted the stick to my left hand, placing the butt end on the ground. With the stick vertical, I lifted the goalie mask up to rest on the top of my head, mesmerized by Samson's dance of passion. For a tiny horse, he was packing some serious schlong. Away he went, working his mojo like it was the last time he would ever get the chance. He was quite impressive for a little guy. All those years of rage was unloaded onto a defenseless piece of gymnastic equipment.

I texted Tyrell to let him know what was happening, letting him know I was all right. He replied with, "K." He was not intrigued by my current situation or cared for my safety, just, "K." Besides being caught off guard by Samson's erotic gyration, I took the circus handler's advice to heart. What was the sense in interrupting him? Had I moseyed over to annoyingly poke him with a cheap hockey stick, he might have turned his attention to me. I figured it was best to let him finish, so he did. With the pommel horse rocking to and fro in place, Samson finished his lovemaking session with a loud, high-pitched neigh. Seconds after the deed was done, the lights flicked on.

"Don't move!" a voice yelled out from the side of the gym. It was Jarod. He knelt near the switch on the wall, flicking it on. As my eyes were adjusting, I closed them briefly, reaching to shade them from the bright light. I heard the sound of a tranquilizer gun firing and a dart slapping into the side of Samson's ass cheek. He let out a lower neigh as the sedative coursed its way through his body. The tiny Rico Suave passed out on top of the pommel horse seconds later.

"Got him!" yelled Jarod.

"Jesus, Jarod, how long you been sitting there?" I asked.

"About ten minutes." Jarod walked over to me with his walkie-talkie in hand, keying it up. "Dispatch, this is Jungle Jarod here. I got him. Send over the big van for transport."

"Jungle Jarod?" I said. "That's your radio handle?"

"It sure is," declared Jarod. "No need to fret anymore. The dart's got enough sedatives to keep this little monster at bay for a couple hours."

"Well, that's good." We shook hands briefly as a congratulatory gesture. "I was searching for you to tell you some news I got out of the circus guy."

"You mean about the steroids?" Jarod said.

"Yeah. How'd you know?"

"Well, with my years of expertise on the job, I saw something in his behavior that eluded to a possible anabolic steroid injection. Samson kept kicking backward and shaking his head violently as if he'd been given a counteractive, attention-heightening drug."

Jarod had some swagger of his own in his deciphering of the situation. He was another career-pompous ass with the whole "I've been doing this job for x amount of years" routine. "I'm sure the dangling, erect pony dick gave it away too," I said.

"Yes, I saw that as well," said Jarod coyly. "It was only a matter of time until he found a suitable tension-relieving object to satisfy his urges. Once he…finished, it was time to take a steady shot."

The two of us walked over to the now complacent Samson. The pony was fast asleep on top of the pommel horse, snoring contently. Surely it was the most refreshing sleep an animal in his position could have. Samson looked peaceful lying there. His black-and-white mane was matted, and he was sweating profusely. Had he not been so much of a roided-out prick, he might have been a sweet little pony, perfect for backyard playtime.

"What's going to happen to him now?" I asked.

"Typically, animals who act out in public are either sold at a humane auction to be retired to a farm or euthanized," said Jarod. "If the courts consider this animal to be a nuisance, then its euthanasia for sure."

"Even if the jerk-off circus guys are at fault because they juiced him up? They penned him up for years, constantly shooting him with God knows what. The circus owners should be sued for this crap."

"That's the way the law is written," said Jarod. "Doesn't make it right. That's the way it goes. I've seen plenty of circus animals get put down due to handler negligence."

A minute later, a few members of the SWAT team rushed into the gym, rifles drawn, along with two firemen. There wasn't much they could do now. They questioned us about the horse and the milky-white substance coagulating on the floor. We had a hell of a time explaining it. Eventually, everything was put into the report with giggles and jokes discussed but ultimately omitted from the final report. Mr. Polotski showed up about half an hour later, looking at me like I caused the whole thing. Yeah, like it was my fault the pony was drugged and humped himself to sleep.

I made my way back down to the cafeteria through the carnage in the hallways. The whole school was a disaster. Broken glass, gerbil food, and about six gallons of horse semen were slowly adhering to the wooden gym floor. In the café, I met back up with Tyrell near the chimpanzee cage. He was saying goodbye to his new friend, wishing him well in his future endeavors.

"Bye, Jeremy!" said Tyrell, waving obnoxiously as the animal control team trucked the cage out of the school. "I hope you enjoyed your salty snack. Don't forget to write me!" The remaining police and animal control workers gave Tyrell dirty looks, which most people did whenever Tyrell opened his mouth. The simple bastard smiled at me, chuckling to himself.

I gathered the other janitors, who were either hiding or oblivious to the whole fiasco. In such a huge school, it was possible to be halfway across the building and never knowing what was happening on the other side. Half the crew didn't have a clue about the pony incident.

We started the cleanup process as the last cop car pulled out of the parking lot. I assigned Tyrell the job of mopping up the gym because he abandoned me. He cursed the whole time, calling me all sorts of colorful names. He got over it, though. The office denied his claim for shoe reimbursement, stating they weren't paying $160 for new Air Jordans covered in pony smegma.

Before long, the cafeteria cleared out. Distraught families took their traumatized children home for the evening, yelling about legal action against the school and the circus, but it was nothing a new PlayStation game and rocky road ice cream couldn't fix! We swept up the littered hay and popcorn kernels, along with red circus ticket stubs. I picked up a stub and placed it in my pocket. I was positive that was the last circus ticket stub I would ever see. The whole big, top experience didn't have the same luster it did when I was a kid. Now I knew what happened in the real world—the drug-induced comas, the ruthless pursuit of profits, and ultimately, the loss of precious animal lives. It was yet another part of my childhood that was smashed to pieces before my naive, tear-filled eyes.

I hoped poor little Samson didn't get put to sleep because of this. He never asked to be paraded around with countless kids on his back, being shot up every time he revolted. In my head, Samson had a happy ending—not a real happy ending but a joyous outcome. You get what I mean. I pictured him running freely in a green pasture—no sedatives or steroids coursing through his veins, no rigid saddle chafing his back, and no metal bit stuck in his mouth, just a big, open field with plenty of female ponies running eagerly with him. I thought he had earned a peaceful retirement. Don't you?

CHAPTER 19

The Gray Viper versus the Bearded Mongoose

I got a call on a Monday morning, early Monday morning, 7:00 a.m. on the nose. A warm and bubbly lady who was way too chipper for seven o'clock on a Monday morning told me that Mr. Sanders would like to have a meeting with me that Friday afternoon. A whole week they made you wait for some dreaded meeting, which I was already expecting. They always did this shit to you; they would call on a Monday and make you wait the entire week.

"Can Mr. Sanders expect you this Friday afternoon?" I heard from the receiver.

"Yeah, whatever," I said and hung up the phone.

Boy, they sure did act fast when they wanted your ass terminated. I had a weekend of peace before Sanders had the meeting set. It took the bastards a whole year to pay me back for overtime, but they got my termination meeting set in less than forty-eight hours.

This had been a long time coming. I knew this day was just over the horizon ever since I got into it with that infant-sized Taylor Gregors and his cave troll friend Cassandra. Those two losers dimed me out for standing up for myself. If I hadn't ever met those two, I would still be sleeping in on a Monday morning, just me and my kitty cats, snuggling under a blankie, dreaming about not being at work. The kitties, of course, were actual cats. I was not making a euphemism or anything. I was talking about real felines who loved to cuddle under the blanket when my wife had left for the morning. Get your mind out of the sewer, man.

Anyway, Taylor and Cassandra fucked me royally with their report to HR. That was where I met the lovely and multitalented Ms. Janet Rillings, who had a hard-on for me before I even walked in her office. Her hostile takeover of the human resources department meant she had to cut some dead weight, as the board of education liked to do. All new bosses tried to do this same thing. They would find people who were at the top of the pay scale and looked for any reason to shitcan them.

The more money she could save the board of ed, the longer contract she would get. It was Business Economics 101. They taught this crap in business administration classes. "Oh, what do we have here, an employee who's near the top of the pay scale and will likely stay here for another fifteen years? Looks like they just aren't what we're looking for in a model employee. We'll just fabricate some awful lie and set his ass up. Time to fire him and save the district beaucoup dollars."

The final blow came from a close friend I had spent too many nights working with, a one Mr. Tyrell Jones. Right after he and I had it out, he made a phone call to his new overlord, Sanders. It was weird how I got a meeting scheduled not soon after Tyrell and I had it out. That slimy Sanders had all the ammunition he needed to bust me up now.

To be honest, I was glad I would finally be leaving this trash heap for good. I wasted so many years working here, and for what? Sure, dental insurance was great and all, but what about my mental health? It had been a long-ass time since I felt happy when I walked into work. I'm not talking about a bad day or even a few days. I felt absolutely abysmal coming to work. Half the day, I looked out the window with a broom in my calloused hands, watching anonymous cars drive by. Where were they going, and who did I have to bump off to hitch a ride with them to whatever destination they were headed? That was never a good sign, wanting to hop in a car with strangers as long as they took you away from your current mess. I hoped they had good candy.

I said this in the last book, but it still rang true to this very day: Working a job you hated to make rent was no way to live. You felt clammed up and stuck in a small space with no wiggle room. I would say it was like suffocating, but not like suffocating. Maybe it was more like a tight-collared shirt limiting your airflow. Over the years, this collar got tighter and tighter, much like a boa constrictor or a viper, another one of God's scaly serpents.

Between that Monday and Friday afternoon, I got my affairs in order. I hit a few doctors' appointments, renewed my prescriptions for as long as the doctors could fill out, and doubled up on my rent payments with the meager amount of savings I had. If these pricks were going to fire me, at least I would have a place to consume my much-needed meds! I also canceled what I could when it came to retirement plans.

Since I started working, I set up a tax shelter and a limited 401(k) plan. I couldn't get all my money out because of my age, but I got a nice chunk out of what I had put in over the past twenty years. I surely wasn't going to make it to retirement age now. It was a damn shame too. I had a lot of money in the market so I could sit pretty during my older years. A few more years and I would have been able to leave on my own terms. Being vested in the system meant you had a future when you finally quit. That was all up in the air now.

Friday morning came, and I prepared myself for the worst. You had to when you worked for a school district. They got unlimited funds and lawyers out the ass. They were good lawyers too. Have you ever watched *The Simpsons*? Do you remember the scenes where Mr. Burns is in court and he's got, like, fifteen lawyers on his side of the bench? That was the board of education. Come to think of it, Mr. Sanders may have, in fact, been Mr. Burns! He got the same decrepit walk, and he was loaded too thanks to working for the board of education. I'm sure one of his minions resembled Smithers in more ways than one. Did that make me Homer Simpson? I do love me some doughnuts.

I woke up on Friday morning not with a sense of nervousness but with a sense of relief. My mind was at peace for the first time in an exceptionally long time. After today, I would never have to work for this unholy job ever again. Saying it out loud, never having to work there again, gave me a feeling of joy unrivaled by any drug. There would be no more shameful feeling of disrespect when I walked in and no more mental torture of having someone stalk my every move. It was truly exhilarating to say this sentence aloud even if the only ones listening were my two cats.

For years, I had been afraid of a life without a mop in my hands. It was all I had ever done as a real full-time job. Besides my writing side gigs, the janitoring life was all I ever had to pay my bills. What would happen to me without a steady paycheck? How would I afford to live, let alone strive ahead? These ideas had been filling my brain on an almost weekly basis for years. Sure, I could pick up a broom and plunger at another dead-end janitoring job, but did I really want that again? More of the same fears and anxiety sneaked into my daily thoughts, causing me to freak out for no reason at all. This job made me a slave to what-ifs.

I learned a lot of things from working here. No, I'm not talking about the proper way to unclog a drain or lift a desk without throwing out your back. I'm talking about how to not live your life in fear anymore. If you gave in to your fears, then that was all you would ever be: afraid. Who wanted to live life constantly walking on eggshells? Thoughts about losing a job or getting sick or even dying only polluted your mind. They held you back from actually living your life.

Sooner than later, you would start to miss out on things you were meant to enjoy. That was no way to live. Once you started feeling afraid of the future, you might as well stay in the past for good. I was done being afraid of things that could or couldn't happen anymore. Whatever the sack of shit Sanders had planned for me, I would meet it head-on. I would go out in a blaze of glory, just like Bon Jovi said!

When Friday afternoon rolled around, I had already come to terms with being unemployed. What was done was done, I assumed. I couldn't change the past or try to fix anything already too far gone. It was me against the evils of the Gray Viper and whatever villainous activity he had laid out for me.

Instead of bringing a binder full of paperwork or a leather attaché to the meeting, I simply walked in with a smirk and a new hat. I had always been fond of porkpie hats, really nice ones with a red or black feather along the rim, so I bought a new outfit with the last bit of moola I had in my rainy day account. I went down to Asbury Park and picked out a sweet hat, along with an offensively worded new T-shirt and dark leather boots. This hat was tits too, real sharp! If I was going to get fired, at least I would go out in style.

I arrived at the viper's lair about half an hour late. What was he going to do, fire me? Ha! Fucker already had my neck on the chopping block. I breezed into the meeting room without a care left in the world, like a gunslinger walking the dirt road into the outlaw's rowdy Wild West town. Ahead of me were several individuals. The board's three midlevel lawyers were decked out in their finest Jos. A. Bank spring collection. All looked mediocre except for the head honcho, the dude they brought in to close out careers.

He was old, and the years of litigation had made him look regal. He was sort of like F. Lee Bailey, only sterner. His suit was superb—pinstriped olive green and reeking of money. The board must have robbed the treasure chest hard-core to bring this reaper in. I bet he got paid per hour what I made in a week. To his left was the teacher's union president, a feeble-looking man many years past his prime. This guy might have had some balls back in the day, but he was a school board lackey now. Whatever the board executives said, he did. Having this dipshit at the meeting was only a formality. He was just someone to document my execution so payroll would know when to stop my checks.

I longed for the day when being in a union actually meant something. The way this country was going, being a union member only meant you had less money in your take-home pay. The unions were in bed with management; unless you were a member of the well-protected bosses, you might as well throw your union dues into a volcano. My only union representation had the intelligence of a mole rat and the backbone of a mushroom. He was in the pocket of the same people gunning for my termination.

On one end of the long meeting table was Sanders's secretary. She was all set up with her notepad and laptop, ready to document the trial. I guess she was there to write in the number of times they expected me to beg and cry during my hearing. *I ain't begging for jack shit*, I thought, *so she's going to have an easy day. She'll be writing down a whole lot of "Cocksucker" and "Useless piece of donkey shit" quotes from me, but that is it.*

At the head of the table, dressed in a brand-new black suit, was the Gray Viper himself. The cheap son of a bitch finally bought a new suit! It looked like a tuxedo, and it was real fancy. He must have splurged a little, treating himself to a new outfit knowing he would finally be able to get rid of me. In his mind, he probably thought he was an undertaker, anxiously awaiting the time to close the lid on my coffin. I wasn't going to give him the satisfaction.

"Please have a seat," said Sanders. His voice was hoarse. He sounded like he had a bad cold, maybe even the flu. There was talk of a new respitory illness going around, possibly turning into a worldwide pandemic. Maybe he had the bug. I hoped the prick choked on his own saliva before the meeting was over.

"Thanks," I said. I plopped down onto a comfy leather chair while folding my arms. I said nothing else, just hawking Sanders down. I stared at him, waiting for him to begin the charade. The three lower-quality lawyers all began shuffling their papers, waiting for him to speak. The secretary started to type nervously. I didn't know what she was afraid of. It was my job on the line, not hers. Both the union president and the head lawyer sat there with their hands folded nicely in front of them. The president was looking downward, at the table, while the head lawyer watched me. This guy had spent countless hours glaring at courtroom defendants. I was just another case file to him.

"Let's get started, shall we?" said Sanders. "Do you know why you're here today?"

"Nope," I said. The room was quiet. Only the noise of shuffling papers filled the closed room setting.

"You're here today because of your numerous infractions against the workers of this board of education," said Sanders. His eyes bounced between the papers in front of him, back to me, and then down again. He was struggling to form words with whatever illness he had.

"Is that so?" I said, still watching him.

"Yes, it is so," said Sanders. He cleared his throat, reaching for a tissue in his suit's breast pocket.

"Huh," I said, shifting my eyes to the rest of the room. "Beats me. First time I heard about it."

"Oh, really? Are you certain about that? Judging from the long list of violations I have in front of me, you should be well aware of your behavioral outbursts." Sanders reached for a yellow steno pad in front of him, adjusting his Dollar Store reading glasses on his wrinkled nose.

"News to me," I said nonchalantly. I moved my high-back chair from side to side with my right leg bouncing up and down in place. Everyone in the room looked down at the table to whatever pile of official papers they had in front of them, everyone except the head lawyer. He kept staring at me with intent. It was starting to piss me off.

Sanders brought forth a sheet of paper from the bottom of his pile, starting to read from it. "Let the record show that Mr.—"

"Tell this dude to stop eyeballing me," I yelled out loud. "I don't give a fuck who he is or how much money he's getting paid for this." I pointed at the head lawyer. The papers stopped their shuffling motion. I stared back at him, undaunted by his scare tactics. He kept his gaze straight on my pupils.

"That kind of language has no place in a formal meeting!" Sanders yelled. "I would refrain from such coarse actions if I were you."

"Well, you're not me, are you?" I said to Sanders. I eyeballed him now, just as the head lawyer was doing to me. I was ready to punch Sanders in his wonky eye. I was already getting shitcanned, right? I might as well go for broke.

"Let's all just take a moment to relax here," said one of the other lawyers. "This is a formal hearing here. No need to get out of control. From anyone." I guessed he was the cooler of the group. He was about my age, I would say, and was fearing for some kind of technicality if Sanders or the head lawyer said or did anything to jeopardize the case. The head lawyer smirked a bit, then looked down at his papers, still not saying a peep. He was getting paid either way. I was sure pushing someone's buttons was his specialty. Sanders, refraining from going back and forth with me, averted his gaze to the wall at the opposite end of the room.

I looked back at the group of lawyers and the union president. "I ain't got time for this," I said. "Say what you gotta say and get it over with. I got shit to do." I folded my fingers in my hands, placing them on my stomach, and leaned back.

"Well, then," said Sanders. "Here it is, then. You're officially being charged with insubordination, insighting a hostile work environment, and causing undue duress on your coworkers and the board of education. We have all the documents to prove your guilt and will display them out here today at this hearing. Upon testimony from eyewitnesses, your employment status will be judged upon the findings."

I kind of missed what he was saying toward the end of his diatribe because of his wheezing. With the black suit and the constant moist sounds from his throat, Sanders looked and sounded like Darth Vader. Once I had the image in my mind, it all came together. I was being prosecuted by the Dark Lord himself. I started to laugh.

"What are you laughing at, mister? Do you know how serious these charges are?" Sanders was getting animated now. He leaned forward to lambaste me further. "If these eyewitnesses prove your guilt here today, you will be terminated on the spot! Do you understand that? Do you?"

Sanders put his left hand up at me, pointing. He looked exactly like Vader when he was using the force to choke out the captains aboard the Death Star. I reared my head back, laughing hysterically at him, which, in turn, only made him angrier. The more he yelled at me, the more I laughed. My head was fully back on the chair, my eyes closed and all. Two of the lawyers were talking over Sanders, trying to get him to stop yelling and me to stop laughing. They got control of the room, but not before I was crying and Sanders was crimson in the face. I didn't know skin could get that red unless sunburned.

Some adult words were exchanged during the outburst. I thought for every curse word I said, Sanders matched me in kind. We pointed menacingly at each other. Then I mocked him, pretending to be choking as he waved his hands at me. At this point, it was a weird pantomime session, the two of us acting out a scene from *Star Wars* while the bloodsucking lawyers tried to persuade us to sit down and shut up.

Sanders wasn't getting my references to the movie. I didn't think anyone in the room did. I believed he was actively trying to air choke me. Five minutes later, with the secretary feverishly typing away, it was agreed by the lawyers that she would edit out the verbal exchange. It was more on their end; I meant what I said and could care less at this point. We all took a breather for a minute. Sanders's breathing sounded even more like Darth Vader's as he inhaled and exhaled through his nose. I sat back after a good, hardy belly laugh, trying to get back on pace.

"Go ahead. Get on with this farce," I said. "Present your so-called eyewitness testimony. I'm starting to get hungry."

With that, the cheaper lawyers did what they got paid to do. Each one presented a piece of paper with a formal write-up against me. The first was a culmination of thirteen major write-ups from my time on the job. They were not smaller infractions. Hell, if they presented those, the meeting might need to be extended a few days. These were major complaints.

They detailed the Bobby Benz debacle, the Brother Wade altercation, and several cases where I verbally or mentally assaulted coworkers. Some of them I had completely forgotten about, like the time I put bearing grease on a faculty room toilet seat so each time someone went to take a shit, they slid off the bowl and onto the floor. The lawyer also pulled out a file from the midnineties. It was written in old-school printer paper, the kind with the perforated edges. Allegedly, one of one my first coworkers brought a case against me because I terrorized him. He claimed he had to seek counseling because I hazed him somewhat. Calling someone fresh fish and spraying him with a garden hose was not appropriate behavior, apparently.

I had forgotten all about this guy, Jesus! I might or might not have said he looked like a future inmate and treated him as such. He was a weird little twerp with not one bit of thick skin on him. Every time he walked down the hallway, I would jump out from an open classroom door, screaming, "Lights out!" scaring him half to death. He started falling to the ground, covering his head, after the first week.

"Mr. Pilles had to undergo years of counseling due to your hazing. He has only now begun to live a normal life after you tortured him," stated Sanders.

"Never heard of him," I said.

"Yes, you have. It has been documented. I reached out to Mr. Pilles to corroborate his story a few weeks ago. He wrote me a detailed letter saying your treatment of him caused him to have nightmares for years. You sure did a number on his psyche."

"Isn't there, like, a statute of limitations on these alleged offenses?" I asked wryly. I kept swiveling side to side in my chair, ignoring them all. The room was quiet. They all watched me with distaste in their eyes. I was blowing it off, waiting for the firing to be official.

Taylor and Cassandra's complaint came next with their accusations about me starting rumors. The second lawyer read their case against me aloud to the room with more silent stares. The union president shook his head, looking like a bashful nun scolding me. I rolled my eyes, brushing off their claims.

"Those two are lying pieces of shit," I said. "Both of them treated me like garbage the whole time I worked at that school. Where's my case against them, huh? I guess the things they said and did to me are overlooked, right?"

Sanders smugly dismissed my claims to the lawyers. "Both Taylor and Cassandra are exemplary workers with no record of complaints against them. I believe both of them are in the clear with all the blame lying solely on the defendant in this case." The lawyers and union president seemed to agree with Sanders.

"Bullcrap," I said in a lax tone. "This is all a bunch of bullcrap, just like this entire job has always been."

"One more outburst like that and I'll terminate you right here and now!"

"Go ahead. Go for it!" I said. "That's all you've been trying to do for years. Grow a set and pull the trigger, pal!"

"Enough," said one of the lawyers. "You'll have your rebuttal in due time."

"Whatever," I said, rolling my eyes, looking toward the ceiling.

The third lawyer presented his part of the case, an incident report from Ms. Rillings. Here, the lawyer went in for the death knell, claiming I screamed her out and trashed her office. I kept swiveling around and around in a circle, resting in a relaxed pose, until one of the lawyers told me to stop spinning. He asked me if her report was true, and I said, "Hell no!" about six times. Each person in the room looked at me as if I was a murder felon at a parole hearing. The stupid union president shook his head shamefully.

"What the hell are you shaking your head for? You cost me all that money for some stupid-ass anger management classes, remember? Don't give me that look. You should be standing up for me against these claims. I didn't do any of these things, and you know it! What the fuck do I pay union dues for?" I said. He put his head down, then looked over at Sanders for guidance.

"I think it's time we bring in our special eyewitness so the board can make its final judgment, shall we?" Sanders pushed a button on the wireless intercom system on the table. "Send him in," he said.

I now knew why there was an empty chair in the room. Across the table, the door opened. In walked Tyrell, fancy suit on with a toothless grin. He had his right hand in his pocket with a padfolio under the crook of his arm. He sauntered in, saying hello to everyone in the room, everyone except me. We didn't make eye contact until he was done shaking hands with the lawyers and Sanders.

"Fucking Judas," I mumbled to myself under my breath. The lawyers shot me a look. Tyrell finally looked at me as if to say, "Watch your tone. I'm still from the hood, and I'll take your ass out." I looked away, turning to the wall instead of the person I had been cool with for many, many years.

Sanders leaned back in his chair, introducing Tyrell to the group. "This is Mr. Jones, a recent recipient of a promotion in the custodial department. He was appointed to the position of head of the department not long ago. Mr. Jones has pertinent information about this case, information that I believe shall persuade this panel once and for all as to what action shall be taken against the defendant. After his testimony, this panel shall make its overall judgment in the case. Is that clear?"

The lawyers nodded their heads while I blew air out from my mouth. My lips vibrated as I did it. It was only a matter of time now. Tyrell's testimony would be all they needed to make it legal. I sat back, slowly realizing how far this had gone. I started to get a cool sensation over my body, the same kind you got when you were nervous and anxious about something. This was it.

Sanders took the helm for this part of the hearing, reading from a prepared statement. "Upon Mr. Jones's appointment, the defendant in the case became very disgruntled, so much so that Mr. Jones was verbally accosted during a routine job performance inspection. The defendant, as acknowledged in this room, began swearing at Mr. Jones. The result of the altercation was Mr. Jones informing the defendant that if he continued to be defiant, he would be written up for insubordination. The defendant then called Mr. Jones several words I cannot and will not mention here today."

Tyrell sat there, staring straight down toward his padfolio, not saying a word. The remainder of the group—the lawyers, the union president, and the secretary—all wrote things down on legal pads. I refolded my arms, adjusting my pose to reflect my carelessness.

"Such insubordinate actions call for an immediate response," said Sanders. "If these statements are found to be true, the defendant shall be terminated immediately."

"Agreed," said all three lawyers in unison.

"Agreed," the union president chimed in.

"Noted," said the secretary as she typed.

Sanders looked up from his statement. His beady eyes lurched upward to address Tyrell. "Therefore, I ask Mr. Jones to verify these statements to be true by speaking here and now." He put down his pen and leaned eagerly toward Tyrell. "Mr. Jones, do you agree with these statements I have said? Are these to be true in your educated opinion? Did the defendant verbally accost you on the job?"

Tyrell looked up from his padfolio. He wasn't writing anything, just looking downward. When he looked up, he looked to his left, into Sanders's crooked face, then looked toward the lawyers, then finally locked eyes with me. He opened his mouth to answer Sanders's questions. "I don't know what the fuck you talkin' 'bout, Mr. Sanders," he said. "Everything you said was a bunch of bullshit."

CHAPTER 20

I Love My Job!

"What?" Sanders cried out, wheezing, his Darth Vader accent full of phlegm. "What did you say?"

Tyrell looked around the meeting table. He was cooler than a snow cone in Northern Alaska. He shot me a look, a familiar "Keep cool, my brotha" look. "I said, I don't know what the fuck you talkin' 'bout." He clapped after each word he uttered. "Everything you said was a bullshit-ass lie."

You could hear the atoms crashing into one another in the meeting. That was how quiet it got. No one spoke for about ten seconds, but it seemed like an hour. I almost pooped a Buick when Tyrell spoke. I jerked out of my chair with a massive smile. A jolt of adrenaline shot into my system, causing my senses to be heightened. I was fully aware now. No more lollygagging here.

"Oh, really now?" I said. I looked at Sanders with glee and unfiltered joy.

"What…what…this man is saying…is…"

"Is this true, Mr. Sanders?" The honcho head lawyer spoke for the first time. His voice was deep and authoritative.

"No!" Sanders said back. "This man is full of deception. He… he doesn't know what he's speaking about." He was backpedaling bigtime, coughing as he reached for a tissue. He shuffled papers back and forth in front of him, barely able to make full sentences.

Tyrell messed him up something fierce when he called him out. "You lyin', and you know it!" he said as he pointed his right index finger at Sanders. "You told me you'd hook me up with a boss position if I went along with your plans. You done told me if I set him up, I'd get a raise and a new company car and a whole bunch of stuff!"

"Sanders, is this man telling the truth?" asked the top lawyer. His words were concrete, stonelike his demeanor. The deep, bass-filled voice put everyone in the room on notice. Serious didn't begin to explain the depth of the meeting now. The other three lawyers began writing all sorts of stuff down. God help the poor secretary. Her fingers were working faster than Liberace on a grand piano.

"I…I never promised this man anything!" said Sanders. His mouth was ajar. His bad eye was twitching in random intervals. He looked like a pinball machine on full tilt.

"You're full of shit!" said Tyrell. He turned to address the head lawyer now. "Look here. Mr. Sanders came to me 'bout a month ago, sayin' he thought I was the perfect man to take the foreman position. I thought he wanted to promote me for all the hard work I put in over the years. He said he'd give me a big raise and a nice office and all sorts of perks, but I had to turn on my man over there. I didn't want to do it at first, but Mr. Sanders kept pushing me. He told me if I did this, he'd be able to help me pay off my credit cards. Everybody knows I've got a shitload of credit card debt. He said something like putting the bills into a school spending account. I don't know. Something crazy sounding like that."

Sanders's face told the story. He looked like a kid who just got caught breaking a lamp. His mouth was still open, speechless. Nothing but a wet breathing sound emitted from the back of his throat. I listened to everything coming from Tyrell with both happiness and sadness. Why would he tell his story now? Was it even true, or was Tyrell covering for me? I didn't have the chance to address any of my questions before a loud slam hit the table. It was the head lawyer's briefcase as he picked it up from the floor to gather his materials.

"It is the finding of this panel that the defendant has been wrongfully accused in all charges and will hereby be placed back on full duty effective immediately. This case against the defendant will be expunged from the records, and all records and files in relation to this case will be sealed under my jurisdiction."

"But you cannot let this man go! He is a menace to the board of education! You…you…," said Sanders. He was trailing off, grasping for proper words to annunciate.

"No, Sanders. It appears you are the menace in this situation," said the head lawyer. He gathered his papers and placed them in his briefcase. He closed the briefcase with authority, latched the clasps, and rolled his chair away from the table. With that, the three other lawyers hastily gathered their materials as well and stood up. "Sanders, I'd like to have a word with you in your office," added the head lawyer, "in private." The three other lawyers all started to leave the room, following one another in order of seniority. The head lawyer shook the hand of the union president, who sat there like a bump on a pickle. He was just as flabbergasted as I was. The secretary collected all her stuff too and made her way out of the room to take notes of Sanders's impromptu meeting.

The union president started to get up and looked at me with his stupid face. "Well, I guess everything worked itself out," he said.

"I guess it did," I said in a victorious tone. "Thanks for all your help, you useless jerk-off. Glad my union dues paid for such stellar representation!"

He slinked out of the room, trying to look back at Sanders. Mr. Sanders was motionless. His hands were planted firmly on the table, palms down. His lopsided face was grimacing in pain—pain from defeat and pain from the ass chewing he was about to receive in the next meeting. He looked up at me, and we locked eyes. He said nothing as he stared. I saw weakness and frailty, the pitiful look you see on the face of someone who had lost everything in a natural disaster.

Sanders turned his head to the right to look at Tyrell, who had his arms folded, smiling away. "You'll never work here ever again. You're fired!" said Sanders.

"Good, 'cause I don't want to work for your sorry ass no more. You lucky I'm still on probation, 'cause I'd have ended your ass long ago, you crooked-faced bitch!"

Sanders started to say something, but he was interrupted by a voice from outside the room. "Sanders! Now!" said the head lawyer. With that, Mr. Sanders, in his new suit, wheezing voice, and twitching glass eye, got up from the table and slowly walked out of the room.

Tyrell and I watched him as he left with his forked tail between his legs. I felt a bit of remorse for him. Sanders would probably face a slew of charges, maybe lose his job, and possibly have legal action brought against him. Plus, he didn't sound too good. He was wheezing like a man on a ventilator. I said I felt a little bit of remorse, but not enough to make me lose a wink of sleep over it. This prick had been hunting me for a long time, and he finally got a taste of his own medicine. I hoped it went down smooth.

"Come on, man," said Tyrell. He stood up from the table and motioned for me to follow him. "We got some talkin' of our own to do. Walk with me for a little."

I stood up, half confused, half elated. There was a tornado of butterflies in my stomach. After Tyrell and I left the room, we walked out of the building, and we did not speak until we were clear of other people's ears. We passed Sanders's office on our left. The door was closed, and the blinds were being pulled closed by one of the lesser lawyers. I looked in right before the blind went shut and saw a hopeless Mr. Sanders sitting down in his desk chair. He stared forward. He wouldn't look out at the hallway as we passed. I believed I was looking at him for the last time ever, and the feeling gave me a rush of jubilation.

We walked side by side out to our cars—Tyrell to his Lincoln with twenty-four-inch chrome rims and me to my much newer yet paid off Ford truck. I was afraid to speak first. I didn't know what to say or where to start. What did one say to make the uneasiness go away? Tyrell knew exactly what to say or, better yet, what to do. He put his right hand on my left shoulder, as he had done many times before, and applied a friendly amount of pressure, the universal sign that said, "Everything will be okay."

"I'm so sorry for how I treated you, my brotha," Tyrell said. "I hope you understand I did it to help you out."

"This was a setup the whole time?" I asked.

"Yes, it was," said Tyrell. "That piece of crap came to me a month ago, tryin' to get me to turn on you. I didn't want to do it, you know. The fact I had to have it out with you really hurt me inside, man."

"But why did you do it? We almost came to blows. What the hell, man!" I said.

"Yeah, man, I know we did. Damn, you almost took a swing at me right before I left the school that night!" Tyrell was getting louder as he spoke, but it was a friendly kind of loud, the kind of voice elevation you had when you were trying to get a happy memory out at a party. "You pushed up on me like you was gonna try some shit. I seen ya!" We started to laugh. Tyrell still had his hand on my shoulder as we faced each other, laughing away as if we had the whole world watching us. To a passerby, we must have looked like two old friends catching up on years of memories. There were a few tears of joy and sadness mixed in to give it a feeling of realness.

"What are you going to do now, Tyrell?" I asked. "You lost your job because of me. Where are you going to work now?"

"Welp, I did it for you, and I did it for me too," said Tyrell. "I hoped if Sanders's plans came true, he'd need me to testify against you in this here meeting. He said he needed an eyewitness to pinpoint you to get the board to fire you. It was luck how it turned out. I was hoping you wouldn't quit or do something stupid before the meeting, or else we'd both be fucked."

Tyrell took his hand off my shoulder and stepped back. He threw his hands up to his sides, palms up, and gave me a patented Tyrell look as he smiled through his teeth. I might have been a smidge emotional from all that happened at the meeting. On my deathbed, I would say that I had an allergy or that a bug flew into my eye, causing it to water abnormally. The same bug must have flown into Tyrell's face too.

"As far as me makin' money, nah, I'm done cleaning toilets, you dig?" Tyrell said. "I think it's time I made my way back to the West Coast for a few years. I've been hearing all this hype over this new CBD oil stuff. You ever dig on that? I hear it's supposed to be better than weed. I'm getting old now, you know. My lungs are all fucked up over the smoke. I might have to indulge on some oil and sling some for a livin'." Classic Tyrell. The man loved to get high, and he was good at selling drugs. It was the perfect combination.

"I still got my connections in Colorado, so I think I can swing a job in a CBD dispensary, maybe head back to Cali for a stretch," Tyrell said. He started to giggle again. I saw his shoulders go up and down like he was a big bear with an itch.

"What?" I asked. "What are you laughing at?"

"Dig this, man. You think I should write my résumé on rolling papers, or nah?"

By the time I stopped laughing, I was wiping some of that allergy moisture out of my eyes again. Tyrell extended his hand out to me, and I shook it with adulation. Two seconds later, we pulled each other in for a big hug. I believed it was the last hug we would ever share together. Something told me it was.

Tyrell walked to his Lincoln, hitting the alarm on the key fob to unlock it. I stood in place, watching him, then called out to him one last time. "Hey, man, thank you for helping me. I'm going to miss you, Tyrell. Take care now."

He looked back at me over his left shoulder, pointing at me with his right hand. "You my brother, man. You always gonna be my brother. You be cool. Maybe I'll send you a care package from my new job when I get settled out there. You feel me?"

"All righty. I will."

Tyrell fired up the pimp wagon deluxe, cranked up his booming bass music, and drove out of the parking lot, his taillights slowly disappearing into the distance. There I was, on my own in the parking lot with my hands in my pocket, not knowing what to do with myself. I still had a job, I guess, even though I was already living in a different frame of mind. Not an hour ago, I was done with the janitor life, ready to embark on a new career, far from the icy hands of this place. What was I going to do now?

It was Friday, late afternoon, almost 5:00 p.m. I had an entire weekend free to do whatever I pleased. Maybe I would work on my résumé or try to write a book about my life. Maybe I would go get a drink at some swanky wine bar, order some tapas, and enjoy my triumph over the evil demon Sanders. Or maybe I would follow Tyrell out west, work in some head shop, and see the Pacific Ocean for a couple thousand tide changes. It would be a hell of a hard sell to my wife to load up the old Ford with our cats and a couple of couches and see what would happen. There was at least one other place I thought I would move to first over California, but the idea was enticing.

Either way, I was still standing in the middle of a parking lot, waiting for my life to change. If I stood there in one place, waiting for a change to come, I would eventually get run over by a car. A lot of good could come from change, if you thought about it. Nothing stayed the same forever. Things were always in motion, fluxing in and out of a rhythmic pattern. Change was good. You would get bored after a while of doing the same thing, and I was tired of being bored.

It started to rain after Tyrell's car vanished. It was just a light rain, but it was building. I needed to get in my truck fast. As I got into the cab, the rain poured down. I just missed getting soaked right before I got into my truck. *Lucky,* I thought. I went to put the key in the ignition, then I stopped. *Where do I want to go?* I thought. Where did I want to go most of all—the wine bar, the airport, or my keyboard? I sat back in my truck seat. I looked into the rearview mirror, stared at myself for a second, and thought about it one more time. *Where do I want to go?*

The End

ABOUT THE AUTHOR

J. R. Warnet is a writer and humorist living in Central Jersey. Yes, there is such a thing as Central Jersey. J. R. writes short fiction designed to be read and laughed at. Please do not take anything in his books too seriously. It's humor. J. R. thinks the world should laugh more, hence his writing style. He has a BA in creative writing and other semi-useful college degrees hanging on his walls. He lives with his wife, Tia Lyn, and two cats, Salem Annabelle and Sophia Alice. Frequent visitors include a mother and a mother-in-law, a New York transplant named John, and various food and liquor delivery people.

Printed in the USA
CPSIA information can be obtained
at www.ICGtesting.com
LVHW041724110624
782943LV00002B/149